Wind In Morning

Other books by Delibia
Bonnie Parker

Soon to be released:
Francine Parker
Gunther

WIND IN MOURNING

Delibia

Wind In Morning

ஒஒஒஒஒ

To my beloved husband
Michael

Generations

WIND IN MOURNING
Father: Chief Omekobee
Brother: Little Claw (Shining Star)

Ira and Anna Parker
Son: Joe Parker (Landonelle Stiver)

Jeremiah Davis: trapper

Frothworth and Emma
Son: Gunther

Ronald Stivers
Wife: Judith Ann – deceased
2nd wife: Delores

Francine Parker: daughter of Joe and Landonelle
Daughter: Bonnie (Kenny Fisher)
Daughter: Lucy Thomasina
Daughter: Phyllis Parker
(fiancé Will Huston)
Daughter: Bernadette Marie
Son: Kenneth Collin
Son: Arnold Alexander
Daughter: Patricia Catherine

Bill and Ruby (foster parents to Collin)

Wind In Morning

ঌঌঌঌঌ

1888

Every time her foot hit the ground her heartbeat demanded, "go faster, faster; keep going, faster" and though her legs ached, and her lungs burned she found herself gaining the distance she needed to be free!

"AnnaBelinda!" His voice bellowed from absolute rage! "You git back here!"

But she ran with the wind. A response reverberated through her entire being even though it was locked in silence through gritted teeth. In her heart she cried, "that's not my name!" The further away she ran, the closer she would get to her real name, Wind in Mourning.

She desperately wanted to look behind her but she knew that moment of hesitation could cost her the freedom she was beginning to achieve. She ran blindly through the trees with only one destination in mind--to be far, far away from the wickedness of her captor, Ira Parker!

Even though she didn't know where she was going, she basically knew her surroundings. Not long ago she had played a game with little Joe in order to get a mental picture of the land around her. When she had been kidnapped they had traveled mostly at night and there were times when Ira made her ride backwards on the mare so she wouldn't be able to identify landmarks. The game with the boy began as she described the landscape where she had once lived in order to trick him into describing what it was like around the cabin.

She had baited the boy. "I bet we have more trees around our teepees than you have around this cabin. I bet our water is cleaner. You probably don't even have a big enough creek to fish in. It probably takes you till the heat of the day just to carry back your water. I bet you don't even have a place for your cattle to graze." It was important to know exactly which direction she'd run so she wouldn't trap herself.

Breaking through the trees she was suddenly in a clearing and directly in front of her was a high bank that dropped dangerously down to a swiftly moving river. In a split second she debated the pros and cons of staying in the clearing or riding the current. Even though she knew Ira's head was spinning, he could still outrun her if she stayed in the clearing. There was always the possibility that he would shoot and a bullet would hit her whether he could aim well or not. It wouldn't make any difference to him. If she was dead, he would just leave her body right where it fell. If she was hurt bad he'd still leave her, letting her die a slow, agonizing death. She feared that as much as she had feared being held captive.

On the other hand, choosing the water over the clearing could be a trap in itself. What if it didn't flow fast enough or if it wasn't deep enough? What if she jumped and merely hit a sandbar or rocks or a log jam that would serve only to cripple her? The boy had told her the water was as deep as the cabin was tall but what if he had just been exaggerating? She kept running, not wanting to think of the negative possibilities. There was always the chance the river was deep and fast and her only hope. In that same split second of debating which way to go she convinced herself she had to trust the river. She knew it would be cold but she also knew she was the only one who could swim.

Ira had warned her one time to stay away from the water; to keep the boy away, as well, because the current could catch both of them and he wouldn't be able to do a thing about it. Of course, he wouldn't have cared if she had drowned but he did care about the boy. That is, if devils could care!

Just the thought of the repulsive man having his hands on her again made her run even faster! If the fear hadn't controlled her thoughts, she might have smiled, knowing that being able to swim was her very own secret. Once they had crossed a river and she could clearly see fear in Ira's face when the horse stumbled and he fell off. If she would have had the chance she would have drowned him herself!

Her lungs were burning as her long, flowing hair was whipped back from her face by the wind. It would have been so much easier if her hair had been braided but Ira wouldn't allow it. When she asked to put it in bands he not only refused but made it clear if he ever saw it that way he would cut it. He did everything he could to prevent her from enjoying any of her Indian ways.

Remembering the cruel treatment, her eyes filled with tears and then her foot caught on a root and she began to stumble, her arms flaying in the air as she tried to regain her balance. Both knees came down hard as the flesh scraped away. The few seconds lost sent a new serge of adrenaline as she could hear him getting closer and mentally could feel his hand getting a firm grip on her. The pain and numbness in her knees was nothing compared to what he had done to her and would do again if he caught her! The terror of that touch coursed through her body, and then the world ceased to exist around her as she focused on the river.

The only sound she could hear was the blood racing through her veins and her own frantic breathing. Every time her foot came down on the hard ground, the sound filled her ears with an inner, thunderous echo that filled her aching lungs and burst from her open mouth. At the same moment she heard the shotgun blast she was airborne. Without hesitation she leaped from the bank towards the rushing water. For just a second she was suspended in slow motion, falling at least ten feet. With arms out and legs braced to hit the water she hung in space, her entire body touched only by the sky around her. Before she closed her eyes she saw the face of the Great White Spirit in the clouds and she imagined herself jumping into the safety of its arms. The shock of the cold water jerked her back into reality as it snatched her breath away. For a second she was not only stunned from fear but from the unexpected cold. Had she been shot? She hesitated just long enough to see if any of the water was turning red. Only crystal clearness swirled around her. Going with the current, she allowed herself to float so Ira would think he had killed her and wouldn't shoot again. As she held herself suspended between escape and freedom she pulled everything into perspective.

Little Joe would be sleeping; she couldn't feel guilty for leaving him. He wasn't her responsibility any more. It seemed like months since she had been planning this escape and now it was all happening. An Indian child of fourteen years could outsmart a white adult! Now, with the water carrying her away, she wasn't fearful for her life or even afraid she'd have to go back. Just as she raised her head, Ira Parker yelled he was going to kill her! Another shotgun blast roared through the trees and then all was quiet. Going around the bend she knew that he wasn't able to see well enough to aim let alone to see the smile on her face! She looked at Ira Parker for the last time; defeat in his expression, triumph in hers!

Regardless of the cold, she felt wonderful! Just a short distance away a large tree branch was riding with the current. Using all the energy she had left, she swam to it and grabbed hold. She was so cold that her hands had a hard time gripping the rough bark but she finally wedged herself in.

"I made it!" She both laughed and cried. "I'm alive and free!"

She clung to the branch, wrapping herself tightly so that she could even lay her head down and keep it out of the water. As long as she could hang on she was going to let the current carry her farther and farther away. Closing her eyes, she offered a prayer of thanksgiving and then for the first time in two years, she closed her eyes in peace.

ↂↂↂↂↂ

Teeth chattering, she finally had to give up and get out of the water. There was no way he would follow her this far. He wouldn't leave the boy alone and by this time he was probably retching and in horrible pain. The affects of the weed she had secretly given him would be worse on him because he hadn't been purified for a spiritual quest. No, she assured herself, he wouldn't follow. Hopefully, his anger and grief had been played out over the last two years. Perhaps he would let her go now without a fight since it would be hopeless to go after her. True, he would be mad because she had outwitted him and gotten away, but she knew there wouldn't be a revenge factor this time because he had no idea that his weakened physical condition was because of her! Besides, if he followed her or started asking questions, people might get suspicious and that was the last thing Ira Parker would want.

As she pulled herself onto the bank she was so cold she couldn't even feel her legs. For a good five minutes she lay still, letting the sun warm her freezing body. But she couldn't stop shivering. She didn't think it would be wise to build a fire so she completely dismissed that possibility of warmth. It would have been good to get out of the wet clothes, but she was too scared and too modest to take them off and risk being seen. How she longed for a blanket!

"This is not cold," she scolded herself. "Cold is when the men come in from hunting with frozen hair. Cold is when the wind blows icicles into your lungs making them burn as though you swallowed fire." She continually rubbed her legs and arms. "Cold is when you have to shake ice crystals from your blanket in the morning. Cold is when your moccasins freeze and the leather is so brittle it cuts your toes! This is nothing."

Finding what energy she had left she began to walk at a fast pace. At last she began to get warm. With every step she talked to herself in her native tongue. She had practiced it every chance she had for fear she would forget. The words were reassuring, convincing, and encouraging. At this moment she was her own best friend! If she hadn't had that positive ability to overcome, she would have never survived or even attempted such a courageous escape!

The wet clothes clung to her skin with a soggy, deathlike coldness which only made her hate them all the more. No, she physically shook her head as though shaking off the negative thought. Hate wasn’t going to be a part of her life anymore. She would run from that as swiftly as she had run from Ira Parker! What if she didn't have the dress? What if her bare skin was exposed to the world? Then she would have to be in hiding! She would have no protection from the briars or from the wind or even from the bugs. At least the dress would eventually dry. She didn’t have to like it, but it was better than nothing. Looking down at her bare feet she realized she hadn't had any shoes for two years. In the winter her feet were constantly blue.

Ira had made fun of her discomfort. "Redskin with blue feet," he mocked her. "We could always put them in the fire so you'd have black feet. Ain't there an Injun tribe by the name of Blackfeet? Maybe you want to be like them, huh?"

She had just glared at him. Her feet weren't blue now! That was another good thing to think about. Her wet hair against her shoulders suddenly made her aware that she could braid it. Eagerly, she parted her hair and pulled it into two sections to the front. Her fingers automatically separated each section into three strands and started twisting it. It felt incredibly wonderful to be able to braid her hair again! She used her teeth to make a nick in the ragged skirt of her dress and tore a small strip off, then bit that in half so she would have two strips to tie around the ends of her braids. Wanting to shout for joy she shook her head and felt the long braids whip against her! Back and forth, back and forth. What a simple pleasure! She gave a sigh of complete joy. Just the freedom of being able to braid her hair seemed to warm her more than the sun.

Blackberries were growing thick so she stopped long enough to pick some and then sit in the sun and eat them. Because her hands were so cold, she didn't feel the briars at first until she saw little streaks of blood where they were scratching her. It was a reminder that she still needed to be cautious. She was constantly listening--if not for another human being, it was for snakes or animals, particularly bears. Whenever she saw a paw print she would always allow either imagination or memory to create the monster that would be big enough to make that print. Then she would add to the story by proclaiming she just saw the baby bear prints! The father bear was always four times bigger!

Wind in Mourning had actually forgotten what it was like to be under the open sky. It had been rare when Ira Parker had allowed her to step foot outside the cabin. He was always afraid that a trapper would be heading out to the lines and would see her. Then there'd be questions. Out of habit she reached down and ran her fingers across the groove that was imprinted on her ankle from the foot chains. Ira Parker had made sure she couldn't escape by keeping her chained up like an animal!

With her foot she began digging a hole, scooping the dirt out with her heel. When it was of decent depth, she stared at it and then closed her eyes and allowed all the hate and anger for Ira Parker to fill her head. When she couldn't stand the pain any longer she stuck her finger in the back of her mouth and made herself gag until she threw up in the hole.

"There, Mr.-Parker-Evil-White-Man. That's what I think of you and that's where you'll stay." Then she stomped the dirt back into the hole and considered that part of her life buried. When she looked up she saw a clear sky and when she outstretched her arms she gathered in the air as though bathing in a spring shower. She rubbed the air into her skin and then listened to the sounds around her. Squirrels chattered at each other, birds were proclaiming territory or singing to a mate. Some kind of beetle was making a popping sound. It was all an unchained, uncaged life, and she was once again a part of it! Just as quickly as she rejoiced in such freedom, she suddenly buckled from the realization that she had no idea where her people were and that she might have to face the realization of never seeing them again. When she had been held captive, she repeatedly dreamed of someone finding her. She had prayed to the gods of the sun and moon and stars and earth and wind and even fire. She even made up a few so she would cover every god that existed and might come to her assistance.

Looking at the landscape around her was overwhelming. She knew that she could walk for days and still be alone. After two years, her people could have traveled to the other side of the world. The best that she could hope to do would be to find someone who would treat her like a human being and then she would be able to ask them where her people were.

She believed there might be good people. She remembered hearing pleasant voices at the cabin when she was in the crawl space under the table. She had never actually seen the individual other than little slivers of shapes and colors through the narrow cracks in the floor, but she had memorized their voices. One man came, not often, but consistently. Ira called him Frothworth. She knew he was a big man because his footsteps lumbered across the floor as though he was carrying an elk across his shoulders and his voice was deep.

He played with little Joe which struck her as peculiar. Sometimes she wondered if the man came to check on the boy instead of to visit Ira. When she asked little Joe what the man looked like he told her he had a long, black beard and deep eyes that sparkled as though touched by raindrops. Actually, Joe said they were sunk and wet but what did white boys know anyway? There were times Frothworth would get mad at Ira and swear he'd kill him or never come back. She figured it was only for Joe's sake that the rugged man would just storm out of the house instead of shooting Ira on the spot! He'd be gone for months, then he'd show up again.

As she let her mind remember, she realized that she wasn't cold anymore and the farther away she went the better she felt. What was life going to be like now? Along with planning the escape, she had also counted on finding people within a moon's change. Staying alive was not going to be a problem. She could build a fire, hunt and kill a rabbit, or chew on pigweed. She had learned long ago that the best method of finding food was to let the animals hunt it for you and then make noise to scare it away. An owl with a rabbit would drop it and even a wolf would run if you didn't stare it in the eyes. This time of year, berries were in abundance and she could even find nuts from the trees.

She kept on walking. Finding shelter wouldn't be a problem either. She knew how to create a windbreak but generally a heavy pine or spruce would cover her with its branches if she stayed close to the trunk. Her brothers had taught her well. They would be proud! The thought of them made her swallow a lump of sadness. What were they doing? Had they searched for her? Had they grown into manhood and were now riding with the war parties? Did Little Claw ever get the horse he wanted?

She liked horses, too, but she was never allowed to ride them as much as she wanted. Squaws were to cook and clean and nurse their papooses and prepare meats and vegetables. They weren't supposed to frolic around the countryside on the back of a horse. She took a deep breath and looked all around her. To her left was an open field that stretched out to rolling hills. To her right was a wooded area. By chance she spotted something that looked like a path. Probably just an animal trail, but she knew it had to lead somewhere. Even though she didn't run into any people she could feel them and smell them. The path cut through more blackberry bushes and then separated into two more paths. On one heavy clump of thorns she touched a torn piece of cloth. It was a blue calico, nothing her people would wear. Just touching the cloth sent shivers through her the same as if she had touched white flesh. Her senses were keen and she listened for even a snap of a twig or movement that would indicate someone coming.

From that fear alone she decided to leave the path and find cover in the woods. At this point in time she felt more confident facing a wolf or even a bear or wild cat than a human being! She had picked up enough English to carry on a conversation, but she didn't trust anyone. In all truth, she had no idea how many white people were like Ira Parker or how many were like Frothworth. She had learned the hard way that once you got close enough to someone to find out if they were good or bad you had gone too far from being able to get away. When she had left her village to speak to Ira on the hillside she had considered him a good man. He had spoken to her father on occasion and even though her brother didn't like him she had never thought of him as bad. She found she was still angry with herself for being so quick to trust him. She would have been better off to have walked into a bear's den blindfolded. She sighed. An encounter with man or beast could change the course of events in your life.

She kept on walking, trying to determine where she wanted to go and what she'd do before night fell. At first she was somewhat confused. There was nothing in front of her but trees. She finally decided that as long as she didn't go in circles, it made no difference what direction she went. With determination she commanded her feet to make a trail. By dusk she felt as though she had walked ten miles even though it was probably only half that. She knew it wasn’t far enough! Feeling twinges of hunger she looked around and saw acorns. She untwisted the gauze cloth from around her belt and started gathering the nuts. For a good ten minutes she debated if she should build a fire or not, and then finally decided against it. She wasn't cold now and there was enough to eat to satisfy her. Her eyes suddenly identified a patch of pigweed. It wasn't her favorite but it was edible. Filling the cloth, she took pride in her ability to survive. Before she sat down to start cracking the acorns she picked a few more berries. All the time she had been in captivity she had dreamed of having the freedom to sit on the ground with her legs comfortably wrapped under her and to get up when she pleased and to do only what she wanted to do. She never wanted to see Ira Parker's face again or smell the mixture of whiskey and sweat and putrid body odor that was a result of pure filth. She burrowed her toes in the grass and leaned back, looking up through the treetops to the sky above. She was just as free as the birds up there.

Suddenly, a cloud of loneliness overshadowed her face as her eyes tired. It was all too clear that the birds had a home but she didn't. Once again, the enormity of the world and her own smallness was completely overwhelming. The birds had a purpose for life, she wasn't sure about herself. She gave an extra hard whack on the acorn with her rock.

"Then I'll just have to find me a purpose. There's got to be some good reason why I'm not dead," she declared.

Picking out the best acorn, the biggest berry and a pinch of the weed she laid them on a rock and then looked up at the sky.

"To the god of the fruit of the land, remember that I was not greedy enough to eat it all. Reward me by giving me more when the pains in my stomach begin to groan."

She ate the remaining handful and shook out the cloth, carefully twisting it back around her rope belt so she wouldn't lose it. Her ankles were hurting so she didn't want to walk any further. The base of a huge spruce tree invited her to sleep under its branches for the night so she accepted. For the first time in years she didn't have to listen to Ira Parker snoring or be concerned about little Joe wetting the bed. She rubbed the callus on her ankle. No more chains. Freedom felt so wonderful!

CHAPTER 1

ஒஒஒஒஒ

1969

They had been walking along the edge of the river. Phyllis had stopped several times just to watch the current and marvel at how beautiful it was. Silently, she was humming the tune 'Peace Like A River'. The water was incredibly clear and inviting; there were a couple places by the shore where she could even see fish. Mesmerized by nature, she realized Will was quite a bit ahead of her.

"Hey, wait up, will ya," she called to him.

He stopped and as soon as she caught back up she slipped her petite hand in his outstretched one. Phyllis truly loved him!

"I don't think anything in life could be more relaxing than this. I just love the great outdoors." Phyllis stopped again and looked all around her as though she could never get tired of the scenery or be able to take it all in. "I don't think I've ever been here before. Whose land are we on anyway?"

"You'll never guess." Will swung her arm in a big arc as he held tightly to her hand and then drew her close to him as he looked down into her captivating, hazel eyes that seemed to reflect pools of festivity. "You'll be so surprised."

She squinted her eyes and frowned. "Then tell me. I have absolutely no idea where we are let alone who might live around here."

He kept her in suspense as long as he dared. "Talk has it that this land first belonged to Herman Parker." He stopped abruptly and leaned forward in a gesture that meant 'figure it out'. Her brow furrowed in concentrated thought.

With tongue in cheek she wrinkled her nose and then made the connection. "Herman Parker? Why does that name seem to ring some kind of inner bell in my head? Are you trying to tell me the owner of this land is a relative of mine?"

Will was beaming. "I'm pretty sure he is. I don't know how many generations ago but I do believe there is a connection."

This time she was frowning as her tongue swept across her teeth. "Oh, if only that were true! But," her eyes enlarged as she sucked in her breath. "If it's the man I'm thinking of he was considered an outlaw. Of course, that was back in the cowboy and Indian days. So, who does the land belong to now?"

Will stooped and picked up a broken twig and then threw it in the water. "I have no idea. It might still be in the family if you could ever track it down."

Her eyes remained large as fragments of memory shinnied down the family tree. She grabbed his shoulder and spun him around. "Oh, Will, who knows, maybe this could be my inheritance one day. Maybe my ancestors left it to me and all this land will be ours. We could build right here by the river."

He touched her nose and then ran his finger up and encircled her eye. Boy, did he ever have a story for her! "I don't think so, funny face." Then he touched her ear. "Listen, what do you hear?"

She wet her lips as she closed her eyes and listened. "I hear birds and the sound of water, and the wind in the trees. Why?"

"I reckon that's who this land belongs to now." Even though he wasn't serious he sighed and pretended to be resolved to never finding out the truth.

"No, Will, that can't be!" She backed away from him and shook her head. "Land can't become an orphan. It's like a wild pony, once you break it, it's yours. Or, like a prospector's claim. You stake it and whatever you find on it belongs to you. We've got to find out who this land was passed down to or sold to." It was obvious her mind was made up. "We can go to the courthouse when we get back and find out."

"It is beautiful, isn't it? And yet--" again, that deliberate mystery in his voice that lured her just as the low rumbling of white water could draw the rafter into its churning embrace.

"Okay, and yet what? Finish your sentence, please." She deliberately batted her long eyelashes at him.

He rubbed his square chin. Fingers that were masterful on a keyboard seemed to play a silent melody through a day's growth of beard. "I hear that the reason no one lives around here or even takes care of it is because the land has a curse on it. No one, but no one dares to say they own this land. If they did, they would immediately inherit the curse! Not even Mother Nature will claim it for fear the beauty would be spoiled."

Phyllis stuck her lip out and exaggerated a pout. "Then who do we have to talk to? Father Gloom or Uncle Despair?"

Then she imitated a mean face as though she was going to attack Will with demonic insanity. "Because I've got to find out who this land belongs to! Whatever happens is all your fault because you brought me here!"

She lunged into his willing arms and then laughed, "If I don't find out I'll be resolved to some haunting myself!" She drew it into a passionate moan while turning her face up towards the dark eyes that could melt a heart of stone.

Will absolutely loved her comical over-reactions. By nature he was somewhat of a serious fellow. Coming from a family of lawyers he had learned to sit quietly during business engagements. In fact, he had a great gift of either taking in everything around him, to the degree of remembering trivial conversations while passing an acquaintance in the hallway, to tuning everything out and not hearing a single word. His father was physically a big man and William Huston had inherited not only the same handsome features of his father but his stately stature as well. At five feet ten, Will prided his ostentatious physical fitness to lifting weights and continually running, playing tennis, biking or swimming. Being outdoors left him with a healthy, bronzed completion.

"Are you sure you're willing to take chances with the curse?" His eyes were so dark they were almost black. "If you pursue this thing you might be bringing down the powers of darkness."

Her mouth dropped open about as wide as her eyes enlarged. "Mr. William Huston, that's got to be a lie if I ever heard one! You're just saying that. Of all things--a curse!"

His expression wore complete innocence. He held up his right hand as though swearing on the Bible. "That's what Rev. Winter told me and I don't think he'd lie about it, do you?"

Phyllis wasn't sure what to say. The peace and quiet that had captivated her now sent a shiver of uneasiness through her. "Why would anyone want to curse such a beautiful place as this?"

Will suddenly became serious which only added to the growing eeriness. "Because of what happened here, I guess. They say that whoever lives here will never find happiness because the moans of misery haunt this land. A long time ago some old trapper turned up missing. Some said he died from natural causes, others said he was murdered. There was even a story about him getting killed by Indians. It wasn't his death that was so bad, but the fact that they never found his body. On full moons some people swore they saw him--or at least his ghost. Don't you remember any of the stories about the Parkers?"

Phyllis looked down as though the ground would help to rekindle her memory. "No, everyone in the family has always hated each other. As a kid I was always told to stay away from my relatives or I'd wind up in trouble. They were bad."

She drew the word bad out to emphasize years of scandalous adversity.

"Even with your curious mind you never wanted to find out what all the rumors were?" Will was honestly surprised.

Phyllis picked at a fingernail; her voice held a nervous quiver to it. "I can't help it if I'm so obedient. Mom said I didn't need to know and I believed her. You know as well as I do that rumors carry just enough truth that if you're not careful you can get sucked into the lies they actually are. Scandal is something else. If I see a woman in the maternal way I don't have to ask for clarification that a man was involved. It's quite obvious, you know? Neither do I have to see actual blood to know that violence exists. Scandal may be a truth exaggerated, but it's still truth. Believe me, my family is full of scandal!"

"I have to admit, I wouldn't want you involved either," he agreed.

"However," she took a deep breath and then dug the toe of her Oxford into the dirt. "All of that is in the past and the past is after all the past."

"Maybe so." Will took her hand in his, playing with each delicate finger that was accented by a skillfully manicured nail. "They say that a place is haunted because the ghost has to prove violence is unjust. And the curse will remain until the ghost can find some sort of justice. Maybe something horrible happened right here on this very spot we're now standing on."

She snatched her hand away and jumped back, lifting her foot as though she had violated a sacred grave by carelessly standing on it. The wind in the trees suddenly sounded hollow and mournful. Phyllis quickly put her foot back down, looking at the ground and wishing she wasn't so gullible. Then she questioned. "Well, what are we suppose to do about it? There haven't been any murders recently and we can't very well go back and connect each generation by a kindness that never existed. What's done is done, Will Huston, and none of it had anything to do with us."

As a thought crossed her mind she stood straight and held her head with an air of defiance. "And I'm not about to let a savage time in history mar the present! That's ridiculous! It's not the land's fault. It wasn't inhabited with spooks but cruel and wicked people. Those people are gone now and we're here, and that's going to make all the difference in the world."

She squinted her eyes and pointed at him. "Besides, I don't believe in ghosts! Only the Holy Ghost." There was a little jerk to her head which meant 'and that's that'.

Will deliberately stayed silent as he looked at the scenery around him and then inhaled deeply. "Some things we may never know, but there's undeniably something different about it."

"By the way, where are we?" She changed the subject. Phyllis knew the general location but they had been walking for quite some time and she wanted to get some familiar landmarks.

"Just about ten yards past that old spruce tree."

"And where are we going?"

"About twenty more yards past that boulder and then down into the valley."

"What's there?" Phyllis felt as though she were pulling teeth.

"Mostly God's exquisite artwork of nature." Then he took her hand. "Plus an explanation for the curse--I mean, if you believe in that sort of thing, which I personally do! If not an explanation of it, at least it's an unexplained mystery waiting for an explanation."

"How do you know all this?" She stopped dead in her tracks and challenged him, sensing that there was more to the story than what he was telling her.

"Actually, I found it quite by accident and then I started snooping around and asking questions. It seemed like something I wanted to share with you because of your uncanny spirit of adventure. Plus the fact there's an excellent possibility that the Parkers still have something to do with it."

"Well, I'm not sure if I want to thank you or say thanks but no thanks."

"You know you love a mystery." He baited her.

That she couldn't deny. With a smile she skipped up to him and ruffled his raven, black hair. "So, what's the big mystery? I can see that I'll never leave here until you show me whatever it is you found."

"Come see." He wagged a finger at her in a gesture to follow him. “We're almost there.”

They walked faster, his excitement taking over. He suddenly stopped and looked around. "Here we go; this is it. I want to see if you have the same reaction I did. Look around and take in all the beauty. Pretty peaceful, huh?"

She agreed. "Well, that's what I thought a few minutes ago before you started talking about curses and bogeymen."

As though sneaking on someone's property, with another's eyes watching their every move, Will tread cautiously forward. Then he stopped and nodded his head as though asking her if she was ready. She eagerly nodded back. Will led her through a copse of trees and then stopped.

"Look over there," he whispered.

At first Phyllis didn't see much, but then a perfectly camouflaged cabin manifested through the thickness of the trees. "Oh, how sweet…" but then she stopped cold. "No, how sad. It looks like most of it has burned down. Does anyone live around here?"

"No, not in the last twenty some years. I asked Dad about it and he said it's just been sitting here. Like I said, absolutely no one will have anything to do with it."

They continued to walk closer and she suddenly got a chill. "Kind of creepy in a way." Then she immediately reverted to her optimistic self. "But that's just because fire is so devastating. How I wish I knew more about my ancestors. If the Parkers sold it, maybe a really wonderful family lived here."

"I don't think so," he contradicted her with his thick eyebrows raised.

"And why not?"

"That's the mystery. Come and see what's left."

They approached the cabin, curious and yet respectful. At first she didn't see anything unusual or even hinting towards the mystery that Will alluded to. But as she looked around, she realized she was actually frowning. Something didn't feel right. Another shiver went through her and she spun around, suddenly feeling as though they were being watched from an unfriendly source. It was a threatening feeling, as though someone was watching them behind a pointed gun. She tried to ignore it, persuading herself that her imagination was merely working over time.

"Wonder what happened here?" Only part of the cabin had been destroyed and they were making their way into the debris through one wall that had been burned, exposing the remaining contents.

"Looks like an explosion of some kind. Either there wasn't a lot of fire or someone was able to put it out in time."

"What's through there?" She pointed at a door that hung limp on only one hinge.

"A bedroom."

For a moment she smiled as she carefully shifted the door so she could look inside. But the smile instantly changed. "I don't like it here. Something really terrible went on in this room. What's that on the bed frame?"

"Chains."

Her eyes widened with terror. "Do you suppose someone was chained up in here?"

Will boldly stepped through the doorway and went straight to the bed where he ran his finger along the rusty link of metal. "Sure looks like it."

"But why?"

"A number of reasons I suppose. Maybe they walked in their sleep, maybe a slave tried to run away, maybe the wife wanted to run off with the milk man. Who knows?"

"Maybe it was used as a kind of torture," she interjected, squeamish at the mere thought of such an atrocity.

Then she shook her head as though to free herself from such thoughts. "Oh, if only the walls could talk. What a story they'd tell, huh?"

She let her imagination roam as she went back into the living room and ran her hand along the wall. "I wonder what kind of story they would tell?"

"What kind of story would you want to hear?"

"Something good, something happy and wonderful."

He cocked his head to one side as though intently listening. "I don't hear anything. Maybe there isn't a good story to tell."

Phyllis scoffed at the idea. "Oh, such pessimism. Now you just look at this."

She picked up a broken basket and handled it gently. "Someone use to carry stuff in this basket and I bet it was a woman. She probably wasn't beautiful but she was strong and had a gentle spirit. And I bet she'd go off and pick berries and load up this basket and sing. In fact, it could have been my great, great grandmother, and I bet she sang a lovely lullaby as she thought about the pie or cobbler she'd make for her children. That would be a good story."

"It most certainly would, but that's not what happened," Will stated matter-of-factly.

"Oh, yeah? Then you tell me what happened." Her back was straight as she put her hands on her hips and waited for his version of the story.

"That basket always sat in that corner, right where you picked it up, because it was always full of rotting cow chips. The woman who had to keep it filled might have been your great, great grandmother but she was two hundred and fifty pounds of redheaded fury that nagged at her skinny husband. When he wasn't around she screamed at her runny-nosed kids. And all the children in the valley spread a rumor that she was really a wicked witch because anyone who went in to visit never, never came back out."

"Never?" She pretended to go along with him.

"No*, never*!"

The corner of her lips curled up to a good-humored smile. "Will Huston, you're impossible."

"Hey, you've got to admit it's at least interesting." They both stood in silence for several seconds as she held the basket and contemplated his side of the story. "Well?" He coaxed her to say something.

"I'm listening," she answered.

"And what do you hear?"

"The walls are telling me that you must have been deprived as a child."

His eyes were wide and his voice playfully gruff. "And what do the walls know, I ask you? If they're going to be insulting they might as well be quiet. Deprived? Ha!"

Then he grinned at her and gave her a moment as she looked around the cabin.

“Walls are never quiet.” She was running a finger along the roughness. “They just speak another language. As sure as my name is Phyllis Parker these walls have a story to tell!”

He had to admit the whole thing captured his attention as well. In the silence he let his thoughts try to imagine life in the little home. What story would the walls share? Where would they even begin? Would it be back at the time when the trees were first cut and hands settled each log in place? It made sense that the beginning would be at the birth of the new home. Then what? Who lived here? What kind of people were they and where did they come from? What dangers did they face and what triumphs did they celebrate?

Will found himself standing in the doorframe, his hand against the roughness of the old planks. As though guardian of the gateway, he held out an arm, beckoning those from the past to come back in. The woman came with her basket. Children came running in and out because they could never make up their mind where they wanted to be. There was an old grandpa going out to hunt so they could have meat for the winter. Grandma was going to the smokehouse for a slab of bacon. The youngest boy, insulted by the fact that he wasn't old enough to go on the hunt, sulked because he knew he had to stay home with the women. The little lad stood in the doorway, under Will's arm, watching his grandfather leave. He yearned for the day when he'd have his own gun and was trusted to endure days and nights in the open. Survival belonged only to the toughest and wisest of men; that's what his grandfather always told him. The boy knew that the old man wouldn't be back for three or four days.

Even though such people belonged to Will's imagination, he believed in their existence. The real inhabitants of the cabin may have looked different from what he imagined, and they would have their own unique name but people were just people, all basically doing the same thing, living the same kind of life. No matter who they were, they got up in the morning, the mother fixed some kind of breakfast, the men went off to work, and the kids had studies or played. Chores were done. They went to bed at night. Life went on in a comfortable ritual.

What Will didn't know is that at one time, the life in this cabin wasn't within the boundaries of daily routine. In fact, those who went in and out of the door he was still touching were far from normal. It all started when Ira Parker came in from a successful hunt and found that the life he had known for ten years had all been destroyed.

1886

Ever so carefully, Ira Parker tucked the knife in his boot and then took off his heavy topcoat for easier access to the handgun in his belt. Then he took a firm hold on his shotgun, squinted his eyes and gripped it even harder. Something was wrong, terribly wrong! As he stood at a distance and looked at his cabin, he knew there was trouble. There was an uneasiness going through his body the same as when he was alone and surrounded by wolf tracks. He might be in danger, he might not, but experience had taught him that when he had this much evidence and unease there was bound to be a carcass close by gathering flies. His senses were alerted as his eyes took it all in. There wasn't a bit of livestock around and everything was too quiet. No lights, no smoke from the chimney. It was as though the place had been deserted, but he knew that was impossible.

Even with the hint of dusk, his eyes could clearly see more than the meager surroundings. He was coming in from a three-day hunt but he could smell blood and he knew it wasn't from the game in his pouch. This was different. Sounds were different—the entire atmosphere was different. He had seen this a long time ago, over at the Mack Ranch. He went closer.

Ira Parker didn't have to go inside the cabin or the barn to know that Indians had massacred his family and taken off with the livestock. Experience had already imprinted the feel of tragedy and slaughter upon his thoughts and senses.

"I'll kill 'em," he mumbled. "I'll kill every last one of 'em that done this."

He didn't know of any Indians on the warpath. As far as that went, neither were there any neighbors seeking revenge. Ira Parker knew that he was probably the most hated man in the country but there weren't any grudge matches waiting to happen. People just hated him and left him alone. That was the way he liked it.

Not knowing why death had brutally stalked him made him mad. Only with a moment's hesitation did he hold onto the door latch. Then, with a violent gesture that seemed to put an exclamation mark to his suspicions, he threw the door back and looked inside.

The dim interior, brightened by the doorway light simply revealed what he already knew. Close to the door was his brother-in-law, his rifle still in his hands. Dead eyes looked up at him as though pleading for him to do something. That made Ira even madder! What was he suppose to do if the fool couldn't even get a good shot off and at least wound one of the savages? It was too late now for anything to be done! Pushing the lifeless leg out of the way, Ira Parker kept his eyes forward as his voice dropped to the floor.

"I didn't like you no ways, Graydon Farr."

Another step into the room and he saw his sister, SaraBeth, crumpled by the fireplace. His wife, Anna was lying across the kitchen table. And from the doorway of the bedroom he could see his daughter, Belinda. All murdered. He didn't see the boy anywhere but he figured he'd be dead, too. No one would have survived this attack. It apparently came swiftly from murderous hearts that were cold to mercy. One lone feather on the floor told him who had done it. Little Claw always dipped the end of his feathers into a mulberry dye. It was his feather and his deed, no doubt about it. Ira's anger exploded as he yelled at the top of his lungs. The sound ricocheted and echoed, coming back to him to lodge in his memory forever. He was a very quiet man so the sound of his own tormented voice would haunt him on lonely lights.

Ira Parker picked up the feather and ran his finger down the spine of it. Murdering thieves! They had no reason to come on his property and shed innocent blood and steal his animals. He'd done nothing to them!

At first he was ready to take an eye for an eye, a life for a life, but even that didn't seem to carry enough justice. A plan began to formulate in his thinking. Little Claw's own father was the chief of the village. Chief Omekobee. For years Ira and the chief had traded and then they had a bitter dispute. Not life threatening by any means but the chief no longer welcomed Ira Parker to the village center.

Chief Omekobee had a daughter the same age as Belinda. Ira decided it would be a child for a child! That would be the deal. What did the chief call her? Cry in the Night? Scream of Terror? He smiled maliciously. Her name was Wind In Mourning. Ira knew who she was and how to find her. He'd snatch her and give her another name; a name she would hate every time she heard it!

He looked again at his wife and daughter, both disfigured in death. They didn't need their names anymore. He'd call the Indian child AnnaBelinda. And every time she heard it she would be reminded that her own brother was guilty of shedding innocent blood. It was his fault Ira was being forced to take the girl for revenge. The name would be a daily reminder of how much Ira Parker hated her and her people! She'd become an object of cruel, living hate. He'd never let her forget. Never! It would be revenge of the sweetest kind. The more he thought of it, the more his determination built to kidnap and enslave her.

The Indian village was only two days ride away. Ira Parker gathered his saddlebags and filled one with food, dropped extra shells into his pouch and closed the door to the cabin. Death wasn't going anywhere. He had two days to plan how he'd take the child and when they got back he would make her drag the bodies to their graves.

Within a half hour he had ridden to the other side of the valley and when he looked to the crest of the hill he recognized a familiar rider. Jeremiah Davis was heading south; away from the cabin even though the home site could clearly be seen once Jeremiah rounded the copse of trees. Ira hesitated, evaluating the situation. It looked like the old trapper was going to ride on by.

The moon would be full that night so chances were that Jeremiah was heading to his lines and would take advantage of the moon. That meant he'd be gone at least five days before he headed back. Ira nudged the horse's sides to go forward as he gently clucked his tongue. He figured he'd be back himself before Jeremiah completed his rounds.

Little did Ira know that Jeremiah Davis wasn't going to the trap lines at all; he was just heading to the creek to wash off before he went back to the cabin to see if he could trade his mule. And so, Ira rode on. Just as darkness completely suffocated all remaining traces of daylight, the memory of seeing his family dead snuffed out any thought but revenge. With each mile his anger peaked because his family had been wrongfully taken from him and then he thought about taking the chief's daughter. For the next hour he kept cycling through anger and laughter, as though lost in a dark forest of insanity.

Noises ahead made him suddenly put all concentration towards what was happening in front of him. It had to be Indians—the language didn't sound like English. Creeping up he discovered three young Indian braves who had set up camp and were talking and eating. He had seen them before. Three rabbits were on a spit over the fire, almost done. Ira Parker was hungry. That, along with the anger and hatred, made him a very dangerous man. His fingers gripped the gun with a fierceness that defied morality. To him, it only stood to reason that even though these braves were nothing but young boys now, they would grow up to be scalping savages like the ones who murdered his family.

Thinking of it as little more than a good hunt, Ira plotted the death of the young boys and then carried it out. It didn't take more than five minutes. The worthless heathens didn't even give him the satisfaction of an honest fight! Leaving their lifeless bodies where they fell, he sat down at their campfire and ate the cooked rabbit meat. Then he ravaged through the few belongings they had, took what he wanted, and journeyed on. He didn't need to sleep. Instead, he plotted exactly the best way to achieve what he wanted.

He wasn't a stupid man and he took pride in carefully working out every detail. If a minor complication came up in his planning, he'd position that problem like a spoke in a wheel and start at a different angle until he had all spokes meeting in the center. The rim and core of this wheel was the means to get in the camp and back out again without being seen. Everything he would do would be aligned for the sole purpose of taking the girl without anyone accusing him of doing it!

Before he reached the village he rode through a town by the name of Fuertes. He hated towns. The saloon was fine but he had no use for anything else. As far as he was concerned banks were a waste. The mercantile was convenient but why pay for something when you could get it yourself? If God had intended for man to buy supplies from a store He wouldn't have provided seeds for gardens or animal furs and pelts for clothes. Not that he believed in God, but he knew how to argue with those who did.

At one end of town he could see a blacksmith, an apothecary and a school. At the other end, way off in the distance like a privy set apart from the house, was a church and a graveyard. Just as he condemned it as worthless he smiled, changing his mind. As a matter of fact, the church was the best thing he had seen all day! Then he spit on the ground as the spokes of the wheel began to gyrate. He didn't want to draw attention to himself so he stayed on the outskirts, checking out the farms.

Seeing a dog casually walk behind a barn, he followed it. The animal was a good size; not as big as a wolf but it's prints would look like a wolf's! During the next hour, Ira Parker was able to secure a shovel, a gunnysack and a long leather strap. Then he approached a chicken coop. He knew he had to be especially careful because he could see the people of the house at the kitchen table and any ruckus in the hen house would alert them. Ira debated about chunking a rock at one of the feathered creatures but he knew if he missed he'd have the whole place cackling in a panic.

Instead, he inched his way to the first row of nests and with lightening speed he jerked a hen off her nest and had wrung her neck before she could even put up a defense. Carrying her away from the others he went to the back of the barn where he quickly tore away the breast meat from the fowl and then discarded the rest of it behind a bale of hay. Then he went in search of the dog which only took another matter of moments.

Ira lured the dog with the chicken breast and easily slid the leather strap around the dog's neck, using it as a leash. The dog followed obediently. Ira had a way with animals; he liked them. The darkness of the night had concealed his actions. Perhaps all the men of the town were in the saloon or sitting at their supper table eating beans and cornbread. Before he got the dog, someone walked past him but he wasn't even interested enough to take a second look. Ira would never understand people. If a man kept his head down and deliberately tried to conceal his identity, everyone on earth would look and watch his every movement. But if a man held his head tall and stared at a passerby first, the other would look away, not wanting to make visual contact. Ira made sure he stood tall and threatening. When talk came about, the word would be that there was a stranger in town but no one would be able to accurately describe him. Ira Parker retrieved the shovel he had hidden then bid farewell to Fuertes.

When he got back to his horse, he didn't even bother to get on and ride. He just rubbed the horse's neck as a friendly greeting and anchored the shovel on the saddle as though it had been a shotgun. With the reins in one hand, the dog and leash in the other, he headed towards the church. Before he left town completely there was one last thing he had to do. Sitting and waiting for the lights to all go out in the town, Ira Parker almost wished he had saved some of the chicken for himself. He was beginning to get hungry again, but the surge of adrenaline kept him too apprehensive to eat.

For a moment he wondered if maybe he hadn't lost his mind. What he was about to do was something he would have probably killed someone else for doing. But he had a good reason; there were five dead people in his cabin! Therefore, regardless of what he did or what people thought, he figured his actions were justified.

The dead didn't need anything but sometimes they could sure oblige the living! Ira swallowed, wishing he had a cigar or something to smoke or chew on. He pulled out a whiskey bottle from the saddle pack. Now, in complete darkness, Ira Parker tied up the horse and the dog, toted the shovel and headed into the graveyard behind the church. He walked around, always watchful for any movement. The night was perfectly still. Keeping his lantern low and with the barest amount of light he could still see with, he began reading the tombstones. And then he found what he wanted. With ears and eyes both keen to any movement, he listened and then began to dig.

The moon was full in the night sky when Ira went back to his horse. He was tired and hungry but he knew he had to travel on and get quickly away from this small community. He didn't want anyone asking questions! Determined to ride for at least an hour, he continued to develop the plans for the kidnapping. In his opinion everything was falling into place.

Ira smiled, "Maybe you do belong to the devil, Ira Parker." He talked to himself and then slapped his thigh. "Come on dog, if you're real good maybe I'll give you a bone." That made him laugh.

He didn't think of too much else as he rode along. His mind was getting rather numb, as though he had fallen asleep even though his eyes were seeing everything around him. Maybe it was just a dream and by morning he'd wake up. He had no idea what time it was but he couldn't ride another mile. Making sure the dog couldn't get lose, he dropped to the ground, put the saddle under his head, a blanket over his body, and he went to sleep.

Morning assured him that he hadn't been dreaming. There was a stench in the air, his belly felt raw, and his bones ached. The dog was staring at him as though anxious for him to get up. He rubbed the grizzle on his chin and found some beef jerky from his pack; he even threw some to the dog who happily chewed on it. He knew the village was over the hill and then about three miles to the west at the most. When the sun was high and he was looking for shade, he could hear the activity from the village long before he actually saw it. From that point on, his mind was focused on just one thing. Revenge. A child for a child!

From a safe distance, he watched every movement within the Indian village. He knew exactly which teepee belonged to the chief and it wasn't long before the child was singled out. His heart beat fiercely and it was some moments before he realized he was making an audible growl with each exhaled breath. None of the Indians were displaying war paint. There was laughter and easy conversation. He didn't see Little Claw. Maybe no one had any idea that the poaching of human lives had just occurred. Perhaps that was to his advantage. If they had known, someone would have been expecting retaliation and therefore ready to counter attack. It was entirely too peaceful for them—and too easy for him!

For hours he sat and thought and watched. No one even looked in his direction. It would take time to determine if she did anything in the form of a pattern. And if she did go off by herself, he had to be ready! Ira Parker knew that he wouldn't get a second chance. He began to think of himself as a rattlesnake. One strike and it had to be for a vein. The only warning she would have was maybe one second of a rattle just loud enough for her alone to hear. Just long enough that fear would course through her veins before his poison followed. Leaving his position he began to scout out the land. He knew the area but he wanted to memorize it. He was looking for a particular area.

The dog was actually a companion for him. Ira kept it fed so it wouldn't whine or try to run off. Leaving the horse, he found the area he was looking for; soft dirt and very little grass. He began to play with the dog, throwing scraps of jerky so it would run off and get it then come back for more. When Ira was satisfied that the area was full of tracks, he went back to his horse and tied up the dog. Then he carried the gunnysack to the area and positioned the contents that he had dug up in the graveyard. Wasn't much more than a handful of flesh and bones but with all the tracks it looked like wolves had made a feast of some poor child – some Indian child! Satisfied, he went back to his spot where he could see the entire village. Actually, everything was now taking a little longer than he had anticipated. He was anxious to carry out his deed and get back home before Jeremiah Davis came on the cabin and discovered the carnage.

Neither horse nor rider were in any hurry. Jeremiah Davis was so tired he almost fell asleep on the back of his horse. The mule was still stumbling along; bruised his hoof somehow and Jeremiah wanted to stop off at the Parker homestead and see if he could trade the mule for a packhorse. There had been times in the past when Ira Parker had helped him out.

Yawning, he stretched his shoulders and back. That's when he had seen Ira heading off towards Fuertes. The man looked like he had a task at hand and wasn't about to be diverted or detained. It didn't bother Jeremiah much, Anna Parker was always nice to him. Often times she'd help him out even when her sorry husband wouldn't! Jeremiah decided to go on down to the creek and clean up a bit before he knocked on the door. Maybe by that time Ira would be back. Anna Parker was a good woman, clean and wholesome and Jeremiah enjoyed talking to her. He would never understand why she had married Ira. He knew there were opposites; black and white, cold and hot, wet and dry. With Anna and Ira it was the opposites of good and bad. Their life together just proved to Jeremiah that he had made the right decision never to marry!

When he was done at the creek, he headed back to the cabin. It seemed strange to him that there weren't any lights or smoke coming from the chimney. Once he got to looking, he even noticed that all the animals were gone. There should have been two horses, a cow and Belinda's goat. Everything was deathly silent. As he got closer, he could smell it! A shiver went through him as he recognized the sickening pungent odor; so thick it was worse than warm manure or a freshly killed skunk.

"They's all dead," he told his mule. "As sure as my name is Jeremiah Davis that's the smell of death left over after grief has knocked on the door!"

For a long time he debated about going inside the cabin. It was actually too dark to see anything without natural light. What could have killed them? He looked in the direction where he had seen Ira Parker riding. Could he have killed them and just ridden off? No, he decided. Ira might kill someone else but not his own family.

Jeremiah scratched his bulbous nose; nothing was making sense to him. Ira had been riding away from the cabin as though he had just left it. A man in his right mind wouldn't come home to death and just ride away from it as though he was going to play poker or something!

The one thing that Jeremiah did know without any doubt or reservation was that he didn't want to get any closer! He had always been a superstitious man and when the Indians told him about the death spirits hovering in the trees and being carried with the night wind, he could actually see them! Maybe those spirits weren't satisfied with just those in the cabin. Maybe they were waiting for him as well. Jeremiah rubbed under his nose so hard he almost took the hide off. Terrible smell! If he got that foul smelling stuff in his clothes and furs he'd never get it out!

Then another thought crossed his mind. Maybe everyone in the house had all been sick; that's why Ira rode away. Chances were that the whole place was filled with some disease that not only wiped them out but anyone else who ventured too close. Jeremiah started to turn the horse and go back but then he couldn't. That wouldn't be right just to ride away. What if someone was alive and needed help? He'd never forgive himself if they were trapped inside and then died because Jeremiah Davis had been too afraid to rescue them!

And so, from guilt and self persecution, he forced himself to ride closer and investigate. His heart was absolutely racing as his eyes continually darted from one tree to the next to make sure there weren't any haints waiting to swoop down on him and possess his body. Maybe he couldn't see them, but he sure felt as though they kept brushing against him! His flesh crawled and he began to sweat in torrents! His hat kept slipping to the side because it wouldn't stay on the few wet strands of hair that he had left. Jeremiah Davis was genuinely spooked! Nevertheless, he finally found the courage to light a lantern and then go up to the door.

"Anybody home?" he called out. "This here is Jeremiah Davis. Anything I can do to help?"

Silently forbidding any voice to call out to him, he held his breath, eager to get away. No sound whatsoever. He was ready to leave!

The chorus of animal sounds in the night broke the silence. Those were sounds that Jeremiah could relate to. Only when there was imminent danger did the animals stay still. The squirrels would freeze on the tree trunks, except for an occasional flickering of their tails. Birds remained perched with their beaks high, listening and watching. They all waited until the danger passed. Well, there must not be danger now because there was too much noise between the frogs and katydids. That gave Jeremiah some semblance of hope. His curiosity got the best of him as he put his hand on the latch, thinking he should probably go in and at least see for himself what had happened.

With unaccountable boldness, he opened the front door, his lantern held high. The body of Graydon startled Jeremiah but the old trapper blew out his breath in four, quick, forceful breaths and then regained his composure. As he held the lantern even higher he could see the shapes of the two women. It was clear they didn't die from sickness. Then he crossed the room and went to the bedroom, still keeping the lantern high. The girl was still, but he had no sooner shone the light on the bed than he thought he detected a movement.

It might have been his imagination. "I'm fixin' to leave this here place," he called out in a shaky voice. "I done what I could and I'm a leavin' now."

There was another sudden movement! It was the boy and he was obviously alive and moving. Jeremiah was so startled he almost dropped his lantern.

"I'm hungry," the boy whined.

"You sick?" Jeremiah asked.

"No, I'm hungry! No one will get up. They's sleepin'."

How did you tell a baby boy the difference between sleep and death? Deciding that it would be okay to touch him, Jeremiah scooped him up and headed out of the cabin. He had to get away in order to think—in order to breathe! With Joe under his arm he quickened his pace and put distance between him and the boy and the cabin. At last he was back at his horse and mule.

"Put me down," Joe squalled and wiggled free of Jeremiah's strong grip.

"What happened back there?" he asked the boy.

"Indians."

Indians? Even though it wasn't sickness, Jeremiah still felt as though his clothes had been contaminated. He could handle dead animals. It was nothing to kill them, gut them, and skin them. He didn't even mind the smell of the chemicals he used when tanning the hides. Human beings were another thing!

"You're coming with me," Jeremiah stated flatly as he pitched the boy up on the back of the horse and started walking back down to the creek. He had to think this thing through. Not knowing when the Indians attacked, they could easily have been in the area, watching, waiting to ambush him and take his scalp. Didn't matter if he had hair or not, he had heard stories about the scalps ripped off with a dull knife! What in the world was he going to do?

He figured that by morning he might have a better idea. A man just couldn't do anything in the dark! Spooks didn't come out during the day so he'd be safe. He'd bed down for the night and by daylight he'd go back and see what all had happened. He was still puzzled about Ira. If the man had known his family was dead, how could he have left the boy? It only gave Jeremiah a little more reason to hate Ira Parker! Little Joe seemed to be okay. He didn't have any wounds on him that Jeremiah could see. If Indians had done it, they would have killed him too or taken him off with them. What had happened in the cabin was a clear mystery to him!

Jeremiah Davis built a big fire that night. Fire always kept away bad things and lit up the area enough you could see someone slipping up on you. He cooked up some beans and venison and he and the boy ate before they fell asleep. The boy did seem to be nearly starved to death. But with their stomachs full they spread the blanket on the ground and Jeremiah propped his head on his elbow. He tried to sleep through the night with one eye open. Around two in the morning he finally gave up. The boy was snuggled next to him and everything sounded perfectly normal.

It was well into daylight when he stirred. Jeremiah got some water from the creek and made some mush for breakfast. Took his time because he wasn't in any hurry to go back to the cabin. Even put his coffee pot over the fire and watched the black, coarse beans floating on top of the water. Coffee grounds never bothered him. He'd just crunch them up or spit them out. When he couldn't put it off any longer he decided to venture back to the Parker place. He knew the daylight would only magnify the scene. Then it wasn't a matter of guessing what he saw. The sun put it all in bright colors that couldn't be denied.

As he got closer, however, he began to talk himself out of it. What good could he do anyway? He was an old man with a gimp leg and no muscles in his arms. It was all he could do to pull the skin off a muskrat! He really didn't have any business digging graves and burying people that weren't even his own kin. There might be a curse on someone who did that sort of thing.

Jeremiah sure didn't want to deal with Ira Parker. When that man found out his family was all dead he'd be worse than a wounded bear! Jeremiah knew that Ira was the kind of man that had to see things for himself. He'd want to know who did it and how and why and then he'd never get the blood off his hands until it was mixed with the blood of those who shed it to begin with. This was definitely Ira's business and not his. If Jeremiah did anything more than keep the boy safe, he'd be stepping in where he didn't belong.

With his mind made up, he rode off in the direction of his traps. He'd go ahead and work the line and then he'd come back. If Ira still hadn't returned then he'd go towards Gough's Ridge and see if he could intercept him and let him know that he had rescued the boy. Not that Ira Parker would probably care. Somehow, Jeremiah knew that taking care of a three-year-old kid was something that no man wanted to do alone! Sometimes you didn't have a choice, though. A man had to do things in his lifetime he really didn't want to do. Like riding away from a cabin full of dead people! Even though Jeremiah was sure of his decision not to go back, he had to wonder if the spirits of the dead were following him. Would they still want to claim him, too? No, he had rescued the boy so the good spirits would defend him. Chances were, he had bought his freedom from the drama of the spirit world.

Jeremiah had always boldly announced that if anyone ever killed him he'd haunt them for the rest of their lives. He didn't think he'd be afraid of the spirit world once he was a spirit himself. Then he'd understand how it all worked. He knew murder was wrong and life had to work on a balance. If Ira had ridden off, knowing his people were dead, the spirits wouldn't even ask questions, they'd just devour him! And where would Jeremiah be? Far away from their clutches, that's where!

Jeremiah looked at the boy sitting in front of him. He hadn't said hardly a word the whole morning. The old trapper had to wonder if the boy would grow up to be just like Ira. If he did, he sure hoped people would leave him alone! No one really knew what had made Ira so mean. Some said his daddy, Herman, beat him several times to just an inch of his life. One time Henry and Buster Brannigan used both Ira and his brother Amos as target practice! They sent the two boys into the woods and tracked them down. Buster was checking the accuracy of his gun and needed a moving object to shoot at.

Another time Herman had taken all three boys out in the woods and after getting them lost made them find their way back home. Didn't matter if there was snow on the ground or not. He figured they needed to learn how to survive and if they didn't, then it was because they didn't deserve to live.

Now, Amos Parker turned out just as mean as Ira did, but the youngest brother, Walter, did pretty well. On one of his survival trips Walter never went back home. Oh, he knew the way, but he finally decided that if he was smart enough to survive on his own, he sure didn't need to live under the same roof as Herman Parker! So, he put distance between himself and his family and eventually found a wife and built his own cabin.

He didn't know if it was a blessing or a curse but his woman always had multiple births. Twins the first time, triplets the second. In the first three years they had seven children. Then she had five at one time but they all died. They had been so small he could put two of them in the same hand. He didn't weep but it sure made him feel sad.

Ira just made fun of Walter's wife. He called her a scrawny barn cat that had a litter once a year. He continually ridiculed his brother Walter and he treated the babies no different than he did livestock. They were good kids though. Jeremiah knew that.

He couldn't quite remember just when Ira Parker and little Anna Rose got together but he knew it had been a shotgun wedding. Anna's daddy had been a traveling preacher. It all started one Sunday when Ira's mother made the boys put on a clean shirt and go to church with her. As soon as Ira had seen Anna he had made up his mind that he was going to marry her. He really didn't care what she thought, but he did play the part of the charming beau.

She fell for it. Maybe she really did like him, but it was more likely that she was tired of traveling from place to place and used any excuse to settle down. Then she got pregnant and her daddy disowned her. Told her she had made her bed and now she had to sleep in it. It was a sin that she would have to pay contrition for, for the rest of her life. Her daddy told her if she ever tried to leave Ira Parker, the devil would only drag her back. Little did her daddy know how true that statement was! And it didn't take her long to know that Ira was the devil himself and she would never be able to get away from him. Ira wasn't happy that she had given him a girl first, but he did gloat that at least she only spit out one at a time! Anna was a miserable person. She tried to find peace in her life by taking care of her child but then she was constantly worried that Ira would get mad and try and kill them both. He had made that attempt several times!

Jeremiah would pass through and at first Ira was insanely jealous. He wouldn't even let Anna make eye contact with him. It wasn't until little Joe was born that Ira Parker settled down. He would brag that he had a son but everyone knew that he didn't care a thing about the boy personally. So, Anna stayed busy taking care of her children and trying to stay out of her husband's way.

It had been a strange situation with Graydon and SaraBeth. Jeremiah had no idea what made Ira agree that the six of them could all live in the same cabin. There was only one bedroom and a small loft area just big enough for the two children. Graydon always slept out in the barn. SaraBeth had a cornhusk mat she could spread out by the fireplace but most times she slept in the barn with her husband.

In all truth, Jeremiah had to wonder if maybe the girl had received one beating too many and was brain damaged. She was as slow as thick molasses in the winter and had absolutely no sense of humor. SaraBeth was a hard worker but she constantly forgot what she was doing. Didn't have any babies either even though she and Graydon had been married longer than Anna and Ira.

Graydon was as dull as an empty bottle of whiskey. Maybe Ira kept them around because they were so easy to manipulate. He had always liked that sense of control and power. Everything had to go his way. SaraBeth would agree to absolutely anything Ira wanted her to do and Graydon either agreed or just looked the other way. Jeremiah spit on the ground. If Graydon had been a deer he would have looked too stupid to mount his head on a wall regardless of how many spikes he had!

The horse walked on, in no hurry, and Jeremiah kept thinking. Now they were all gone. The devil couldn't play poker with their lives anymore. Come to think of it, maybe that wasn't so bad after all. But then, here was little Joe sitting in his lap. His life was just beginning. How much had he seen in his three years that he would remember? How much did his head know that he would never forget? Was he going to be like Ira or Anna?

Jeremiah continued to ride on. It was all too much for him to figure out. The only thing he had to keep on his mind was his traps and surviving through the winter. He was getting to be a crippled, old man and it was getting harder and harder for him to work the lines.

The days wore on and he did the best he could to keep the boy happy. Joe seldom talked and Jeremiah only talked to the mule so they were basically a quiet lot. No questions were asked and no answers had to be given. Having accomplished all he could, Jeremiah Davis decided to head back to the Parker place. He had no intention to get too close unless he saw some form of life. By this time Ira should have come back. So, he and Joe loaded up all the critters they had trapped and silently wound their way back to the river.

CHAPTER 2

ঌঌঌঌঌ

1969

Will stepped back from the doorway and sighed. He knew this poor, demolished cabin would intrigue Phyllis. Now he smiled as he watched her carefully stepping over boards and debris as she gently touched different items. He loved how she furrowed her forehead in deep concentration. Her mind seemed to actually whir as thoughts were spinning. Even though she looked troubled, he knew that she was mesmerized and enjoyed each smell and every spot of roughness against her fingers. A couple of times she had outstretched her hand to touch something only to recoil as though not having enough courage. Could there be a source of energy from the past that was causing resistance?

To him, the cabin was lifeless but to her there was a heartbeat in everything and if she touched it, it was like resurrecting it. Courage raised, she would reach out again and this time ever so lightly run her finger against it. Somehow, she seemed to either identify with it or absorbed its importance before she moved on to the next thing. Or, she'd shudder as though repulsed by it. He leaned back against the doorframe, watching her intently, with no intention to interrupt her.

"Will," she drew his name out with a hushed voice. "Do you think it's possible to know who all lived here and to really discover what happened?"

"Who knows? I mean, we can ask a lot of questions and maybe fill in some gaps, but I don't know if the past will give up its secrets. It's the same way with our lives; how could anyone know exactly what you and I have experienced unless they walked in our shoes?"

"I know what you're saying, but there was history made in this cabin. How tragic if it was all lost. If our generation doesn't even know who lived here, then these people have disappeared…and yet, they're still here. Can't you feel them?"

As soon as her eyes met his she knew he didn't. At first she was disappointed but then she shrugged. "I'm being foolish, aren't I?"

He looked at her lovingly. "No, of course not! It's the same as walking through a graveyard and reading the tombstones. All those names belonged to real people who lived a real life, and it's a shame when someone is forgotten. It's almost like their life didn't count. But we know that's not true! Every single one leaves his or her mark; every one influences someone else and has the potential to change the course of history."

Phyllis picked up a broken bottle. "Even something as insignificant as this bottle has a purpose. There were hands that held it, and there's a reason why it's broken. Not something that is earth shattering mind you, but there is a story behind it."

Will couldn't help but laugh. Now she had gone too far. "Yeah, a drunk came through here and pitched it."

She scolded him, "Even a drunk has a story! What was he doing out here in the first place? Does he come here frequently? If so, why? Does he know something we don't know? What tragedy happened in his life that made him start drinking? Don't you see how everything leads to something?"

Will went to her and lifted her up, swinging her in a half circle. "I'm just thankful I was led to you! By golly gee, I love you!" As soon as he put her down she laughed and went right back to exploring. He was amazed with her. "Do you know that you can make something out of absolutely nothing? That's truly a special gift! So, what are you going to do? Touch each stick and stone and try to put life back into this old place?"

She vigorously rubbed her fingertips against her jeans and then held out her hands, wiggling each finger. "My fingers are ready! Oh, remember Ezekiel and the valley of dry bones? Out of a chalky dryness would come tendons and sinews, and blood and flesh, and a beating heart! And whalah! There he would be, Mr. Herman Parker himself, the builder of this mysterious fortress."

Will protested, "Oh, no! No, no, no! No one in history would ever want him to resurrect! What do you want to do, unleash the devil himself? Well, that's what would happen because it's his fingerprints that you'll find all over this cabin."

"Whose? Herman's?"

"No, my dear, Satan's! I'm telling you, if there's a curse here then there's a reason why someone cursed it. Talk about a story!" His eyes widened.

"There you go again, Will Huston, you're just tryin' to scare me."

"But it's the truth my little, sweet thing. If you go diggin' up the history of this cabin, I bet you'll be diggin' up more trouble than you'll be able to deal with."

She remained stubborn. "You say there's a curse on this place, well, I say either put up or shut up." She puffed out her cheeks and let out a long, slow breath as she looked around.

What she was seeing right then was a demolished cabin, but what did it look like when all the walls were solid and the roof didn't leak and there was a fire in the fireplace? She walked across the debris to the kitchen area. A square table had lost one leg so was bowing to her. A beam from the roof was propped on the other edge where it had caved in. The chair was completely destroyed, lying underneath like discarded feathers from a plucked chicken. She looked closely at the chair pieces, trying to imagine what it looked like when it was whole. Then, something caught her attention. Her gaze was intent as she dropped to her knees.

"What in the world are you looking at?" Will watched her, trying to see what had drawn her attention so intently.

"Probably nothing." She tried to give the table a little nudge with her shoulder but couldn't budge it. There was something odd about the wood grain. In places it didn't match. With one finger she traced the board suddenly discovering an edge. "But then, again, maybe there is something! Move this table for me, okay?"

"Sure, but what is it you think you've found?"

"Maybe a trap door. I've heard about them. Oh, Will, don't you remember that story about the pioneer family that dug a hidden room under their kitchen floor so that when Indians came they could put their women and children down there for safety? I bet you anything this is exactly what it is! If you can get that beam off and move the table we can open it."

"What you found is probably just an empty, old, crawl space. Or maybe a cold storage for jars." But even in protest he heaved the beam off and then pushed the table over. Then he saw the outline of the trap door, too.

Finding a way to open it was more difficult. It fit too tightly to get a solid grip with his fingers and he couldn't find anything like a crow bar or tool to try and pry up the edges. There was just a sliver of an opening where a leather strap may have been used as a handle. Will took off his belt and carefully threaded it through and then shook it to try and force the belt buckle to lay horizontal, giving him some leverage and therefore allowing him to pull up on the door. It took not only skill but also ingenuity to accomplish such a task! At last it caught and being careful not to break the buckle, he pulled as Phyllis used a broken board as a wedge. With each fraction of an inch that he raised the trap door, she was able to dig the board into the opening until there was enough space for Will to get his fingers under it. With a solid grip he curled his fingers around the edge and began to lift the trap door over his head. The wood screeched in protest. Or, as Phyllis imagined, it was shouting one of the stories that had unfolded in that very room over eighty years ago!

1887

"So help me, girl, if you even cough loud enough for a cricket to hear I'll make sure your throat will be slit and your tongue fed to the buzzards. Now, get down there!" Ira Parker gave her an unnecessary shove and then dropped the trap door back into place, pulling the table and rag rug back over the top of it.

He stomped the floor as though adding finality to his threat. Just then, a heavy knock came on the door and without waiting for Ira to answer, the front door was opened as Jeremiah Davis walked in.

"Mornin', Ira, you got any coffee still on the stove?" The old man dropped his armload of furs, propped his gun in the corner and went to the stove. Shaking the coffeepot he set it down with a disappointed thud. "Whoever heard of draining the pot before the sun's even high? You got any grub in this place? I'm as hungry as a coon caught up in a tree during a rain storm."

Ira just stared at him. "I reckon that's your problem, not mine. What do you want?"

He was mad because in the first place he didn't like unexpected company and in the second place Jeremiah had nearly slipped up on him before he had enough time to get AnnaBelinda hidden. Ira never had been one for surprises.

Jeremiah ignored the cantankerous mood. "Look at my furs there. Want any?"

"Now what do I want with a bunch of smelly beaver furs? I can get them on my own; it don't take a whole lot of effort."

"Maybe not, but it takes more'n what you're willin' to put out. You ain't gonna trap 'em or preserve their hide." He pointed at them. "Somethin' else there you might want to see."

He sat down at the table and threw his feet up, leaning back on two legs of the chair. Reluctantly, Ira Parker went over to the furs and sorted through them. Beautiful furs. Jeremiah was always the best furrier he'd ever known; though he wouldn't openly admit it. He pulled out an unfamiliar pelt.

"White fox?"

"Nope. You'll never guess. It's a skunk."

Ira threw it down as though it was full of fleas, which got Jeremiah to cackling so hard he nearly lost his balance.

"Are you crazy?" Ira yelled. "There is no such thing as a white skunk!"

"You just had your hand on it didn't you? I reckon it did exist if I got it's pelt to prove it. One of a kind. You remember Benjamin Malone? He told me he'd double the pay if I found a rare fur. Well, I found one, didn't I? Kind of pretty, ain't it?" He was obviously pleased with himself.

Ira wasn't impressed. "Who in their right mind would go around wearing a skunk? That's darn nigh brainless if you ask me. Might as well hang chicken feet around your neck and call 'em hairless bear claws! You're a fool, Jeremiah."

"Fool or not, I'll have the extra coins in my pouch, not you. None of my business what he wants to do with the fur; I just got it for him and that's all I care about. Never seen a white skunk before. Probably never will again. Kind of like them white buffalo, if you ask me. It's an omen of good luck."

"You and your omens. How do you know it's not just the opposite? Maybe there's some legend going around that says whoever kills a white skunk will be damned!"

Jeremiah hadn't thought of that and the possibility of it made him a little uneasy, but then he quickly shook it off.

"Guess I'll just have to burn me a poultice of herbs and let the spirits know that I didn't mean no harm. A man can't be blamed for doin'somethin' he didn't know was wrong."

"Suit yourself, now I got work to do."

Right then, little Joe appeared in the doorway, watching the old trapper; not saying a word. Jeremiah immediately perked up.

"Well now, there's the young whipper snapper. Good day to you, Joe. See my furs there?" He stretched a moment as though his bones were aching. "You sure you don't got nothin' to eat? How you and the boy survive? If you ask me you'd be better off livin' with your brother for awhile."

"Well, I didn't ask you. As a matter of fact, I didn't even ask you to come in my house. You just walked through that door and put your skinny rump on my chair like you owned the place."

Jeremiah's voice suddenly grew solid with offense. "You sayin' I ain't welcome here?"

"Well, what good is sayin' somethin' when the other ain't even listenin'? Don't much matter what a man says, does it?"

In a quick, unexpected movement, Jeremiah Davis dropped the chair legs with a thud. The sudden noise surprised AnnaBelinda and she made an audible gasp. The space was small and her head was brushing the top of the trap door so she had felt the impact of the chair coming down. She could have gone down farther into the cellar but she hated it. There were crawly things; spiders and worms and roaches. In the dark she couldn't see them but she could feel them.

The first time Ira Parker threw her down in the cellar she had gone to the bottom of it but no sooner had she stretched out her legs, thinking she would enjoy freedom from the chains, than things started to crawl on her. Things with sticky legs and a smooth, hard-shelled body. She hated those things. Some felt like they had wings when she brushed them away.

One time Ira had made her go on down to the bottom. He was still on the steps, going back up when she let out a little holler as something flew right into her face and sticky legs scraped against her nose. Suddenly, Ira was on top of her, beating her about the head and then kicking her. Then he went back up and slammed the trap door down and made her stay there all night. By morning the inside of her lip was bleeding where she had continually bitten it instead of crying out. Oh, how she hated him! When he did let her out she was ready to kill him and then let his body rot down there with those bugs and things. Her mind swept out of memory back to the present. There wasn't any noise above her, no talking, no movement. Nothing.

Jeremiah's voice boomed out in an accusatory tone. "What was that I just heard?"

"How should I know? It was probably nothin' more than your old gut rumblin' because you're too sorry to fix your own grub. Instead, you come here lookin' for handouts."

"Tweren't any noise from my body, Ira Parker. You're there and the boy is there. You got someone else around here that no one knows about? Is that how come you've been actin' so sneaky and hidey like?"

"You're losing your mind, old man. The only thing around here besides me and the boy are spooks. I like spooks." Ira spit through the open front door.

Jeremiah Davis began to cross the room, keeping one eye on Ira the whole time. Not seeing signs of anyone, he looked into the bedroom. "You're the devil himself, Ira Parker. What do you do all day?"

Ira was getting restless; he never liked anyone asking too many questions. The only reason he tolerated Jeremiah Davis was because he was some kind of second-generation distant cousin or something. For as long as Ira could remember the old man had worked his traps and traveled the countryside. There had been a time when Jeremiah saved his life. There'd been a fire and Ira had gotten himself trapped. If it hadn't been for Jeremiah he would have been burned alive.

A smile teased the corners of his mouth as he considered that thought. Some folks had said Jeremiah hadn't saved a life, he'd merely cheated the devil. They whispered among each other that Ira Parker was meant to burn in hell. Well, Ira didn't care what they thought. He turned slit eyes towards the trapper and frowned.

"I don't do nothin' but live here with my boy and keep us both alive."

"What's them chains on the bedpost for?" Jeremiah's bony finger shook as he pointed to the contraption.

"You've been out in the woods too long, Jeremiah. Awhile back I had me a wolf dog chained up so's he could tear anyone apart that tried to sneak up on me through the night. If you'd been around you would 'ave seen him. Dog was so mean he even attacked me."

"What happened to him?"

"Killed him, of course; deader 'an a skinned weasel. Joe closed the lock and then lost the key. You know how boys are. I don't pay no mind to the chains anymore; they ain't hurtin' anything. Maybe I'll get me another wolf dog if I find the key."

"What would you do if he turned out just as mean as the first one?"

Ira actually smiled. "Eat 'im for supper I suppose. Or, I'd let you skin 'im and pass the pelt off as some rare breed of somethin' or another. Might get triple the money if you make the story good enough!"

By this time both men had forgotten the strange noise and AnnaBelinda quit holding her breath. She was safe as long as Jeremiah didn't ask any more questions. She wiped at another crawly thing and then drew her knees up to her chin as she waited. She would have liked to have been that imaginary wolf dog and chew right into Ira Parker. She'd go straight for his face and rip it apart and then she'd chew off his fingers. She wouldn't kill him, though. A quick death was too good for Ira Parker. Once he was mangled she would chain him up and then toss him down here in the cellar and let things eat on him until he died real slow. That's what she'd do to him if she could! Just the thought of it made her smile.

The men continued to talk and then Jeremiah left. Ira went outside with him to see him off. She couldn't hear Joe at all. Then she heard the boy get up in the chair, doing something at the table.

When Ira came back in, he was suddenly besieged with anger. "Go to your room, boy," he demanded as he jerked him away from the table.

AnnaBelinda could hear all the commotion as the boy fell and then Ira grabbed him and practically threw Joe across the room towards the bedroom. In one quick movement he had the table moved and was tugging up on the door. AnnaBelinda started to get off the steps but Ira was too quick. With one hand he reached down and grabbed a handful of hair and started pulling her up, yelling at her all the time that she had gotten him in trouble.

As soon as she regained her footing he shoved her across the room and started to hit her but then stopped with his arm still in the air.

"What did I tell you if you made any noise down there? Didn't I tell you I'd cut out your tongue?" He glared at her as he pulled his knife out of the sheath and ran his thumb down the blade. "Maybe I'll do just that. There's no reason for you to talk any way."

With terrified eyes she looked back at him, fully convinced that he would do it! She automatically curled her tongue in her mouth as though her teeth could protect it. She avoided Ira's advances as much as she could, her eyes always looking to the door to see if she could escape.

"You sure do want to get away from me, don't you girl? Well, I bet my Anna ran from your brother, too. And how do you think my little girl felt? Don't you reckon she was as scared as you are? So, why shouldn't I cut your tongue out? I would like to kill you outright, but I won't. It gives me too much pleasure just to see you suffer! That fear in your eyes is as sweet as honey butter on cornbread!"

She ran from him again and he chased her. He had no intention of grabbing her right away; he loved the fear that dictated her responses. Even if he caught her, he let her struggle and then get away from him. It was like a snake cornering a field mouse, just playing with it until it was ready to devour the helpless rodent.

But then, everything changed! All of a sudden the front door burst open and there was Jeremiah Davis with a knife in his hand, posed as though ready to attack.

"I knew you were up to somethin' Ira Parker. I knew it the day I brought little Joe back. Who is that girl? How'd you get her?" Jeremiah allowed his eyes to quickly look at the girl before he put his focus back on Ira. "You white devil! That's Chief Omekobee's daughter, ain't it? I should have known."

"So what if it is?" Ira yelled at him. "My family is dead! She's just helpin' me out in raisin' Joe here. You ain't never heard of an Indian slave? Sure you have."

"It's wrong, Ira, and you know it. You stole her and the chief thinks she's dead. Come here, girl, you're gettin' out of here."

Ira blocked her way. "Oh, she is? And just what do you think you're going to do with her?"

"I'm going to take her back to her people. You can't chain her up like that so-called wolf dog you was tellin' me about. You're still livin' on revenge, Ira Parker. No more, I tell you, no more! Come to me, girl."

AnnaBelinda started to move towards Jeremiah but Ira quickly stopped her. "You'll only take her out of here when I'm dead and gone."

Then he backhanded her so hard she fell. She knew better than to get up. With her ears ringing and her head spinning she could hear them arguing but the voices sounded hollow and garbled. She had to shake her head hard to clear her vision. When the men started fighting she thought it might be her chance to get out the front door and run for it! Inching closer to the open doorway she watched for the chance to make her move. Suddenly her hopes were crushed.

Ira's hand came up with Jeremiah's knife and it was red. The old man lay still a moment and then with eyes that stared at Ira before they lost all focus, he gasped "I curse you, Ira Parker! You may kill me but I'll haunt you all your life. I'll join them spirits and see you in hell!"

He coughed and then his body went into spasms. Jeremiah Davis died right there on the floor.

AnnaBelinda just stared in horror. Ira had actually killed the old trapper. She believed in curses, especially those from a dying man's lips! But Ira didn't seem to be phased by any of it. Joe was standing in the doorway of the bedroom watching, too. Ira got up and looked at the knife, then down at Jeremiah. He shook his head as though disgusted with the whole thing.

"I ain't diggin' you no grave." Ira grabbed hold of the man's collar and started dragging him out the door. Then he stopped, remembered that AnnaBelinda was still huddled against the wall.

Dropping Jeremiah he went to her, grabbed whatever he could reach and got her into the bedroom where he put the leg chain on her, the key to the lock in his pocket. Then he went back to his business with Jeremiah. AnnaBelinda tried to see what was going on but she couldn't. Joe moved to the front window and looked out.

Her mind was trembling. What was he going to do with the body if he wasn't going to bury it? White people didn't build pyres and burn their dead. AnnaBelinda believed that if the body wasn't taken care of the spirits would reject it. Then it would become an evil, restless spirit that would continually search for another body to possess. Throughout time it would moan and howl and wait until life was about to leave another body so it could find refuge in the shell and be buried properly. If it took too long, the spirit would torment any living being just to hasten the time of death. She shivered again. If Ira would do that to Jeremiah Davis, what would he do to her when he killed her? Would she forever be a restless spirit?

Her teeth were chattering as she heard Joe go out the door to follow his daddy. From that moment on she was determined that somehow she would get away from Ira Parker. Whether she had a tongue or not, at least she was going to protect her spirit! And so, she started plotting her escape.

~~~~~

A week had passed and Ira Parker had basically left her alone. She had no idea what he had done with Jeremiah's body. Even though she had asked Joe, the boy wasn't about to say anything. Maybe he honestly didn't know. Sometimes Joe talked easily with her, other times it was as though he didn't understand his own language. She had never known a child to be so mysterious.
~~~~~

He never laughed, never played like the Indian boys did, making up games or playing with rocks or rope. Maybe it was because he didn't have brothers or sisters. Ira seldom gave him the time of day. There were times when AnnaBelinda felt sorry for him and she would try to get him to do something with her. Every once in awhile he would respond in a positive way.

He did like for her to tell him stories. Even though he didn't talk much he seemed to like to hear her voice. If she didn't know the English word for something she would say it in her own language but he didn't so much as frown or wrinkle his nose to indicate he didn't understand. When Ira was gone, she even sang to him; songs that she had heard mothers singing to their little ones. She really didn't care if Joe liked them or not. It was important to her she didn't forget them. How she yearned to hear the familiar chanting and singing to the drums. The dancing and the stories that were all a part of the colorful headpieces and rituals had always fascinated her. Here, there was no color or even any reason to dance. Days grew into endless weeks because there wasn't much to do. Her only challenge was to keep Ira from getting mad at her.

AnnaBelinda cooked and cleaned and took care of Joe. Most of the time she was tied to something. Every once in awhile Ira wouldn't take time to secure her and that's the time when she knew she was going to make her escape. She never involved Joe or told him what she was planning to do. When she got angry or scared she would shout at him "one day I'll be gone and then you'll be sorry!" She'd never let him know she was actually planning to escape because he might tell Ira. He might do it deliberately, he might accidently let it slip. Either way, it would be the death of her. She was just hoping that with Joe's silence and innocence, Ira wouldn't blame the boy for her escape.

Ira's movements had a sort of consistent pattern to them. He had certain chores that he would do at the same time every day. She made scratches on the wall to see how many days went by between hunting trips as well as how long he would be gone. She knew when he was getting ready to hunt because he would make sure there was enough food brought in from the smokehouse and barn. Then he rigged up a system of chains and sliding loops that allowed her to go from room to room.

She was never close enough to a door to open it and look outside. The only window in the cabin was also out of reach. When Ira was there, he would leave the shutters open so she was able to at least see outside, but when he went on his trips he would bolt them shut. Not even Joe could open them. She hated those days because the intensity of being trapped was magnified. It was always so dark at night! To add to the discomfort, there were times when Ira would bolt the door from the outside to make sure Joe didn't go outside and get lost or hurt. When he did that it usually meant he would be gone as long as four days. At least he left two buckets for body waste. Joe slept a lot while he was gone. AnnaBelinda knew she'd have to ration the food because it was all they would have until Ira got back.

No matter what time of the day it was when he returned she had to help him prepare the meat. He never allowed her to have a knife, but she was good at rubbing salt in the meat and preparing it for the smokehouse. It was also her duty to clean the rabbits because she didn't need a knife for that. All she needed was a stick and a bucket.

Little Claw had taught her how to prepare rabbits. She would dig her fingers under the rib cage and tear open the hide to reveal the guts. And then, holding the front and back feet in one hand, bending the body like a horseshoe, she'd snap the rabbit forward and all the entrails dropped into the bucket. She'd clean out the cavity really good and then poke a stick through a loose fold of the hide on the rabbit's back, making a finger grip. With all the strength she had she'd snap both hands apart and the skin would peel off like a glove. Then it was just a matter of breaking the legs and the rabbit was ready for the kettle or to put on a skewer over the fire.

All the time she worked on the rabbits she would let her mind substitute the carcass for Ira. It was his guts she was spilling into the bucket and his skin that she was peeling away. The anger kept strength in her hands so she never tired. When she thought of the animal as Ira Parker, she delighted in the stiffness of death and her ability to snap the body right in half! She could even mutilate it if she wanted to. Later on in life she would understand that the rabbits had been a good outlet to vent her hostility and to feel as though she did have some control over her life.

The time for another hunt had come. AnnaBelinda had stayed out of the way as he brought in extra provisions and started rigging up her series of chains.

Joe watched in silence, then finally asked, "You gonna be gone long this time?"

"Might be. I've got one extra stop to make."

"I don't want you to bolt the door this time."

AnnaBelinda stopped what she was doing, surprised that Joe had actually spoken his mind. Did he possibly feel the same sort of caged in feeling that she did? She had never really stopped to think that he was old enough to have feelings or even an opinion.

Since Ira didn't say no right away, Joe continued to state his request. "I won't go nowhere 'cept the outhouse. I don't want her watchin' me!" His tender but hardened, brown eyes seemed to plead in a way his voice couldn't.

Ira studied the boy a moment and then the corner of his mouth raised in a smile. It would have been another channel of torment if it had been AnnaBelinda's request to keep the boy's eyes off her. His reply was a shrug and a grunt. Ira shut the door behind him and both Joe and AnnaBelinda waited, listening for the bolt to go into place. It seemed like an eternity, but the silence prevailed. The next sound was Ira's footsteps going away from the house.

Whether he was gone one day or four, the man never said goodbye or anything; he'd just leave. AnnaBelinda listened for the horse and heard him ride off. He was gone. Even though she was chained, she felt a sense of freedom. She could eat, sleep, drink, sing and do whatever she wanted until he came back. As long as Joe was safe and taken care of, nothing else was demanded of her. By the amount of provisions left, she judged that Ira was going to be gone at least five days.

She carefully inspected her chains. He had been thorough in securing her so she knew she wasn't going to be able to get away. If a trapper did come up to the cabin and see that the door wasn't bolted he just might step in. That was always a hidden hope in her heart. Every day AnnaBelinda prayed to the god of the forest and the god of direction "Send someone to the cabin when Ira's not here." But then she had to pray to the god of safety to protect that same person from Ira's anger. She didn't want them to end up like Jeremiah Davis!

AnnaBelinda had a plan of escape established in her mind; a good plan. Looking at the extra supplies, she chose those items she could carry in some sort of pouch around her waist. She knew she could only store little things. Most important was a piece of flint and a small knife.

Ira would allow her a knife only when he was gone but it had to be on the table, in full sight when he returned. If he didn't see it, he would pull his gun on her and threaten her until the knife was where he wanted it. Little did he know that she had been making her own knife. Indians weren't stupid! She had her secret hiding place and without Joe watching her she got it and wrapped it securely in her belt. Pleased that it would serve her well she hid it again, knowing she could get back to it when she needed it. She now had an adequate weapon.

Knowing that Joe could go outside, another plan developed. Sitting at the table, she began to draw a leafy plant that grew as a shrub. When she satisfied herself with the reality of it, she called Joe over to her and explained that she needed that herb to put into the cooking. AnnaBelinda started pulling out his favorite foods, whetting his appetite.

"Have you ever seen this plant?" she asked him. He just shrugged. "I bet you have; it grows close to moss and has a white, bell-shaped flower. You might have even seen little berries but I don't want them; they're bitter and just the birds eat them. Do you think you can gather a handful?"

"I can only go to the outhouse." He stared at her with no expression on his face. Her response to his uncooperative attitude was to put all the food away.

"Okay, mush and beans for supper." She knew he tired easily of both. He didn't say anything but opened the front door and just sat there looking outside. They had mush and beans for supper.

Morning came and the only thing she gave him was mush. For lunch they had mush and beans. Joe complained and she emphasized that if he wanted her to cook something else she had to have the herbs. She wasn't about to tell him that her supply of mush was already dwindling and she couldn't keep up the bland diet much longer herself!

"You get this for me and I promise you we won't have mush and beans any more until Ira gets back."

Her bribe worked. When Joe headed to the outhouse he didn't come straight back. When he did come into the door he had a handful of the plant she wanted. Setting the leaves on the stove she once again started pulling out the potatoes and venison. She never used the plants, though. Didn't dare! They had nothing to do with flavoring a meal.

The clear liquid in the leaves and stem were dream makers. If you had just a little bit, the room would be hazy and a tingling went through every vein in your body as your mind started seeing whatever the god of the unreal world chose. Ingesting the leaves were a part of a ritual in a ceremony for the braves. Only a strong man of mind, body and soul could endure the nightmarish agonies that would spin in their heads alone. AnnaBelinda remembered hearing the groans and gasps from the sacred teepee from those who were involved in the ceremony.

There was a harsh punishment if any of the boys tried to eat or smoke the plant on a dare. It was only through a series of cleansings and sweatings that the plant could be used. Handled carelessly, it was a poison.

As AnnaBelinda held the green leaves in her hand, she had every intention of drying them and putting a good pinch in everything Ira ate. When dried and crushed, the leaf lost a lot of its hallucinatory qualities, but she knew there would be enough to give Ira a nightmare he'd never forget! There was no way he would connect it with her. She planned to put it into his biscuits every morning. She'd have to be careful to section out enough dough for her and little Joe to eat and not get the two mixed up. If he did get some she'd just give him enough mustard water to cause him to throw up.

She had to smile at the thought of Ira having a tremendous headache! Chances are he wouldn't be able to think straight and he'd blame the bad dreams on the headache. He'd have a dry throat that would make him terribly thirsty, and yet, it would be hard to swallow. So, he'd drink more to try and relieve the ache. She knew that his face would turn red and the black of his eyes would devour the color as though trying to make a hole big enough for the pain to escape!

AnnaBelinda had to wonder what the god of the unreal world would place before the evil man's eyes. Was there anything that would truly frighten Ira Parker? She didn't think so. It wasn't just the fearful visions that he would experience during sleep. His joints would grow stiff, eventually leading into a temporary paralysis. At some point in time he would neglect her chains, either because of the pain in his head or from swollen fingers. As he attempted to close the lock he'd find he wouldn't have the strength to push it down firmly enough to catch. She tried to think through every possibility. The worse thing that could happen was that Ira would put her under the table and leave her there until he felt better. Even so, strong coffee would ease the pain and if he threw up, the effects of the poison would wear off within a day's time.

She knew she had to be healthy and strong in order to escape. If she were starved or weakened she wouldn't be able to get away from him. Even though she took a chance in running out of food, she ate more than usual because she knew she would need the energy. If Joe left anything at all on his plate she finished it for him.

When Ira didn't return on the sixth day she began to worry. The servings for her and the boy were smaller. Even though she didn't want to, she had to get into her little supply of food that she had stashed away. Several times Joe left the house and even though she wasn't sure where he went, she figured he was in the barn. When he came in he wasn't hungry. Curious as to what he was finding to eat she decided to trick him. She took some of the flour and meal and make a dough from it, wrapped it around a stick and put it above the fire so it would cook to a fluffy, golden brown. Then she heated a little dish of butter and honey that she dipped the bread in. She made noises of exaggerated pleasure; even smacked her lips and then licked the stick as though anxious to get every little taste.

"I want some." Joe watched her. His eyes were cold and his voice demanding.

"This is mine. You've been eating out in the barn and not sharing anything with me, so I don't have to share this with you." She began rolling another pinch of dough to put on the stick.

"You do, too!" He had his hands on his hips and bent forward to yell at her.

"I do not, and you can't make me." She deliberately turned her back to him and then licked her fingers.

"I want some!" He stomped his foot.

"Then fix it yourself," she challenged him, knowing that he couldn't.

"I don't know how! You do it!" He reached over and hit her shoulder but she ignored him. "You have to share it; you're my slave!"

AnnaBelinda hated that term as much as her white name. "No, I'm Ira's slave, not yours," she corrected him.

"Well, you have to take care of me or I'll tell Pa when he gets back and you'll be sorry."

"You're right." She let him think he won. "If you share what you have in the barn, I'll not only make it better but I'll make you a dough stick."

He didn't waste any time. He came back with turnips and ears of corn. The kernels hadn't dried out yet and she knew how to keep them wrapped in the husk and cook them. That night she and the boy had a good meal! From then on, she kept sending him out to the barn so they wouldn't go hungry. If the front door had been locked both of them would have probably been close to starvation.

Two days later, Ira rode up. The moment she heard him she scrambled to switch the knives and to get everything out of sight that might raise suspicion. As usual, Ira stood in the doorway and looked on the table.

"Girl, put that knife on the table where I can see it." He wasn't about to move until she did.

The shotgun was aimed at her head. She obediently got it, put it on the table and then backed off to the bedroom door. He grabbed it up and then looked around to make sure everything was in order.

"Where's the boy?"

AnnaBelinda had to think a minute. Had he come back inside? She didn't remember hearing him for quite some time. If he came in from the barn with food in his hands she knew they would both be in trouble.

Ira's voice became threatening. "I asked you, where's the boy?"

"Here." Joe was suddenly standing in the doorway, empty-handed.

"Where you been?"

"I had to go." His eyes darted over to AnnaBelinda and then back at Ira.

"You said he could," she defended him.

"You go anywhere else?" Ira grabbed a handful of hair and pulled the boy close to him.

"No, sir," he answered with gritted teeth as he tried to wiggle free.

"She take good care of you?" Ira let him go and then headed for the fireplace to see what was cooking. He was a little bit surprised to see turnips and rabbit. "Where'd that come from?"

"You should know, you left it for us! It's almost gone and I'm gettin' tired of turnips," Joe complained.

Ira didn't care. "I was gone longer than I thought I would be. I want some coffee. Dish me up some of that and be sure to put some gravy on those cold biscuits, you hear me?"

Ira Parker never asked if anyone else wanted to eat, he just took what he wanted. AnnaBelinda was quick to get the coffee heated. She rubbed her fingers together as she went to the hidden place with the crushed leaves. It was now or never. Ira wasn't paying attention to her so she quickly got a pinch of the leaves and mixed it in with the gravy on his plate. She had no idea if they would create a bitterness or not. As he waited, he puffed on a cigar.

"What's takin' you so long?" He suddenly looked up and started watching her.

"I got it for you." She put the plate in front of him and immediately sensed that he wasn't satisfied. He sat back as though suspecting something. Or was that just fear peeking over the rim of her imagination?

"What's wrong?" she asked.

"I told you I was hungry; this ain't enough! Gimme all that rabbit and put on some more gravy!"

He gave the plate a shove across the table and she had to catch it before it slid off. With a sigh of relief she went back and doubled his portion, this time dishing up all the rabbit. When he was finished he left his plate and then sat by the fireplace, lighting up a cigar.

"That cigar smell is makin' me feel kind of sick. Makes my head hurt," she lied. "You never smoked those things inside the cabin before."

"Well, now I do! Benjamin Malone gave me this here cigar. Made it hisself. Since you don't like it, maybe I'll get me a whole handful. Maybe I'll smoke one twice a day."

He deliberately stood and blew the smoke directly into her face. Little did he know that she was exaggerating her discomfort. After that he ignored her as he took off his boots and then sat back again, puffing on his cigar. Joe was sitting in the open doorway, angry that Ira had taken all the rabbit and he had been left with nothing but turnips and only a spoonful of gravy.

"My head hurts, too," Joe gave him a cold stare.

AnnaBelinda looked over at him, wondering why he chose to say that. He hadn't complained of anything since Ira had left and in all truth, there wasn't anything unpleasant about the cigar. It was better than some of the weeds Ira had put together! Unknowingly, the boy was helping her pull off her scam.

"You kill much?" the boy asked.

"Fair amount. Did kill a bear. The fur is on the packhorse; it'll make a good rug. You and me will have bear stew for the winter."

Ira never included AnnaBelinda. She wasn't allowed to eat until they were both finished. Often times there was nothing left in the kettle but a spoonful in the bottom and leftover scrapings on the sides. She'd get all she could and be content with the little bit on her plate. Not once had she ever been allowed to sit at the table to eat. Not that she really cared! Indians didn't need a table or chairs or even beds. She did feel resentment when Ira would toss her food as she was sitting on the floor. It made her feel like a dog. There had been times he wouldn't give her a dish, he'd just dump the food on the floor and she had to eat it the best she could. In one of his nasty moods he had made her lick the floor clean. She had no choice but to obey.

The fact that Joe and Ira ate everything that night, leaving her without, didn't affect her. Before he had ridden in she had made three sticks of dough for herself, dipping them in melted butter and honey. She was only eating the turnips to keep her breath from smelling so sweet. If Ira got down in her face he would know she had been into the honey.

As soon as Ira finished eating he left his plate at the table and went back outside to start curing the meat. When he came in he was squinting as though his head hurt. AnnaBelinda had to bite the inside of her cheek to keep from smiling. He immediately went to his coffee and sat down as he drank it. Out of spite he relit the stub of the cigar and kept blowing the smoke in her direction. The smoke gave her an idea.

"I smelled that before," she said matter-of-factly.

"So?"

"We call it sykichanomie. It's a devil tobacco. If the horses eat it they fall over in their sleep. It makes them sick for many days."

"Yeah well, what do you know? You're just a stupid child."

"I know that my people don't smoke it in their pipes."

"That's why your people are outcasts. They don't have good breeding. Benjamin says there's three blends of tobacco in this one cigar. Cost me six bullets." His eyes narrowed to slits as he sneered. "Can you even count that high?"

"I can count as high as anyone."

"Then count how many seconds it takes me to leave your ugly face and go back outside." Once again he blew smoke in her face and then stomped out the door.

Chances are he was so tired the poison would hit his system a little quicker. When he finally came back in for the evening he didn't even bother with her chains. That meant she had to sleep where she was without a blanket. The little bit of discomfort she would feel was nothing in comparison to what Ira was going to go through. That brought a smile! Feeling rather proud of herself, she curled on the floor and slept comfortably. By morning, she would put another pinch in the dough for his biscuits.

Ira Parker was moaning through the night and he didn't get better. On the third day he was still on his feet but it was obvious he wasn't thinking clearly. Often times he staggered and he was continually rubbing his eyes or the back of his head. She heard him tell Joe that he thought he had been poisoned or something. The stub of the cigar had never been relit. To her relief, he had fallen for her lie and his painful condition was attributed to bad tobacco. She watched with anticipation each time he opened and closed the lock on her leg chain. His fingers were getting stiffer and she knew his eyes were really bothering him. He blinked continuously, as though trying to focus.

And then it happened! Ira came in moaning and didn't even bother to shut the front door. Doubling over for a moment he had to wait for the queasiness in his stomach to subside, then he looked for her. He moved with a stiff awkwardness as the world apparently spun around him.

"Get me something to eat, right now!" Even his voice was weak from a scratchy, constricted throat.

"I can't reach the stove, you'll have to switch the chain," she said as she held the chain up and rattled it, knowing that small sound would echo in his head!

With her heart beating frantically she retrieved her hidden knife before he got any closer. For the last week she had been wrapping a long gauze cloth around her robe belt. Now she concealed the knife in that cloth. She had already knotted one end of it, securing a precious piece of flint. This was her true means of survival. There was a small pouch of food hidden in the back of the stove but she didn't know if she could get to it or not. It didn't matter; she knew in her heart that she was about to be free and even if she starved in that freedom all the preparations would have still been worth it!

She had doubled the pinch that morning in his food and as he bent to open the padlock he lost his balance and fell backwards. It took him a long time to regain his balance. He swore as his body seemed to work against him, but he finally managed to get back up and fumble with the lock. Just as she felt the pressure being released she moved in such a way that she made him fall backwards again. Only this time he had a harder time getting back up because his head rammed into the stones of the fireplace as all his weight forced him down. In one swift movement her foot was free and she was out the door!

CHAPTER 3

ᘏᘏᘏᘏᘏ

1969

Phyllis was standing at the front door of the cabin looking out into the yard. It truly was a beautiful setting. They really hadn't found anything in the cellar. To her disappointment Will had been right. It was really no more than a crawl space. The dampness had created a lot of mold; one wall being covered in moss. Neither one had gone down the steps even though Phyllis tried to imagine all the feet that had trusted those wooden slats as they went into the coolness of that earthen hole.

"Are you about ready to leave?" Will asked her.

She chewed on the inside of her cheek and raised her eyebrows, "I don't know. Why, are you in a hurry to get back?"

She was paying more attention to the scenery and smells. Looking off in the distance she wondered if the trees had always been this thick and the foliage so dense. Maybe there was a time when the land had been cleared and the living space was broader. When someone went out the front door, did they have a yard to cross? How far did they have to go before the trees swallowed them? Did they have to walk all the way to the river just to get their water? It seemed like she and Will had walked quite a distance before they had actually come upon the cabin. Even two buckets of water would have made your shoulders sag at that distance. Of course, Will may have taken her the long way for the "perfect effect" in discovering the cabin among the trees. Seemed to Phyllis like everything had a short cut, whether you knew about it or not. Maybe this family used a horse and cart. Huge wooden barrels could have sat outside the door to catch the rain. How many people walked in and out of this very doorway she was standing in?

Will's voice brought her back even though his words didn't make sense. "You don't have to do that."

"I don't have to do what?" She turned to face him, her nose squinched up as she quickly searched through memory but couldn't find anything to hang onto. He slipped his arm around her waist and pulled her to him. Somehow she knew he wasn't going to be honest.

"I asked you if you were ready to go and then you asked me if I was in a hurry to get back. And I said kind of. Then you said you were ready to go back to town and get a root beer float and I agreed. Surely you remember saying if I was hungry enough for a steak dinner you'd foot the bill. I truly appreciate the offer, but you don't have to. That's what I said 'you don't have to do that.'"

Her smile beamed. "You should be ashamed of yourself Will Huston; you're making every bit of that up."

"I might be stretching it a bit. Even so, are you?" His eyebrows raised like restless, twitching caterpillars.

"Am I what?" Phyllis got lost again without turning any corners in her thinking.

He loved aggravating her. "Are you ready to leave?"

"No." Her expression was such that she had just come up with another idea. "I want to look around just a bit longer. This place really intrigues me."

"All empty houses intrigue you."

"That's because they're never really empty! You know what? I never understood how people could just move out and leave so much stuff behind. You see it everywhere! Abandoned houses are often filled with furniture and left belongings. I don't think I could do that."

Will knew that Phyllis was about to get into a long story because she sat down on the fallen beam and was messing with her fingernails.

"Do you remember my best friend June? When her aunt and uncle moved from Rochester they put sheets over all their furniture and just left. I mean, it was the perfectly logical thing for them to do because they didn't need those things since they were moving into a much grandeur house. Do you remember Miss Myrtle at all? She came to church one time and was really decked out! Hat, gloves, and a pocketbook the same color as her heels. She could have easily been on the front page of some glamour magazine. Was I ever impressed!"

"If I remember her right she was quite beautiful."

"Oh, yes, you remember right! Her husband was just as ugly as she was beautiful; what a contrast! I always wondered how he felt about that. Men don't like women making more money than they do, but what about appearance? Is it okay if she looks a million times better?"

"A good looking woman always makes a man feel incredibly proud." Will wet his lips and winked. "Voice of experience."

"Thank you, but don't get me sidetracked. Back to this neat story I want to tell you. As it goes, Miss Myrtle said the rustic, country furnishings would never compliment her city décor. Besides, I think she was selling the house to a newly married couple who needed everything they could get! I don't know who was more thrilled, Myrtle in getting rid of all the old stuff or the young couple starting their new home!

"Now, it was a little different with the people who sold Myrtle their house. They were going overseas and they couldn't take a thing but their most prized treasures and their luggage of course. Can't you just imagine how sad they were to leave all their furnishings? There were beds that her great grandchildren had slept in, and baby furniture passed down from one child to another. Plus all the pictures on the walls! Glory sakes! The same people they knew and loved would become strange and foreign to those who didn't know them. But there's no way they could get those things on the ship.

"I bet you anything that old pictures get stacked up in a dusty old corner because they lose their appreciation. Kind of like uncared for tombstones in a cemetery."

She paused a moment, looking at a broken picture frame lying on the floor. The photo had long since been damaged beyond any kind of recognition. Sighing, she left that train of thought and went immediately back to the house she was describing to Will.

"I remember that house had three floors and an attic that was so large in itself it would have swallowed the entire house that Miss Myrtle had just moved out of. I went up to the attic once and of all things, there was the head of a moose! Its rack was so wide, I couldn't touch both of the antler tips at the same time. Of course, I was fairly small then, but still! Anyway, Miss Myrtle just loved the house. Well, who wouldn't?

"I wish you could have seen all the belongings in that place. It looked positively ghostly when we first went in because absolutely everything was covered in sheets. And in the upper floors that were seldom used there were tons and tons of cobwebs that had to be cleared out. They left a sofa that was long enough to be a bed and there was a dining room table and chairs that could sit sixteen people! Can you believe it?

"The best thing was the pump organ! It was a massive thing and of course no one in their right mind would want to move it. It had at least six shelves and in the middle was a huge photo of Miss Florence, the grandmother, sitting on her mother's lap when she was a baby. Everyone had such a dour expression on their face and they were all dressed in black like they had just come from a funeral. There was an older son who was maybe six or seven standing prim and proper; not a smile on his face, either. I think that's because of the starched collars. The boy probably couldn't breathe." She stopped for a split second to catch her breath, becoming more and more animated as she continued to swing her arms and bend down and bounce up and spin around.

She was enjoying reliving the memory as much as she was in telling it. Phyllis put both hands on her hips and then they went up to caress each cheek.

"Nevertheless, it was a fabulous photo. And you would have marveled at the scrollwork throughout the organ and the intricate lace pattern in the wood. Little curly queues here and there and spiral columns and touches of elegance carved everywhere. Whoever made it had been a true artist. Anyway, this superb instrument was included in the price of the house and Miss Myrtle felt like she was moving into a palace!

"And then! I remember there was a washroom all by itself! You went in on a side porch and there was the mudroom like you'd expect but next to it was a room just to wash clothes. There were shelves to put folded clothes on and Miss Florence had strung up a line so she could hang clothes right inside the house. What a marvelous idea during the rainy season. Of course we take that for granted now, but back in those days people didn't have that kind of convenience. Come to think of it, this was the first indoor plumbing they'd ever had.

"Mr. Stanley, that's Myrtle's husband, was funny but quite crude. He stretched his suspenders and boasted 'first time in my life I could drop my britches without having to worry about bees coming up the hole.' He's such a riot. Oh, how I loved to visit them. You know them, don't you?"

Will started to say he thought so but she was on a roll. "Of course you do! We met them in Chicago one time and I remember that Mr. Stanley took you to an auction."

"I remember. I bought an old iron kettle to hang in the fire place." He finally got a word in.

"One day it will hang in our very own fireplace, too." She stopped talking and let her thoughts swim just in the liquid pool of his sensuous eyes. In that one quick second she realized that she had been endlessly talking for the last five minutes, not letting him get a word in edgewise.

Now, being calm and quiet and with tenderness she reached up and kissed his chin. "I love you William Huston."

"I love you, too, Phyllis Parker." He leaned forward and brushed his lips against the soft moistness of hers. Her lipstick always had a pleasing cherry taste to it. They kissed for a long moment and then she broke away with a big smile.

"Told you there was something good in this cabin! The love we have for each other is filling up these walls and little rose buds are just popping up all over." Her eyes grew round as they started catching memories like one carrying a net catching butterflies.

Will squeezed her with anticipation, he knew what would happen next! If her mouth could have kept up with her mind she would have lived in a time warp that not only broke the sound barrier but the speed of light as well! He had to admit, though, he loved to hear her talk because she had a pleasing voice that was easy to listen to. More than anything he loved how involved she got as she spun each lively tale. Every inch of her body became a part of the explanation as her eyes and mouth expressed emotions, her hands drew the dimensions and her body twisted or turned with heavy, giant steps or a delicate pirouette. This time she began by simply freezing as though the memory would disappear if she moved even an inch.

"Will! Oh, Will! I do remember a story about one of my relatives. Oh, wow, let me think a minute." She turned and buried her head in her fingers as though trying to massage her mind to bring out the memories. She sat down next to the fireplace and ran a finger along one of the stones.

"She would have been my great grandmother and if I'm remembering the right person her name was Francine Parker. She had the most beautiful voice people ever heard. I think she began singing when she was only three years old or something. I want to say there was a time when she would only sing love songs. I don't know why, I guess she was either secure in love or so lonely that it was an endless dream. I'll have to find out which it is because that will be a story in itself. The point is, she wasn't evil!" She glared at him as though daring him to contradict.

"Okay." He held up both hands in defense. "I didn't accuse every Parker throughout history of being bad. I believe you; Francine Parker was a good person."

"Yes, she was." Phyllis suddenly frowned, "No, she wasn't. She started out good and then life got bad which made her bitter and cruel. Or, was it the other way around? Oh, Will, this is terrible! How I wish I would have learned more about my family. You're right, my insatiable curiosity should have been a better guide because if I had listened to it I would have asked a million questions until I found the whole truth and nothing but the truth so help me God!"

She had her hand raised as though taking an oath. The smile continued to droop, "Then I would know who is who and I wouldn't feel so bewildered right now."

"Are you sure her name was Francine?" Will questioned.

"Yes, that I'm sure of. Now, don't make me lose my train of thought because it's important that I don't mess it up too bad." She was silent as she thought. "It's just sketchy, you have to understand that, okay?"

Will sat down next to her and crossed his arms over his chest as he leaned back against the fireplace. "Okay. I'll excuse all contradictions and I won't rub it in that you have no idea what you're talking about."

"You're oh, so kind!" She playfully bumped his shoulder with hers. "This is the story of Francine Parker, as far as I know it. At some point in time, I don't know if it was before or after she got bad, something really sad happened to her; there was this big city hoopla event going on and something happened."

She closed her eyes so she wouldn't be distracted. Will knew that she was trying to put fragments of memories together. "I know what it was; she was singing and someone got shot. Yes, that's right, it was her lover that no one else liked. Right after that she went to New Orleans to sing in a theater. She didn't have any money to make that kind of trip but there was a big man who was there to hear her sing and he said he really cared about her.

Naturally she asked why. Why should he care, she wanted to know. And he said that it was a sin not to care. And he opened his wallet right there and gave her the exact amount she needed. This big guy apparently knew her father, whose name, I believe, was Joe. Gosh, I hope I have the story right. There was some kind of bond between this guy and Joe. I know they weren't relatives or anything, and they didn't even live in the same town, so they must have been good friends. There were some pretty horrible stories about Joe, just like most of the Parkers, but back to the other guy."

"Whatever his name was, he was a man of wisdom and compassion. There was something about him that was almost..." she had to stop and think of the right word. Religious? No. It was like she would mentally write the word in the air, study it, and then erase it. Divine? Closer, but not quite. Almost saintly. Though that wasn't the word she was looking for, either. Then an invisible word suddenly appeared in front of her eyes. "Prophetic! That's it! This man talked as though he knew exactly what was going to happen to Francine."

Once again Phyllis stopped with the story to try and think through the details. She chewed on a fingernail trying to remember.

"I'm sorry, Will, I can't really tell the story because it's kind of like a dream that doesn't make any real sense. One minute there's a big guy who came from some town event and then there's an Indian who was or wasn't real and then her life is threatened in the theater but she gets sick and almost dies while she's singing to people living in the streets. Somewhere along the way she's working in a library of all things and yet lives on a yacht. You figure it out. The thing that Mom was willing to talk about was that this prophetic man warned Francine of danger and sure enough it happened! I think it was Francine's selfishness that made Mom hate her so much."

Phyllis suddenly shot up as though a new memory made her burst out of her seat. "Francine had a daughter but she never wanted her! Oh, yes, that's what made Mom so furious with her! Not that Mom can win any award for Mother-Of-The-Year herself. Anyway, this Indian woman was like a ghost or guardian angel or something, even though I can't imagine an angel looking like an Indian. I suppose they could, all things are possible and of course in the heavens there's no such thing as race or creed or the such."

"You're starting to chase a rabbit." Will touched her nose.

Phyllis took a deep breath and then sighed. "You're really bored with this, aren't you?"

"Actually, no. You've sparked my interest. You said it all goes together kind of like a fragmented dream. The absolute eerie thing is that I know this story! But I don't know why I know it. I think we need to ask some questions and maybe try and fill in some blank spaces. This is good stuff."

Phyllis had to stare intently into his eyes to see if he was being serious or making fun of her. He was serious! She couldn’t believe it.

He continued deep in thought, “Good chance that Francine lived in this cabin at one time, at least when she was a child. I'm thinking she moved when she was about fifteen or sixteen years old.”

“What makes you say that?”

“It was in the news once; something about a local girl making it big in New Orleans because of incredible talent. If I remember right the scandal tabloids got a hold of her, too, and for awhile she was the talk of the town.”

“You're right! The talk was that she was wealthy but wouldn't share that wealth. Then the country went into depression and she found herself at the other end. Of course, no one was about to help her! I wonder what it's like to be so popular that other people want your autograph and yet your own family won't even speak your name?”

“I hope you never know! It must be as tragic as having your lover shot and die in your arms.”

Phyllis sat down with a deep sigh. After a moment she looked up, slapping her knee as though she had made up her mind. “Well, no more of this nonsense about not knowing my relatives! I'm going to find out who my aunts and uncles are and maybe even track down all my cousins! Oh, Will, I’m so thankful you brought me here. So much of my heritage is right here in this poor, demolished cabin, and I’m determined to find out everything I can. And I don’t care how bad it is because it’s just too important to discover the good as well and to make sure that’s as much a memory as the so-called curse.”

She made a ghostlike moan and then wiggled her fingers in front of his face as though imitating a scary monster.

“But where do we even begin?” She sighed. “I wonder who that big guy was and what his connection to Francine was? Do you suppose he came along just by accident?”

“God never does anything by accident. You know that every person in our life is put there for a specific reason. No doubt he was a predestined part of the whole miraculous scheme of life.”

“I bet so, too. Oh, I wish these walls could talk! How I would love to know the true story.” She sighed again as she propped her elbows on her knees and then cradled her face in her hands.

ஓஓஓஓஓ

1888

The huge man sat at the table, his head tilted back and his chin up, eyes slanted and forehead deeply furrowed. Every once in awhile his spatulate hand would come up as his callused and scarred fingers rubbed his chin or nose. He had lost half a finger to a trap years ago but he never seemed to be bothered by it. He was listening intently to the conversation going on around the table next to him. He had heard the three men talk before and even though he had wanted to know more, he had remained silent. At this point in time he didn't want to seem too interested or too eager to know what was going on. If he asked any questions they might try and get him involved. He was the type of guy that watched, listened, and only moved when necessary. No one could have ever accused him of doing anything on impulse. Everything he did was carefully calculated.

That's what made him such a good hunter. He could be quiet long enough to think like the wild creatures. He not only knew their habits and survival skills but he also knew their patterns and why they did everything they did. As a matter of fact, he could outguess what they'd do eight times out of ten.

Now, he was calculating the next movements from the trio at the table. Henry Russell was about to leave. He was a hard working farmer who lived at the east end of town and always seemed to boast of the biggest and best crop of corn in the whole district. He wasn't conceited but he knew a good thing. Neither was he a cheat but his prices were high. Quality, he said. A man paid a price for quality. Henry had a wife and maybe eight young'uns. They were good folk. But Henry was over protective and a follower. If someone hollered 'wolf! Go kill it!' he'd be shooting anything that moved for fear his family was in danger. What they had been discussing the last couple of days sounded to him like a threat to his family so he was ready to take defensive action. Made no difference to him if the threat was real or not, he was going to be ready for it!

Then there was Ezerius Miller. He didn't have a family, only a pack of wolves that seemed to travel everywhere with him. He liked setting up dog fights and made a fistful of dollars at it. Miller wasn't a man to deal with. He didn't listen to reason and he never listened to advise. No one dared cross him! Usually he came into town, carried out his business and then left. It was Conifer there that got him to stay on a bit. Conifer was really the ringleader and agitator.

Ray Conifer was known to the townsfolk as a waste of a man. Short in stature, mere skin and bones, always wearing a suit and tie. Typical banker. Looked like someone had grabbed his chin and just stretched his face, elongating his nose and drooping his cheeks. His mouth had a perpetual curve to it; not because he was smiling but because a scar side winded from jaw to jaw. Got that as a young man. On a moonless night he had tried to cross Smith's pasture and had a run in with the bull. Story went that he was gored pretty badly. A horn had caught the corner of his mouth and ripped him from ear to ear. It had been a wonder he had even lived through it.

Even the ladies had a hard time looking at him. Deciding he'd never make it in life by his looks he decided to get rich. If people didn't respect him for his appearance, at least they'd tip their hat to him because he had money! He was the most educated man in Gough's Ridge and he quickly established himself in the banking business. Conifer wasn't much of a sociable man but people did trust him with their money because he knew what he was doing. Everything related to the bank in some way or another for him. Conifer was saying "folks'll get wind of this and they'll move right out of this territory. I might as well fling the bank doors open and let everyone just come in and get all their money. I ain't about to go broke without takin' a stand."

Henry Russell spit and then wiped his mouth with the back of his hand. "Well, there ain't gonna be no Injuns comin' into town as long as I'm here. We run them off two year back and we'll run 'em off again. They don't have no right to be here among decent, white folk."

He slammed his fist down on the table as though to emphasize how strongly he felt about it. He was ready to fight and just waiting for someone else to make a move.

The big man lowered his chair so that all four legs were on the floor. He leaned forward, shaking his head and then raised himself to his full height of six feet four inches. It was time to leave; he'd heard enough. Now, he had to find out what tribe was heading his way, if in fact, there really was one.

"Hey, Frothworth, leavin' so soon?" The bartender called out, but no answer was given, just a wave. Actions always spoke louder than words.

He had to work everything through in his mind. Why was the tribe coming into Gough's Ridge? Did they just need supplies or were they possibly looking for someone? Like a young girl, per chance? He had listened to Ira Parker's boy talk about his imaginary friend. Rumor was that little Joe Parker was addled because of his mama dying but Frothworth knew better.

He never saw the girl in the cabin, but that made never-no-mind to him; he still knew she was there. From the very first time he suspected Ira was up to something he was determined to find out what it was. At first he suspected Ira was stashing money, then he suspected that he had a woman in the cabin. By watching and listening to little Joe, Frothworth figured it out even though he couldn't prove it.

Everyone knew Chief Omekobee's tribe had been run off because Little Claw was always on the warpath. To Frothworth's surprise, Ira Parker admitted that Indians killed his family but he didn't name names.

Wasn't long after that when word came around that the Chief's daughter was missing which was about the same time little Joe came up with an imaginary friend. But then, the remains of a child were found not far from the reservation. There was too much decay and mutilation to actually identify it, but the Chief declared that it was his missing daughter who apparently had been killed by a pack of wolves. Forthworth hadn't believed that either. The chief refused to make eye contact which was unlike him. But it did settle all the unrest. Little Claw and Ira seemed to have been pardoned for atrocities neither admitted to but had sure been guilty of.

Times got hard and some of the tribe came into town to start trading goods. That was just too much for Gough's Ridge. The Indians were threatened and eventually run off. Frothworth hadn't heard of any other Indians in the area so he figured it had to be the Chief.

That's what the three men were talking about. If the tribe headed toward Gough's Ridge there would be trouble for sure. The townsfolk just wouldn't hear of having Indians in the area again, fearful that there would be more bloodshed. Frothworth knew it was foolishness. He'd traded with the Indians all his life. He'd even spent nights in their teepees and had found them to be considerate and cordial people; not to mention intelligent and fair!

He honestly didn't believe that the Chief's daughter had been killed. Couldn't have been, he spat on the ground. For the last couple of weeks he had been watching her. At least, he suspected it was her before this situation came up. Now, he wasn't so sure. Maybe the girl he had been watching was someone else. There was a possibility that she was from some other tribe and had gotten separated and they were looking for her. That would have been a believable story and an explanation why the girl wasn't moving on.

But…no. Frothworth shook his head. Bears may look different when they come out of hibernation but that's only because time and elements have a tendency to make a crucial change in behavior and appearance. The child he had been watching belonged to Chief Omekobee. Frothworth's gut knew it even if his head wouldn't admit it. And if that were indeed true, he would reunite them. That's why he had listened so closely to Henry, Ezerius and Ray. There was absolutely no explanation where the girl came from or even how she got there; but none of that really mattered. If her people were coming, then he had to make sure she got safely to them.

As he continued home, he thought about her. She was always careful to stay out of sight…or so she thought. Even though the girl wore the dress of a white child, Frothworth could tell by the hair and mannerisms that she was Indian bred. He never let her know that he was around and watching, but he made sure she was okay. Every once in awhile he'd leave a blanket laying around or a heavy shirt or a sack of potatoes or something that he knew she could eat. One time he tossed a pair of Emma's shoes in the shed along with a worthless hat and a broken harness. That way she wouldn't suspect he was leaving her something. Next time he saw her she was wearing the shoes. He had smiled.

He figured he didn't have to interfere; she was doing just fine. She was sleeping out in an old shed that he had basically abandoned years ago. It was just too far from the barn and he kept a few farm implements in it but that was about all. There was a bit of concern because he knew snakes liked to inhabit that shed, especially when the weather changed. He was hoping her constant activity had scared them away. This was one time his reasoning should have coincided with logic. In a way, he blamed himself for what happened next.

It was an unusually dark night. He was almost to the house when he saw her up at the barn with something white in her hand. Looked like a dead chicken. He picked his tooth with his knife blade. She must be getting pretty hungry to get that close to the house. She had built fires before so he knew she could cook. He never let his actions betray the fact he was watching her as much as she was watching him. Instead, he always looked busy, making himself visible at all times. As long as she could see him, he knew she'd skirt around and stay out of the way. On this particular night, however, he kept her in sight and it didn't matter if she saw him or not!

When she had gotten back to the shed he circled around so he could watch her. Didn't take but a moment to size up the situation and he was mighty tempted to step in but he forced himself to stay back and watch. Scared him pretty bad, but then he marveled at her ability to handle the situation. When she was gathering wood for the fire she picked up a snake among the twigs and birch curls. He knew she was bit even though she didn't cry out. It wasn't one of the poisonous kind but it had a nasty bite. It would make her sick and feverish. He hated snakes! All snakes!

Without any more movement than absolutely necessary she gutted the chicken and laid the entrails across her arm. Frothworth wanted to applaud! Chicken entrails would draw out the venom every time! She seemed to settle in, patiently waiting for the affects. Oh, how he wanted to help. He wanted to go to her and tell her that she'd be okay. He wanted to give her a cold drink of water and wipe the sweat off her brow. But he knew he couldn't. When she finally went back inside the shed, he did the next best thing. He went for his wife.

Emma was just a little woman with a short, squat body. The kids called her a roly poly but she didn't care. Her sense of humor was as tall as a ten-foot giant that was always laughing and praising the good Lord. Frothworth was as much of a church going man as his little woman was. She'd read her Bible every day and make him take his hat off at the table. Didn't a day go by that he didn't bow his head in prayer to offer thanks and to ask for the simplicities of life. Everyone respected him and Miz Emma.

Now it was time for the both of them to get involved. Frothworth remembered the first few times he had seen the child and how she had troubled him. Emma had been quick to pick up on his mood.

She had been in the kitchen, busying herself. "Might as well tell me about it now and save the waste of time when it's later," she had coaxed him. "What's so heavy on yer mind?"

"Don't know for sure." He had sat back and watched her as she carried the iron kettle back to the fireplace. After she secured it she turned towards him, wiping her hands on her apron.

"I reckon you know enough that you've been workin' it in yer mind and it troubles you." She contradicted him with a smile as warm as the fire.

"That it does." Still, it had taken him a good two minutes before he actually formed the thoughts into words and was able to share it with her. "She's out there. I been watchin' her."

Emma had known exactly who he was talking about, but it was more important to allow him to express his mind first. "Who's out there?"

"That bit of a girl. I think it's the Chief's daughter; Wind In Mourning."

"The one they say got killed 'bout two years ago?" Emma had opened the flour bin and carried a scoop to the table where she was preparing biscuits.

"So they say but I never believed that story. I seen her, Emma, she's down at the shed. After a couple days I figured she'd move on but she hasn't yet."

Emma had carefully scattered the flour so she could roll out the dough. "So, what are you going to do about it?"

"I been thinkin' on that. If I do more than just show myself it'll scare her off. I would hate to even imagine what Ira Parker put her through; chances are she don't trust no one, especially men."

"I reckon you're right about that. You want me to go to her?" Emma didn't look up but kept her eyes focused on what she was doing.

Her hands had worked so effortlessly she probably could have made biscuits with her eyes shut. Frothworth had watched her, wondering how anyone, even an Indian child, would be blind to Emma's warmth and goodness. His little woman had always been a patient and compassionate mother to their son and a wise and understanding wife to him.

"I'm not even sure she'd trust a woman. The weather's turnin' cold and I'd hate for her to take off and not be ready. And yet, I can't imagine her thinkin' she can stay hidden in that old shed. Somethin's keepin' her around, though."

Emma had smiled as though the secrets in her head couldn't stay there any longer. "She's been watchin' me, too, Frothworth." She had finished kneading the dough and then plopped the mound onto the floured surface and started spreading it. "And I been lettin' her know I see her. Oh, she'll be quick to hide but I just smile or nod my head at her. I think she might want to trust us but it will take time, like you say."

And that's the way it had all started. They had agreed to just let the girl do what she wanted, as they kept a watchful eye on her. Now, things were different. Frothworth couldn't leave that child in the shed, snake bit, knowing that she may have disturbed a nest and could suddenly get more than she bargained for. One time he had counted twenty-three snakes in that shed! He had been tempted then just to burn the thing down.

When he got back to the house he found his beloved Emma at the fireplace, stoking the fire, ready to put on a kettle of bean soup. "Put your pot down, it's time we step in." His voice seemed level even though his heart was racing. "She's gonna need our help, Mother, she's been snake bit."

Emma didn't need to hear another word. Everything else was forgotten as she and Frothworth hurried down to the shed. Both were asking the good

Lord to guide them so they could approach her without scaring her to death. They had no idea what to expect. On the way, Emma was almost wringing her hands in her apron. They paused for only a moment.

"Let me do this." Emma knocked lightly to give warning that they were there and then she boldly opened the door and stepped in. The child was huddled in the corner of the shed, curled into a tight ball. There was obvious fear in her eyes as well as pain, but Emma had a special way about her that just seemed to pulsate trust.

"Come to me, child; it's okay." The little woman approached carefully. "That snake bite needs more attention. We won't hurt you."

Emma bent down and touched the sweating forehead. "Don't be afraid. My good man here…" she emphasized good, "Is going to carry you up to the house so we can take proper care of you. You don't got nothin' to worry about anymore."

At that, Frothworth scooped up the frail, little body in his arms, noticing that she was as light as a feather. He could feel her fear as her entire body tensed but she didn't fight him. He carried her in such a way that she could feel safe and secure in his big arms and even before they reached the house he felt her go limp and relax. Emma had to admit that it was easier than she had feared and she gave all the glory to God! At least they weren't dealing with a savage.

The young girl seemed to know that everything was going to be okay as Frothworth put her down on a daybed they had set up by the kitchen a long time ago, and then he headed to the barn. Emma kept the lights low and every time she touched the child she spoke in soothing whispers. By morning, her little patient was sleeping peacefully. At the first crack of dawn, Emma was in the kitchen putting on breakfast. The sounds and smells woke the child. Just as she was stirring, Frothworth came in from milking the cow.

"May be frost on the ground in a couple nights," he called out.

The girl's eyes opened wide and full as she gasped and then her head rolled from side to side as she tried to figure out where she was and where the voice had come from.

"It's okay, child." Emma was immediately at her side. "No need to be afraid."

"I know that voice!" She had to sit up in order to look around and see him. Emma gave a quick praise to the Lord that the child could speak English but then she was quickly drawn to the realization that even more important than words being understood was the fact his voice had been recognized. How could that be, she wondered?

At that time, Emma had no way of knowing that it was the voice the girl had heard so many times talking to Ira Parker when she had been under the table. It had a distinct quality to it; one she knew she'd never forget.

When he came into the room she just stared at him. So, that was the face the voice came from. True, she had seen him and the fat, little woman countless times in the yard but she really hadn't paid much attention to either of their distinct features. Come to think of it, she had never been close enough to even recognize his voice. Up close, he looked like a giant, especially compared to his woman. Little Joe had told her he was a big man but she had never seen any human being as tall or as broad as the man she was looking at now. His size definitely drew her attention to him, but it was his voice that made her stare. Without even knowing it, she had ended up at Frothworth's house; the one man she had thought might be a real human being!

"What's your name, girl?" Frothworth asked.

She hesitated and sank back into the bed. Throughout the last couple of weeks she had repeated her own name time and time again because she loved the sound of it. But she wasn't prepared to tell someone else who she was. She knew that her people thought she was dead. Ira made sure of that! And he had her convinced that no one else would believe her if she did tell them.

With absolute malice Ira had taunted her, "White folks think you're dead. And you know what they'd do to you if you tried to tell them who you were? They'd call you a liar and liars don't deserve to live. We hang 'em or drag 'em behind a horse until all their flesh is scraped off and they beg us to let 'em die. You want that to happen to you? It will if you go around saying your name is Morning Grief.

He didn't even know her real name! How she had hated him! Now, as she faced Frothworth she remembered all too well who she was and the precarious situation she was in.

"It's okay." Emma continued to soothe as she brushed the long, black hair away from the child's face. "We know you're an Indian child and we haven't told a soul you're here. You can tell us; what's your beautiful name?"

There was no explanation for it, but she suddenly had to blink back tears and to bite her lip to keep it from trembling. Then she shuddered and stared into the tender, brown eyes of the woman who she wanted with all her heart to trust. She finally got the courage to answer her.

"My name is Wind In Mourning."

"I knew it!" Frothworth stepped closer. "I knew you was alive! Little Joe wasn't as addled as his daddy made him out to be. How long did that man keep you there?"

She didn't answer; she just stared at him. He stepped even closer; in fact, so close he bent down and she could smell him. He didn't have that sour odor that Ira Parker had, but a combination of sweet tobacco and hay. There wasn't even a hint of whiskey on his breath! She could tell he wanted to touch her but he didn't. At that moment there was a kind of silent communication going on between them. Almost like when the wild animals just looked at each other and knew there was nothing threatening.

"We'll get you back to your people if we can, I promise you that." He squared his shoulders and stiffened his chest so that he had to look down past his nose at her.

"You would do that?" Her heart seemed to stop beating at such an unbelievable possibility.

This time Emma answered, "Yes, child, that's where you belong. Not out there in that God-forsaken shed full of snakes! How long have you been wandering around on your own?"

Before she could even count up the moons and answer the question, Frothworth had cocked his head so that he was now looking at her sideways with a frightening look of cold hatred in his eyes. His jaw was set as he clinched his teeth. Even though she knew this emotion wasn't directed towards her, just his look sent horrible shivers through her!

With a deep, level voice he thundered, "It was your brother that killed Ira's family, wasn't it? And because of that, Parker took his revenge out on you, didn't he?"

She remained silent. Memories suddenly turned into black, hairy hands that were reaching down from the ceiling and clamping onto her throat, keeping the breath from her mouth. His intensity seemed to make those hands squeeze harder and harder.

"What'd he do to you child? Did he starve you? Did he beat you? How did he manage to keep you hidden all this time? Were you caged up like some animal? What all did he make you do? What'd he tell you to frighten you so?"

It was too much! With painful whimpering she curled into a tight ball as though fending off the questions in the same way she had once fended off blows from Ira's clenched fists.

"No, no, you're scarin' her too much." Emma sat on the bed, wedging herself in between her husband and the child. Frothworth immediately backed off. The little woman drew the child up to her, cradling her in secure arms. "There, there, now, it's okay. We don't need to know everything that happened. You just rest right here in my arms because you're safe and sound and that Mr. Ira Parker will never, never touch you again! No one knows you're here and we'll do our best to get you back to your people as soon as we can. Don't you worry about a thing. Let's just think on the things you need right now. Are you still feeling sick from the snakebite? Are you hungry?"

"No." She had quit crying and liked the feel of being in the woman's arms. She knew she was too old to be held like a little papoose but she didn't care. The gentleness of someone touching her was as warming to her heart as honey was sweet to her lips.

Emma continued to hold her close as motherly fingers threaded through the black hair and then stroked her temple. "Well, let me change that dressing and put another poultice of onion and salt on it. That will help the soreness. And then, would you let me give you a bath and wash that dress before you put it back on?"

"No!" She almost shouted as she pushed away. Her eyes were wild and Emma was taken by surprise. "No," she fought back tears, "Don't make me put it back on!"

"What's wrong with the dress?" Frothworth knew there was a good reason why the child had reacted the way she did. Now that he was close to her he could see that the dress was patterned with numerous colors that weren't a part of the design.

Ugly stains crisscrossed it that even he couldn't identify. The skirt of it basically hung in shreds, in some places the material was so threadbare he was surprised that it hadn't rotted off her.

He reached out and touched the course material. "Where'd you get this from?"

Tears came to her eyes even though she desperately fought not to cry. When the knowledge was simply in her head she could deal with it, but when she actually had to put it into spoken words, it was as though all feelings resurrected as well. It made her think of a smoldering fire whose fierceness lies in silence until stirred. Then it rises up in searing flames that can burn and destroy. Her own words might turn against her and her joy could become blackened as memories charred her fragile mind. And yet, now that she had been asked, the answer could no longer remain in silence. The words were fighting to get out no matter how tightly she was holding her lips together. She even put her hand over her mouth to try and keep them in!

Emma was well aware of her inner struggle, and took the small hand from the trembling lips and then lightly kissed the fingers. With a voice so soft she could barely be heard she looked directly into her eyes.

"The truth, child. Nothing will happen to you and I won't let Mr. Parker near you. Tell us, where did you get the dress?"

Wind In Mourning took a gasping breath, "Off his dead daughter." She almost choked over the words, pulling her hand back and then holding both hands in tight fists against her throat. "He gave me her name and her dress; she didn't need them, he said."

Then, in sobs she told the story, the words spilling out. "We went in the cabin and he made me look at each one my brother killed. They'd been dead a long time! Then he stripped me and threw my dress in the fire. I never stood in front of a man like that before. Then, I watched him take off the girl's dress so he could put it on me. It stunk so bad! Made me feel dead, too. He tied me to a chair for a long time; he was outside digging graves. Then he got a blanket and made me drag the bodies out to the graves. He just dumped them in with no words or songs. His own kind!"

Emma stood upright, her face red with agony and rage. "Oh, my Lord! Oh, my good, Lord!" Then she stomped out like she was going to be sick at her stomach. Both Wind In Mourning and Frothworth could hear the little woman moan and cry out as though her heart was being wrenched. They had no idea what she was doing as she went from room to room, hitting and stomping and throwing things, wailing and sobbing.

Frothworth raised his eyebrows and explained, "She's okay. She's just sharin' the grief that you carried alone. She'll be back in a minute." He was right. When she came back in she was carrying a simple, muslin nightgown. Her voice was soft again even though her eyes were puffy and the muscles in her chin quivered.

"Daddy, please leave this kitchen. I'll call you shortly."

He obediently left. Emma composed herself, wiping her nose with the tail of her apron. Then she took a deep breath and tried to smile. "This is all I got; it won't fit you but you'll never wear that dress another day. Let me help you take it off."

Wind In Mourning only flinched once when her arm was moved. As the woman held the dress in her hands, tears were streaming down her face but this time she didn't make a sound.

"Frothworth can bury it. It should have been in the ground a long time ago!" As the gown went on, Emma also washed the dirty flesh. The water was warm and Wind In Mourning almost went back to sleep. In fact, as soon as Emma called Frothworth back in, she heard his voice and then gratefully closed her eyes and slept for the next four hours.

❧❧❧❧❧

It had only taken Emma two days to make a dress for Wind In Mourning. The girl had stayed in the gown during that time, not going past the kitchen. Emma was smiling as she shook out the soft, gray material and motioned for the child to raise her arms over her head.

"It's all they had at the mercantile but it's going to look just fine on you." Emma slid the dress over her head and then pulled it down into place.

She hadn't made a dress in a long time, especially a child's! It took a little imagination because she didn't sew it in the usual fashion. Without a bow or ruffle it had a strange waif look to it. Emma had debated the style of the dress even before she threaded the first needle. There was no way the child could ever fit in with a group of children so it was of no value to design pleats and puffs or a fancy collar. No amount of pretense would help this child blend in; the black hair and sharp facial features would give her away immediately! With the impossibility of passing her off as a visiting niece, Emma decided to honor her by allowing her to be as close to her heritage as possible. Therefore, the dress was created to fashion the styles of her own people.

To Wind In Mourning it was beautiful! It wasn't much different than her own dress that Ira Parker had thrown in the fire. All it needed was bead work and colorful designs of red and green or a shade of turquoise. Even though her pride wanted to show off her new dress to the world, she knew she couldn't be seen. Otherwise, Frothworth would be in trouble. But this time she didn't mind staying out of sight. If she wanted to leave, they wouldn't stop her. Therefore, restrictions on her activities had no bearing on her freedom, only on her safety.

Gunther was their son and she could show it off to him. He had ridden up the day after she had gotten snake bit. She had liked Gunther immediately! His eyes beamed with an inner light and his blond hair was long, pulled back with a leather strap. Wind In Mourning had never seen blond hair. At first she wondered if somehow he had stuck corn silk on his head!

He had actually seemed eager to meet her. In a peculiar kind of way, if Gunther had darker skin and had let his hair go free, he could have been mistaken for an Indian himself. His chest hair was so light and curly it could barely be seen. In her innocence she had asked how it had gotten that way and if he had deliberately curled each hair. Natural curls were something else she had never seen. His eyes smiled first, and then he did a most peculiar sounding thing. He laughed!

Wind in Mourning had a hard time understanding laughter because she had never experienced it herself. Sometimes the girls her age had sniggered with their hand covering their mouth, and once or twice she had even heard her brother laugh with just a single 'oh ho', but never had she heard anyone laugh like a waterfall! And it wasn't just Gunther that did it. They all did! He would say something and then laugh and then Emma would laugh. And then Frothworth laughed. Of course, Frothworth was more reserved with his laugh, but his eyes were still splashing in the same pool of merriment. Wind In Mourning discovered strange gargling sounds coming from her own throat that they said was the birth of laughter. That only made Gunther laugh harder!

At first she was embarrassed and shied away, but then he let her know that it was good to laugh. He wasn't making fun of her at all. They all said it felt good to laugh. Once she laughed so hard she got a stitch in her side and it was hard to breathe. When she groaned from the pain they all laughed even harder! The more she gasped for breath and wiped the wetness from her eyes, the more they all laughed! It was as though she had been given a special gift and she found herself falling asleep at night with a big grin on her face.

For three days Gunther had stayed with them, then he rode out early the next morning and didn't return until the following evening. Wind In Mourning didn't want to see him go and yet she knew that he was going to ride out and try and find the tribe of Indians supposedly heading their way. His presence reminded her a little bit of her brother and even though her heart ached for the young brave, she was strangely comforted by Gunther's presence. One morning, Gunther came to her with something in his hand.

"Wind In Mourning, come a minute." She liked it that everyone called her by her real name. Every once in awhile Gunther would call her Winny. She didn't understand why, but she knew it was a name that carried respect and affection so she didn't care. He was holding five beads.

"I traded these a long time ago and plumb forgot I had 'em. Maybe we can attach them to your dress some way."

Her voice was speechless. She didn't understand why this strange man with hair like the sun should be so kind to her. Standing incredibly still, even in her excitement, she watched him thread the beads. "Here, Ma, come and sew these around the neckline."

It became a special time of bonding, even though no one realized it as such. Gunther was smiling as though he had given her the richest treasure in the world. And in a way, that's exactly what he did! Emma was concentrating on the stitching and yet the smile she wore wasn't just for the beads, but for the love in which they were given. She was proud of her son! And Frothworth sat against the wall leaning back on two legs of the chair. There wasn't a smile on his face but his eyes were dancing.

Wind In Mourning was so happy she thought she would float! Every time she looked down, Emma would tilt her chin back up so the needle wouldn't stick her. At last, Emma knotted the thread, bit it off, and then sat back and looked at her handiwork.

"Excellent," Gunther beamed. "You done good, Ma." Then he held Wind In Mourning at arm's length and spun her in a circle. "Now you're starting to look like Chief Omekobee's daughter again! He will be so proud of you!"

"How close are they now?" She suddenly took her attention away from the beads to the coming of her people.

"Heard tell that they were less than a day's ride. I think you'll be all better and tomorrow I'm going to go out and meet them."

"Can I go with you?"

Gunther picked her up and spun her in another circle. "Do you think I would leave you here my Indian princess? Now that you have decent clothes we can let you ride a horse and be away from here before anyone even sees you. But, once you're reunited with your people you've got to tell them not to come into Gough's Ridge. If they need supplies or something you sneak word to me and we'll take care of it for you. I'm happy for you but we'll have to say our goodbyes."

Wind In Mourning didn't want to say goodbye! "The townspeople don't want us here, do they?" Her eyes were downcast as she feared the anger that she had seen in the white people before.

Gunther frowned, "No, they don't. There would be trouble for everyone." Then his eyes brightened. "But this world is bigger than Gough's Ridge! The sky is open and says 'come, Wind In Mourning, the earth is yours! Come and be happy!' Can you hear it?"

"No." Her smile was doubtful. "The sky is dark and silent because it's asleep."

"So, wake it up! Holler and yell and dance and sing! It's great to be alive and free!"

Wind In Mourning believed him! The times the four of them shared were good. In fact, it was only at night when the wind moaned through the trees that she remembered when life had been ugly and dark. She thought she had walked far from the fear she had once known and that Emma had washed away all traces of harm.

Little did she know that the simple act of Emma buying the gray material over a week ago had started the women in Gough's Ridge talking. They tried to reason it out; Emma and Frothworth basically lived alone. They also knew that Emma rarely sewed. Their only son, Gunther, wasn't even married so there was no way she could be sewing for grandchildren. He was rarely even home but out riding the range. He was known to scout for the wagons and be gone for months at a time. And then, the amount of material had been questionable. There wasn't enough for a tablecloth and certainly nothing for Emma to wear. It was totally inappropriate for a shawl or even a curtain.

"What in the world is she up to?" One woman looked at another, not willing to let the episode go unsolved.

Even though Emma was respected she had just done something that was suspiciously uncommon. The gossiping women stood huddled in the back of the store, trying to be inconspicuous and yet so obvious that Emma had had a hard time keeping a straight face.

Bernadine Russell finally decided that it wouldn't hurt to ask at least one question so she left the group of ladies and tried to look as though she was interested in the dry goods.

"That is a pretty piece of cloth you have there, Emma. I had my eye on it but there just isn't enough yardage to make anything except for one of the young 'uns. But they wouldn't like that material; it wouldn't pleat worth a nickel. Whatever do you have in mind?"

Even though her smile was innocent enough, Emma knew the woman was just meddling. She had already thought of the answer she would give. "I'm going to make a bib the size of Frothworth's appetite!" She chuckled. "I don't sew much, you know."

"Yes, we know." Bernadine was at a complete loss for words and looked at the other women still in the back of the store to see if they would help her out. None moved. GloryLynn simply shrugged. Emma quickly busied herself and headed to the counter where she could pay for her select items.

Going into the street with her parcel, she laughed to herself. Maybe she should have told them she was going to make Frothworth some underwear! That would have shocked them so badly they wouldn't have dared ask another question!

A couple days later, GloryLynn Conifer mentioned it to Ray. "Now, what in the world do you make of Emma buying that material? In the last three years she hasn't bought so much as a straight pin. I wonder what she's up to."

Ray was bored with the conversation even before she spoke. "Maybe she's gettin' so big she has to add another panel to her dress."

GloryLynn's mouth dropped at hearing such a crude remark and then her shoulders sagged as she uttered a disgusted humph. "And what do you know about sewing?"

"Not a thing, so why even ask me?"

"Why indeed?" She busied herself as she filled her lap with peas to shell. "Well, I can tell you this, it's nothing meant for her. That can only mean she's got someone visiting. They got any kinfolk around? Who do you reckon is there?"

"Why should it matter?"

"Maybe it don't, but then again, maybe it do." GloryLynn snapped a pea pod as though highly insulted by her husband's disregard for her opinion.

Ray tried to feign a lack of interest, but the more he thought about it, the more he began to get curious. He didn't like anything happening in Gough's Ridge that he didn't know about. He needed to know if new people came to town because they might need his services at the bank. If Emma was sewing for someone she might have to take some money out of her savings. Company always meant extra expense and he knew that Frothworth never carried a dime on him.

Even though Ray Conifer told his wife he was going to the bank to get something, his intention was to walk down to Frothworth's place first and just see if there was any unusual activity. It was dark and the lights were on. Frothworth was just coming in from the barn. Ray made small talk, tried to persuade him to go back into town and get a drink with him and the boys. It was a usual request in which Frothworth always declined. The whole time they talked, Ray kept Frothworth's back to the house so he could continually watch the doors and windows. And then he saw her! A child crossed by the window! GloryLynn had been right; something was going on! And it was something that quickly got his attention because it had only taken that quick second to ascertain that the child wasn't any relative of Frothworth or Emma. That was an Indian as sure as he was the bank president!

"Suit yerself then." Ray tried to keep his heart from racing. Frothworth immediately noticed Ray's change in character and how the tick in his jaw intensified to a nervous spasm. The big man looked up at the house a moment, almost expecting to see Wind In Mourning standing on the front porch. He didn't see her and nothing looked out of place. But Ray was obviously unnerved about something.

"Emma's waitin' for me," Frothworth excused himself.

Ray Conifer was all too glad to leave. The little man quickened his pace down the road and headed straight for Henry's place. Twenty minutes later the Russell household was in an uproar. The men had decided that Frothworth had already met with the tribe of Indians that were coming and was so endeared to them that he had opened his home to their comings and goings. Ray pointed out that he had actually seen an Indian squaw in a nightgown! Maybe Frothworth was going to be hospitable to the whole tribe. Everyone knew he owned nearly a hundred and fifty acres. Chances are he was going to let them set up their reservation for the winter right there on his land.

Ray scratched his balding head; there were probably five other Indians in the house that he hadn't seen. And Emma was getting the material for them. Frothworth had probably already sold his furs so they could have money to buy whiskey. Then they'd come into town and get so drunk they'd get in a fight and start scalping innocent citizens! All it took was just one Injun to overstep his boundaries, then there'd be a massacre. Another family would be slaughtered, just like the Parker family had been. History was about to repeat itself. Only, whose family would it be this time? Henry Russell was going to make sure it wasn't going to be his! The fury escalated. Henry and Ray went to the next house and then the next and the next. It wasn't difficult to get everyone riled and suddenly there was a mass of men in arms, heading for Frothworth's place.

They were all there on a mission. Someone hollered, 'Henry, you talk' and that's all he needed! But he did more than just talk. Stepping forward from the group he hollered for Frothworth and then in one unexpected swift movement he had pulled a gun from his holster and shot into the air.

"And bring all them Injuns out with you or we'll come in there and get them ourselves!"

Emma froze! She looked out the window and saw almost twenty men!

"There's blood in their eyes." She immediately went to Wind In Mourning and wrapped her arms around her. "Frothworth, what are we going to do? How did they know she was even here?"

He knew. In fact, he had started to say something earlier that evening but then decided against it. "Doesn't matter."

He had already planned what to do in case they did show up. He pulled his shotgun from the mantle and loaded it. All the time he was doing it, the men outside were hollering and threatening their very lives. With his hand on the door handle, Frothworth turned and looked at Gunther.

"Can you get her out of here? I'll hold them off as long as I can if you can ride out."

Wind In Mourning was terrified! She looked at Frothworth and then at Gunther, then at Emma. No one was about to give her any false hope. Her life was in danger and they all knew it.

Nevertheless, Gunther refused to look at the situation as hopeless. "Looks like we're going to take our little trip sooner than we expected, Winny. We'll both ride out on my horse. You with me?"

She couldn't speak but he didn't expect her to. Fortunately, the mob of men was in the front of the house, their attention now on Frothworth who had just stepped out on the front porch.

"Have you all lost your minds?" He called out to them. "Ray, what do you think you're doing?"

"I seen her, Frothworth! You're hiding a savage in there and none of us will allow that. Our lives could be in danger and we don't want our women and children killed by a bunch of heathens. You bring her out to us and none of you will be hurt."

Frothworth's voice boomed out, "You're right, none of us will get hurt. But you're wrong about everything else. There's no one here but Emma and I. Go on home, I don't have nothin' or no one that you want."

"Not true," Henry yelled. "We ain't leavin' until that little redskin is in our hands. We all saw her and you can't deny that you been shelterin' that abomination of flesh."

Gunther knew it was time to leave. He pulled his hat low on his head and his collar up high. He had learned the hard way that his hair was often a giveaway when the moonlight cast its beam on him. He threw an old blanket over Wind In Mourning and instructed her to walk directly in front of him as though they were only one person, walking in the same shoes. They were going to sneak out to the barn and get his horse. Then they were going to walk into the trees so no one would hear them. Only when they were out of hearing range would they get on the horse and ride. It seemed like a good plan. As they walked, he kept his voice low.

"If anything happens, you keep going, you hear me? Don't you let this horse stop until you get to the river. And then you walk softly down the river. Let the current be behind you. And when you get close to the dam you get out and you ride that way." He pointed to his left. "Go as fast as you can and as long as you can. You'll find your people. I know you will."

"Nothing can happen to you." Her voice cracked as she suddenly clung to him.

There were mixed emotions. Never had she held on to a white man for protection! And yet, in all the time she had been with Ira Parker, she had never feared for her own life as much as she feared for Gunther's at that very moment.

He had to pry her hands off his arm. "Keep going, we can do this together."

But they couldn't. It got crazy all too fast. Gunther had just untied his horse and was heading to the woods when one of the townsfolk spotted him.

"There goes two of the heathens now, trying to get away," a voice cried out.

The mob descended on them and Gunther pitched Wind In Mourning into the saddle and slapped the horse, which sent her off by herself. With tears blurring her vision she got to the trees but then stopped the horse and looked back. She couldn't believe the scene before her. Frothworth and Gunther were fighting for their lives! She had never expected her freedom would cost someone their life. The shouting frenzied as Gunther suddenly had three men on top of him. He got back up but there was blood on his face. His hair had gotten loose and was flying about his head in chaos. In that moment Wind In Mourning saw him as an Indian brother. He was strong and brave and protecting what he believed in. Both he and Frothworth were picking up anything they could to try and even the odds, but she knew they were outnumbered. How could the very same people who had one day shouted his goodness turn around and the next day be ready to kill him?

And then, the night air was split by a gun blast. Wind In Mourning looked just in time to see Gunther's body flying backwards. He had been shot! She gasped in horror and then kicked the horse and took off through the trees. It couldn't be happening! It just couldn't! In a wild panic she kept her body low to the horse so he could run. Another shot rang out after her! They were trying to kill her, too! Get away! Get to her people! She'd never look back again. She knew Gunther had died for her, but why did that have to happen? Had he felt disgrace because his father had trusted him to escape and he had failed? Why had he even allowed himself to be put in such danger? She was no one. She didn't even have a purpose in life.

Nothing made sense to her! Did Frothworth die, too? Would the mob go after Emma as well? What was going to happen next? A part of her wanted to go back to help, but she knew she couldn't do anything. And if those men didn't kill her they would treat her just like Ira Parker had. She had to keep riding. The directions had been so simple when Gunther had told her where to ride to. Now, her head was reeling from the blast of the gun and her thoughts had frozen on the sight of Gunther being blown backwards. She couldn't hear another sound or see anything else. If she tried to think of what happened before that she saw Frothworth fighting with his eyes glazed over like a wounded, trapped animal, anticipating death and yet denying it. And then she immediately heard the gun and saw Gunther again. It was like a viscous cycle that she couldn't stop replaying.

The tears had stopped and her entire body was numb but the horse rode on. And then she came to the river. What had Gunther told her to do? Go upstream or downstream? She had to think hard to remember. It was only at that moment that she worried about the men following her. After they realized they killed Gunther would they go home and get their horses and then track her down? Would they make sure she could never live among white folk again? Would they pursue her as she tried to find her people? Then she had another terrifying thought; if she led them to her people, would they kill everyone? She had heard one of the men holler 'the only good Injun is a dead one!'

Totally exhausted from fear and heartbreak she slid off the horse. There was no way she would lead them to her people! Frothworth had told her that the townsfolk would lay in ambush and if any redskin even got close to Gough's

Ridge they would shoot to kill. She'd rather go somewhere and live with snakes all her life than to put her people in unsuspected danger.

So intent on trying to make the right decision she was suddenly aware that the sound that slowly became identifiable was that of horse's hoofs getting closer and closer. Someone was riding her way! Not a fast ride, but a deliberate movement as though they were searching. They were after her! What should she do? Send the horse off and hide the best she could or ride like the wind? She didn't know. As the rider got closer she suddenly made up her mind that she wasn't going to be easy prey. No one was going to take her without a fight. She quickly mounted and started riding again, knowing she was making a lot of noise but hoping that the other rider could only hear his own crashing through the trees. It was too dark to really distinguish a good hiding place. She had no idea where she was.

Wind In Mourning looked back only once and she could see the rider behind her. He was gaining fast and she was terrified. And then, out of nowhere came a hanging tree limb that caught her! It slapped her with an incredible force across her chest and face and she went flying off the horse, rolling on the ground as soon as she hit. Numb and dizzy, unable to take a deep breath, she tried to scramble up but her body was too clumsy and disoriented and she fell back down. She could hear the rider getting off his horse and then his figure was suddenly swooping over her as strong arms grabbed hold. She fought with all her might, kicking, hitting and even biting!

"Stop, it's me." A familiar voice demanded in a hushed tone.

She froze. "Frothworth?"

"Hush now, they're right behind us." He let her go so he could scramble to get the horse out of sight. Then he grabbed her and pulled her under a spruce with him and they huddled together tightly.

She didn't fully recognize how terrified she had actually been until his arms were holding her so tightly she could feel his heartbeat. Off in the distance the riders clambered through the trees but passed them and kept on going. As soon as he released his grip on her she bolted from him.

"Stop! What are you doing?" He took off after her and quickly caught up but she still fought him. He had to hold her down with force. "Have you gone mad, girl?"

How could she explain her fear? She had watched him fight and it wasn't at all the man she thought she knew. Maybe he would turn on her, too!

As soon as he let go of her again she took off but then stumbled. He caught her before she fell.

"What's wrong with you?" He raised his arm and she immediately interpreted it as him getting ready to hit her with a violent blow.

She fell to the ground in a broken heap as she covered her head. "No, don't hurt me!"

Frothworth was truly puzzled at her outburst but then realized that it was his arm in the air that had scared her. "What? Wind In Mourning, what's wrong with you? I would never hit you. Never!"

She slowly stood upright, her arms hugging herself as though she were freezing. She was shivering but he knew it was from fear and not from the cold. She finally got the words out. "I saw you fight. You hurt those men bad! Your eyes—."

All he could do was stare at her. "I had to fight, to protect you. To protect myself and Emma and Gunther."

Then she wailed, "But Gunther is dead! And you must hate me because it's my fault."

Frothworth dropped down to one knee so he would be more on her level. "No, girl, Gunther is not dead; even if he were, I would never hate you. Nothin' is your fault."

"I saw what happened! I heard the gun! I saw him fly through the air." Her arms were like outstretched wings flapping in the air as though pounding each statement into the ground.

Frothworth sighed and nodded, "He did get shot but he ain't dead."

"No?" She stood still, trying to determine if that was really the truth or if he was just telling her that to calm her down.

"No. Gunther will be just fine; it was just a flesh wound. Emma's takin' care of him right now. As soon as he went down the men knew what they done and they quit. They didn't really want to hurt any of us. Only two of 'em took off after me because they knew I was comin' for you, but Gunther is alive."

"I gotta see him with my own eyes. I gotta touch him."

"Then you'll have to go back with me, but I can't guarantee your safety. It's either that or you'll just have to believe me and we'll leave from here right now and try to find your people before morning."

She couldn't decide right then because she was torn both ways. The more she looked at her surroundings the more she didn't want to spend the night in the woods, knowing the men might come back at any time. If she went back, however, she'd be putting the family in danger again. Next time the mob just might kill someone. She'd never forgive herself if they hurt Emma.

"Gunther didn't trade his life for me? I mean, he really didn't die?" The weight in her heart was beginning to lighten so she didn't feel like it was pushing her into the ground.

Frothworth shook his head, "No. He would have if it had come to that. It's no shame to die for someone you love."

"How could anyone love me, Frothworth? I'm nobody."

The same face that she had been so afraid of because of its intense harshness suddenly melted right before her eyes. The firm mouth drooped and the eyebrows slanted sad like so that his gaze upon her seemed to look not just at her but right into the sore spot inside, that was hurting. It was as though he could see her lungs moving and her heart beating! That look softened so much that tears just spilled over the edge.

"Me and the family all love you, little girl. And we're going to really miss you," He spoke.

The same man that could laugh from the belly and then avenge with the aggression of a she-bear, could also shed tears from the heart. It was hard to put her thoughts and bewilderment into English words. She had heard that her father shed tears when her mother died and that's how she got her name. She touched the warm wetness on Frothworth's cheek and then stared at her finger.

"You mourn for me?"

He didn't say anything; he just took her in his arms and snuggled his hairy chin into her hair. She didn't understand, but then she decided she didn't have to. White folks had a strange way of expressing how they felt. But she knew this was good.

The sun was now full in the sky. Wind In Mourning was thirsty but they hadn't passed by any form of water hole for the last several hours. She wasn't about to complain, however. Being with Frothworth was both a happy and a sad time. Even though no one had given her hope that the small group of Indians was in fact her people, she believed they were. And if they were, she knew she would have to say goodbye to this white blood brother. Well, even if they weren't her people, she knew she would never be able to go back to Frothworth's house. She'd have to ride with the tribe anyway and hopefully they'd take her to Chief Omekobee. But that wasn't what was troubling her. Something had stirred her curiosity and she had been trying to find the right words and to ask the questions that were creating a whirlpool in her mind. Several times she had looked over at the huge man and then bit her lip because the words wouldn't stay still long enough for her to choose which ones to say.

"I want to ask you something," she began, deciding that it would be easier to let him help her with the right words. Frothworth looked at her, waiting. "What makes you a good person instead of being like other men?"

He smiled, shrugged, smiled again. Then he looked up into the sky as though he would find an answer there. (She knew he wouldn't…she had already looked to the sky countless times to find that same answer and it simply wasn't there.) Then he looked straight ahead and after a moment his eyes glanced over at her.

"Well now," he looked again in front of him. "I don't think I could say I was just born that a way, but I was raised that a way. My mama and papa were good people and I learned a lot from my pa. He always treated others right no matter how old they were or what color they were. I reckon I just took after him."

"Does that mean Ira Parker had a bad papa?"

Frothworth made a face at her that almost made her laugh, but then he rubbed his chin and kind of laughed, but not at her. "Well, little lady, truth was, his papa and then his papa and then his papa before him were all very, very bad!"

"Does that mean Joe will be bad, too?"

"I reckon so. One generation sorta follows the next."

"Does it have to be that way?"

"It just comes sorta natural. It's kind of like breedin' cows or horses. You start with a bad one and breed with a bad one and there ain't no choice but a bad one comin' out."

He scanned the area in front of him and turned the horse a little. "On the other hand, every once in awhile you'll have a good one come out of the stock. I don't know why because it's against all odds. Now, that don't happen very often. Mostly the bad breeds so much bad that nature refuses to give any more life and the bad dies off. But ever once in a while I believe Almighty God steps in and says 'enough is enough' and somethin' new is born. A different creation from all the others. And then the bad cycle ends."

"Do you think Almighty God said 'enough' to the bad in Ira when Joe was born?"

"I reckon we won't know 'til the boy grows up."

"How old do you have to be before you know if you're good or bad?"

Frothworth watched her a moment, rather amazed that at her age she was trying to understand adult thinking. "How old are you?"

"I've seen fourteen years now."

"How long have you known you're a good person?"

Her eyes were wide. "Well, I'm not real sure that I am a good person. I wished Ira Parker dead plenty of times. I even dreamed about doing horrible things to him and watching worms comin' outta his eye sockets."

Even though she said it in all seriousness, Frothworth had to laugh! Even slapped his knee. "That don't make you bad, little girl. I know I've dreamed about cuttin' his throat or bashin' him in the head or pushin' him in the river myself!"

Wind in Morning clamped her hand over her mouth and then took it away as she confessed. "One time I dreamed of cutting off both his legs and leaving the front door wide open so a bear could come in and get him!"

Frothworth picked up on the humor. "Now, I'll tell you the honest truth, girl. You know what I wished? I wished that he'd get into some bad mushrooms or somethin' and poison hisself and just die a miserable death but even that didn't seem fittin' enough. I don't think that makes either of us bad to think of them things. Now, if I actually did hit him or try to kill him off, then I'd be bad. It's against God to murder someone. Besides that, Joe don't have nowhere else to go. I think he might have an uncle somewhere but who knows even if he's still alive."

"Sometimes I think about Joe and wonder if he's cold or hungry or if Ira beat him." She rode on, her eyes constantly scanning the countryside for even a hint of Indians. She sighed, "Do you think Joe could ever be good like you?"

"That all depends on who helps him grow up. If he only has Ira all his life then I reckon he'll grow up and be just like his pa. But if someone else is there, showin' him the right thing and teachin' him good from evil, then I reckon he'll be good."

She watched a hawk in the air and then looked at Frothworth again. "The hawk only kills to eat. My brother killed because he thought it made him stronger. Now, I think he did an evil thing. How do you know if what you do is, in truth, good or evil?"

"That's somethin' you got to learn from God."

"The great, white spirit?"

"No," he drew it out, trying to choose his words carefully. "Your great, white spirit is in the sky there, but God is even higher than that. I'd say God is even God of the great, white spirit. It's like climbing to the very top until there ain't no place higher to climb. That's where God is; at the very, very top. He's not only everyone's Chief but even the Chief's chief."

"Can we go to the top and see him?"

"Not in this life. We save that for when we die. Gotta have a new place to live I reckon."

For the next couple of hours they talked. Wind In Mourning had one question after another. At times it was difficult to find the English word but Frothworth seemed to know what she wanted to ask, sometimes even before she did and he generally had an answer that she could understand. There were times when he admitted he didn't know the answer but he explained that probably no one else did either. Some things in life didn't have explanations and weren't meant to be figured out. Frothworth had been talking about Jesus and she suddenly stopped him.

"Is that Gunther's second name?"

"No, Gunther is all his ma and I gave him, why?"

"I thought maybe he was a Jesus, too."

Frothworth turned the horses head and changed direction. "What makes you say that?"

"It's on the count of what you been telling me. How Jesus loved everyone and even died for them. Gunther did that for me."

"But he didn't die," Frothworth emphasized.

Wind In Mourning didn't want to sound like she was arguing but she wanted him to understand. "My heart felt his death when he got shot and my mind replayed it so many times it became real. But, he came back to life. He's your only son and he was trying to do good. If I hadn't known Gunther to do what he did, I probably wouldn't understand much of this Jesus you talk about. Are you sure he loves Indians, too?"

"Indians, the French, the black slaves. Everyone." They rode in silence for a bit.

"Can I ask you a mystery?" Her heels tapped the horse as they went uphill.

Frothworth nodded even though he had absolutely no idea if she was going to ask or tell. At that exact moment he saw smoke along the horizon. Though he couldn't explain it, he was convinced that he had just located her people! He tried to get his attention back on her as she explained.

"Even though I hated Ira Parker, there is a spirit in me that worries about Joe. And I think I must have eaten locoweed or something because there's times when I miss him. If I'm a good person, maybe I was supposed to help Joe be good. But I won't ever go back so if Joe becomes a bad person, is it my fault?"

"No!" Frothworth spoke sharply but then caught the tone of his voice and softened it. "I mean, no, it ain't your fault. Now, I'm the one who don't understand somethin' and I have a question for you."

"You would ask me?" Her eyes were wide and then she sat up straight, with her head held stiff and high. "I am now the wise one. Ask your question, big, white man, Frothworth."

He knew that two years of taking care of a child would naturally bring a bond between them, like a brother and sister, but her concern for Joe seemed to exceed normal expectations. Keeping his focus on the smoke he listened to her more than observed her.

"If you had the opportunity to be with Joe and Ira wasn't anywhere close by, would you want to?" He watched for her reaction.

"I think I would. But it kind of scares me that one day Joe will be a bad person and then turn on me. A wolf looks like a dog but you can't tame him. I mean, you can break him but you can't really take the instinct out of him and that instinct is to kill. I would only watch at a distance. But, yes, I would choose to be with him."

"You shur do take the cake, little girl."

"What does that mean?"

He laughed. "It means God made you so special that in all my born days I've never known no one like you and I 'spect I never will again! You are a very, very good person Wind In Mourning. No matter what anyone else says, you must believe that."

"Well, if you say it, I have to believe it. Emma says you never tell an untruth."

"To my knowledge Emma never tells an untruth, either."

Frothworth nudged the horse's side and sped up. Wind In Mourning nudged hers, too, wondering why they were quickening their pace.

He pointed up ahead and off to the right of them. "Your people are right over that hill, yonder."

Her eyes beamed as her mouth dropped open in disbelief and yet incredible expectation. "Are you sure?" Then she broke into a gallop as she yelled over her shoulder, "Of course you are, you never speak the untruth!"

Frothworth quickly caught up with her and when they reached the top of the hill they looked down into the valley. Six or seven Indians were milling about. Frothworth watched her expression as she watched them. Suddenly, recognition broke through her demeanor the same way the sun pushed itself away from gray clouds and broke through with a radiant beam! Wind In Mourning turned to Frothworth and looked at him with her eyes bright and her mouth almost too excited to speak.

"It's him! It's Little Claw!" Her voice cracked as she pointed towards them.

"Go," Frothworth nodded towards her people, with a smile that assured her everything was going to be okay.

Without another word her excitement dug her heels into the horse's side and she was racing down the hill towards the reunion she had been waiting so long for. Frothworth only watched for a short time and then he turned his horse to head home. She was okay now, and Emma would want to know everything that had happened.

CHAPTER 4

ꕥꕥꕥ

1969

Phyllis was sitting on the floor, her back against the stones of the fireplace. “This is just so great. Just think, my very own ancestors lived here at one time. I suppose that’s why this whole thing intrigues me so much. It’s a connection, isn’t it?”

“Definitely.” Will was standing at the window and watching some squirrels scurry around an old tree.

“For just a moment I was sitting here wondering what it would be like if we lived here. I mean, the walls would be rebuilt and all and it would be a cozy, little place to live. Come here and close your eyes, Will, and just listen to all the sounds around us.” She seemed to melt against the stones as she totally relaxed and closed her eyes, listening to each individual sound.

“Our place, huh?” Will sat down next to her so that their shoulders touched.

“Ssh, the birds are singing to us.”

He played her game for awhile, listening to all the familiar sounds of nature, then playfully nudged her.

“It’s gettin’ late in the day, Ma, do you s'pose I should go out and chop some more firewood so you can start crankin’ out some vittles? The kids'll be fussin’ 'fore long. Seems like they have bottomless pits for stomachs!”

At first she squinched her nose and looked at him, then seeing his eyes still shut she knew he was pretending with her. With a broad smile she answered, “Well, Pa, I reckon so. You go out yonder to the smokehouse and fetch a couple of them possums you kilt the other day and I’ll make us some stew with dumplin's so thick you'll have to cut 'em in three pieces 'fore you can put 'em in your mouth! Hot, steamin' stew that'll stick to your ribs by golly."

Will opened his eyes wide and got right in her face. "Possum?" He was suddenly serious. "Have you ever eaten possum in your whole life?"

"I don't think so, but my grandmother did. It just sort of fits with this cabin, don't you think? Possum belly and hog grits, cracklin's and coon? How about squirrel eye gravy and biscuits? For breakfast we'll have crawdads on buckwheat toast. Don't they say a way to a man's heart is through his stomach?"

Will made a face and shuddered, "That's only when you're talkin' about meat and potatoes and pie and cakes! Don't you be makin' that other stuff; I don't care how hungry the kids get!"

Then he tickled her and they rolled about the floor until she had to beg him to stop. They both stayed on the floor and she snuggled into his side as he slid his arm under her head. Looking straight up, they could see right through a damaged part of the roof into the sky above.

"Sure hope it won't rain," she frowned.

"Yeah, we'd get wet for sure."

"I wonder what it was like to live this far out in the country? I don't think anyone lives close for miles."

"Used to, though. I'm not sure just when, but I saw the foundation of a house not too far from here. Who knows what happened to it? Maybe it just blew over from old age. Maybe it burned, too, though I didn't see any evidence of incineration or anything. It's possible that it could have been moved. One day I was driving down the road and there's this huge, huge truck and on the back of its trailer is a house. The whole house! Sure did look strange going down the road. Didn't seem natural."

"It stands to reason that throughout time there would be neighbors. But now they're gone and so is most of this cabin. I bet no one will ever rebuild it. And when it finally crumbles to the ground, it will be a forgotten memory of a time long ago. Hey, that makes it even more special that we're here right now, doesn't it?"

"Why do you say that?" He swatted at a bug that was crawling on his arm.

"Because we just updated it and brought it out of the throes of the past. And now it will be in our memories the rest of our lives. We have to show this place to our children so it can live on in their memories as well."

"And then to our children's children and to their children?"

"Why not?" Phyllis sighed and they were silent again. "I wonder how long it took them to put on that roof? Do you suppose just one man did it?"

"Oh, I wouldn't think it would have the same roof after all this time. Herman must have lived almost a hundred years ago. That roof doesn't look more than maybe thirty years old."

She started which made him jump as well. With wide eyes she grabbed his shoulder. "Then someone did live here recently! Surely it wouldn't be that hard to find out who it was."

She sat up and looked around again. Something caught her attention and she crossed the room, carefully stepping over the fallen boards. With the near destruction of one wall, there was something partially exposed between the stones, as though a hidey-hole had been revealed. Will watched her as she carefully approached it. As soon as her fingers touched it she pulled back.

"What's wrong?" Will was instantly alert to any danger.

"This is so weird. Nothing is wrong, but I just felt a surge go through me as though I was touching something alive. But we both know that's impossible!" Her fingers closed tighter on the rough hide and as she tugged, a small satchel slipped out from the stones. "Look!"

The excitement began to build as she realized what she had. "Oh, Will, this is so fantastic! Do you know what I have here?"

He hadn't stood up yet. "The lost inheritance? The deed to the ranch? What?"

Treating the leather with delicate care she unwrapped the strap from the button and opened it, then drew in her breath.

"It's full of old papers! Maybe a journal of some kind. And to think we were just joking about the walls telling a story. This is even better!"

She bent down and looked at the small space she had pulled the satchel out of and how the wallpaper had obviously covered it. "It was a secret place, like a wall safe or something. Only, there isn't a door or anything so it must have gotten stuck in here and then sealed in with the intent that one day someone would find it!"

Her eyes were huge. "The only reason someone would do that is because they have something to tell."

"Or to hide," Will interjected but she ignored him.

"Someone's hand put it in place, and now my hand brought it back out!" She physically held the satchel close to the opening again as though she were drawing it back out.

"Oh, wow, I wonder how long it's been here?"

"Long time!   Whatever made you see it?" Will was now interested.

"Just the corner of it caught my eye and it didn't look natural. I mean, how many times do you see leather sticking out of a wall? At first I thought it was a lizard or something. Oh, Will, this is so incredibly exciting! Look at these old pages. Someone wanted to keep them hidden, but I wonder why?"

He stretched for a moment as he stood, working his neck and shoulders and then watched her as she carefully handled her treasure. He may not have any ready answers but he knew this was definitely worth finding!

1908

If Landonelle wasn't talking she was writing. Years ago her father had discarded an old, brown, leather satchel and she had quickly salvaged it for her own use. It was always filled with paper and she was constantly asking for pens or pencils. Once she found herself stranded with nothing to write with. Her solution was to keep burning the end of a stick and using it to scratch out rhythmic words to a poem that almost breathed with musical quality.

She was almost adamant about being called by her given name, Landonelle. It was a big name for a little person. She was only five foot two with wild, curly, red hair and sky blue eyes, mirrored by freckles playing leapfrog across her cheeks and nose. The elaborate name came from her father, Landon Bennet Stivers, IV. She was the only girl in three generations of Stivers. Perhaps that's why she was such an individual, determined to place her mark in the world for who she was, not just because of her name.

She introduced herself to strangers as Landonelle Catherine Grace Stivers, the first! She had to impress upon them that she was indeed feminine and the first and only daughter of the wealthy and prominent Landon Stivers. She had a mind of her own and a determination that wouldn't quit. All too often it got her into trouble, but she was also quite good at getting herself out of any predicament that arose.

Delibia

Landonelle was looking out the kitchen window, watching some kittens out in the yard. It wouldn't be long before the sun would be setting and the walls seemed to be closing in on her. Looking for adventure, she decided to go exploring. As a writer, she was always looking for a story and a means to exercise her tremendous imagination. To Landonelle, a tree wasn't just a tree. It was a majestic oak with arms and face lifted towards the heavens to embrace life itself! She didn't just walk anywhere; she strolled along the pebbled path as the autumn breeze kissed her cheek and then tickled the fallen leaves so that they swirled around her feet, giggling in their dizziness.

To Landonelle, everything had a vivid description, every movement was an adventure in itself. There was never a smell that went undetected or a touch that went unfelt. In some way or another it all found an endless existence in the brown satchel that was stuffed with pages upon pages of writing.

"Please, dear, don't wander too far," her aunt warned. The aging woman stood at the kitchen sink, drying the last plate, then gave it to her niece to put away. At last the kitchen was clean and their chores were finished for the day.

"No farther than the river, I promise." Landonelle's eyes glistened with excitement.

She was just visiting while her father was taking care of a business transaction in Gough's Ridge. It had been a marvelous trip and she had always adored both her Aunt Hetty and Uncle Glenn.

"Aunty Hetty, would you like to walk with me?"

A warm smile helped light up tired eyes. "No, no dear, you go on ahead. I'm a little tired and I'd just like to rest. Besides, I have my knitting and we're finished here in the kitchen."

Landonelle gave her aunt a quick kiss on the cheek and off she went, never giving second thought that trouble could be lurking. Yet, trouble there was and it happened long before Landonelle ever neared the river. Every once in awhile the breeze brought a pungent odor. It was no concern because she often smelled dead things. Looking up, she scanned the sky for any birds of prey. Not seeing any didn't surprise her because when she thought more about it, it wasn't really a 'dead' smell but something mighty close to death. Her mind was activated; this was the beginning of a story! She imagined the words on paper as she described herself. *Her nostrils were assaulted with an offensively rancid odor! Rotting, permeating, macabre, and yet strangely—alive.*

She stopped so that she could listen to the sounds around her. How strange that the birds were suddenly silent, even the crickets. Nothing was moving. That definitely meant there was some form of danger close by! The hairs on her arm seemed to bristle. A fist of tightness in her chest began to uncurl as though fingers of fear were stretching and reaching out for something to grasp. Even though the sun was shining she found herself in the darkness of an encompassing trepidation. Her heart skipped a beat when she heard a shuffle in the leaves and then a labored moan. It wasn't a human moan, but neither did it sound like a familiar animal that would have been in these parts. Her eyes searched for the slightest movement. Where was it? What was it? *Her throat became dry as the palms of her hands became clammy. Now her legs felt weighted down with each cautious step. The carpet of leaves became a bog of apprehension as her feet became entangled on the imaginary semi-protruding vines of a formidable chimera reaching out for her!*

Landonelle swallowed again, her senses now assaulted with an odor so abhorrent she became nauseous. Tears came to her eyes, not only from fear but also from the stench. Her head began to spin, creating a confusion of vision and rationalization.

Then she heard the low growl and suddenly she was not only seeing clearly but also understanding just as explicitly that she was in a dangerous situation. From dense brush emerged the most pitiful creature she had ever seen. She couldn't move in spite of the fact that a pathetic mass of mangled, bloody fur approached her. Something, that at one time was probably someone's pet.

"Nice doggy." She looked around for a stick or something to use as protection but found nothing. She knew the dog wasn't nice. It was hurt and sick and probably crazed from starvation. All the trees were too small to climb or even hide behind and there was nothing but an open field in front of her.

Her voice quivered, "Help? Anybody?" She tried hard not to panic.

The dog continued to growl and advance towards her, showing bloody, slime covered teeth. She couldn't take her eyes off him and yet the mere sight of him was painfully terrifying. And then, just as quickly as the situation had presented itself it ended. As though he materialized out of nowhere, there was a man behind her with a gun.

"Don't move," the voice commanded in an even tone as she heard the hammer pulled back.

"Wouldn't think of it," she mumbled, preparing herself for the blast of the gun.

The dog lowered its head as the growl became even more threatening. Perhaps it knew the power of the gun. Not as an enemy but now as a blessed relief. The moment it gathered enough strength to attack, the gun went off and Landonelle flinched. She didn't want to look so she stood firm, her eyes squeezed shut as she held her breath.

It wasn't until the man snapped the gun and fed in another shell that she realized her shoulders had been tight against her neck.

"It's okay now." He seemed to dismiss the entire episode as though it had been no more than catching your shirt on barbed wire and with a twist and pull you're freed. But to her, it wasn't completely okay, not just yet. Her ears were still ringing from the shotgun blast; her heart was racing and she wondered if she would ever get the smell of the creature out of her nostrils. Memory would give life to the beast even when breath couldn't.

"Is it dead?" Landonelle still refused to look.

"Quite."

She spun around, letting out her breath in an avalanche of gratitude. "Oh! Thank you! I don't know what I would have done just now! I mean, there's nowhere to go and no telling what he might have done to me!"

Just the mere thought of the blood and slime on her skirts and sleeves made her knees weaken. She would have had heart failure if the beast had bitten her. No doubt she would have taken to her bed for three days just from the shock and horror of it all!

Landonelle had expected the man to be like her Uncle Glenn, in his fifties, tall and strong, broad shoulders, a true woodsman. Instead, her undaunted hero wasn't much older than she was. Even though he wore a flannel shirt and tattered jeans his over-all appearance was far from that of a hunter. He didn't have a beard and he wasn't even wearing a hat. In fact, even the gun looked out of place in his hands. Her first impression was that he would have held a rake or hoe much easier. Or, if he had worn a white shirt she could have easily mistaken him for a lawyer or a banker.

She didn't want to stare, but she noted that he had gorgeous, brown eyes that were somehow distant and yet penetratingly close! He blinked and then looked down at the creature.

"I was following it. As soon as I saw it I knew I had to put it out of its misery."

Without a second thought he reached down and picked up the dog, not like it was a worthless carcass but as though it still reserved the dignity of a once devoted companion. Landonelle admired him for that. But when the animal's body was moved, the stench and blood became unbearable and she suddenly put her hand over her mouth to stifle a gag.

"Will you be fine, Miss?" He paused for only a second as he situated the animal in his grasp.

"Yes, thank you. I'm just a little shook. Who are you?"

Her creative mind was already turning him into a royal knight in shining armor (in spite of the blue jeans and flannel). Surely his name would boast of military prowess and authority. Generation after generation must have passed down a title that he would wear with proud distinction. Perhaps he was a Montgomery or a Vincente or Rutherford, or…

"Joe. Joe Parker. I'll be gone now." He tipped his head, turned and strode off as though she had ceased to exist.

Just Joe? Nothing more grandeur? Not even a Joseph or Josephus? She held up her hand to call out to him but then withdrew it quickly, knowing that it wasn't proper. Besides, what would she say? He obviously wasn't the kind of man who would stand around being idle for simple chitchat. Even though he didn't seem to be in a hurry, Joe Parker had the kind of walk that exemplified business and direction.

Landonelle quickly returned to her aunts and went into a lengthy and somewhat exaggerated explanation of what had just happened.

"Who is Joe Parker?" The young girl paused just long enough to catch her breath, nearly tearing off another fingernail from all the excitement.

The smile Aunt Hetty had displayed while listening slowly drooped as the corners of her eyes pulled back visions of memory that sent a crow's feet pattern of pained experience.

"He's Amos and Walter Parker's nephew. Now, I don't think you ever met Amos but he was mean. Sometimes I think the devil just took over his body so he could have a voice to yell with and a fist to strike out. Amos was a real fighter. He got killed a couple years back because of it, though no one paid mind. Many said he got his just dues and it was a good riddance. Walter's not as bad but even your Uncle Glenn won't reckon with him in the dark.

"They got a brood of young 'uns and there's not a one of 'em that's going to amount to anything. Shameful. I haven't seen Joe in years even though I've known he's been back. He's not as bad as his uncle but he sure is a rightly troubled soul."

There was a spark of mystery in the air and Landonelle could see a new chapter going in her journal. "Why? Tell me his story." Her fingers rolled an imaginary pen.

Aunt Hetty straightened her apron on her lap and then went back to her knitting as though the story would be woven into the afghan she was making, word by word, stitch by stitch.

"I can't remember all the details because those Parkers don't talk much and I'm afraid that a lot of the story has been embellished along the way. Joe's daddy was Ira Parker. Just his name brought darkness into your soul! Oh, the stories told about that man even makes the wind moan through the trees. Well, Ira died when little Joe was about five; got mauled by a bear or something.

"Joe struck off by himself and walked nigh on to fifteen miles to his Uncle Walter's to tell him that Ira was dead. It's amazing that the little lad even made it! Now, there's some strange stories about that, too," she nodded as though agreeing with herself. 'Yes, siree, some real strange stories!"

Aunt Hetty let out a long sigh as her knitting needles froze in mid air. Landonelle wasn't sure if she was counting stitches or trying to put her thoughts together so she could remember everything in the right order. Hetty flipped the afghan over and started working the stitches again.

"Makes no never mind now." She pulled out a long length of yarn, letting it fall loose at her side. "Walter took the boy in. You would have thought that with a family of fifteen young'uns little Joe would fit right in, but he didn't. All them kids looked alike. Darlene Parker had two and three at a time. No one could tell who was who. Poor little Joe was just an outsider who didn't look like none of them so they blamed him for everything. It was pretty easy because Joe never stood up for himself.

"From the day he showed up it was like Joe had some dark secret and just wouldn't tell no one. Now some folks remember Joe growing up when his mama was still alive and there wasn't anything wrong with his voice then. In fact, he had told some stories to the trappers that no one believed. After the boy got to Walters he just up and quit talking all together. He said 'my pa is dead' and that was it. Not another word out of him for years and years. They tried to get him to talk but he just wouldn't do it. Not, no ways, until he was good and ready. Then he talked. But he never told the whole story. It's still a mystery to this very day I reckon."

Landonelle had her chin in the palms of her hands, listening intently. “A mystery?” She hung on the words. “I would think it would be impossible for a child so young to travel that far by himself!” She couldn’t believe it.

“I guess Ira knew he was going to die so he drew a map and that little boy followed it. Then the stories go that he had some kind of guardian spirit helping him. Well, anyway, Joe lived with his Uncle Walter until he was about fourteen and then he got into some kind of trouble with the law and spent a few years in something they call a reform school. When he got out he went back to the cabin where he and Ira had lived and since then lives no better than a hermit. He says he don’t need no one. I guess he doesn’t; he’s still alive and doing just fine.”

Landonelle sat upright in a posture of disagreement. “But everyone needs someone. I bet he’s miserable deep down. You don’t know why he was in that reform school?”

Aunt Hetty rubbed her chin a minute, looking more into the past than she was at the yarn. “No, there are stories about it but who knows the real one? Some said he stole some money, others say he beat up one of his brothers pretty bad, and then there are some who say he burned down someone’s barn. Maybe he’s done all three, who knows? The Parkers stay to themselves and no one will ever accuse me of being a busybody. I have to respect their privacy. Besides, my dear, it’s none of my concern as long as he leaves me alone.”

She yawned and Landonelle knew she would end the conversation soon because the sun was setting. Aunt Hetty was never one to stay up late. Her day began long before the sun ever came up and ended just as soon as the sun went down.

“Do you think Joe is a good person now? I mean, he did put the dog out of its misery and he was very nice to me!” Landonelle busied herself with a ball of yarn so that she could hide her curiosity while still exploring her feelings.

Aunt Hetty stopped knitting a minute, the needle poised in the air as she thought. She wasn’t even paying attention to what Landonelle was feeling. She took a deep breath and then her voice softened.

“Well, darlin’ I think everyone is basically a good person if they’re given half a chance. It’s just that I don’t think Joe Parker’s path and mine will cross often enough so I could find out if he’s a good person or not. I am thankful that he was nice to you today.”

Landonelle could still smell the dog and hear the blast of the gun. “I’m thankful too! He didn’t say much but he was polite. Maybe I’ll see him again.”

Aunt Hetty squinted her eyes and clucked her tongue. “Don’t you be looking forward to it, you hear? There’s a dark past with that young man that doesn’t concern the likes of you no more than it concerns the likes of me. Like I said, I don’t see no reason why our paths should cross. He stays to himself and we stay to ourselves.”

Standing and stretching, Landonelle felt a weariness in her bones. “Don’t fret, I’m not going to do anything foolish. I’m just curious. Besides, as soon as Dad finishes his business we’ll be heading back.”

Landonelle knew she had said it just to pacify her aunt. The hidden truth was, she desperately wanted to satisfy her curiosity and discover more about Mr. Joe Parker. Mysteries were the good Lord’s way of keeping boredom from spreading like some plague. She couldn’t explain it, but there was something about Joe that had captivated not only her imagination but also her entire thought process. Was it because he had rescued her from the dog or because there was a remote chance that she could rescue him from the deadly creature called ‘the past’?

As soon as she could, she went off by herself and sat down with her brown satchel and began writing. Growing up with so many brothers she felt as though she had somewhat of an advantage in regards to understanding how a man thought.

When Landon Stivers returned from his business he expected to be bombarded with questions and never given a moment’s quiet on the way back home. The questions never came. In fact, Landonelle greeted him and then without another word jumped into the carriage and immediately absorbed herself in writing. To Landon’s complete surprise, his daughter was content with silence. She would answer any question he asked, but there was no idle talk as they slowly headed for home. He had to smile though because he could tell that she was incredibly happy!

It was months later when Landon Stivers had to plan another business trip. Always enjoying her presence he asked Landonelle if she would like to accompany him.

“Can I stay with Aunt Hetty,” she asked.

“Not this time, I’ll still be on this side of Fuertes.”

“How many days?”

“Four.”

“Then drop me off and come back and get me.”

“It’s twenty miles out of the way,” he protested.

That didn’t trouble Landonelle. She knew she could wrap Landon Stivers around her little finger and get anything she wanted. So, it didn’t take her by surprise when he told Samuel to hitch up the horses a day before he had intended to leave. Neither did it surprise him when she stood at the top of the stairs with luggage in hand, ready to go.

Landonelle couldn't explain why she was so excited about the possibility of meeting Joe again. But knowing that Aunt Hetty warned her not to pursue it, she knew she couldn't say anything. She tried to let the course of events come natural as she kept her thoughts in secret.

When she arrived, she kissed her aunt and talked about trivial things. For the rest of the day she helped in the kitchen as Aunt Hetty canned blackberries and then made a cobbler that could have fed twenty people. Landonelle had to bite her tongue so she wouldn't verbalize her desire to take some over to Joe. When she finally retired for the night she eagerly took out her brown satchel with paper and began writing.

It was noon the next day when Landonelle announced she was going to go for a walk. Her heart's desire to head towards the Parker place seemed almost impossible to hide. There were times she imagined her thoughts were so obvious Aunt Hetty would see them as clearly as if they had been etched on her forehead.

Even worse—lost in her own musings, Landonelle would snap back to reality only to realize she had been holding her breath! In that moment of stillness she had heard something erratic thumping and then laughed at herself when she discovered it was her own heartbeat and not someone outside hammering! What if Aunt Hetty suspected all that was going on? Surely it was all so obvious the truth would soon be discovered. Yet, nothing was mentioned.

Trying to avoid any suspicion, just in case she was being watched, she took off in the opposite direction of where Joe Parker lived. It was a beautiful day and she had a briskness to her step that secretly indicated her excitement. As soon as she could she circled back and began looking for the landmarks that Uncle Glenn had mentioned.

She knew that the cabin was way off the road, nestled in a wooded area. Landonelle found the road she was supposed to turn off on as well as the mulberry bushes that Uncle Glenn said he liked to pick from. She looked about, remembering his directions “once you go past them bushes you're almost there. It's only fifteen yards or so due north and then you go down a culvert. Now, that gets pretty slippery come winter. I don't like for your aunt to venture that far because it comes up so unexpected like. At the bottom, you go another fifteen yards, no maybe twenty, and just when you think you're totally lost, there it is!"

Past the bushes...go north...down...where did it go down? Landonelle was getting totally frustrated. The land was flat, it didn't go up or down! She went back to the bushes for the third time and with a renewed determination she closed her eyes as though blind. How far was fifteen yards? One yard was only three feet and that was like one giant step for her.

Looking around in all directions she made sure there wasn't anyone watching her. Then she pulled up her skirts a little higher and closing her eyes again, paced off fifteen of the longest strides her short legs could possibly accomplish. And then, to make up for her shortness and for good measure she added another stride. With an outstretched arm pointing like a compass needle, she spun around and to her complete surprise stumbled and was suddenly falling down a steep slope.

As she opened her eyes she found herself looking at the top of the trees and then at the ground as she tumbled down the culvert. At the bottom she stayed perfectly still for a moment, scolding herself for falling and yet congratulating herself for finding what she wanted. Words formed for the journal pages. *She found she couldn't rely on eyesight alone; it was only when she followed the guidance of her heart that she was able to discover its desires.*

And then! There they were right in front of her nose; two brown shoes that were suddenly accompanied by two strong hands that were shaking her shoulder.

"You all right miss?"

Embarrassment brought her into motion as she frantically pulled her skirts back down and sat up. "Yes, thank you, I'm fine."

Landonelle checked herself over before she looked up. And then, to her surprise and added embarrassment, she found herself looking into the same distant brown eyes she had found so mesmerizing only months before. The face of Joe Parker was right in front of her.

"I can't believe I fell, perfectly clumsy of me..." she looked into the depths of his eyes and her mind shot back to the journal. *She would have totally defied gravity by floating into a bottomless chasm of titillation if she hadn't blinked. His tone was dry and yet the words came from full lips that remained parted as though yearning to be kissed.*

Joe Parker looked away from her. "It's understandable, especially if you aren't familiar with this area. Here, let me help you up."

She took his outstretched hand and the strength of his grip sent waves of admiration and security through her like an electric charge. She knew her heart was skipping a beat and it certainly wasn't because of the fall. For a delayed second she deliberately kept her hand in his and then snatched it back before he realized it.

"I can't believe it, we meet again." She fumbled for something to say.

"You're not hurt or nothin'?"

"Oh, no, not even scratched; not that I know of." She was examining herself.

"I believe you've torn your skirt."

Her eyes followed the direction of his eyes and with horror of possible exposed modesty she looked at the irreparable tear. She gave a sigh of relief that only the color of her petticoat showed and nothing more. In all truth, Joe probably saw more as she fell than he ever would from a simple tear in the cloth. Because of that, she felt somewhat awkward and her mind was spinning with what to say next. Landonelle looked up only to discover that Joe was gone!

"Well!" She gave a humph with her hands on her hips. He had done it again—appeared and disappeared just like that. Wadding up the torn pieces of fabric in a frustrated fist she was determined to find the cabin, hoping that's where he had so rudely gone off to.

Breaking through a copse of trees she froze. There he was, getting ready to split some rails for the woodpile. The love story in her mind continued. *A symphony of satisfaction rumbled down at her toes, as it made a breathtaking crescendo and then exploded through her head, sending shivers and tingles throughout her, and then showering her with a mist of exhilaration. She found she was perfectly drenched in the moment. He was so strong! Splitting logs looked as easy for him as running a fingernail through cold butter was for her.*

Landonelle stepped out of the trees and went directly to him. He didn't look up so she called to him. "Joe?" She was so nervous her voice managed to crack on the one syllable and she had to retrieve it like she would an eager puppy running up on an old cat.

He held the ax in midair and then swung down. The crack of the wood was clean and sharp. Then he kicked the wedges over to the side. With penetrating eyes he held her gaze in his own and then swung again. He ignored her as he split three more logs, then he wiped his brow and set the ax down.

"You want something," he asked.

"Well, ah, no, actually I was going to go back home but I don't think I had said thank you for helping me when I tumbled."

"You said enough."

She took a cautious step forward. "Well, since we seem to keep meeting, may I at least properly introduce myself?"

He shrugged and started loading the wood into his arms. "I know who you are. I reckon everyone in these parts knows of Landon Stivers."

She became bolder as she stepped closer. "You might know my daddy, but do you know me?"

"I know you." It had taken him forever to answer her. Then she remembered Aunt Hetty telling her that he had just quit talking. Well, he was going to talk now! No way would she allow Joe Parker to remain silent in her presence!

"Then, what's my name?" She decided to try and beat the odds by forcing a conversation that wasn't held together by a simple yes or no. He looked right at her and then through her. She knew he was debating if he wanted to be rude or if he was actually interested in her.

He cleared his throat and spit, which was a disgusting thing to do, but she refused to give him the satisfaction of showing shock or repulsion at such a crude display of disrespect. Her brothers had done the same thing. Seeing that she didn't so much as flinch, he stared a moment with raised eyebrows.

"What really matters is not so much what your name is but what others call you. Landonelle sounds far too big and high phalutin' for a little girl like you. Yet, I never heard you called nothin' else. Don't know why, the name sure don't fit."

Her first impulse was to strike back and tell him that Joe, just Joe Parker wasn't any kind of a fitting name either. But she quickly checked herself and decided it would be to her benefit to humor him.

"Then what does fit me? A girl like me can't go walking in the woods alone without being called something proper and fitting."

He didn't even look at her. "You go walkin' in these woods alone and you'll be called simple minded, no matter what your name is."

That did it! The fire of a quick temper leaped into a starter flame; just big enough to let him know that it existed.

"Not true, Joe Parker. I heard tale that you walked fifteen miles alone when you were only five years old and no one called you simple minded."

The stern look in his eyes let her know he had no intention of acknowledging her statement, let alone talk about it. If there had ever been any warmth in his eyes it had vanished. In fact, before he looked back down at the wood, his eyes had turned cold, transformed into a menacing pool of liquid anger. That anger was poured out as he split the next log. As the ax came down, he took in a deep breath and then blew it out with a force that would have been equal to a sneeze from Paul Bunyan's blue ox!

Landonelle made a fist at her side as she scolded herself. Stupid! Stupid! Stupid! “What I meant is, it made you a legend in these parts.”

He was still breathing heavy and she had to calm him. “That's a compliment you know! No harm meant. I'm truly sorry, I guess I was out of line.”

Her voice carried a genuine apology as her fingers fidgeted in her skirts. For a moment she couldn't bear to meet his eyes and see the anguish that had been mirrored. But, no! She wasn't going to succumb to feminine sheepishness; he wouldn't relate to that or appreciate it. Landonelle stood straight with her head held high.

He finally looked her way and acknowledged that she at least existed. This time his voice was stiff but the anger had subsided. “I don't have no more to say to you,” he told her flatly.

Joe Parker had composed himself and positioned his ax over his shoulder. Then his eyes slanted as his voice mumbled a warning. “You go walkin' around here and likely as not you'll get shot for trespassing. I got signs 'round and I shoot those who want to poke and pry their nose into my business.”

The change in his character bothered her and she was desperately trying to think of some way to break the tension and repair the damage. When her brothers were angry she knew how to soothe the beast in them. Perhaps men were men and an air of innocence, charm, and humor would quench the flames she had unintentionally flamed.

“Well, don't shoot me on an empty stomach. There's a blackberry cobbler on the stove at home and I'm starving. Besides, I'm not a snoop and I don't pry, and I certainly never intended to cause any trouble. I'll leave, but it's a shame that I have to go around with a name that doesn't fit.”

Joe Parker remained silent for a moment, and then he looked straight at her, long enough so that he could have memorized her appearance. Then he put the same gaze down on the wood as though transferring her image to the rail. He swung the ax again but this time it didn't split the wood in half. A small end was severed just as neatly as Aunt Hetty's knife could cut the end off a string bean.

"Landonelle Stivers?" He said her name as he reached down and picked up both pieces of wood, then tossed the longer one to the side as he held the tiny end out to her. 'No, you're just Nelle, that's who you are."

He tossed the end piece and it landed right in front of her feet. Then he immediately went back to the last rail that he had to split. "That name fits you just fine."

"How so?" She picked up the piece he had thrown and ran her thumb along the rough bark and clean cut edge. She defended herself, "Landonelle is a name about as tall as that pine tree over yonder. Nelle is no bigger than this here plug."

As soon as she said it, she realized that it was that precise symbolism that he had intended. How ingenious! The man was truly remarkable. Under the disguise of a backward, hardened hermit was a genuine scholar. The depths of his imagination were no doubt dictated by his inhibitions, but once released she just knew that Joe Parker would be another Henry Wadsworth Longfellow!

So absorbed in her own reverie she almost missed the fact that he was talking to her. Her attention snapped back to him as sharply as the splintered wood had responded to the ax.

"...doesn't matter," he was saying. "It fits for the fact I said so. Now, get off my land Nelle Stivers; I got chores to do before nightfall."

Even though it was a rebuff of sorts, she smiled and for just a second their eyes locked. How strange that when he called her Nelle, such a simple name suddenly had a magical quality to it. She liked it. Nelle Stivers and Joe Parker. Such simplicity painted a noble portrait of uniqueness. And that's what image was impressed upon her mind in that quick instant before he looked away. She raised her hand in a gesture of a pleasant farewell.

"Okay, I'm going. But I'd like to see you again, if that's okay." She broke all rules of etiquette by being unashamedly honest. He didn't take the time to even look at her.

"Reckon I can't stop you from opening your eyes and seeing what you will. But I don't have time to prune any feathers."

Lightening slashed through the sky and blazed through her mind and right into her fingers and on to the next written page in her journal. He did it again! Such profound sagacity came with a flash and a thunderbolt that nearly knocked her off her feet! She understood completely. From an early age she had learned to give a quick answer, and her desire to constantly read only nourished an insatiable imagination. With boldness she hoisted her skirts and faced the sorcerer of this atmospheric clashing of imagery.

"Not even your own, Joe Parker?" she asked.

He was obviously impressed but turned before she could see the smile he couldn't hold back. Staying in control of a gruff voice he replied, "Especially not my own."

And with that he walked around to the other side of the cabin; he had dismissed her from his sight but most definitely not from his mind.

It was time to go. On the way home, Landonelle was exceptionally careful to mark her way. She couldn't very well close her eyes and just by chance fall into his backyard again! Once she climbed back up and stood on the road she wondered how she could have missed it. But after walking another thirty yards and then turning back around, it looked like flat country again.

"Like it's just an illusion of my mind. There is no Joe Parker, no cabin, no woods, nothing." Then she fingered the tear in her skirt and smiled. "Oh, yes there is and he hasn't seen the last of Landon—Nelle Stivers!" She caught herself and changed her name.

With that, she couldn't wait to get back to her aunts and seclude herself in the bedroom where she could daydream and feast on every word she was about to write. This was going to be a terrific story!

CHAPTER 5

ஓஓஓஓஓ

1969

Will was watching Phyllis on the floor with the brown satchel and the handful of papers but she didn't have his undivided attention until she let out a wild squeal of excitement.

"Look! Oh, Will, look at this old paper! You can hardly make out the handwriting. Isn't this exciting?" She took just a few pages and went to an area where the light was better. "It's got to be something terrific; I can just feel it!"

He had to laugh at her enthusiasm. To him a couple pieces of paper in a leather bag were just old worthless documents; to Phyllis they were an invaluable treasure.

"Can you make out anything?" He finally asked as he made his way over to her.

"Just bits and pieces on this page. There's something here about the weather; wait, this is clear enough to read:

> It hurts my thoughts to remember, so I shall hold fast to the determination of my heart. I will see him when the sun sets and my only fear is that he will turn from me and my heart will set deeper than the sun. If there is a new day to dawn

"I can't make it out, Will, help me. This is so incredibly exciting! It was written long ago and yet, here it is in my hands; from that person to me! This is monumental!"

He joined her and carefully lifted a page, fearful that it would crumble at his touch. Being tucked away within the wall had preserved it from the damaging effects of air or water. The paper in itself was quite durable, it was mostly the fading of the ink that gave them the biggest problem. Nevertheless, he handled each page with extreme care.

"Here you go, this page is better. I bet we can read the whole thing." He sat down on the floor as he read silently for a moment and then started laughing.

"What is it?" She begged him to share the humor.

He finally looked right at her. "I guess this proves that no matter who it is or the time period they live in, life doesn't change. This whole page is talking about a wedding and all the hassles that seem to come with it. For a minute I thought I was reading about our own upcoming marriage." His eyes were still large.

"Let me see, too. Come on, Will, I'm dying to know what it says."

He pointed to a line at the top of the paper and leaning close to it, began to read:

> They didn't know that would happen. But the plans had been made and it would have been impossible to have changed them. Uncle Arthur was traveling from the far coast especially for the occasion. It seems a shame that so much money is spent on a wedding and yet, for a solitary daughter among seven brothers, what is a father to do? At least he consented and gave the young man his blessings. For a time, such an acknowledgement was somewhat irresolute. There were rivers of resistance to cross, chasms of conflicts to bridge, and far too many guests to gratify. "Too fast," they all cried. You're too young to know what you're doing," others chided. But the truth? Sadly it was there among the voices but the one who should have listened became deaf. Who can give advice to the one lost in love? Who can talk fact when the ears only hear fantasy? But those who talked only had a mouth, not eyes! They had a voice, not a heart. I know, because I was the one who fell in love. I was the one who refused to listen. Do I have regrets? Do the trees shed their leaves in the winter? Some do and some don't, you say. Well, same for me. Some days I do have regrets and some days I don't. Surely that is not unusual. Joe is a good man. The words he doesn't say are right there under his fingertips and come through his touch. The emotion that he doesn't show is surrounding his heart. Only I have the key. And when we're alone, I take the same key that unlocks my heart to free his. I would leave it as such, so that he could be open and free at all times, but he won't allow it. He is a very private man. He has told me many stories but hides many more. If memory doesn't take residence in your heart, does it merely lodge forever in your mind? If so, where does it go when your mind forgets? Is it then lost from your soul? Whether I knew his secrets or not, I was determined to win his love. I was prepared to leave my family and to face all objections. I would have died for him if necessary. Fortunately, for both our sakes, it didn't come to that.

Phyllis was nearly holding her breath as she leaned over his shoulder, reading along with him. "Turn the page, this is fabulous! But who are these people? Not enough names are given. Oh, Will, I've just got to find out who wrote this."

He was trying to turn the page but it was stuck to the page behind and when he lifted it, a piece broke off.

"I sure don't want to lose any of this but look how old the paper is. Maybe we should read it later, under better conditions." He started to put the papers back in the satchel, but Phyllis couldn't bear it.

"Not yet," she stopped him. "One more page, please. Look at this one, the ink seems to be a little darker. Please, Will, see if you can read it and then we'll put it away."

He couldn't deny her. Once again he bent over close so he could try to make out each written word. At least the handwriting was legible. If it had been a doctor writing in a journal they probably wouldn't have been able to decipher anything! Carefully, keeping all the pages in the right order, he separated the page she had pointed to and began reading:

> There was no one around and I desperately needed comforting! If only Aunt Hetty had been close by! She knew the baby was coming and told me not to worry but Uncle Glenn got kicked by a horse and he nearly died. She couldn't very well leave him because he was still choking from the blood he coughed up. So, there I was, by myself. For awhile the pain was so intense that I wondered if I was going to lose my mind. And then the strangest thing happened. I do not know if it was real or not. There hasn't been a moment to go by that I don't question myself. The baby was coming feet first and I was terrified! I'll never forget reaching down and feeling a tiny, little foot. At that moment I was afraid the child would die and so would I! Tragically we were going to be alone! I remember my head was spinning and my heart beating with a force that seemed to explode within my chest. There was a force underneath me that was wringing my back like two people wringing water from a towel—one twisting one way, the other twisting against it. I heard someone in the room and I tried to see who it was but it was too dark. There was only one lantern lit but I'm sure it was a woman, though no one I knew. I remember now that her voice was firm and yet soothing. Because of her presence and her perfectly calm manner I began to breathe normal. She knew exactly what she was doing. As though she could feel my pain she touched my forehead and then whispered 'bite down hard' as she put a knotted rag between my teeth. I suppose it was then the baby was born. It felt as though my back separated and my head burst from the pain. When I came to, someone was changing a cloth on my forehead. I thought it was still the woman but it wasn't. It was the doctor. I asked about the woman; I wanted to thank her. What woman? He asked. There was no one with me when he arrived. I panicked! Where was my baby? Right there in the cradle, all cleaned up and sleeping peacefully. I told him that she had been born feet first and he said that was impossible because I would have been too weak to take care of her after she was born. In fact, he says I probably would have died but we could all see that I was fine. He said he was proud of me for giving birth to my child all by myself. But I hadn't! I just know there was a woman with me! She delivered the baby and swaddled her.

But no one would listen to me. The doctor said I must have dreamed it. What he says makes sense but what I remember makes sense as well. Yet, both can't be true. Joe said he believes there is a walking spirit that becomes a guardian in times of danger. He said she visited me in my time of need just like she visited him once. He couldn't explain it, and no one else believes it, but he knows she's there. I'm comforted and at the same time disturbed. Haunted. One day I hope to understand this strange occurrence. Who was she? Was she even real? Was she flesh and blood or just a spirit? I touched her and I know she felt real. Oh, this is greater than my imagination! The baby grows. My daughter. My Francine. She's beautiful. I'm thankful she does not have my red hair. She's dark like Joe and I think…

Will tried to turn the page but couldn't. “That's all I can read on that page; they're stuck again.” He carefully put the pages back in place. “Well, just in the few pages we read we fell in love, got married and had our first child. Kind of boring, huh?” he teased her.

“Boring!” Her eyes were so large her face disappeared in her expression. In fact, her seriousness was so comical he burst out in laughter. As though put out with him she carefully took the papers away from him. “Say what you will, but we now have names! And wouldn't it be a miraculous coincidence if the Francine that was born turned out to be my very own great grandmother? I bet it was!”

Now her expression was one of uncontained excitement. Her fists were clenched and shaking as though she were doing everything humanly possible not to burst. Then she giggled and poked him.

“What,” he asked when she didn't say anything.

“You're just as excited as I am. Don't even try to deny it! You should have heard your voice when you were reading those few pages. Yep, you're just as interested as I am.”

“Well, yeah,” he admitted. “I thought it would probably be just a bunch of blank papers or figures of livestock sales or something. I never dreamed you'd have something so personal. Actually, I'd like to try and separate the pages so we can read it in its entirety. What do you think?”

“I think you've got a great idea! I'm just positive that this will be the key in putting together the history of this place. Oh, Will, my heart is just racing I'm so excited! How I wish I knew who wrote it and when. At least we have two names and it won't take long to find out who Francine's mother was. How I wish I could remember. No matter, I'll probably have it figured out in another twenty-four hours.”

"It's got to be a woman writing but that satchel is definitely not feminine. Maybe Joe or someone kept all his wife's love letters as well as her journal. Isn't that romantic?" Will rolled his eyes as he closed the flap over the papers and handed the satchel back to her. "Am I going to be doomed if you ever write to me and I don't save your letters so that our fourth generation can discover them?"

"Of course!" Her eyes were large with merriment. She hugged the satchel close to her heart. "Somehow, some way, I'm going to do my best to read every word I possibly can. It's really important, don't you think?"

He tilted her chin up and looked deeply into her radiant, brown eyes. "Yes, my darling adventuress, it is important. I have an idea!" Will offered his thoughts. "Let's go back to the river and sit under the cotton tree with our picnic lunch and try to read a little more while we eat. How about it?"

"I am getting kind of hungry. Sure, let's do it!"

"And if I can't tear you away from the journal I'll sacrifice and let you read a little longer while I stay out of your way. I bet there's some great fish in that river and I just happen to have my pole."

"I was wondering how you were going to get a fishing trip in." She took a deep breath and bounced on the balls of her feet. "You didn't slip anything by me, I saw you hide your fishing pole in the trunk of the car. Which is fine! I'll be quite content to read while you drown the worms in that sour cream container in the cooler."

"What makes you think it's not sour cream?"

"Neither one of us puts it on our sandwiches, do we?"

He smiled; she was absolutely right. As they went back outside, they retraced their path and headed for the car. Earlier that morning they had packed the picnic basket and now she was eager to dig into its contents. Will loved to eat and she had brought his favorites.

"I really am glad you brought me out here." She closed her eyes a moment and spun in a circle. "It truly is rapturous! Everywhere you look could make a perfect calendar picture. I wonder how much it's changed throughout the years?"

"Well, like I said, there's the foundation of a house and barn way over there." He pointed to an area about a quarter of a mile from where the cabin was. "Other than that, I haven't seen any other structures. No, wait!"

Will looked around and tried to get his bearings. "Somewhere around here is a newer house. Actually..." he spun in circles, "I think it's on the other side of the river. So, I guess that doesn't count. As far as I can tell, there's no bridge anywhere around here and I haven't found any shallow places where a person could cross. Doesn't make sense though that a house would be cut off like that. You'd have to go for miles and miles if you wanted to get to the other side; which is what I did! That's how I know!"

"Another mystery perhaps?" she teased.

He nodded, still trying to figure it out. "In fact, if you're on that side I'm not even sure if you could get to Gough's Ridge. The next town on that side is a good ten miles away."

"Could there have been any stores or anything over there?"

"Who knows? Well, it only makes sense that at one time there was a bridge, had to have been. Wonder what happened to it?"

Phyllis hugged the satchel close to her. "Maybe the answer is right here within these pages."

"One thing at a time my sweet. Just like you unravel a mixed up ball of yarn we'll start at one end and eventually get to the other. It's just one continuous story, with a lot of loops and twists to unravel."

For the next half hour they enjoyed their picnic lunch and then Will went down to the edge of the bank where he could fish. Phyllis put everything away and then leaned back to stare up at the sky. The day was incredibly perfect. She couldn't remember when she had been happier or more excited about life. Looking down at the satchel she tried to imagine herself as the person who had written the priceless pages of the journal. When she picked it up, she looked at her own hands as though they were the hands of the writer and little by little she transported herself back to that time period. She tried to go beyond the pages about the marriage but before the child was born.

> I didn't mean to pry. I just wanted to know the story. Joe seemed to understand even though some things just couldn't be put into words. So much of his memory seemed to be from feelings and fears. There were times that none of it made sense to him. Reality had become like a dream; bits and pieces of conversations blended as though there were no commas or periods or beginnings or endings! He couldn't even remember who said what or why so how could he explain it to me? People and places were all jumbled together. Except for one. The Indian girl. He's never forgotten her even though he was forbidden to speak her name. He said she secretly lived with them for a long time. His daddy told him she had drowned close to our cabin but there was a man living in Gough's Ridge who swore he saw her alive. Well, whether she was alive or her ghost lived for her, I guess we'll never know. Joe seems to think he saw her, too. It was during the time after Ira was killed and he had to walk to his uncle's.

ꕥꕥꕥꕥꕥ

1888

The sun was just beginning to set when Ira finally saw his cabin through the trees. He had made it! It still took him almost ten minutes to drag himself to the front door. The pain was unbearable! His left leg was only attached because the bone hadn't been broken completely but the flesh and meat was gone between his knee and ankle. His left arm was broken; his right was badly chewed, like his leg. He wasn't sure how many fingers he had left. If he had had his gun he would have put himself out of his own misery, but it was somewhere in the ravine. He didn't even have the satisfaction of knowing he had gotten a good shot at the bear. He had been following the tracks with his gun ready but the creature must have doubled back on him. Three hundred pounds of raging beast suddenly came out of nowhere and attacked him before he knew it was coming! With one sweep of that mighty paw, the gun went flying and then Ira found himself smothered in black and silver fur as it came down on top of him, followed by teeth and claws.

Knowing that he had to get back to his son, Ira somehow managed to get home. Now, he was almost at the door. He tried to call out to the boy but all he could produce was a gurgling sound deep in his throat. He knew he was in trouble when he spit out a mouthful of blood. Picking up a rock by the door he scraped on the weathered wood with all the energy he had left.

"Who's there?" The small voice called from behind the safety of the door. When there wasn't any answer but the scratching sound, the boy timidly opened the door and in horror questioned what had happened.

"Bear." Ira coughed again. "I'm dead."

Between the two of them, Ira finally got to his bed but Joe had no way of knowing what to do. One eye was already completely swollen shut. Little by little he finally got Joe to understand that he wanted paper and pencil.

"Walter. There. Go." Ira had sketched out a crude map, then dropped the pencil, satisfied that he had done the best he could. He took a pained breath and then closed his eyes. In less than ten minutes, Ira Parker was dead.

Joe kept looking at the man and then at the map. He didn't want to go to his uncle's but he was now afraid to be alone. He knew Uncle Walter and didn't like him. But then, he didn't like Ira very much either. He decided to follow the map. Pulling the covers completely over Ira, he stood at the foot of the bed and stared at the lifeless lump under the blankets. He had seen enough faces of death to know that his father would never breathe again. He was totally alone.

He had to have someone to take care of him. How he wished AnnaBelinda was there. She would have known what to do. She had been gone so long it was almost hard to remember her. He squeezed his eyes shut, straining to see a glimpse of memory still imprinted on the inside of his eyelids. What did she look like? He remembered her long, black hair and deep, brown eyes. Sometimes her eyes were so cold and so full of hate that he was afraid to look at her.

She had threatened him one time. "My eyes will burn you alive, white boy! You won't burn on the outside of your skin but on the inside. And it will be too late when you see the flesh starting to ooze off. Your whole insides will be black and you'll die with great pain!"

That scared him because she picked up a charred stick from the fire and hit it against the table. It exploded on impact and as each splinter went in a different direction Joe thought his own body parts would shatter in the same way. He was afraid that with her Indian powers she had burned his insides and if he looked around the room he'd see an arm there, a leg there, and his head over there, shattered like the stick.

But he wasn't always afraid of her eyes. One time he had a nightmare and she was there by his bed, stroking his forehead and her eyes were soft and warm. They coaxed the dream back into the night and for a moment they seemed to embrace him even when her arms wouldn't. He felt secure and safe with her. Then there was another time when he got in trouble and Ira beat him with the strap. After Ira left, he looked up and saw AnnaBelinda looking at him. He didn't know the word compassion but the look in her eyes told him he wasn't the only one hurting. He couldn't explain it but her spirit blinked through her eyes and made the hurt go away. He thought it was magic. Even if he couldn't remember exactly what she looked like, he didn't think he'd ever forget her strong determination to hold on to her Indian heritage. Her name wasn't really AnnaBelinda. He knew that. But he couldn't remember her real name. She had told him what it was but it sounded dumb to him so he forgot it. Besides, Ira had warned him that if he ever spoke her real name he'd get the worse beating of his life. From the very beginning Joe had been forced to call her his made up friend. That way, if he accidentally said something no one would believe him. Ira explained that in Joe's grief he had made up a special friend to replace his mother and sister.

"And he believes every word of his story." Ira's eyes had widened in mock concern. "Sad. I got a deranged boy because of those heathens. He don't even know what's real and what ain't!"

Joe didn't like when Ira talked that way and he never fully understood why AnnaBelinda was such a secret. All he knew was that Indians had killed his mother and the girl had been given in exchange.

"Somebody's gotta cook and clean for us." Ira laughed. "But we don't want no trouble, so just keep yur mouth shut."

Joe could remember a little of the attack - not faces or the things they did but the fear. He had gone to the outhouse when the Indians rode up so he knew to stay hidden. There wasn't even that much noise but what he did hear terrified him! He curled up against the wall of the outhouse and refused to look up. At one time he thought he heard someone else ride up, but he was afraid that it was another Indian coming back to find him so he stayed where he was. He finally came out from hiding and headed to the house. He didn't remember the blood or how they had been killed. All he could remember was that his mother didn't blink. There was something about her eyes that deeply disturbed him.

Joe Parker had been far too young to comprehend the situation he was in. Neither did he have any idea what to do. So, he wandered around. At first he'd go back in and tug on an arm trying to get someone to respond to him. When that failed he ate whatever he could reach and then he crawled up in his bed and went to sleep. When he did wake up, he was startled as he looked into the face of Jeremiah Davis. That was it. He couldn't remember another thing. He had no idea what Jeremiah had said or done from that point on.

He did remember that Ira use to keep the girl chained so she couldn't escape. Even though she was able to move around, she was limited in how far she could go. At times, Joe would stay just out of reach and taunt her.

Ira was gone a lot so it would be just the two of them. It was during those times they discovered they could be friends. AnnaBelinda told him stories and the ways of the Indians. She always told him what the young boys were expected to do, and how she would grow up and be proud of who she was.

"When you grow up, Joe Parker, people should think of you as a brave man, not a murdering man like your father who hates life."

Actually, Joe didn't care what he grew up to be or even what people thought. But he didn't like being alone. Now that Ira was dead, he felt overwhelmed with loneliness. He shut the bedroom door and looked at the map again. It was a long, long ways but he had been there before and he was pretty sure he could get there again, even if he didn't have anyone to take care of him.

The map was crude but it looked like he was supposed to follow the river until he got to an abandoned gold mine. Then he was to go over a hill or mountain and at the bottom there was a lake. He had to go around that and then he'd be at his uncle's.

Joe went over it again and then put the map down and started putting food and things he thought he'd need in a leather pouch. Then he slipped his poncho over his head because he hated to get caught in the rain but he didn't want to carry it. Just like he had seen Ira do many times, he slipped a knife down into his boot. Knowing he didn't have a choice, he didn't dwell on the dangers that were out there. All he knew to avoid was the bear that killed his dad and poison ivy. Even though he didn't know the psychology of his actions, the sorrow of Ira's death and the anger of being left alone was what motivated him to start out on that fifteen mile journey.

Joe didn't mind walking along the river. When he got thirsty he just went to the edge of the bank and drank as much as he wanted. He even stopped to eat some berries but his mind really wasn't on food. After walking another two hours he was ready to quit. His legs hurt and then he really was hungry! He sat down and wondered how long he'd have to sit there before someone came along and found him. If Jeremiah had been alive, Joe would have just waited for him. It wasn't the right time of year for Frothworth. He yawned; he'd wait anyway.

Other than the birds and squirrels there were no sounds around him and hardly any movement. In his mind he had been waiting for at least six hours! He opened the pouch and began to eat. Then he sat around until the sun went down and he started to get a little cold. He put the poncho back on and then used his hat as a pillow and curled up to sleep.

The night was long and he hated it! He got madder and madder that Ira had to have gotten killed. He wanted to be home in his own bed and he wanted someone to make hot biscuits and beans. When morning came he still waited. But the longer he waited, the madder he got! Now, he was really hungry! He dumped everything out of the pouch and started eating. Before he quit, he had nearly eaten everything. His jaw was set; he didn't care. From complete boredom he decided to start walking again, thinking that if he started moving, his chances of being found were better. When his feet started hurting again, he got mad because Ira had never given him a horse. With a deep frown he looked up at the sky in case Ira might be listening from up there.

"You should have thought about me! You were stupid to get killed but stupider not to give me a horse! Now, you're makin' my feet hurt!"

When there wasn't any sound or any acknowledgment to his outrage he looked down at the ground as though addressing Ira in the pits of hell.

"You down there? Well, I hope you're in so much pain you can't stand it because I sure am and it's all your fault!" He stomped the ground for good measure.

Satisfied that he had gotten his message across he kept on walking. As he walked, he snapped off dry stalks or hanging branches. He kicked at the dirt and shuffled his feet so that he was leaving an obvious trail. Jeremiah had once told him that if he got lost in the woods and wanted someone to find him then he had to make his presence known. Joe was hoping that someone would just happen to cross his trail and be curious enough to follow it.

The map said he had to go past the gold mine. He thought he remembered seeing it before but it was such a vague memory that he didn't know if it was a mine shaft or his aunt's storm cellar that he remembered. Whichever one it was, there was darkness and a musky smell with a sticky, closed in feeling that he didn't like. Maybe he'd find the gold mine and find him a nugget so big that he could buy a farm and have a cook and someone to take care of the horses. He'd run it the way he wanted to. Doors would never be locked and no one would be allowed to kill anyone. He didn't like death. Besides, he didn't know where dead people went when they no longer moved or saw through their eyes. They never came back to tell him.

He remembered he had yelled at his mother to come back but she didn't. And he kept going out to the barn to see if Uncle Graydon had gone back out there. Whenever he walked up to the gravesite he was afraid to step on the mound of earth for fear a hand would reach up and grab his ankle. Jeremiah had told him that a lot of times people didn't really die they just turned into ghosts. AnnaBelinda had told him a ghost story once.

Joe found a good boulder to climb up on and look around. At the top of it he searched for the gold mine but he didn't see anything. He sat down, weary. He was like the unlucky Indian that had to walk a long distance and talk with a lot of strange beings in order to kill an otter and wear its skin so he could be lucky. Actually, he had always liked that story. AnnaBelinda must have told it to him a dozen times because he kept forgetting if the ghost people came first or Coyote or Beaver. So, she acted it out with him once and then he remembered.

Joe smiled and then, out of habit, looked around to make sure no one was watching him so he could pretend to be the unlucky young boy from the story. Ira had caught him pretending one time and kicked him in the stomach so hard he fell over.

"You some kind of baby?" Ira had mocked him. After that, Joe never let anyone know what he was doing. He decided it would be safe here in the woods to pretend. Joe could do exactly what he wanted because no one was around to make fun of him. He closed his eyes a minute and sucked in his cheeks as he put himself in the story. Then he took off his shirt so he'd be more like the Indian brave. Poor Indian brave! He could hear AnnaBelinda's voice telling the story, and that was somehow comforting to remember.

No one liked him, he couldn't find a bride, and every time he tried to shoot an arrow his bow broke. He was forced to walk because his horse was lame. Instead of his name being Joe Parker, he was now The Unlucky One. There was an old woman in the story who was gathering wood by the side of the river.

Joe walked to the water's edge and sat down, pretending to fish and then lose his pole. All of a sudden the old woman in the story was behind him. He turned and asked her 'who are you looking for old woman?'

She answered, 'I'm looking for the strong, young boy they call the Unlucky One.'

'Well, I reckon that's me.' Joe continued to pretend as the imaginary old woman talked with him. 'What do you want with me?'

'Follow me.' She bent over as though she was carrying a buffalo on her back. Her eyes stayed focused on the ground as she walked. Only once did she stop and look back to make sure he was following her.

Joe imitated her slow shuffle. At last she stopped and faced him, pointing to the ground for him to sit. 'Before you go anywhere else you must learn this song.'

He could distinctly remember when AnnaBelinda taught him that song and they had sung it together. Once again, making sure that no one was watching, Joe stretched out his neck, holding his head high and then let his voice sing out the strange little song. He had to stop and think about some of the words, but the more he sang, the easier it was to remember. He was actually proud of himself for getting all the way through it!

Then, the little, old woman gave him moccasins and a bag of food and told him that he had to travel a great distance. 'Go down the river until you get to a great beaver village. Not a little one but one of such great size that you could get lost in it! When you get there, stand still and then sing the song for all to hear.'

Joe pretended that he put on the moccasins and then headed off as he followed the river. As soon as he found the beaver village he would speak with the great, white Beaver who would tell him what to do next. The story went that the Indian brave sang the song to the white Beaver and then the Beaver told him that he had to find their brother the Coyote and sing the song again before Coyote would help him out. He was to carry a big stick because it would be a long journey.

Joe looked around and picked up the biggest stick he could find. He had pretended to come upon the beaver village and darted this way and that as though dodging beavers who would have otherwise run into him. He squared his shoulders as though determined he wouldn't get lost in such a huge village. And then he bent over as though talking with the Great White Beaver. With the stick in his hand he pretended that he was walking for miles and miles, days and days! But he was brave and strong and could keep going. The Coyote stopped him again and said, 'I'm hungry.'

Pulling out the pouch, Joe found it nearly empty. 'I'm hungry, too, but I ate up all the dried meat the old woman gave me and if I wasn't so brave and strong I know that I would die from starvation,' he told the Coyote. Pulling out two pieces of jerky, Joe pretended to share with Coyote. He sat still long enough to eat both pieces and then he jumped up as the imaginary coyote took off, calling back to him, 'Our brother, Wolf just killed a doe and we have plenty to eat. Come on, come on, there's enough for the three of us!'

As Joe continued walking he kept cramming imaginary pieces of venison into his mouth and chewed greedily. 'No more, I'm full,' he protested but Coyote told him to eat more that he would soon be lucky and able to change his name.

'Now we must go to the Old Man's lodge,' Coyote told him. Joe wiped his mouth and straightened his clothes so he would be presentable. It was getting dark. At least in his imagination because that's the way the story went. They walked a long time without stopping, over plains and mountains.

Joe thought about the map he had accidently left on the kitchen table. He knew that as soon as he found the gold mine he was supposed to go to the top of a mountain. In AnnaBelinda's story the Unlucky One also traveled through great forests and across rivers until they finally came to a cave in the side of the mountain. Joe looked around. Maybe the gold mine could really be the cave of the Old Man. It still wasn't in sight. How much farther? Nothing to do but keep walking and playing out the story. He definitely was an unlucky one! His pa was dead and he was alone. This journey was taking forever. Joe put his hands over his eyes so he could only see darkness. He pretended that he was looking inside the great cave. Slowly, he began to creep inside the cave, feeling his way in the darkness. Joe pretended to be afraid because the story went that as the Unlucky One got farther and farther into the cave, his heart was beating like a tom-tom at a dance. And then he saw a fire way back into the cave. As he got closer, shadows danced about the stone sides of the cave and then he saw the Old Man whose long hair was snowy white.

'How, young man, I am Old Man, what do you want?'

Joe stood tall. 'I don't want to be unlucky anymore. I learned the strange song from the old woman and I ate meat with Coyote. I have this stick to prove I have spoken to them. Can you help me?' Joe continued to speak out loud, gesturing with his hands as though there was really someone in front of him.

'Smoke? Is that what you want me to do? Okay, we'll smoke on it.' Joe pretended to take a pipe from the Old Man and he took a long draw on it. He was experienced at this and never coughed. Old Man was indeed impressed.

'I'll tell you what to do. On the top of the great mountain that you have to climb live the ghost people. Their chief is the Great Owl. Take this arrow and show no fear. If you are unarmed they won't hurt you.'

Joe picked up another stick from the ground and pretended that it was the magic arrow. He held it out and examined it as though he had never seen one like it before. Once again he started walking because he had to travel through the night and fight the north wind and trudge through two feet of snow. No, at least four feet of snow, since this was his story! The wind kept swirling the snow and he climbed the mountain higher and higher until he was actually in the clouds. And then he couldn't tell if it was the swirling snow or if the ghost people were flying around him. It didn't matter because he was brave! No fear! He walked boldly right to the top of the mountain where he soon found hundreds and thousands of ghost people. They were singing a warlike song but still he wasn't afraid. In the center of them sat a mighty owl. When the ghost people saw him they rushed him with ice spears but the Owl-chief cried out,

'Stop! For this Unlucky One is brave and carries the magic arrow.' And the ghost people stopped at once.

Joe stood still and folded his arms, his back straight. 'I am unarmed—kill me if you must but I am not afraid to die.'

'We kill no unarmed man.' The Owl-chief held out his hand and beckoned him to come closer. Even though the ghost people were frightening, Joe took firm steps and walked boldly into the circle. The Owl-chief held out another pipe. 'Smoke with me and tell me what you want.'

'I want to get safely to my uncle's and end this journey. Do I like him? No, but I am obeying my father and that is a good thing to do. But I am unlucky. Only you can help. The old woman taught me the song and I have the stick and the arrow, but I still need luck.' Joe cocked his head as though listening.

The Owl-chief was telling him, 'I can help you but first you have to go down this mountain to the river towards a cottonwood tree. Then follow the bank of the river and travel north for days and days without any rest. You have to keep going until you hear splashing in the water and as soon as you hear it, you must shoot this bow with the arrow that Old Man gave you. If you don't kill the splasher, you will never, never have any good luck for the rest of your life. You'll never have enough food and you won't get to your uncles. But, if you do as I told you, the splasher will be killed and you must skin him and wear his hide across your shoulder until your journey is over.'

Joe waved goodbye and kept walking. He was tired but the Owl-chief told him he couldn't rest so even when he wanted to, he continued to play out his story. Every once in awhile he'd holler out 'I'm too tired to keep going but I will! Do you hear me? I won't give up!" And the little boy kept walking, searching for the gold mine. And then he decided he had walked far enough. He pretended that he heard splashing and put the stick in the imaginary bow and holding it with one hand he pretended to pull back the bow string with the other. He made a sound like an arrow whizzing through the night air and hitting something! And then he made a little animal squeal as though it had just been hit. He pretended to walk through high reeds and then search for the otter that he had just killed with the magic arrow. There was his brother Wolf watching, and after Joe pulled out the arrow from the heart he skinned the otter and threw the meat to the wolf. Then he secured the otter hide on his shoulder and wore it with pride. The end of the story was that the Indian hunter changed his name because from that time on he was always lucky.

"My name is now Lucky Joe!" he yelled at the tree tops. At that moment there were two things he didn't realize. Not more than a quarter of a mile ahead was the abandoned mine that he had been searching for. The other thing was that he wasn't alone.

Wind In Mourning was following him. When he had first started acting out the story she had wondered if perhaps he had lost his mind but as she dared to get closer, she could hear him and it didn't take long to recognize the very popular Indian story. So, he hadn't forgotten. She had watched him pretending one time in the cabin and as soon as he was aware of her he stopped and just stared at her, refusing to do anything else. Now, as she watched, she found that she was proud of him. For him to remember the story this well after two years meant she had taught him well.

There was a feeling in her heart that she couldn't explain. Something that made her want to hold the boy and smell his hair and touch his fingers. Wind In Mourning sighed, realizing how much she had missed him. He was growing up into a fine male child. In her Indian beliefs she would have thanked the god of the guardian worshippers that their paths continued to cross but now she knew that it was God Himself who directed this course of events.

With Frothworth's help she had never given up on keeping track of the boy. She would never get too close for fear of running into Ira. Either Frothworth or Gunther would always accompany her. Since she couldn't see him that often, Frothworth would often go down and talk to Ira and get an update just as he always did, and then he would tell Wind In Mourning how the boy was doing.

This time she had waited under the protection of a spruce as Frothworth had gone down to the cabin. To her surprise he had come back immediately.

"Wind In Mourning," he called her name openly. She knew something was wrong for him to be without caution. "He's dead."

Holding her breath and yet at the same time sighing with relief she stepped out from her hiding place. "Dead? Are you sure?"

"There ain't no doubt about it." Frothworth had quickly approached her. He rubbed his nose as though trying to be rid of the smell of death.

"What about Joe?"

"He's nowhere to be seen. I found this map on the table. Looks like Ira must have scratched it out before he died and sent the boy on over to Walter's."

"How long dead?"

"Stiff. Bloody stiff. A blanket was over his head. Looks like he must have been mauled by a bear. What do you want to do?"

"I've got to find Joe. I'll take the map and make sure he gets to where he's going."

"You do that and I'll bury Ira. Should just let his body rot like his soul so they can both go to Hell, but since I'm a God fearin' man I'll do the right thing. Don't know if I'll say a prayer or not."

"Maybe a prayer for Joe; he deserves one." Wind In Mourning still couldn't believe that the most wicked man on earth was gone.

Frothworth went to his horse. "You go on now and take my food pack from this here saddle pack. You have your bow, right?" She acknowledged she did. "Good, then you can get fresh game if you need to. Is there anything else you might need?"

"I'll take an extra blanket in case Joe doesn't have one." She tried to think of the next couple of days and how to offset any obstacles Joe might have.

"You be careful, girl." Frothworth kissed her forehead. "Once you get the boy safely to Walter's you come back and let me know what happened. You know how to keep yourself out of sight."

"I'm good at that." She returned his special smile.

Without delay, Wind In Mourning had set off with the map in her hand. Riding her horse she made good time and Joe's trail was easy to follow. Before she had actually spotted him she had said a prayer for herself. It seemed a little awkward, this white man's faith that she had accepted, but Gunther had told her there was a lot to learn. He explained that her spirit had been reborn and she was like a baby learning to walk and talk. She smiled at the thought of Gunther; the white Indian who was more like a brother to her than her own flesh and blood. When Frothworth was telling her about the savior Jesus, she didn't understand until she realized that Gunther had acted out that same kind of love when he had risked his life for hers. That helped her to understand.

Her thoughts were pulled back to the boy as she watched Joe dragging the walking stick behind him, still pretending. And then he saw the gold mine and his entire demeanor changed!

"I made it!" He whooped and hollered. Wind In Mourning had no idea he had a voice that loud! She watched him as he ran down to the mine and explored the two huts that were barely standing. They couldn't even be called a decent shelter anymore. Joe went inside the mine but didn't stay long. He came back out and looked around. Wind In Mourning was careful not to be seen. Since Ira was dead she knew she was safe but there was an uneasiness to her about actually confirming her existence to the boy. It was something she couldn't explain.

Joe sat down on a horse trough and opened his pouch. He pulled out the last stick of beef jerky and then threw the pouch on the ground. "How can I be lucky if I'm going to starve to death?" He shook his fist at the sky.

"Where are you Coyote? Where is brother Wolf? Call him so we can share the venison. The real stuff!"

Then he kicked the dirt as though frustrated with the story and pretending. It was starting to get dark and Wind In Mourning knew that he would start looking for a safe place to sleep. She didn't like the idea of him going to bed on an empty stomach. Going back to the horse she took out three corn cakes and smoked fish. She had to smile at the thought of Joe trying to explain to someone how he came up with the food. Then she pulled the blanket off the pack so he would have something to cover with. This would make a good story, even better than imagination. It wouldn't do anything for his credibility but no one could deny that he was well fed and had safely traveled the distance.

Joe went back to the mine and as soon as he was out of sight she slipped down to the old hut. She put the fish and corn cakes on top of his pouch so he would be sure to see them. Deciding that there was no way he could miss the food and blanket, she slipped back around to the mine, listening carefully to make sure he wasn't coming. Right before darkness folded over the landscape she found a good hiding spot and imitated the wolf's howl. It sounded rather sickly but that didn't matter. Joe immediately emerged from the mine and looked around. Wind In Mourning walked towards her horse and howled again, leading Joe towards the hut. She could tell he was scared. Just as she predicted, he found what she had laid out for him. He stooped to touch it, making sure it was real. He tasted the corn cake, then sat down and arranged everything on his lap.

"Oh, I am so lucky!" Looking around again, he was obviously trying to figure out how it got there. Then he reached over to his walking stick and shook it in the air. With a big grin he shouted "Thanks Coyote and Wolf. It was supposed to be venison but that's okay. Fish is just fine. And you even brought my blanket! I am so lucky!" He took three more bites and then gathered up the food and pouch and went inside the hut. Not more than two minutes later he came running back out as though he had forgotten something. He cupped his hands around his mouth and called out “I’m not afraid! If you’re close by, ghost people, I’m not armed either.” Then he went back inside.

Wind In Mourning rubbed her horse’s neck and then unstrapped her blanket. Once she was sure where Joe would sleep, she would set her bed down at a safe distance and make sure that he wasn’t disturbed through the night.

CHAPTER 6

1969

Phyllis stretched her back and rolled her neck a bit; she was getting cramped from sitting in one place for so long. Then she rubbed her eyes and yawned.

"Will? Have you caught enough fish for supper yet?" She stretched her legs out as well and leaned back on her elbows, looking across her nose so she could see him down at the bank.

He called up to her, "I think this date has been officially declared as a beef and potato day. Are you getting restless?"

"No." She made sure the papers were secure and then she left the blanket to walk over to him. "It is getting a little bit late though. Do you suppose we should be heading back?"

"I'm ready whenever you are. Did you want to go back to the cabin before we leave?"

"What about walking over to that foundation you mentioned? In the journal the woman talked about neighbors. I'd kind of like to see for myself just how close, or how far they actually were."

"Sure, we can do that," he agreed.

"I've decided that the Francine mentioned is definitely my great grandmother."

"And what brought you to that conclusion?" He cast the line for probably the fiftieth time. It had become so automatic he could have probably read a book or eaten a sandwich without missing a toss.

"I read where she started singing when she was just four years old. Apparently, Joe frequented the saloon in Gough's Ridge quite often and he'd take her up there and she'd stand on the tables and sing. The patrons would flip coins on the table for her. What a life, huh? And then, as she got older, she sat on the piano."

"And they tucked dollar bills in her anklets, right?"

"Wrong!" Phyllis frowned at him, then mischievously grinned with her eyes wide. "In her neckline!"

"Are you serious?" Will stood perfectly still for a moment as he considered what she said.

"No," she laughed, enjoying the fact he had been gullible enough to even consider believing her. "I don't think she did. I mean, after all, great grandmother Francine must have been a stately lady! I can't imagine how she got any polish around here but she must have acquired it some way for her to travel and do concerts and such. Can you imagine starting a singing career in a saloon? Well, she did. And then, when the little community around here had social events she would sing for them, too."

"What about at church?"

"You know, nothing is ever mentioned about church. And yet, our writer is definitely a God fearing woman. Makes you wonder how these people maintained their faith. We sure take church for granted. I wonder if there was ever a church building around here?" She stretched up on her tiptoes and looked around as though expecting to see something.

"Doubtful. I think the closest one is in Gough's Ridge. But you've heard about traveling preachers. Maybe they had a regular man-of-the-cloth pass through and during the community events maybe he had a chance to preach a little extra hellfire and damnation. At least enough to carry them through until he made his next circuit. Could have been months and months in between. Then, if anything happened to him, I guess they had to wait until some other brave soul decided to take up the call to preach."

Phyllis sat down in the plush grass and put her elbows on her knees with her head in her hands. "We sure do take a lot for granted, don't we? I bet Francine's life would have been totally different if she had been raised in a church and was able to sing for the Lord."

Will totally agreed with her. "I wonder if you look anything like Francine? Family traits and characteristics seem to be passed from one generation to the next. Maybe there are parts of you that are exactly like her -

like your hands, or chin, or maybe even your smile. Wouldn't it be neat if we could find some old pictures or something?"

"Definitely. Right now I just have to use my imagination."

"Well, that puts her in a unique category." Will over emphasized each word.

"What do you mean by that?"

Will laughed. "She could look like anything from Poor Pitiful Pearl to the Queen of England! Your imagination doesn't know any boundaries or limitations."

She upturned her nose and looked in another direction in mock offense. "You should be thankful for that; at least it's kept me with you."

Will threw the line out again. "And here I thought it was due entirely to my charisma and sense of humor. No, wait! I forgot, you were going to marry me for my money."

"You're right, I was! Now, how could I have possibly forgotten? Oh, I suppose it's because I have to rely totally on imagination for you to even save a dime! I don't let that bother me though," she winked at him and then got up again. "I mean, I love poor, pitiful paupers, too."

"Well, I guess I can't lose either way. So what else did you read in the journal?" Every once in awhile he felt something nibble at the bait and would instinctively play with the line.

"It's really quite fascinating. Joe must have been a very difficult person to get along with and yet he wasn't mean or anything. Our little missus really had to work at hooking him!" She was watching the bobber, too, and deliberately used the play on words. Will acknowledged her quick wit and then his attention went right back to the rippling water.

Phyllis continued, "She often writes about her little short legs and that she had a hard time keeping up with Joe. I think she was the kind of person that could think up twenty questions if someone had asked her to do a simple task like dusting. What do you want dusted? Do I dust around each item or under them as well? What do I dust with? Is that the green dust cloth or the yellow one? Is there really a difference? You know, that kind of thing. But she wasn't complex. She strikes me as a woman who didn't let people push her around and she accepted whatever life seemed to dish out. Wonderful writer! Oh, my, the phrases and descriptions she comes up with! Definitely not a shallow mind!

"In fact, her writing has some of the most beautiful analogies and metaphors as I've ever read. Nothing I've learned in English class can even compare. She seemed to be a natural at it, which makes me wonder how in the world she had that kind of education. I mean, I bet she was teaching the teachers by the time she was twelve. Anyway, her writing sure does make the journal more interesting to read. Seems like I really get into it, heart, mind, and soul. In fact, I find myself rooting for her!" Phyllis gave a little bounce and a deep shrug of her shoulders. "Whoever she was, she was one incredible woman, I can tell you that much!"

"Well, she's probably been dead a long time, but I think you've probably inherited some of her talent and therefore she lives on. Have any more children been mentioned besides Francine?"

"No, not yet, though she's mentioned that she would like to have a house full of little ones. I think for awhile she was feeling quite barren as though God wasn't going to bless her because she was so short. Actually, I think it's next to a miracle that Francine lived. Who do you suppose was the woman who helped during the birth?"

"Well, if it had been a neighbor she would have recognized her, don't you think? Not only that but the woman would have admitted to being there and would have talked about it. And if it had been someone just passing by, you'd think they would have stayed until the doctor got there. I have to wonder if she was hallucinating. It just doesn't make sense for a midwife to suddenly disappear."

"I have a really wild speculation." Phyllis had debated if she had wanted to tell him or not, but now that they were talking about it, she couldn't keep it to herself.

"Which is?" Will was eager to hear her idea. The invisible, nibbling monster had gotten away so she had his undivided attention.

"Well," she drew it out as she leaned back against a tree. "I think it was the Indian girl that Joe grew up with."

"The one that Joe didn't know was alive or dead, or if she had drowned or was reunited with her people?"

"Right. My vote is that she was reunited. I mean, there has to be some substantial evidence for someone to say that she had been seen alive and well. Now, I don't know if she was reunited with her people or not, maybe she spent some time in the area but I do believe that she kept an eye on Joe as he was growing up and then she just happened to be there for Francine's birth."

"Was she an Indian or an angel? If the story is going to be logical you have to come up with a reason why she would even stick around. No, sorry, Babe, but I don't bite into it. If my memory is right, cowboys didn't get along with Indians and I don't think there's any way that an Indian girl could survive such a hostile environment. If she went back to her people, why in the world would she want to leave them? Chances are, she would be risking her life to even be seen!"

"Exactly what I was thinking, that's why she didn't stick around for the doctor to see her. She saw what was happening, and she intervened and when everything was okay she left. I bet you anything she stood out among the trees and waited until she was assured that Francine was going to live."

"Why should she even care about Francine? That's what I'm getting at."

"Because, that's Joe's daughter! And she just happened to be in the right place at the right time."

"And just happened to deliver the baby and just happened to be able to leave before anyone else came?" He finished her sentence. "And what was her next angelic adventure?"

Phyllis wanted to hit him. "Now, quit! You're making fun of me and I really am quite serious. I don't know all the particulars, I told you it's just a speculation. But I think I'm right. I think the Indian girl--for who knows what reason--became like a special guardian to Joe and his family."

"I would almost tend to believe you but there's a serious discrepancy here. You're putting Christian traits upon the girl who was probably raised with many gods and witch doctors and all kinds of rituals that involved drugs and torture! That would have been something so inbred in her that to try and change her would be like trying to teach a dog to moo. As a matter of fact, some tribes were not only barbaric but cannibalistic."

Phyllis wasn't going to be swayed. "I know that, but this is different. This girl came from a tribe of peaceful Indians who were incredibly skillful and they survived because they weren't at war all the time and the white man got smart enough to realize that they could learn from each other and who knows, somewhere along the line maybe she was converted." She stopped, seeing that Will was actually waiting for her breathe.

"Is that so?" He took a deep breath with her and then just smiled and waited.

"It is! I know it for a fact."

"Do you really? Well, I'm certainly glad we got this little issue straightened out. But, just in case you're wrong, would you do me the honor of considering my speculation?"

"Oh, sure. Just because I'm right all the time doesn't mean I'm rude; go ahead." She teased.

"I think that one of the neighbors or maybe even a trapper helped Joe during that fifteen mile trek and there was nothing miraculous or mysterious about it. Joe just turned it into a good story. You know as well as I do that people always invent new legends because it makes their town famous. As far as Francine's birth, I think our little mother was either dreaming or just a wee bit delirious and wasn't getting her story straight."

"That's the best you can come up with? I can't believe you could be so—so—bland and so—practical! I think I'm actually disappointed in your realm of reasoning."

"Why, because I'm not a romanticist that sees butterflies and silver linings and everyone skipping through the tulips living happily ever after? I have to be practical because that just doesn't always happen."

"It will in my life. And I think it happened in the Indian girl's life. She was involved, I really believe that. But you don't have to agree with me. I won't get mad or anything or call you names or degrade your shiftless character. I have much too much integrity to do that kind of thing." She was walking in a circle around the tree with her hand sliding against the bark.

"I certainly am fortunate, aren't I? Well, who knows, maybe you are right—this time. Wait! Of course you are because today is the twenty-third. I almost forgot that this is the day that Phyllis Parker is right no matter what anyone else says!"

"Why the twenty-third?" she asked.

"Because on the twenty-fourth day, Will Huston will be right about everything!"

"Sounds good to me." She yawned and absent-mindedly picked a flower from a weed and then smelled it. To her disappointment it smelled like a weed.

Will was tired of the conversation so he diverted his attention back to his fishing. "Do we have time for me to go around that bend right there and drown about ten more hooks?" He pleaded like a little boy.

"Sure, I'll occupy myself for awhile longer and then let's go find that foundation, okay?"

"I promise you, we'll do just that." He quickly kissed her and practically skipped around the bend. She could just see the top of his head as he ducked underneath an embankment and found his footing on no more than a two-foot ridge of dry ground.

She sat down and thought about reading but changed her mind. "Hey, Will, I'm going to see if I can find where a bridge might have been." She waited for him to answer but he didn't.

"Will? Did you hear me?" Impatient with still not getting an answer she got back up and looked where she had last seen him. He wasn't there. "Will?" For just a moment her heart stopped because he didn't play games with her and yet he had been there just a minute ago.

"Where are you Will?" she called out. His bait bucket was right where he left it. She searched the water to see if he had waded in. It was quiet and she knew she hadn't heard a splash or anything. Now she was getting a bit spooked.

"William Huston!" Phyllis spoke his name as a demand, not as a question wanting to know where he was. Again she waited and again there was complete silence. A burning sensation filled her chest and sprung up into her eyes in the form of tears. She was so incredibly intent on looking at the water that she didn't hear him come up from behind her.

"Don't get in an uproar," his voice teased. She spun around and nearly toppled into him.

"Where were you?" Her tears were now from anger more than fear.

"Right over there," he pointed. "Come see this. I'm sorry I didn't respond right away but I found something and was completely captivated by it. I'm truly sorry if I scared you."

"Scare me," she wanted to hit him. "William Huston, you terrified me! All of a sudden I was in this world totally alone and defenseless. Don't you ever disappear like that again!"

He was sheepishly grinning. "You do love me, don't you?"

"Well, of course I do! Okay." She took a deep breath and then released it and tried to get all the shivers out of her system as she shook out her arms and hands. "Okay, now, what did you want me to see, I'm ready."

He was excited as he went back a few feet to an embrasure. "I cast my line over here and the hook caught on something and I had to come over and try to release it. That's when I saw—that." He pointed where the embankment jutted out a good two feet and beneath it was a natural hollow that looked like the entrance to a cave.

"Weird." She hesitated even though her adventurous spirit was eager to investigate.

"It gets even weirder. Follow me, but stay low because there's not a lot of space in there."

There was adequate light but it felt somewhat cold as though it had been existing in shadows and never felt the warmth of the sun. She ducked low and put her hand on the arch of Will's back. Together they crawled through the small space and then he sat down. Phyllis started to question him but then she saw they were in a hollow, like a room. Papers were up against the dirt walls, there was a cot with an old, patchwork wool blanket on it with an old pair of shoes under a makeshift table. Someone had definitely lived here.

"Look over there." Will pointed to an area that was cluttered with small bones.

"How awful!" She screwed up her face and bit her tongue. 'Okay, explain that one to me."

"Well, when your eyes adjust to the dim light in here you'll see all kinds of dead things. There are claws and a couple wings and even a rooster's beak or at least something that looks like a beak. It's all little animals. There's a chipmunk skull or maybe it's a rat. Can you see them?"

Phyllis looked closely and her eyes gradually depicted the earth colored forms. "How long do you think they've been in here?"

"Ages! I touched the blanket and it just about disintegrated in my fingers. Whoever came in here did it a long, long time ago."

"A kid maybe?"

Will shook his head no. "I don't think so. Even though I can't imagine an adult being comfortable in this little space. I'm sitting here because it's easier than trying to stay hunched over, but I sure wouldn't want to stay in here for very long.

"Maybe for someone the closeness was a form of security. You can go back outside to stretch." They were both silent for a moment, just looking around. "I wonder what he did in here?"

Once again Phyllis's imagination raced into unknown territory. "I bet he was a real loner and no one understood him and maybe he was just a little off in the head. Not retarded and not particularly perverted, but really, really strange. What do you think those papers were for?"

"Maybe he had drawn something. I tried to see any markings on them but the ink is long gone."

"Let's say you had found this place, what would you have done with it?"

He shrugged again, "Probably the same thing, make it my own private hideaway. I would imagine that the chances of anyone else knowing about this place is incredibly remote."

Phyllis was trying to put the pieces together. "If you came here often, then you'd have to live close by. So, process of elimination, who lived close by? Do you think it was Joe?"

Will shook his head, "No. I may be wrong but I don't think this has his personality. Before he got married he'd been a hermit in his own cabin, so there's no reason why he would need a place like this, too. Right?"

"Right. So it had to have been one of the neighbors. I've got it; I bet it was someone who was maybe a little devious." She looked over at the bones. "Maybe a little violent or vengeful. Someone you really wouldn't feel too comfortable being around. You know the kind of people that you look at them and just naturally get the creeps? I bet it was someone like that." She shivered at the thought of it.

What would it have been like to have a neighbor like that? Would you always be looking over your shoulder? Always suspecting evil lurking in the shadows? It was a thought that she didn't like. There was an uneasiness about being there in such a cramped, closed in space. Phyllis looked at the cot again and her imagination placed a young man there. Suddenly his eyes opened and he was looking back at her!

"Let's get out of here, okay?" She started moving.

~~~~~

1917

Nelle was in the garden picking peas. Joe and Francine had just left the barn and walked the horses over to her.

"We're riding into Gough's Ridge. Be back by dark." Joe helped his young daughter get into the saddle and then handed her the reins. "What do you want me to bring back for you?"

"Just soap. We'll make do for awhile yet."
~~~~~

He didn't say goodbye; he just swung up on his horse and nodded at Francine that it was time to go. She watched them ride off and then went back to the peas. The row looked endless. She knew she'd be busy for the next few hours just with those she had already picked.

Once when she stood to wipe her brow, she looked off towards the grove of trees and saw Thomas Gardiner. He was just standing there watching her. It wasn't the first time she had noticed him like that. He was just a kid, no more than eighteen, but he had the growth of a man. Even though she hadn't gotten close to him, she figured he was a little under six feet tall and no doubt more robust than Joe. Not a bad looking boy, but no outstanding features that would have set him apart from the other boys in the area.

Nelle went back to picking peas. It wasn't long before Thomas walked over to her. "I watched your husband leave," he stated. She stood and looked at him without commenting. "I thought you might like some company."

"I'm doing just fine, thank you. There's plenty here to keep me busy." She continued picking as though she had just dismissed him, and had nothing more to say.

"You're a fine lookin' woman, Mrs. Parker."

"My husband thinks so and that's all I need."

"Can he meet all your needs?"

There had been no hesitation in his voice whatsoever and she was taken totally by surprise. She found she was insulted and on the defense. "Has so far even though it's none of your business."

"Now, don't be rude to me Mrs. Parker. I'm just being friendly. Your first name is Nelle, isn't it?"

"To you I'm Mrs. Parker and I would appreciate it if you would call me that. Don't you have work to do Thomas?"

"I finished it and I'm just waiting till evening so I can deliver it. I could help you pick some of those peas." He snatched a handful even though he hadn't really looked at what was in his hand. Then he strode over to her and instead of putting them in the bushel basket he dropped the handful in her upturned apron she was using.

Nelle was deliberately rude as she pushed his hand away. "No, thank you." Then she went over to the bushel basket and emptied the contents in her apron into the basket. "I'm almost finished for the day."

He was frowning as she kept her distance. “Something wrong with me?”

She was getting frustrated. ‘No, Thomas.”

He walked up to her again, deliberately standing too close and crowding her. “You smell real good, Nelle.”

“I think you’d better leave.”

“What for? Your man is gone along with the kid. No one is around. You could scream but no one would hear you.”

Her heart momentarily stopped. “Why would I want to scream?”

“Most women do.”

She tried to stay calm but his look penetrated her defense and courage crumbled around her feet. So the stories she heard were probably true. Thomas Gardiner was thought by some to be a cruel, dangerous man with a short fused temper and a long history of instability. One woman had escaped him and she said it was only because she talked to him with dignity rather than succumbing to the terror that he could instill.

With that thought in mind, Nelle Parker stretched to her full height, mentally turning the mere five feet into the same height as the young man in front of her. As she took a deep breath, she imagined her petite body swelling to the strength of a blacksmith. She would be more of a match than what young Thomas had anticipated she would be!

“You’re not going to do anything to me, Thomas, and I have no reason to stand in this garden and scream. Now, please go home.”

“I can’t do that, Nelle.”

“Kindly address me as Mrs. Parker. And why can’t you go home?”

“I have to do what I came to do.”

“And what is that?” She looked at him as though he was a stubborn boy that she refused to give in to. He didn’t answer but he touched her collar and smiled, which resembled more of a sneer.

“I want to feel your tiny, little hands on me and I want to put my big, strong hands on you.” He whispered almost demonically as he leaned close enough his breath was hot on her face. “And you’ll give me what I want or those little hands will never be able to work in this garden again.” He grabbed her hand before she could pull away and he nearly crushed her fingers. Then he let go and laughed as though it was a big joke.

Even though she was a bit terrified, Nelle fought to keep her composure as she vigorously rubbed her aching fingers.

"You left your house with the sole intent to walk over here and do me bodily harm? Whatever for? I certainly haven't wronged you and if Joe has then you take it up with him, not me." With every ounce of courage she could muster she deliberately turned from him and started picking peas again. Her fingers were trembling so badly she couldn't even get a good grip on the small, green pods. She fought back tears, not wanting him to see how terrified she really was.

He sighed. "No, Ma'am you haven't wronged me." His voice was suddenly gentle and calm.

Nelle stopped and looked directly at him with indignation. "Then for Heaven's sake, Thomas, what's going on with you?"

"I find you very attractive. You're always laughing and staying so busy. I watch Joe put his arm around you and I want it to be my arm. I want to feel your body against mine."

"You do and you'll be feeling Mr. Parker's arm around your throat and it will be his body crushing against yours! Not a wise thing for a young man to do. You'd best leave this thing alone and go home where you belong."

Thomas wasn't listening. "I just want to touch you, Nelle. I want to hold you and kiss you." He reached out to touch her but she slapped his hand away.

"Don't do it, Thomas, I'll fight you all the way."

His voice changed again as he got that arrogant attitude he was known for. "You'd lose. I'm very strong, Nelle, very strong."

"No, you're very foolish, very, very foolish. The consequences of your actions will land you in some unmarked grave. Joe may not get you right away but he will. And if he doesn't then I'll come for you. Either way, you'll be a marked man—a dead man—and you should know that."

They both stared at each other a moment. She was having a hard time making sense of the situation. One minute his voice was casual, the next it was harsh. His mood seemed to swing like a pendulum. He blinked hard and grimaced from pain as he shook his head. It reminded her of the conversation she had had with his mother when they had first met. Even as a small boy, Thomas Gardiner suffered from excruciating headaches that changed his behavior. Alice had told her that whenever he got them she would put him in a dark room and stroke his forehead, softly talking to him. He seemed to respond to darkness and would always put the blanket over his head and curl up as though he was inside a little box. If the headaches went ignored, Thomas became cruel and vindictive.

But then, Alice rubbed her cheek and talked to the ground. "I don't pay no mind to him anymore. He just has to work it out his self."

"Why's that?" Nelle had inquired.

"Cause sometimes he uses those headaches as an excuse. Sometimes even when I'm trying to help he turns on me. It's times like that I hate him and wish him dead." She was mumbling but Nelle understood her. She also understood that Alice lived among violence every day of her life and had basically given up. It didn't matter to her anymore if she lived or died. Life was meaningless.

Not true for Nelle. Joe was a handful at times and once she had threatened to hit him in the head with a skillet but she loved him. And Francine had always been the joy of her life! She had been so afraid that the Stiver's blood would produce nothing but boys. Even as a child she had dreamed passionately of the day she would have her own daughter even though she had no idea how to respond to a little girl. The farm was going good and Nelle was happy to be alive. She wanted to keep it that way!

The maternal side of her reached out to the boy's pain. With a tender and caring voice she nearly cooed, "I'm worried about you, Thomas. Does your head hurt right now?"

Her question and change of attitude took him completely by surprise. He rubbed his temple. "Now that you mention it, yes, it does hurt. It hurts a great deal of the time."

She responded as though the previous conversation had never taken place. "Does your mother ever grow any Lady's Slipper? It's an excellent herb for headaches. I have some dried roots and all you'd have to do is brush them into a powder. Why don't you let me give you some to take home?" Nelle quickly walked out of the garden and went to the little outbuilding she used to dry her herbs. Thomas followed but never overtook her.

"Here, now, you give these to Alice and let her fix you a decoction and then you find some place that's quiet and dark and sleep for awhile. It will work quicker if you mix a half ounce of powered catnip, a bit of skullcap and then this yellow Lady's Slipper. Alice knows how to do it. Real simple. Just pour on a pint of boiling water and infuse for fifteen maybe twenty minutes. I'm sure that will help these headache attacks."

The distraction worked. She continued talking to him like a hurt child and his mood mellowed as he followed her to the end of the garden patch as she waved him on home. For a moment he looked as though he didn't know why he was even standing there with her.

"Thank you, Mrs. Parker, I'll make some of that tea right away. I appreciate your kindness." He slowly walked away from her, holding the herbs as though he had a handful of eggs that would break.

The farther away he got, the more Nelle began to fall apart! Tears were streaming down her eyes and her entire body started trembling. She knew what a close call it had been! She was now convinced that Thomas had inherited the family's insanity. For a moment she was afraid he'd come back, but then she knew Joe would be back by dark and Thomas never came around when he was home.

Going about her business, she thought about the strange conversation between them. Well, if she could talk him down once, she figured she could do it again if she had to. Maybe all he really needed was someone just to listen and to care about him. Goodness knows his family didn't! She sighed, she wasn't about to be tormented by all the imaginings of what he 'might' do. It was clearly a case of temporary derangement and she would just have to be on her guard and not let him scare her.

The row of peas didn't seem so endless now. Even though she had come to terms with how to deal with Thomas, she wasn't ready to go back inside the house or to be closed in by walls. Somehow she felt safer in the open, with work ahead of her. It was easier to think.

When she finished picking the row of peas, she carried the bushel basket to the front porch; went inside and washed her hands and found a big pot. Then she went back outside and started shelling peas. She tried to keep her mind off the strange encounter with Thomas but it kept coming back as though she needed to ponder it some more. Possibly five hours slipped away and before she knew it, it was getting dark. She kept looking up towards the crest of the hill to see if she could catch a glimpse of Joe and Francine coming back. Nelle knew that Joe took her there to sing so she must have been singing up a storm! She wasn't worried about them being late because Joe could never stay to any kind of a schedule. If there was something he thought needed to be done, he'd do it. If Francine had wanted to follow the river he would have taken the long way home instead of the shortcut. Time just didn't matter to Joe Parker.

Nelle stood up and stretched, noticing how peaceful everything was. She rolled her sleeves back down and watched the dog a moment. Duke was nudging a big toad as though trying to get it to play with him. She was tired and her back hurt somewhat from spending so many hours bent over in the garden. The dog ran around to the back of the cabin and all was quiet again. Nelle debated if she wanted to go inside or not.

Deciding to milk the cow a little bit early she headed to the barn. Looking for another bucket, she went into a shadowy area of the stall and caught her ankle against a piece of barbed wire. Nelle wasn't sure what triggered her nervousness, whether it was the shadows or the unexpected sharp pain against her ankle, but something alarmed her. Trying to dismiss her apprehensions as foolishness, she went back out to the cow, sat down and positioned the bucket. For some reason, even the cow seemed somewhat spooked.

There was a strange sound from the back of the barn and Nelle's attention was instantly alert. She strained to hear more and then she stood and looked over the cow's back to see if she could see anything. Her heart began to beat frantically and for just a second she realized she was holding her breath. And then the dog came running from behind a bale of hay after a rat. Nelle let out her breath and then scolded herself for being so skitterish. Had Thomas really disturbed her that deeply? She started talking to the cow, occasionally rubbing the soft, brown and white fur, talking to alleviate any uneasiness. It was just a small barn--only two stalls and a feeding area for the goats when they weren't out in the meadow. Joe had built it himself. When he and Ira had lived here the barn had only been a three-sided structure. Joe had always made sure that the out buildings and farm implements were all well taken care of. He intended to keep them a lifetime and he never let anyone borrow from him. Nelle thought he almost had an obsession about those things that he considered his belongings. He wasn't even too keen on someone crossing his land for a shortcut.

Once again her thoughts went back to Thomas. Joe didn't hide his feelings. He didn't like the boy and often times he was blatantly rude. Her back was to the door and she kept looking over her shoulder, halfway expecting someone to be standing there. Was it merely her imagination or a premonition that she kept seeing Thomas leaning against the door, waiting and watching.

Deciding that it was nothing more than an overworked imagination, she tried to focus on what she was doing, but the cow simply would not cooperate.

Nelle finally gave up because the old Guernsey was too restless. Nelle had milked her enough to know that when she refused to stand still, the bucket would either get knocked over or she'd get kicked herself. On this particular night, Nelle simply didn't want to hassle with it. She patted the cow's rump and removed the stool she had been sitting on.

"Okay, girl, I'll see you in the morning." She made sure there was enough grain in the bin and fresh water in the bucket. The cow looked at her with huge, brown eyes. What were those eyes saying? Why such a forlorn look?'

Nelle closed her eyes a moment and then forcefully blew out her breath. "I can't do this to myself!" She longed for Joe to come home so she could get her mind back on daily routines. Francine would talk nonstop and then they'd sit out on the front porch for awhile and listen to night sounds. Often times they would look at the stars and Nelle would come up with some far-fetched story about an imaginary person or animal that would become a hero. As easily as Nelle created stories, Francine had a talent of creating songs, making her mother's characters come alive through music.

Going into the house, she set the milk bucket down and searched for a bottle to pour it in. Joe insisted that no food or drink ever be wasted. It didn't matter how hard they had to labor. Food was considered a gift and if you thought less of it then you'd soon find yourself starving. She had asked him why he believed that so strongly and he told her that it was just an old Indian saying."

"Did that Indian girl teach you a lot of her ways?"

"What girl? I learned that old saying from a trapper by the name of Jeremiah Davis who learned it from Indians. I always liked to listen to him because he believed in spooks. I remember one time we passed an Indian burial ground and he painted our faces black so the ghosts wouldn't recognize us. He was so nervous I could hear his knees shaking like two spoons in an empty bowl."

Hearing a noise from the back of the cabin she called to the dog, thinking it was probably him scrounging for food. She remembered she hadn't put food out and she didn't want him to get into the garbage.

"Duke? Come on boy, I'll feed you." She kept a pail of scraps under the sink that she gave him every evening. Something had spilled over the side and she tried to clean it up somewhat before she pulled the pail out. When she heard a movement behind her, she turned to let Duke know his supper was coming.

Turning from the sink, with the pail of scraps in her hand, she found herself standing face to face with Thomas. She gasped! The look in his eyes told her that there would be no talking this time! He was breathing hard as he knocked the pail out of her hand and then grabbed for her.

"We're going to do it my way, now, Mrs. Nelle Parker."

When she tried to get around him, he grabbed her and literally threw her across the room. Either he hadn't considered how light she actually did weigh or he was completely out of control. She landed against the chair next to the table and it fell against the impact. For a moment she was entangled with the four legs.

"Why are you doing this?" Her eyes filled with tears. She knew if she fought him she'd only intensify the anger within him and he might kill her. Yet, there was no way she'd just give in to him without a fight.

"No more talking." He quickly overpowered her as he got hold of her and lifted her off the floor, carrying her into the bedroom. Tossing her across the bed, he let her go but just long enough to pull out his knife. When she saw it she froze. Hitting her was one thing, cutting her was an entirely different story! She had a horrible fear of knives!

"Okay, okay," she surrendered. She needed time. "Tell me what you want."

With a calm voice he simply stated "I want you to take your clothes off. Slowly."

Her eyes darted to the door and then back at him. "Joe will be walking through that door any minute now and I swear he'll kill you for this."

Thomas yelled at her, his face a scarlet red. "I said, no more talking! Don't make me mad, Mrs. Parker." He waved the knife as though he would slice her apart if she spoke another word. When she remained silent, he seemed to catch his breath, taking time to evaluate the situation. She couldn't hide her intense fear as her eyes stayed transfixed on the knife.

"You think I'll cut you?" He cocked his head so that he was looking at her from the corner of his eyes.

"Yes." She was nearly breathless. "I think you could but you don't have to. Please, Thomas, put it away, you don't need it. If you continue scaring me or if you hurt me, I won't be able to do what you want. Blood is messy."

He looked at the knife again as though someone else had put it in his hand, then he looked back at her. When she wasn't resisting him, he seemed to have almost a lost look. Nelle could see that he was struggling between personalities. At that moment she honestly didn't know if she was more saddened for him or afraid of him. This was not normal behavior and she would have to be exceptionally cautious.

He almost started to put the knife down but then something snapped him back to his vehemence. "Shut up! I told you not to talk to me!" With his eyes now boring into her mind and flesh he pointed to her clothes. "No stalling. Take them off." Through clenched teeth his voice raised a bit as he motioned with the knife for her to start undressing.

Nelle looked down, refusing to move. His violent response came more swiftly than she had expected. With one quick and calculated movement he grabbed her hand, pulling her closer to him and he deliberately cut her arm. It wasn't deep, but the streak of blood brought her danger into full focus!

"I'll cut you bad." He threatened, delighting in the power he had over her. She knew her stalling time had just run out. For a moment she was angry with Joe for not being back when he said he would. Because of his selfish carelessness she had to face this on her own. Thomas had told her to undress slowly, so she did exactly that. With steady eyes she stood before him, her hands went to the waistband of her skirt.

A wild idea suddenly engulfed her thinking. Shortly after she married Joe she had tried her hand at writing a steamy, love story. Closing her eyes, she wondered if she could transport herself into fiction in order to escape reality. What if she simply acted out a scene from the story? She had watched a woman at the saloon flirting with a man and Nelle had written a scene where she was taking off all her clothes for him. Somehow, it made it less terrifying to think she was just 'acting' out a part in the story.

Men were just little boys with a huge imagination and an endless quest to transform desires into reality. She loved having the power to lure him into her own realm, whether real or not! With each movement he was captivated…it was her choice whether to kill him or to love him.

Nelle was going to lure him! As soon as Thomas thought she was going to comply, he stepped back and leaned against the wall, anxious for his own private show.

Carrying out almost the same movements she had thought only belonged on the pages of her imagination, she unfastened her outer skirt and dropped it to the floor. She stopped, not touching her petticoats. Thomas nodded for her to continue and she slowly unbuttoned her blouse, letting his eyes hang on every intricate movement as her fingers rounded each button before she slipped it through the eyelet. With an absolutely straight face, she stood still a moment as she let it fall open. Thomas didn't seem to be in any hurry and neither was she. Then she slipped the blouse off one shoulder, letting his eyes feast on her bare flesh before she eased the other side off. As she slipped her arm out of the sleeve, she lifted her other hand so that the soft material hung suspended for just a second before it fell gently from her fingers. Nelle kept her eyes fixed on him the entire time. He didn't move even an inch.

His eyes focused on her bare leg as she pulled the petticoat above her knee to remove her shoes and stockings, slowly, carefully, contemplative. She held each stocking up for a second before she dropped it and then with one bare foot she pushed them over to the side. Standing before him in her camisole and petticoats she stopped again as though waiting for instructions. Her ears had been constantly keen to the return of Joe but the yard remained silent.

"Loosen your hair." Thomas told her, pointing the knife at her head.

Meticulously she took out each pin, once again never taking her eyes off him, never showing any emotion. Her long hair fell about her shoulders and as she leaned over to put the handful of pins on the dressing table she shook her head so that her long, flowing hair cascaded down her shoulders. Thomas let out a moan as though the sight of her had just soothed his angry soul.

Adding words to the story she had written long ago, she ran her hand once again through her hair. *My movements had not excited him; on the contrary. He had just turned to butter and probably would have had difficulty swinging a hammer or even carrying in an armful of wood. In fact, he had to hold onto the back of the chair because his knees had weakened and he was about to stagger.* In her story the couple had embraced and slipped off into the shadows. What happened next, however, had never entered her imagination.

His voice was level and quiet. "Now, wrap yourself in that blanket and take off the rest; so there's nothin' under it."

Nelle wasn't expecting that request and couldn't help but reveal her confusion as she frowned. Thomas seemed to know exactly what he was doing and repeated the request. It took a little coordinated effort but she was able to keep herself modestly covered as the remainder of her clothing dropped to the floor around her bare feet. She hadn't been able to keep her eyes on him so she was somewhat surprised to see that there were tears in his eyes.

His face contorted into an agonized expression as he watched her. Again, there seemed to be that inner struggle of personalities. He started to say something in a whiny, pitiful voice but then shook his head and the voice became harsh and strong. It was as though the forceful side of him was constantly overpowering the meekness.

"Sit down on the end of the bed." He demanded, brandishing the knife again. She didn't move fast enough for him and the knife was suddenly against her throat! It's edge made her eyes sting just from fear. There was no doubt in her mind that he'd cut her again so she quickly sat down and took a deep breath to try and clear her head from the webs of fear. He stood over her. With his finger he traced the outline of her cheek, then ran his finger down her throat, then across her bare shoulder. He bent down and she was frozen as he kissed her neck, his hands never touching the blanket. He smelled her and delighting in her scent, he closed his eyes and once again she saw the anger in him subside. His hand relaxed on the knife. He dropped to his knees and looked into her eyes. The dark eyes were the personality of the Thomas that was kind and considerate.

His voice was soft and almost pleading. "I just want to be loved, Mrs. Parker. My own mother hasn't touched me in years. I see you with Mr. Parker and my heart just aches from loneliness. Can you even begin to imagine how it is to go year after year and not share your life with anyone? I don't want to hurt you; I just want you to love me."

He looked at the knife and threw it across the room. "Please, Nelle, just touch me as though you care about me." At that moment he was just a hurt and lonely child. She still didn't move.

"Don't be afraid and don't move; not even an inch," he almost whispered and then he began to adjust the blanket so that the side of his face could touch her bare skin. His hands embraced her like a boy would hug his mother. He made no other movement. "This is all I wanted," he sighed and then pushed himself away from her and the blanket, ever so careful to keep her covered.

Nelle wasn't afraid for her life anymore. She still couldn't allow him to do everything he thought he wanted to do. But, at the moment she was still able to stall for time. In a strange sense, she was in more control of the situation than he was. With both hands she cupped his face and lifted it so she could look into his eyes. With one finger she wiped a tear from his cheek.

Such a simple gesture totally weakened him. If he had been standing, his knees would have buckled right out from under him. She felt his body shudder as he quickly looked back down. Was it the forceful personality returning? Nelle immediately tensed as the little boy suddenly reverted back to the crazed man. Only this time it wasn't in his actions so much as in his breathing.

"Could you ever love me like you do Mr. Parker?" There was almost a threat in the sound of his voice.

"No, Thomas, he's my husband and I will always be true to him, and him alone. No one else will have my love."

The strength returned as he suddenly stood and grabbed both her shoulders in a grip so tight she winced. "He doesn't deserve your love! I want you to love me!" His dark eyes glared at her.

"It could only be by force and then it wouldn't be love. You'd make me hate you, Thomas."

"No!" His hands flew up and in a fit of outrage he began striking out. One blow caught her in the temple and she actually saw stars before she passed out.

When she came to, the pain in her head let her know that Thomas had hit with all his strength, but she knew even then he had not deliberately aimed the blow at her. It took a moment to register where she was and what was now happening. She looked down at herself, fully expecting to see the blanket removed. Not only was it in place but her head was on the pillow and the bedspread covered her as well. There were lanterns lit in the kitchen and living room and a candle burning by her bedside; half of them hadn't been lit by her hand.

Once more she began to cry. Other than hitting her in his fit of rage, he hadn't inflicted any further harm to her. In his demented way he had actually taken care of her. It didn't make sense. Had it all been just a nightmare? She dropped the blanket and quickly slipped into her nightgown. What would she tell Joe? If she told him that Thomas had attacked her or even made advances towards her, the boy would be dead by morning.

Was Thomas even accountable for his actions? Would he remember what he did when his head quit hurting? In his quest to be loved, would anger and violence and rejection send him further over the edge? If he hadn't forced his way with her this time, would he try some other time? What did he really want? A mother figure who would hold him like a child and say I love you, or a lover who would hold him like a man?

There didn't seem to be a simple answer or even a solution. She looked down at the cut on her arm. It was a vivid reminder that the man could be dangerous! Should she do everything possible to prevent him from coming to her again? Mentally ill or not, she didn't want him to think he could have liberties with her. She certainly didn't want to repeat this nightmarish incident!

And then a mental realization hit her as hard as the physical blow had. If she told Joe what had happened, would he accuse her of encouraging it since she hadn't fought tooth and nail? Had she been temporarily insane as well to allow Thomas to put his face on her skin? She suddenly felt extremely ashamed. How could she possibly tell Joe that she had allowed Thomas to touch her without putting up a fight? Would he understand her fear of the knife or the strangeness in the boy's behavior? Maybe she had been wrong. Maybe she shouldn't have considered the childlike nature in the boy. Joe would interpret the whole incident as though she had wanted Thomas to touch her! Maybe she should have been willing to wear her injuries like badges of bravery.

Nelle walked through the house. Thomas had even cleaned up the mess with the dog scraps. Duke was sleeping peacefully at the hearth. She looked out the dark window at the even darker countryside. Where were they? Going to the stove, she lit the fire so she could warm up the coffee. That's what she needed. Her head was still spinning and she had to think clearly. The guilt she felt imprisoned by seemed far worse than the chains that stayed at the end of the bed. What was Joe going to do to her? She wasn't positive that Joe wouldn't be just as violent as Thomas was.

If she said anything, she would have to face Joe's anger and possibly the death of Thomas. If she didn't say anything, she would have to constantly be wary of another attack, and she knew there would be a next time if given the chance!

It was just then that she heard Joe and Francine riding up to the barn. Their voices were low as they put the horses away and then came inside. By that time, Nelle was at the stove, pouring Joe a cup of coffee as well.

"I thought you two got lost." She tried to sound excited to see them.

"No, but have we ever got a story for you!" Francine was bouncing as she ran to the sink and washed her hands.

"You doing okay? You look a little strange." Joe dropped his parcels on the table and then took the cup of coffee she was extending to him. His smile turned into a hardened frown.

Nelle tried to conceal the cut on her arm but he had been quick to notice that as well as the discoloration around her face. Setting the cup down with an angry thud he jerked up his gun and checked to make sure he had at least one shot. He was ready to kill someone without hesitation.

"Who done it to you?"

"No one, it's okay, Joe." She reached out and grabbed his hand. "The cow kicked me when I was milking tonight and I fell against a piece of barbed wire. It was my own fault; I should have moved that wire a long time ago. Remember when I warned Francine about it?"

"I remember." Francine's voice was small and scared.

Joe settled back down but the way he had cocked his head, Nelle wasn't convinced that he believed her. He put the gun back down. "You're my woman Nelle Parker, and you know I'd kill anyone that even so much as breathed on you."

"Yes, Joe, I know that." She forced humor into the situation. "But the cow did it, and if you want to kill the cow we could have steak for supper but then we wouldn't have milk for breakfast. Guess we better let her live, huh?"

"I'll milk tomorrow." Francine's eyes were wide. "You okay, Mama?"

"Oh, I will be, come morning. I'm a little dizzy and my head hurts but that's all. At least I got some milk from the old girl first!" She pulled her daughter to her and brushed her bangs out of her eyes.

Joe finally smiled. "You get any more clumsy on me and someone will think you got the palsy or something and can't manage yourself. I'll have to put you down like a lame horse if you can't fix my meals and hoe the garden." He teased.

"I'd be worthless for sure." She swallowed the lump of lies that was building up in her throat. Her first desire was to get alone and start writing everything down in her journal, but this time she was afraid that it might get into the wrong hands. There was no way she could risk anyone reading her thoughts and fears and know her deceit. The day that she would write it all down would be the day she would have to conceal her journal so that the words would remain hidden from those who could be hurt the most! "You'll have to excuse me, I've got to go back to bed." She left her cup by the sink. Without another word she left them and crawled back under the covers, putting the pillow against her mouth to muffle the sobs as she curled into a tight ball.

CHAPTER 7

ঌঌঌঌঌ

1969

"That was depressing!" Phyllis took a deep breath of fresh air as she and Will came out of the sod sanctum. "I don't think I could ever get use to a place like that!"

Looking up at the sky she figured they only had about four more hours of daylight. "Come on, put your fishing gear away and let's go for a walk."

As he did, Will was thinking about the dweller of the little hideaway. He wondered if the man could possibly still be alive. Had he ventured back to that place and crawled inside to let his mind remember the countless times he had probably spent in there? Did he still live in the area or had he moved far off? Had anyone known about the place or was it a well-kept secret? One day the place would probably cave in and then all would be lost. He smiled. Archeologists might discover it hundreds of years later and think it belonged to some Indian tribe. Indians. He just had another thought.

"Phyllis? I wonder if the Indian girl stayed in there so she could keep an eye on Joe and his family. It could have been like an earthen teepee or something. Maybe that was the meaning of all those little bones in the corner.

"I don't follow you. What do the bones have to do with anything?"

"Maybe she was casting spells or something or doing Indian witchcraft stuff, I don't know. I've read that they had a lot of rituals and things where bones were used.

Phyllis scoffed at the idea. "My Indian girl was much too civilized for that! No, that wasn't her place. For one thing, I doubt if she would have been bothered to have carted a bed in there; Indians sleep on the ground. And then there's the man's shoes. How do you explain those?"

"She might have stolen them, or maybe someone else left them and she never threw them away."

"Be serious," she scolded him.

"It's not such a totally impossible idea. Maybe she had the shoes to leave tracks so no one would see little, girlie, bare feet in the mud. No one would pay attention to a man's shoe prints. If she was trying to stay hidden she sure wouldn't leave any evidence that she was around. Maybe someone had been using it but abandoned it and she just took over."

She bounced her head from shoulder to shoulder as though thinking of each possibility but then dismissed it. "If she knew about that little hidey-hole she might have used it for a night or two but I guarantee you she didn't live there. I still believe the resident was a man who couldn't adjust to the real world."

Then she laughed, "Besides, if you think the Indian girl stayed there then you're admitting that I'm right about her concern for Joe! I thought you said she was barbaric and would never leave her people once she went back to them."

"Well," he wasn't willing to give in completely. "I was just trying to make your theory more plausible."

"I see." She grabbed his hand as they continued to walk. This had been such an incredible day for her. She was kicking herself for not paying more attention to the family tree. Her mother had never been cooperative about filling in any of the blank lines. If Phyllis asked, Lucy would simply tell her 'it's not important; it won't change a thing'. Phyllis had dropped it because at the time it just didn't seem worth the effort. Now, a name would mean everything! In her mind she could see an open book with the father's side of the family on the left page, completely blank, and only a few names on the mother's side. But even those written in had not registered in her memory other than Herman and Francine.

"And Bonnie!" The sound of her voice made her suddenly realize she had spoken out loud.

"Bonnie who?" Will gave her a puzzled look.

"My grandmother Bonnie. She would have been Francine's daughter."

"Do you know much about her?"

"No, very little. I told you, I was always told to stay away from the relatives." Phyllis searched and searched her memory. "The only thing I can remember about Bonnie Parker is that she got married at the age of thirteen, went insane, divorced, and went by her maiden name the rest of her life. Did her husband die mysteriously or did she just leave him in a mysterious way? Oh, I wish I knew!" She was obviously frustrated.

"Your mom never talks about her?"

"No, Mom hated her and I honestly don't know where she lives or if she's even alive. If she is, maybe she's in New Orleans with her daughter. She couldn't be all that old. What? Maybe in her fifties or something?"

"If Lucy has never mentioned her even in casual conversation it could be she may not be alive."

"No telling what her last name is now. I've just never heard Mom saying she died or anything. I mean, surely she would have made a snide remark like 'the old witch is finally dead' or something like that. Oh, wow, I wonder what would happen if I tried to find her?"

"Guaranteed your mother wouldn't be happy about it. If she's spent your whole twenty years keeping you away from your family there must be something she's trying to protect you from. I mean, there has to be a reason for all this. Maybe you don't want to find out."

Phyllis wasn't so sure though. "But aren't I old enough to make that decision for myself?"

"I don't think age has anything to do with it. I think the issue is more about responsibility. Are you now able to handle the consequences of such a decision?"

Will stopped walking for a moment and looked all around the area. "Maybe that's what the curse is on this place. Maybe you're lured into the past that joins with the present. Only thing is, the hands of the past aren't holding on to your hands, they're choking your neck!"

Phyllis stopped and looked at him, totally surprised. "My goodness, Will you're becoming almost poetic! Your imagination is actually working like mine. A little more macabre, but that's okay." It was hard to think of danger or distress when everything around you was so peaceful and beautiful.

It didn't take long to find the place where Will had seen what was left of a house's foundation. Phyllis was intrigued with it. She walked around the borders and then across each floor pattern, determining what would be the living room and kitchen and bedroom.

"No indoor plumbing. I'm so glad I didn't live back then! Outhouses are for the birds. I wonder how many feet crossed these floors?

Will didn't particularly find anything interesting about it. "A whole bunch. It was a big house by the looks of it so I bet it was a big family as well."

"Then people would have been all over the place. Children would have been playing in the yard; livestock would have been grazing. A garden would have been planted somewhere close by and I bet the windows would have been open all the time. From here, you could see company coming from miles away. Except from that direction. What's over there?" She faced a heavy growth of trees and thick shrubs.

"The cabin."

"Okay. Well, you sure couldn't spy on your neighbors from here could you? But, going back and forth, you could easily hide among the trees and no one would even see you, right?"

"Right. But what makes you think along those lines?"

"I bet you anything that the weird guy who became the cave dweller lived here in this house. And because he was so strange, maybe he watched his neighbors and because of the trees no one was able to see him."

"Why would he want to spy on his neighbors?"

"Because." She had to think up a good explanation for the uneasiness she felt. "Because he was just that type of guy. He had lots and lots of secrets and I bet no one but no one trusted him. Probably not even his own mother."

"Now who's thinking on the edge of the macabre?"

"Alright, alright," she reversed her thinking. "Let's see, if there were a lot of kids over at the cabin and a lot of kids at this house, maybe those kids got together."

"Well, before you get too carried away, let me show you how tricky it is to get over there to the cabin. Now, I understand that the terrain has probably changed throughout the years but even back then I bet you really had to watch your footing."

Before she followed him she looked one last time. "I wonder what happened to this house? It looks like a tornado just picked it up and took off with it. Like Oz."

"But this isn't Kansas. We'll just add that question to our list of mysteries to solve when we get back home."

As Phyllis left the foundation she pretended that she lived in the house and was going over to the cabin to check on the Parkers. Maybe she would even carry some bread or something to share with them. Then she frowned. No, the Parkers probably weren't that sociable. Seems like you'd need a definite reason for going over there, but she couldn't imagine what it would be. But then she watched Will securing their way through the trees and she had an idea. Love was the best reason for anything! Maybe a young boy had lived in this house and just maybe he had fallen in love with Francine and they secretly made a path so they could see each other.

1918

Francine watched Thomas Gardiner from a distance. Even though they had been neighbors all her life she had never thought that much about him until now. There wasn't anything specific that happened to actually draw her attention to him, but now she noticed how jet-black his hair was and how straight it fell except for one definite curl at the nape of his collar. His eyes were equally dark even though they never looked sinister.

More times than not they had a vacant look to them which was impossible to read. Other times he would laugh and his entire countenance would reflect a completely carefree levity. When he concentrated on his work there was an intensity and a bulldogged steadiness that would keep him tireless even through the night. Other than a general greeting he never talked to her or even acknowledged that she was around.

There was a distinct memory, however, when she was only ten. It had been at a Christmas party and her mother, Nelle, had made her a beautiful green, velvet dress. Thomas had bumped into her and made her spill the eggnog. Without thinking he had grabbed a napkin and started to wipe off the front of her, but was only making it worse as the milk absorbed into the velvet. Suddenly, he pulled his hand back and gave her the cloth.

"You can do it much better than I can, my little budding magnolia."

It wasn't until days later when she was talking with her friends that she understood the meaning of his words. Martha exaggerated everything and now as they talked, her eyes were wide with fantasy and embarrassment even though it was quite obvious she was thrilled as well. The younger girls believed that Martha's fifteen years made her an expert on everything!

"Didn't you realize what he was doing?" Martha McKenny gasped, holding her hands crisscrossed in front of her dress.

Francine shrugged, "I spilled the eggnog; he was merely coming to my assistance."

"Francine! Don't be such a child! He put his hand right on…" she stumbled at the full realization of what she was saying and lowered her voice. "Right on your breast! I would have died! Just simply died right there!"

"I didn't really notice." But she had noticed how quickly he had pulled away. She looked down at her front as though remembering and then she let out an embarrassed squeal. "So that's why he snatched his hand back the way he did! Oh, Martha, what do you suppose he thinks of me now?"

She batted her eyelashes, mocking Thomas in a flirting way. "That you're not a little girl anymore. In three more years you would be old enough to marry him."

"Marry Thomas? He's already in his twenties! Why would I want to marry such an old man?"

Little did she know that at that moment in time, Thomas had no more interest in her than she had in him, but life seemed to keep putting them together. One day he told her she was just like a little sister to him. Every once in awhile he would hug her or help her with a chore. Once she was fishing and he stopped to help bait her hook. She didn't think about it then, but his hand did linger on hers a little longer than maybe it should have. And he did look at her in a peculiar way.

By the time Francine turned thirteen her body was rushing her appearance a good five years! It was at this time in her life when she became fully aware that Thomas regarded her differently from the others. There were times they would get into a conversation and talk about books as well as farming. She was fascinated with his carpentry skills and would watch him for hours. It didn't matter if they talked or not. There were times when he had terrible headaches and asked her to leave. Even though she didn't want to, she obeyed.

Francine wasn't sure when she quit thinking of him as a brother and more as a friend. Thomas had seemed to quit growing so he wasn't changing much. But Francine was blossoming in body and spirit. And his eyes were always on her. She didn't feel uncomfortable but she often wondered what he was thinking.

And then, the day came when their relationship changed drastically. Francine had just turned fourteen. She had been singing quite frequently for the last year and she had been surprised how often Thomas seemed to be there to listen. He never said anything to her but when she sang, his eyes were constantly on her. She wondered if he ever blinked! Right before the program was over, he would slip out, but, she didn't know if he had to get back to work before someone missed him or because he didn't follow the usual custom of putting money on the table. As long as he was there, it really didn't matter to her. Over the last year she especially looked forward to seeing him whether he verbally acknowledged her or not. Just his presence seemed to assure her that she was special enough for him to take time from his work just to listen to her sing.

And then, Francine began to flirt. Martha had told her that men loved special attention and that she would probably double her profits. "It will really, really make you popular. Oh, how I envy you."

"But I'm too young to be flirting," Francine protested, even though she didn't want to do anything to change the fact that Martha envied her.

"Who needs to know your age? You look older than Rebecca over there. And your body! Oh, Francine, older girls would kill to have your body!" she shook her head as though saying the absolute truth. "Listen, if God is going to give you that kind of body and that voice, it would be a sin not to make the most of both! It would be like cheating the homely and pitiful from the beauty they've never had themselves. You're only adding pleasure to their poor lives. Who knows, maybe you're going to die before you're thirty and that's why you grew up so fast. If that's the case, you've got to do a lot of flirting real fast! Go ahead, drive all the men crazy! You'll love it and so will they."

Francine liked the excitement of it but wasn't convinced. "I thought you only flirted with the man you wanted to marry."

A disgusted look crossed Martha's face. "Oh, Francine, maybe you are just a baby." She started to walk away but then turned back. "Did your mother tell you that?"

She wasn't going to insult Nelle and when Francine said no, she plunged in. "Then you must have heard that from someone who didn't know what they were talking about. Flirting is just having fun, it really doesn't mean anything serious."

Martha took on the role of the wise expert. "Let me explain it to you. When you sing it's so easy to get the words and the mood of the song. Especially the love songs! Men like to be a part of it and face it, Francine, you are beautiful and men want you!"

"Why?"

"Because they like to fantasize that you're really in love with them and only them because it makes them feel real special."

"But what if they think I'm serious?"

Martha gave a 'humph' as though irritated that she had to explain everything in detail. "Everyone knows it's just play acting. Surely you don't think they believe you when you sing about being left at the altar or being dumped for some pretty filly in Philadelphia, do you? No, of course not, they're just songs. And your audience doesn't take the words seriously, they just like the sound of them. Flirting is just putting a motion to the message. Once the song is over, it's forgotten. It's a game with no winners or losers so how could it be wrong?"

"I just have one more question." Francine tilted her chin up with a serious look. "Why are you so interested in what I do?"

"You're my friend, aren't you?" Martha acted as though she was shocked at the question. Little did Francine know that Martha's boyfriend had dared her to talk Francine into it. If she succeeded he was going to buy her a heart bracelet that she admired. What he didn't admit was that he loved to hear Francine sing and longed for her to wink at him!

Martha won the bet. Francine had thought about it and the next time she sang she took the advice. Francine quickly learned that she could move her hand or hip in a certain way and make the men nearly howl! Her eyes and lips could melt a cold face in a fraction of a second. Within only a matter of months she had totally forgotten her own age. She was being treated like an adult and it was exciting. It didn't take her long to learn the language of manipulation.

At first Joe was upset but the extra money that came in quickly disarmed any hesitation he had about what his daughter was doing. She kept assuring him that it was all a part of being on the stage and performing. As she got older, Joe stayed less and less in the bar room with her. It became a habit for him to go to the back room and play poker. His absence made her even more daring.

Whenever Thomas was there, Francine would always make eye contact with him and sing directly to him. And then she would play the audience and even walk among them and touch the men in an innocent way. Except for Thomas. For some reason she never got that close to him. Though she kept her distance, she allowed her voice to embrace him as her eyes pulled him closer and closer to her heart. Even if her hand was on the shoulder of another young man, her eyes would always go right back to Thomas as though pouting 'I wish it were you instead'.

On the day of the Mayday Festival she sang and was surprised to see that Thomas didn't hurry away. Everyone seemed to have gathered at the park and Thomas even took part in the water contests. Francine had signed up for the canoe race and was delighted that Thomas and two of his friends were next to them. Everything was going fine until one of her team members stood up and tipped the canoe over. Fortunately, they all could swim. The others quickly got the canoe turned back over and crawled in, anxious to get on with the race. The current had taken them quite a piece before they realized there was any trouble. Francine's long hair had gotten tangled in the submerged branches of a fallen tree.

Only Thomas realized what was happening. He dove out of his canoe to her rescue. Even though she was half drowned, he finally got her safely to shore and was horrified when she didn't look like she was breathing. He immediately started mouth to mouth resuscitation. She responded quickly but he kept his face low to hers so the others couldn't see what was happening.

"I thought I had just lost you," he whispered.

Then, to her surprise he kissed her. It held passion and tenderness as his lips lingered on hers. When he raised his head, his eyes remained on her. No apologies or explanation for the sudden display of affection. He merely smiled and then turned to all the others as though nothing had happened.

"She's okay," he called out and waved them on. For just a moment neither moved. Her wet clothes were clinging to her and she suddenly became aware of his eyes coursing the length of her body.

"I'm just fine." She struggled to get up and he helped her.

"You sure you aren't hurt anywhere? I don't see any scratches or cuts or anything, even though you did tear your sleeve."

She gave a little sigh of relief. That's why he was looking at her that way; he was just making sure she didn't have any injuries. "Thanks to you I'm just fine. You saved my life, Thomas."

"It was nothing; you saved mine first." He didn't say it clearly enough for her to understand so she just smiled and dismissed it.

Together they started walking along the edge of the shore towards the dock where the race ended. All eyes were on them as they rejoined the gathering. He told them she had taken in a lot of water but seemed to be okay. Nevertheless, he insisted that she rest and stay out of the water the rest of the day. Even though she felt perfectly fine she enjoyed the pampering.

Francine wasn't sure what to think. It was fun to play up the scare of nearly drowning but she couldn't wait to be alone so she could relive each moment with Thomas in slow motion. She ran the episode over and over in her mind and finally concluded that Thomas loved her, though she couldn't understand why.

She tested this realization by deliberately finding reasons to be alone with him. And then, she discovered that he, too, was luring her to places where they could be alone. He was just going into the barn when Francine approached him.

"Thomas," she spoke his name.

It was almost as though he had been waiting for her. "I'm glad you're here. Follow me and let's talk."

He looked around the yard to see if anyone else was wandering by, then he and Francine ducked into one of the stalls. With an unusually firm hand he pushed her back up against the wall and then bent to kiss her with a hungriness and urgency to his desires. There was absolutely no protest to her response. Her trust was so pure that it almost unnerved him. She looked up at him, simply waiting to see what he wanted to talk about.

"You aren't afraid of me, are you Francine?" He deliberately towered over her, placing his hands on each side of her head and bringing his body uncomfortably close, deliberately trying to intimidate her. She responded with an innocent giggle as she moved his arm and edged away.

"My goodness, no, why should I be?"

"Because your mom…"

"My mom? She doesn't know a thing! Besides, what possible reason would I have to be afraid of you?"

He started to say something but then switched his thinking. "To begin with I'm much older than you." His demeanor returned to the friendly, easy going Thomas that she enjoyed.

"Age? I don't see that it really matters. Not since I've—matured. Perhaps you've noticed."

"Yes, I've noticed," he laughed more to himself. "You're very beautiful, Francine."

He obviously wanted to touch her, but this time he restrained himself. Then he cleared his throat and frowned somewhat. "Tell me, do you know what love means?"

"Of course I do. I love my father and mother."

"No, not that kind of love. I'm talking about the intimate love that your father has for your mother. When no one is around and their door is shut."

"You mean as husband and wife? How could I possibly know that?" She pretended to be embarrassed and shy. He knew better.

"I could teach you." He outlined her chin with his finger and then kissed her nose.

"Why would you want to do that?" Her smile dazzled him.

"Because I want to marry you one day."

Francine was not only flattered but she felt incredibly lucky. Thomas had a sister that was almost twenty and still not married. In fact, Rebecca didn't even have an admirer! And so, Francine was willing to give one hundred percent of herself to this new, promising relationship.

"Then I'm yours, Thomas Gardiner: heart, soul, and mind." She closed her eyes as he bent again to kiss her. Only this time it was gentle and he held her tightly but not so much she couldn't get her breath. The inside of her emotions exploded with joy and security. She didn't want to leave his embrace. But she eventually did, and she was quick to tell her friends she had been kissed. Of course her friends were envious and ecstatic but not everyone shared their excitement.

Francine finally told her mother, "I plan on seeing Thomas Gardiner."

"I simply forbid it; he's much too old for you," Nelle had just brought in a basket of towels from the clothesline and set about folding them.

"Really, Mother, no one even cares about age anymore. Dad is older than you."

"Not by twelve years! Besides, Thomas just isn't right for you."

"Why not? He works hard, he's responsible and he makes me happy. I've been around him all my life, Mother."

Nelle shook her head, disagreeing. “He’s lived down the road, you haven’t been ‘around’ him.”

“Yes, I have,” she sheepishly admitted. “I’ve been around him quite a lot lately. We’ve been doing some—things.”

“What kind of things? What’d he to do you?” Nelle’s head shot up from the towels the same as if someone had backhanded her.

Francine quickly realized she had said the wrong thing. She didn’t want to make it sound worse than it really was. Friends could handle exaggeration, mothers needed the truth!

“Nothing wrong; all we’ve done is talk. I’ve been going over there a lot and I watch him make things in his shop. Really nice things. He’s good at his carpentry. We enjoy each other’s company.”

“Well, I better not hear of you going round him any more. You stay away, Francine Parker, or I’ll have your daddy tear you apart and you know he will!” Her voice almost reached a frantic pitch.

“Why are you yelling at me? What have I done wrong? Thomas is a very special friend of mine and I—I really like him. And what’s more, he likes me! There is nothing wrong with that!”

Nelle shook out a towel with a popping, deliberate force. Then she gritted her teeth, debating what she was going to say. Brushing a strand of hair from her face, she gave Francine a cold look as she got up and went over to her.

“What is this, some kind of hero worship or something because he pulled you out of the river on Mayday?”

“I don’t think so. We never even bring it up any more. I’m old enough to go out and he needs a friend. I think he’s really lonely and he enjoys being with me.”

“Yes, I’m sure he does.” Her tone was harsh as though spitting out each individual word. Then she looked up at the ceiling and shook her head as she lowered her voice. “Francine, think about it. Have you ever wondered why Thomas isn’t married yet?”

Nelle sat down beside her daughter with a serious expression. She patiently waited for an answer.

“I figured he just hadn’t met the right woman. He’s always so busy making cabinets and tables and all and helping out on the farm. There’s nothing that says you absolutely have to get married by the time you reach a certain age.”

Nelle Parker sighed. Her daughter looked like a young woman of twenty but her mind was still barely past puberty. She approached it from a different angle. "Francine, what do you know about the Gardiners?"

She honestly hadn't paid that much attention. "Well, Rebecca is kind of strange and she's never really gone out with anyone, but she's always nice to me. She's a lousy cook! His brother Rubert stays in the woods all the time and I suppose I'm a little bit afraid of him because he's always talking about killing something. But Ernest just says that's boy talk and perfectly normal. And his folks? Well, I admit they're both strange. I don't like his father very much. In fact, I avoid him."

"And why is that?"

"I think he beats up Alice all the time. She says she falls a lot because she has seizures but I can't figure out how in the world she could fall in order to get some of those injuries she comes up with." She rolled her eyes. "I mean, really! Wallace has always been nice to me, too, but sometimes he looks at me real strange."

"Strange as in odd?"

"No, strange as in perverted."

"I bet you never sing to him, do you?" Nelle was blunt, letting her daughter know that she knew exactly what she was doing by flirting.

Francine didn't hide her feelings or her opinions. "No, I think he's entirely too dirty. I bet that man never bathes! And his eyes—his eyes undress me all the time. Sometimes I have to look down to make sure I have all my clothes on and that everything is in place. He's absolutely revolting. No one in their right mind would want to flirt with him. He's—he's—"

"Crazy," Nelle finished the sentence. "He's crazy, Francine. The whole family is. That kind of thing is passed down from one generation to the next."

"Well, Thomas isn't," she adamantly protested.

"You don't know that! He's nice to you right now but I know what he wants!" Nelle's voice had that edge to it again.

In all truth, Francine knew better than to argue with her mother, but this time she felt her happiness was at stake. With her heart racing she suddenly blurted out "I know what he wants! He wants to marry me one day; that's what we both want!"

Nelle froze. “Marry? How did marriage get into this conversation? You said you were just friends. You said you only talked.” Nelle stared at her daughter until the girl broke.

“Okay, so he’s kissed me, but so what? I’m old enough to be kissed, aren’t I?”

Nelle was furious! “You’re not old enough to do anything until you know what it is that men want from unblemished young girls! You should be running from Thomas, not right into his sick arms!”

“How dare you say that!” Francine had her jaw set in defiance. “He’s gentle and kind. We can talk about absolutely anything. He has never, never…” she raised her voice to emphasize it, “never hurt me! And I don’t believe he ever will. It’s just not in him to hurt anyone.”

Her mother stared at the floor for the longest time, rubbing her face and then running her fingers through her hair. Then she looked up again, her face stern and yet with an underlying pain.

“He has, Francine. Okay? He has hurt someone before and I don’t want the same thing to happen to you.”

“Who did he hurt?”

“You don’t need to know.”

“Mother! How am I supposed to grow up and learn things if you’re not willing to tell me?”

“I can’t tell you right now.” Suddenly there were tears in her eyes and she was trembling. Nelle grabbed hold of the basket to steady her hands as she carried it to the next room. Francine knew that she was crying once she got in the other room but she didn’t care. In her opinion her mother was blowing the whole thing out of proportion. She didn’t say another word, just patiently waited for Nelle to come back. It seemed like it took forever. But, she needed that time to build up her courage for what she was going to say next. Nelle had no sooner cleared the door frame than Francine raised her voice.

“When can you tell me? Thomas and I are going to get married. If it’s something I need to know then don’t wait until my wedding day!”

Nelle swallowed hard. She knew she had lost. Even if she was to forbid the marriage she knew the two would just elope. Joe had no idea what had happened in the past or what could happen in the future so she knew he wouldn’t be on her side. She was on her own - so totally alone! Looking at Francine she saw herself in those round, wondrous eyes. Youth had a way of growing up real fast when faced with harshness of reality. There was no way she could prevent it. At that moment she felt completely helpless.

"You wouldn't understand," Nelle mumbled. "Some things in life just don't make sense. You'll just have to believe me. Thomas is not good for you. I had so hoped for better."

"I think that's my decision to make, not yours."

Francine waited again, trying to hold out until her mother broke the silence. Nelle refused to speak and Francine didn't want to wait any longer. "So? Are you gonna tell me or not?"

"I'm not."

"Then we don't have anything else to say to each other, do we?" She flippantly turned her back and walked out of the room.

Francine went to her room and the words to a new song began to float through the musical channels of her mind. A song of true love that was ripped from her grasp. In the end, perhaps both lovers would kill themselves. No, she liked one-sided tragedies better. Her parents would send her off to Australia or Siberia and Thomas would pine for her. He'd never marry and he'd spend a fortune looking for her. When he was only a few miles away, he would die from a broken heart, never knowing how close he was to the only woman he had ever loved! She would quietly bury him and faithfully take flowers to his grave. And everyone would marvel at the love they had felt for each other. Their names would become immortalized and famous! She'd name the song "If I Could Have Only Loved You Longer." Good song.

Francine sighed. Her mother's apprehensions weren't about to stop her from marrying Thomas. She didn't care what others said he did or didn't do. The only thing that mattered was that he loved her and wanted her. The affair became clandestine as she continued to slip around and see him. Being secretive and scandalous fed her desires of temptation and defiance. Determined to prove that he loved her, she extended the flirting to calculated and deliberate advances. There was no teasing now, she was quite serious.

She wouldn't admit it, but there had been times she was somewhat afraid of Thomas. He tried to warn her. So many times he had looked down at her and trying to control his breathing would demand 'don't do that!' or, once he told her, 'you're asking for more than you can handle, little girl'. So, she admitted it was her fault when she got herself in a precarious situation. Thinking it all in fun once, she ran her finger down his thigh and his aggressive response made her catch her breath. It didn't take long to discover there was a lot she didn't know! But then, he retained his composure and just shook his head as though she'd never learn.

"Why are you doing this to me?" Thomas took her hand in his and studied her fingers.

She looked at him through the eyes of a child again. "Because I want to learn all there is to learn and I think you can teach me."

"You think I have all the answers and all the knowledge?"

"All that I need. You said you wanted to teach me."

He looked deeply into her eyes, kissed her passionately, and then stood up and shoved her away from him with a fierceness to his demeanor that she had never known before.

"Get out of here, now!" He shouted at her, pointing to the door.

"No, I won't. Why are you treating me like this?" Tears were instantly blurring her vision.

"You're just a child, Francine! I'm a grown man."

"But you said…"

"I was wrong! Get out of here before I hurt you!" He grabbed hold of a railing as though it took all his strength just to hang on to it.

"I don't understand, Thomas. I know you would never hurt me."

"How do you know that?" He spun around and faced her with the eyes of a beast.

He approached with almost a roar but she didn't move; she wasn't afraid. She knew he was deliberately trying to scare her even though she had no understanding as to why. In his violent helplessness she loved him all the more. Words sang in her head 'kill me with your love, and I'll sing to you from above; just don't send me away where I can't kiss you each day…"

Coming back to reality she swallowed and then softly answered.

"I know that you won't hurt me because you love me. I can see it in your eyes and I can hear it in your voice. It isn't me that's afraid of you," her soft voice was comforting as her eyes wrapped him in tenderness. "You are the one afraid of me, aren't you Thomas? Tell me why."

He choked on the words, "Because you don't know who or what I am!"

She stood up and straightened her clothes. "Don't be ridiculous. I've been around you all my life and I've watched you and listened to you and even helped you with your work."

"But you don't know me--the me, inside, that no one can see. The me that I have nightmares about! The me that I'm afraid of myself. You'd be wise to leave and never come around me again. You should listen to your mother…" his face was buried in his hands.

Why was he saying that? Had something happened in the past? Had he hurt Nelle in some way? Is that what all this talk was about? If so, her mother must have been at fault. At that exact moment, Francine put a barrier between her mother and herself and swore that she would never let Nelle or whatever happened in the past interfere with the present. Her mind was made up.

"I can't leave you, Thomas. I love you too much. Maybe I can't see the same as you, but I know what I'm seeing right in front of me. I'm seeing a lonely, frustrated man who needs nothing more than someone to believe in him. I'm seeing someone who needs to be comforted after those nightmares. I'm seeing someone who needs a companion to laugh with, to have dreams with, to make a family with. We can do it together, Thomas, I just know we can."

"That's the thinking of a child," he continued to protest.

"No, it isn't. Admit it, you've thought the very same thing or you wouldn't have kissed me like you did on that day you thought I had drowned. As far as that goes, you wouldn't have listened to me sing all those times. And you wouldn't be here, now! Admit it, you want me as much as I want you."

She was bold enough to step forward and touch his face, and then to gently stand on her tiptoes so she could kiss his trembling lips. He didn't return the kiss, but neither did he prevent it.

"I must be a fool for listening to you." All resistance drained from him. "Yes, I admit it Francine. Marry me soon. Don't let me run away from you. I'll try to run, I know I will. I'm scared."

His manner suddenly crumbled right in front of her as he curled into a ball and wept. She didn't say or do anything. His weakness was actually strengthening her. After a moment she didn't feel young. She felt mature and maternal and she was ready to devote her life to this man. She ran her fingers through his hair and began to sing softly.

Months had passed. Nelle was aware of what was going on even though Francine hadn't said a word. She had even confided with Joe and though she didn't admit that she had dealt with Thomas years before, she did try to express her fear. She explained it as a mother's intuition that probably didn't make sense but she had to respect her feelings as valid. Fortunately, Joe had never liked Thomas so it wasn't difficult for him to forbid his daughter to marry the young man. Nelle and Joe both knew, however, that Francine was determined to continue the relationship. There was a time when it looked as though the natural course of events may change their plans. Francine was continually moody and always upset with Thomas about something.

Joe had gone to Gough's Ridge alone and while sitting in the saloon, he watched Thomas and one of the girls come out of an upstairs room. He was hoping that this was clear evidence that Thomas had lost interest in Francine. When Joe shared this event with Nelle, she acted as though she had been waiting for it to happen. From that point on, Nelle took matters into her own hands and wrote to her brother who lived a good hundred miles away. She knew she would need help.

Joe was quite blunt in telling Francine exactly what he had seen at the saloon and what it had meant. He wasn't about to allow his daughter to be deceived. Then he left her with the ultimatum that she either willingly break off the relationship with Thomas or he would force her to. Hurt that Thomas had not been faithful to her, Francine agreed to stay away from him. But, the more she thought about it she questioned the gossip and entertained the idea that her father was making it all up because he didn't want them together.

It took nearly two months before Nelle got a response from her brother, but their plan had already been put into motion. She wrote in her journal:

> Instead of ending this horrible relationship, we have pushed our daughter right into his arms and into his bed. I've watched, I've listened, and I know that she is now carrying his child. I'm sure that Francine will hate her father and I but we feel as though we must take matters into our own hands. We will force the separation by taking her to my brothers. She will stay with him until her baby is born and she will be told that Thomas either moved away, is dead, or married someone else. The reason doesn't matter. She can either raise the child or allow her aunt to provide. My brother is quite wealthy and will be able to accommodate all needs quite sufficiently. He has agreed to do this. My heart is broken for my daughter. If I can save my daughter from the clutches of insanity, then the continuation of my own lies will deem it all worthwhile. My prayer now is that she will forgive me and that her child will not be born in the same mental darkness that Thomas seems to exist in. God forgive me for wishing that this child will never be born!

Nelle quit writing and took a long, deep breath. Two days later, her brother Ronald and his wife Judith Ann arrived. What happened, in a chain of whirlwind events, seemed to be directed entirely by the hand of God and had very little to do with the plans Nelle had made. It was growing dark when Francine sneaked over to see Thomas in their "secret" hide-away, which was more like a bear's den by the river. But when she got there, she found that he was not alone. Martha was wrapped in his arms!

"What are you doing?" she screamed at Martha.

In the confined space, which limited all of their movements, she had to stoop over just to enter the dugout. Next to her was a table with paper and scissors where Thomas had been cutting out paper hearts. Sizing up the situation, Francine grabbed the scissors.

"I'll cut your heart out, you thieving tramp!" Francine attacked Martha and felt the scissors sink into flesh even though she doubted she had reached her heart. At that moment she didn't care! When Martha screamed, Francine crawled back out and with tears streaming down her face, she tried to clear her vision enough to see who was suddenly in front of her.

To her surprise it was Ronald and Judith Ann out for a ride in the buggy. They had heard the commotion and when Francine ran frantically towards them, they quickly intercepted. At the very same moment, Martha's husband appeared and when Thomas stepped up to the top of the embankment, Oscar pulled out his gun and fired. Francine screamed as the blast of the gun seemed to shake the ground. She didn't have to look back to know that Thomas had been shot. Judith Ann quickly got her head turned from the scene as Ronald cracked the whip and got the horses to run.

As soon as they got to the cabin they burst through the door with the horrible news. "He's dead!" Francine screamed. "Oscar shot him! Give me Daddy's gun and I'll go after him and finish off Martha, too!"

"Finish off? What did you do to Martha?" Nelle demanded as she spun Francine around before she could get her hands on a weapon.

"I stuck her, that's what! But she's not the one who's dead, Thomas is!" Her eyes were wild. "I'll kill her; I swear I will!"

"No!" Nelle was horrified at the violence in her daughter. "You can't do that!"

It was all happening too fast! "The best thing for you to do is just to get out of here!" Nelle and Judith Ann both started packing Francine's few clothes.

Nelle cradled her daughter's face in the palms of her hands. "You can't stay here. It's going to get really ugly and they'll come after you next and there's nothing you can do! For your own safety, you've got to get away."

"But where would I go?" Francine sobbed.

Judith Ann was quick to persuade her. "You can go home with us; we'll leave right now! And when all settles down we'll bring you back."

And then, using Francine's hysteria to their advantage, they left swiftly! Francine never knew that half of this scene had already been planned.

Nelle watched them go, praying that Martha only had a superficial wound. She choked back tears watching her daughter go out of her life. No one had ever let on that they knew the young girl was pregnant. As soon as she had started getting moody and nauseous every morning, Nelle had known what was going on. If Francine had stayed even another week it would have been difficult for her to conceal her bulging waistline. Suddenly things were a lot more complicated and now it wasn't just the pregnancy she had to conceal!

Nelle and Joe both waited to see what was going to happen. Thomas was immediately taken to the hospital in Gough's Ridge in critical condition. Martha was stitched and bandaged with a serious wound to her thigh. Revenge prompted her recovery so she could get back at Francine. The community was ablaze with talk and rumors for several days. Everyone wanted to get in on the action. Oscar was arrested for attempted murder and the sheriff whispered a silent warning "wherever Francine took off to, she'd better stay there for awhile; for her own sake."

Nelle sent a letter off to her brother, informing him of the sheriff's advice. Since Francine had believed Thomas was dead, she didn't say anything about him being in the hospital. Judith Ann was very good about corresponding with Nelle and letting her know exactly how things were going. Francine had no choice but to confide in Judith Ann about the pregnancy but she refused to tell her parents. Nelle found it interesting to compare the letters from her sister-in-law and her daughter. Judith Ann would write:

> *She's doing very well considering she's having to waddle around with such a heavy child! But the midwife will be here and there's nothing to fear. She had to quit singing because she couldn't get her breath. We laugh about it. Francine talked me into going for walks with her and*

when my legs quit hurting I found I rather enjoyed it! There are times when she's terribly homesick and miserable. She hasn't made any friends yet but I think it's because she doesn't want to have to explain about the baby. I know she struggles with the decision to keep the baby or allow it to be adopted, which I gladly told her I would do. You must believe that she doesn't want to hurt you, she just wants to make up her own mind about the child. No matter what I say, she refuses to talk about Thomas.

Whereas, Francine's letter simply read:

Life is truly wonderful here! I'm so busy I lose track of time. I'm constantly singing and Aunt Judith talked me into going for walks with her. It's strange to walk down streets of stone! I've never seen such wealth before. Imagine having a closet of ten dresses! I met a young man who is just the opposite of Thomas. Maybe we'll get married and start a family. I don't want to mess up again so I won't rush into it. Don't look for me any time soon.

Nelle had anticipated a year that Francine would be gone, when in all truth, it stretched out to almost two years! Throughout that entire time there was never any admission from Francine that she had a child. If it hadn't been for Judith Ann's faithfulness, Nelle would have never known she had become grandmother to little Bonnie Eugenia Parker. Francine did talk about a 'child next door' whom she had fallen in love with and was going to become a nanny to. So, at least she acknowledged her and it gave Nelle opportunity to ask how the child was.

It was in late summer when Francine asked about Thomas for the first time since the shooting. Her letter read:

> ***It's time that I want to know about Thomas and his death. Where was he buried? I just couldn't bring myself to talk about him and I appreciated your silence over the matter. But now, I must know. I deeply regret my dishonesty and lack of discretion in my affair with him, so I know I don't deserve your honesty, yet I do plead for it.***

Nelle studied the letter for three days before she made up her mind what to do. The event had changed everyone! Oscar had nearly beaten Martha to death and wouldn't even discuss the matter of divorce. He was going to see to it that she honored her marriage vows until the day one of them died—and he didn't plan to go first!

Thomas had been shot in the head but he had lived. He had no memory of what had happened. He didn't even know Martha's name, let alone Francine's! The doctor said there was still a bullet fragment in his brain and that he'd never fully recover. He retained his skill in his carpentry and learned to walk again, but he seldom talked. People were still afraid of his quick temper.

In her descriptive way, Nelle told Francine the truth, only exaggerating Thomas's condition a little bit. Even though she desperately wanted her daughter back, she still didn't want Francine to have anything do with the young man. Therefore, Nelle said nothing to encourage her daughter to return. Nevertheless, a letter came from Judith Ann that informed her Francine and Ronald were heading that way; Bonnie was going to stay with her.

Nelle was disappointed that she wasn't going to be able to see her grandchild but she would honor the secret a little longer. Her hand went to her abdomen for the thousandth time. If she could only have another child! She felt as though God had punished her for her lies through the disheartening and humiliating means of being barren. She reasoned that God didn't feel she was fit to be a mother so He wouldn't give her any more children. Having a grandchild in her arms would have alleviated some of the emptiness.

Nelle deeply regretted stating that she had hoped Francine's child wouldn't live! So many times tears would come to her eyes as she read Francine's letters, telling her how Miss Bonnie, the little girl next door, was eating by herself, and walking, and giving little kisses. How Nelle yearned for that touch!

And then, Francine was home! It was a good reunion. Looking more robust than ever, she was obviously glad to be home. She and Nelle talked for the longest time but Francine didn't waste words when asking about Thomas. Nelle told her as much as she should know and then the girl took off through the woods towards the Gardiner home.

Francine was amazed how things had changed! The trees weren't quite as dense; neither did they look as tall as she had remembered. It didn't take as long to cross over the creek and head up to the farm site. But Francine's heart was pounding harder than it had ever done before! Her legs were heavy and she found herself almost dragging along. How could her emotions be in such conflict? She was eager to see Thomas and yet she wasn't convinced she was doing the right thing.

Alice answered her knock and just stared at her. "He's out in his shop but don't expect him to recognize you."

Without another word, Francine turned and headed to the familiar little carpentry shop, which was nothing more than a little lean-to off the barn. She could hear him sanding something. His back was to her when she stood in the doorway. She remained silent. He looked so different to her and yet her heart was fluttering as though the two years had never existed. Sensing someone's presence, he turned around, looked at her, frowned, and then cocked his head as though trying to place her, but couldn't.

"May I help you?" He stood posed with the sandpaper in his hand.

"I…I came by to see you, Thomas."

"Well, I'm working. Do I know you?"

Tears welled in her eyes and she had to blink hard and turn her face away from him for a second. She pretended to sneeze.

"It's probably all the sawdust stirred up. Sorry." He apologized.

"Oh, that's okay. You look well, Thomas."

The corner of his mouth twisted into a half smile. "They say I'm doing pretty good. I don't remember much; I guess you must know that."

"Yes, they told me."

They continued to stare at each other. With a faltering voice he asked, "Did I know you before…before the accident?"

It was almost more than she could bear! Oh, the pain! Before she could catch herself she answered, "No, I…ah…just came by to inquire about a rocker. I understand that you make comfortable and sturdy rockers. Someone gave me your name."

His whole manner changed now that he perceived her to be just another customer. He showed her some of the things he had made and sketches of other items he could make. It was all business talk and his eyes seemed to hold an emptiness. Francine remembered how he used to look at her with eyes full of lust and how he had grabbed her and kissed her passionately. Now, he was afraid to even stand too close or even to shake her hand.

Francine didn't want a rocker but she told him she did and he said he'd get right to it.

"Well, thanks for coming by. I appreciate your business." He stood perfectly still.

She begged him to recognize her, to touch her! Her impulse was to run to him and embrace him as though her love for him could make him remember! Francine hadn't fully realized how much she had loved him until this very moment. The hurt and pain she had suffered, knowing of his infidelity and thinking him to be dead had made her angry for so long! Then, that anger had ebbed into passiveness. Now, she had to wonder why she had kept Bonnie such a secret. At the time of her decision, it had seemed right. For months, Francine had considered allowing Judith Ann to adopt her. There had been times that she hated Bonnie because the child was a living reminder of betrayed love. But as soon as she seemed convinced to give her up, then she was also reminded of the fact that this child was the only thing good that she had from Thomas. And so, the child had remained in the same household with Judith Ann and Francine, calling both of them Nanny.

It became quite clear that Thomas would never understand he had a daughter. Even if she told him; even if she admitted that they had been lovers and were going to marry, he still wouldn't know her. Nothing she could tell him would change things. Her only hope was that one day they would marry and then Bonnie would be considered legitimate. It was Francine's hope that the innocent child would carry the name of Gardiner.

As Francine left the shop she tried to work out what to do next. Later on that very same day she went back to see Thomas again.

"Do you remember me?" she asked.

"I think so, but I must apologize because your name escapes me at the moment. It's my memory, you see."

He laughed at himself. "You could tell me your name was Elizabeth this very moment and in five minutes I might call you Gracie. You must excuse me, I wish I could remember! It's so odd, there are things I don't think I'll ever forget and other things that elude me completely."

"What happened that caused you to forget?" she dared to ask.

He frowned. "They tell me I was shot in the head but I don't remember any of it. The human brain is so strange, don't you think? If I had gotten shot in the arm or leg it would have mended and I would have regained full use of it. But the brain? It's damaged for life they say! I don't know why that is. Even if I had been a doctor I doubt if I would have understood that. I suppose it's just as well I'm a carpenter! At least I didn't forget any of my skills! I had to learn to walk again and even to feed myself but as soon as this saw was in my hand, I knew what to do with it. Same thing with speech. I had to learn how to talk but I knew all the words to say."

"Then you've made incredible progress. Your work is excellent." She ambled around the area, remembering the countless times she had been with him and handled all his tools. It was so familiar and yet at the same time so foreign.

"What's it like not to be able to remember?" She was running her thumb across the top of a level.

He stopped and looked at her. "Why do you ask? Is your question out of morbid curiosity so you can make sport of me, or is it genuine concern?" He was quick to be on the defensive.

"I assure you, with all sincerity, it's from concern," she answered.

"But you don't know me," he challenged her. "So, why should you care?"

She found herself telling another lie. "Because my grandfather is forgetting, too, only he wasn't shot. His mind just seems to be disappearing little by little. I tried to ask him but he couldn't tell me what it was like because he couldn't compare it to anything."

"Oh, I see. I suppose the same is true for me. It bothers me when others talk about me and I can't defend myself or even promote myself for that matter! I have no idea what all I'm capable of because I can't remember dates of things happening. I can recite all my math tables but I couldn't begin to tell you what direction Gough's Ridge is and yet I can draw a map that could only come from some tidbit of memory. I have no memory of growing up and yet I know that Alice is my mother. When I was very small I would crawl up in her lap and she would rub my forehead. I don't know why. She tells me that I had terrible headaches but I don't remember what a headache feels like. There is no pain now."

"What does it feel like?"

"Kind of like when your hand goes to sleep. It's tingly and numb. I can touch certain areas," he demonstrated, "and there's no feeling whatsoever. You could hit me with a two by four and I would simply look at you and wonder why you hit me."

She smiled. "Well, I won't hit you. It must be terrible."

"Not all the time," he shrugged. "Very few people get to start completely over and not have to be accountable for their past. No matter what I did, I can't very well make amends for any wrongs because I have no recollection of the past. I suppose my greatest concern is in being someone's scapegoat. Oh, how easy it would be for someone to steal from their neighbor and accuse me of doing it! They could say they saw me there, even committing the act, and I couldn't defend myself because everyone knows I can't remember."

"But at least they couldn't punish you."

"No, but the guilty party would be free and there's really no justice in that."

"You're a good man, Thomas, you would make such a wonderful husband!" She found herself mesmerized by him and spoke her thoughts before she even realized what she was saying. Her outburst took him completely by surprise. Did he blush? Yes, he did! Thomas Gardiner blushed! Obviously more than just his memory had been affected by the bullet! This was a totally different person standing in front of her. Francine wasn't sure she knew him after all.

"Well, that's kind of you to say. I have to admit I feel rather strange standing here talking to you. I seldom talk to anyone and yet there seems to be something about you that just draws the words out. Are you sure we haven't met before?"

"Yes, I'm sure." She had to shut her eyes for fear he could see into her soul and know she was lying.

"How strange. Will you come again soon? I don't want to sound forward, but I enjoy your company. Sometimes, I get a little lonely."

She consented without any reservations. As she crossed the yard to return home, Alice stopped her. The woman wore a suspicious look in her eyes. "I don't want you toying with his mind," she hissed through stained, broken teeth.

Francine stood her ground. "I don't believe he has much of a mind to toy with."

"You know what I mean you snippy little girl!" Alice pointed and glared.

"For goodness sakes, he doesn't even know me. To him I'm no more than just a customer. If we choose to get to know each other then it's the present, not the past that unites us. Does that meet with your approval?" Francine forced a smile.

"I don't trust you Francine Parker. I didn't two years ago and I don't now."

Francine turned on her. "I don't think I was the one who was ever in question! I believe it was your son who couldn't be trusted!"

"Oh, so you did come back for revenge, didn't you?" she gloated.

"No, I didn't." Each word was deliberate.

The old woman laughed sarcastically. "Maybe you think you got healing powers or something and can make him like he was? Is that what you're up to?"

Then her laugh turned into a vicious cackle. "You wouldn't want him like he was! You'd best be happy with the way he is! But I'll tell you this," she pointed her finger and got right into Francine's face. "You may think he's all nice and friendly right now, but when he gets mad, he explodes! I've seen him rip a chicken apart and kill the dog with one swift blow! Darned near killed the doctor once. Probably would have been put in jail if he had known what he was doing. One day he'll be put in some institution. I guarantee you this one thing; if he ever lays a hand on me, I'll kill him myself! You hear me, girl?"

"I hear you." But Francine wasn't listening. Her daughter needed her father's name and Francine was determined to make that happen! She left, but she came back the next day and then the next. Soon the days turned into weeks and then months. They had reversed roles.

With unusual boldness, Francine asked him "Thomas, do you know what love means? Not just love for your family, but the kind of love between a husband and wife."

Her question took him by surprise. "Well, I honestly don't know. Maybe I do, and maybe I don't. Why do you ask?" He stopped what he was doing.

"Because I could teach you." Her voice was level and confident.

"Why would you want to do that?" Thomas was suddenly nervous.

"Because I want to marry you one day."

"Oh, you do, do you?" Then he frowned and backed away from her. "Aren't you being rather brazen?"

He shook his head as though memories were trying to fill his mind but they were the wrong size. They were either so large they squeezed his thinking or so small they made his mind rattle. "Maybe you just better leave."

"Are you afraid to love someone, Thomas?" She took a bold step toward him.

He breathed deeply and then focused all his attention on a board that he was carving. "Not afraid. But there's something in my head that might be a memory but I don't know if it was a dream or reality. Ever since you came by that first day and asked about a rocker I've been reflectin' on it. It's like you stirred up a memory that refused to be damaged by the bullet."

He still refused to look at her. His movements were deliberate as he carved a deep groove.

"I wouldn't tell this to no one else, you hear? And I probably shouldn't be tellin' you now, but I will." Only then did he stop and make eye contact with her as he nearly whispered, "I think I was in love. My heart seems to tell me that. It's always the same girl I think about. I can't remember her name or even her face. Like I said, it's more like a dream. But I can see her long hair blowing in the wind and her touch was always…delicate. I know this one thing as surely as I know how to carve this piece of wood—if she does exist, I would like to find her again."

He listened to what he had said and then he threw down his tool. "Oh, the rambling of a mad man! What am I saying? It's probably no more than some fantasy that I made up! My life is fenced in by loneliness and frustration. You or ten other ladies could tell me you were the one and I wouldn't know! Don't even listen to me!" He walked away from her, and she knew not to pursue him.

But you're not mad! She wanted to tell him. I am that girl and I'm right here in front of you! You just don't know it…yet! At least, she wished with all her heart that she was indeed the one he had loved. Even though Thomas had been with Martha when he got shot, she was hoping that it had been no more than a physical attraction and that he hadn't really loved her. She silently begged, remember me, not Martha.

The following day she went back to the shop, but before she got close she could hear loud, angry voices. By the time she reached the door, there was a horrible crashing sound and then a man burst out of the door as though he had been pushed. Thomas was right behind him ready to attack him with a broken chair. Francine quickly dodged out of sight and watched what was happening. The fury in Thomas was indeed frightening. If the man hadn't been quick, he would have been severely injured! Wallace responded to the commotion and started yelling as well, then Alice and Rubert stood and watched.

Thomas had drawn his knife as Wallace hollered that he had better drop it. He raised a shotgun and leveled it at Thomas's head.

"I mean it, son. Drop the knife and back off." They stared at each other and then Thomas threw the knife down and ran off.

Only then did Francine step away from her hiding place.

"What are you doing here, girl?" Wallace demanded an explanation.

"I'm going after him." Francine didn't wait around for any more discussion.

"He'll kill you." Alice warned her. "He gets like this and he'll kill anyone that gets in his way!"

Francine turned and glared at them. "No, he won't! He won't hurt me one bit!" Then she ran off.

No one pursued. She knew where he was going. He would go down to the river and sit by the bridge. She gave him time to get there and to calm down a bit. Then she approached.

"Thomas?" She called his name as soon as she was close enough.

"Go away!" he turned on her. "You take another step towards me and I'd just as soon kill you."

"No you won't, Thomas. I know you're upset but you don't have to hurt me." She advanced slowly.

"I will! You don't know me!"

Francine stopped only long enough for him to see her smile with a cunning twinkle in her eyes. "I know you well enough."

"I'm warning you!" His hand was shaking as he pointed at her, but his voice didn't hold much conviction.

She shook her head no and held out a hand as though she was approaching a wild dog. And then she started humming. He used to like to hear her sing to him. Instead of just talking, she made up a tune and sang the words.

"Let go, Thomas. Life is going to be different. You go ahead and hate the world but with me, there's a refuge, a haven of rest, a calm within the storm of your heart. Take my hand, Thomas, take my hand and you'll see." She quit singing and just stood and tried to look into his eyes.

He hesitated, but the closer she got, the more he seemed to calm down. He finally took her outstretched hand and held it gently for a moment, but then with a violent gesture he gripped hard and swung her towards the water's edge as though he was going to throw her in. She started to lose her balance but she never lost her confidence.

"Hang on to me, Thomas."

"I could hurt you bad!" His eyes were darting back and forth but his grip was strong.

"But you won't!" Her voice resounded with authority and then mellowed. "You can't."

He stared at her, totally dumbfounded. She whispered, "See you can stay in control. You're okay, Thomas. You're not going to hurt me and I'm not going to be afraid of you."

She almost slipped by saying 'I never have been' but she caught herself just in time. Then she touched his shoulder and when he didn't object she put her arm around his neck and drew him to her. He was still just a little boy.

When they walked back together, Wallace totally ignored them. Alice waited until she was alone and heading back home before she approached her. "Think you're somethin' don't you little missy? Your turn will come. He'll turn on you, too, you'll see. Well, don't expect me to weep at your funeral."

"How could you? Yours will be first!" Francine raised a shoulder, with her head cocked to the side. Then she felt foolish for being uncivil.

"Is there some reason why you're so hateful to me?" She changed her tune.

"Let's just say I don't trust you."

"You've never trusted anyone, Alice Gardiner, so I reckon there's nothing either of us can do." Francine turned and went back to the cabin. She was beginning to feel a bit emotionally drawn.

As the days wore on, Francine found that she desperately missed Bonnie. She wanted to go home but she couldn't leave Thomas. If she had to choose her child over the man she loved, would she be able to do it? Or, could she go back, get Bonnie and have both? The problem was, she didn't want Thomas to make a decision based on a child. She had never told her mother that Bonnie even existed. There would just be too many complications to try and bring a child into the picture at this particular time. So, she allowed the days to stretch into weeks and before she knew it, another month had passed.

Francine spent as much time as possible with Thomas. On warm evenings, they would often lay on a blanket along the river's edge and talk. At first he was overly cautious about touching her. One night she was actually in his arms and he had bent his head to search for her lips. But then he pulled away.

"What's wrong?" she asked.

"If I kiss you, I might be betraying the woman I had loved."

She yearned to tell him right then and there who she was! She wanted to tell the whole story!

Francine sighed. "I see it this way. Maybe I am the woman of your dreams. If you kiss me, and you don't like it, then you'll know I'm not. But what if it's so good it brings back a memory you're searching for?"

He thought about it. "But if you were my woman, why didn't you just say so when you first came to the shop?"

"Would you have believed me?"

"I don't know who to believe."

"Then let your heart decide for you. It will know; even if your head is confused."

For a moment, as his lips drew closer and closer, she was afraid that in her nervousness she might be too tense and spoil the moment. She had to put everything she could into that kiss without being overbearing. How had she kissed him when she was a child? Would he be expecting that kind of response? If he wasn't the same aggressive, passionate man, what was he? Would he remember his "skills" as a lover in the same sense he remembered his carpentry skills?

Suddenly she quit thinking and merely responded! She would be able to read his actions far better than his mind. It was a kiss that made her entire body go weak. For a moment she thought she saw stars or heard bells!

"Francine Parker?"

"Yes?" She was hopeful that he had suddenly remembered.

"I don't know you, but I think I could love you." he kissed her again.

That was all she needed! Now her hopes soared. When she thought of Bonnie, she knew the child would soon have a father! Then she wouldn't have to stay secluded or be afraid of what people might say.

Time continued to pass and there were often times that Thomas went into rages, but Francine knew how to quiet the beast in him. Alice even acknowledged her in a decent manner, though Francine knew she would never receive an apology from the woman.

One night Joe came into the house and told Francine that she had an engagement in Gough's Ridge at the theater. It was nothing but a barn with a stage and wooden stands for the audience, but they were planning a gala event and Francine had been asked to sing. She was thrilled with the idea and looked forward to it. Thomas had promised to go with her. Deep down she wondered if it would stir any memories. Her own head couldn't keep up with all the times she had sang to him and teased him and lured him into her affections.

Soon the night came. The publicity of the event had been spread throughout the region and the crowd was expected to be in the hundreds! They even had her name on a banner! It was truly the high point of her singing career. Before it all started, she was standing backstage with Thomas when a smartly dressed man approached her.

"Francine Parker?" His voice was that of a tenor.

"Yes?"

He introduced himself and let her know that he had been sent as an agent to listen to her sing and then offer her a position in New Orleans at the Rosemont Theater. It would be a high paying position and she would be singing and acting every night to crowds of fifty or more. During the festivities it could easily surpass three hundred and off season would require a great deal of traveling. Her heart was ecstatic! Even Thomas caught her enthusiasm.

"Would you go with me?" she asked him, breathless.

"That wouldn't be proper for two unmarried people, would it? Especially with the traveling part?"

"No, but what would prevent us from being married?"

Thomas smiled. "Would I be able to open a carpentry shop there?"

"I don't see why not." She could see endless possibilities.

He became almost animated. "Then Mr. and Mrs. Thomas Gardiner shall move to New Orleans and become the talk of the town with her voice and his art work."

She wasn't about to mention Bonnie yet. For an irrational moment she considered leaving the child with Judith Ann until they were settled in New Orleans and had a chance to really get to know each other. Only then could Bonnie become involved. Francine wanted to have more time with Thomas as a husband before she sprang it on him that he was also a father!

"It's a pity we can't get married right now at this wonderful moment." She held his hands and looked into the warmest eyes she had ever seen. She looked down at her stage clothes. "I'm all dressed in white."

"And I'm all duded up in my Sunday-go-to-meeting-clothes. Does it matter where we say our vows as long as we mean them? Francine Parker, will you marry me right here and now? Will you take me as your beloved husband and love me until death doth us part?"

"I will! And will you, Thomas Gardiner, accept me as your beloved wife and love me until death doth us part?"

"I will!" They sealed their vow with a kiss and then he threw his head back and gave a war hoop! "What's done is done! Our vows will be much stronger than a preacher's words! He reads from a piece of paper, but we have spoken from our hearts. From this day until forever, I will love you Francine. I really mean that."

Then he teased. "And as long as I can remember your name and your face, you'll be the only one I'll love!" He deliberately frowned "What's your name again?"

Francine giggled and hugged him tightly. She had never known him to have such a glorious sense of humor! Oh, how she loved him! But then she had to ask a nagging question.

"What about the woman of your dreams?" she smiled at him and touched his nose with the tip of hers.

He didn't even hesitate. "I'm holding her in my arms this very moment!"

"Francine Parker! Time to go on stage." Someone called to her.

For the first time in her life she didn't want to sing. He knew she was hesitating. "Go on, now, and sing for me!"

"All my love songs will be for you, Thomas."

"Then sing them for the rest of your life and I will listen." They kissed again and then parted as she took her place and he went to the stands to find a seat in the front.

There was only magic for the first three songs and then tragedy struck. As Francine was singing, a drunk stood up and tried to approach the stage. It took three men to finally hold him back. He was escorted out of the building and everyone settled back down. Not more than five minutes later he was back, but this time with a gun. Thomas was angry as the drunk tried to reach Francine again and threatened to kill anyone that got in his way.

"Just go home and sleep it off." Thomas demanded as he stood in front of Francine.

"Yeah, well, who are you?" the drunk bellowed.

"I'm her husband!"

The drunk laughed and waved the gun. "Well, you just made her a widow!" With a hideous belch he aimed and fired.

Thomas looked down at his shirt and watched the red suddenly covering his pocket. He staggered and the screaming echoed around him as though he had been in a hollow cave. Francine fell upon him but with her white dress he couldn't tell if she was his bride or an angel come to get him. He temporarily focused on her face which was becoming a blur.

"I only loved one girl," he was struggling to speak. "I remember now, I use to call her Frannie and she always sang to me. It's you, you are my one love! I know that for a fact!"

With that he closed his eyes and smiled as he slipped into eternity with the memory of her name and her voice comforting him.

Francine couldn't believe what was happening! She held him until she knew without a shadow of a doubt that he was dead. Two years ago she thought she had watched him die. This time she wasn't going to leave the scene. Her mind was completely shocked and numb! There was commotion around her but she couldn't hear it. People were talking to her but she couldn't respond. Finally, someone pulled her backwards while two men carried Thomas away. The next thing she knew she was in a back room and someone had gone to get her some water. The man she had met earlier, with the tenor voice, was sitting next to her.

"I know this isn't the time to talk about it, but this doesn't change the offer I made. I'll wait for two weeks and then expect an answer from you. Can I do anything for you?"

"Just let me be alone, please." Even her voice was numb.

He consented, knowing that someone else would be right outside the door in case she called out. Francine found herself completely alone and she buried her face in her skirts. The blood was drying on her clothes and she touched it, almost in disbelief! She vaguely heard the door open and felt the presence of someone in the room.

A woman's voice softly spoke. At first the words didn't even register but there was an incredibly soothing quality to the voice. She was saying how she had come from a long distance to be able to hear Francine sing again. And then the woman spoke of how tragedy was often like a fragile egg in God's hands, and the sufferer was the chick struggling to get free. Once the shell broke, a new life would be exchanged for the previous captivity.

Without looking at the person, Francine listened to the voice. A hand was touching her hair and then gently rested against her back.

"I know this to be true." The voice was even softer. "It is not just an old saying of my people. The shell of tragedy will soon be chipped away and you will become a new creation, Francine, don't be afraid of the world you are about to enter. You will never be alone."

At last, Francine looked up at the stranger before her. Her hair was done up on the top of her head like the ladies of the town, and she wore a blue, fashionable gown, but there was no doubt that she was an Indian. Breaking into sobs again, Francine buried her face in her hands, only vaguely aware that someone else came in the room. When she looked up again, the Indian was gone and Mr. Miller was close to her.

"Where did that woman go?" Francine was looking around the room.

"Who? I haven't seen anyone else."

"It doesn't matter; I didn't know her anyway."

"Probably just a fan. Are you about ready to leave? Your dad is here to take you home."

"What did they do with Thomas? I don't want to leave without him."

"The coroner won't deliver him to the family until morning. Why don't you get ready to go on back home, there's nothing more you can do here."

But what did she have at home? No one. Nothing. Her dreams had just been shattered. She had come so close to winning Thomas back. They had said their vows to each other. Did that mean her daughter had a name? Was she indeed a widow? Or, just a bride left at the altar? What would Alice and Wallace think about it? Well, she didn't want any of Thomas's possessions. They didn't have to worry about her taking all his things. Francine couldn't believe that Thomas was dead. It had all happened too fast!

In her grief she made a decision. She would accept the offer to go to New Orleans and she would sing love songs for the rest of her life in honor of the only man she had ever loved-- and lost twice! Francine decided that she was going to keep the past where it belonged and think only of the future. Singing and being on the road was no life for a child so she would allow Judith Ann to raise Bonnie. The Indian woman had been right. She was going to break the shell of tragedy and emerge as a new creature, and she wasn't going to be afraid!

CHAPTER 8

ꕥꕥꕥꕥꕥ

1969

"Watch where you're stepping." Will's foot slid about ten inches in the soft soil and as soon as he knew he was sure-footed he reached up to take Phyllis's hand to help her down. "I bet this place could really get tricky after a hard rain."

"Yeah, but when you're in love you'd swim the deepest ocean and climb the highest mountain…you know, that sort of thing. A six foot drop is really nothing!"

"What made you think of that?" he queried, holding tightly to her hand.

"I was just imagining two kids in love, going back and forth from the cabin to the house."

"Maybe so," he went along with her. She suddenly stopped and with a puzzled look she started counting on her fingers. "What are you doing?" Will asked.

"Trying to figure up ages. This is really something; I'm beginning to feel like an old spinster lady."

"Why, because I helped you down that little drop off?"

"No, I'm already twenty years old. Mom had me when she was just sixteen. Do you know what I was doing when I was sixteen?"

"Trying to stay out of trouble in school I imagine."

"That's exactly right! No way was I mature enough to get married and have a child! I remember still going to the school playground and swinging so high the chains sagged! Jerry always boasted he could go over the bar but I tried to do it and found it to be impossible. For goodness sakes, Will, even at twenty years old I'm not sure if I'm ready for marriage, and children, and all! How did women do it back then?"

"Stamina, I guess, or maybe it's because they didn't have a choice."

Phyllis scoffed at that. "No choice? It's hard to imagine anyone feeling like they didn't have a choice. That's because Mom has harped on me every day of my life that 'it's your choice; so be ready to live with it!' By my figuring, my grandmother Bonnie was thirteen when she got married which means she probably had Mom when she was fourteen or close to that anyways. What could possibly be going on in your life to make you want to get married at that age?"

"I figure you're either running from something or into something. My question is: why did your mother hate her so much? Was Bonnie always a delinquent child that turned into a troubled adult? Now, that's a story I'd kind of like to find out."

"Yes, me too. People sure did get married young back in those days."

"They had to because they usually had eight to fifteen kids in one family and with that many mouths to feed you were in the fields working by the time you were ten. And you'd been raising brothers and sisters your whole life so having a baby yourself wasn't anything remarkable. It just lengthened the chain of survival. Know what I mean?"

"But that's like saying all there is to life is just survival! Where's the joy and adventure and love? I'm really glad I didn't live back then. It's tough enough the way it is now."

"I hope you know I'm planning on at least seven children myself," he raised his eyebrows.

Phyllis shook her head, "Not if you're going to marry me! Four is the absolute limit! This is almost the seventies, you know, not the depression. Wow, just think of everything that happened in history between Joe Parker and me. That's over sixty-five years! The railroad went through, men served in a couple of wars, Chicago burned to the ground, the holocaust destroyed millions, and think of all the inventions! Makes you wonder what's still to come, doesn't it?"

"I do know this for a fact; regardless of what the world is doing, we'll have our children, then their children, and their children. One generation will keep on following in line one after another. It's the only sure thing we can count on."

"I hope they'll know us. Look at that cabin and all that's lost." They now stood in front of it. Somehow, it seemed even sadder.

"Don't you think it's important that we leave a good legacy for those who go on after us? I'll tell you what I'm going to do." She paused to step over a fallen tree.

"Tell me." He automatically reached for her hand as he helped her cross over the tree.

"I'm going to record all the family history I possibly can in a kind of book that we can keep adding to. We'll pass it down to the next generation and they can add to it and then keep passing it down. I want my fifth generation great grandchild to know that Phyllis Ann Parker was madly in love with William Reginald Huston and that they lived a good and sensible life. No, a wonderful, Christian life! That's really important. I wouldn't call our ancestors heathens or anything like that, but it seems like they didn't allow God to play much of a part in their lives. Oh, they may have believed in Him, but there's so much more than just knowing He exists! Our lives are going to change history, Will! We're going to remove this stupid curse!"

His eyes darted back and forth and he began wringing his hands as though anxious to get started. "I just can't wait! Tell me, my lovely, how are we going to do that?"

She totally ignored his antics, "By finding out who owns this place and if it is still in the family. I just made up my mind that I want to live here."

Seeing that she was totally serious he found himself frowning. "We would have quite a bit of rebuilding to do. Or, we could bulldoze the whole place and start over."

Her eyes became astonished saucers. "No!" Phyllis suddenly became animated as she exaggerated her movements, describing what she was thinking. "We'll save as much of this house as we possibly can and then we'll add on another wing to it. We'll have a dining room and extra bedroom and a beautiful porch! Maybe even a gazebo off to the side. Of course, the addition will compliment what's already here. We have to keep as much as possible. When I stand here at the kitchen sink," she located herself in the kitchen at what was left of a window. "I want to look out and imagine that I'm looking through the eyes of the writer of the journal, or Francine, or maybe even Bonnie. Do you think Bonnie ever lived here?"

"Chances are she might have."

"If she did, she would have looked right out of this very window, too. It's so quiet out there."

ঌঌঌঌঌ

1943

She stood at the sink, her hands submerged in water, but her eyes looking out the window at a world that was motionless. There wasn't a blade of grass bending to the wind, not a cloud in the sky, not a bird or even a cricket moving. It was as though time had stopped and was standing perfectly still. At least, there in the world outside.

Bonnie's mind was in the middle of a windstorm of thoughts. She could go from one thought or image quicker than she could blink. The idea of him coming back was like a fierce wind that could instantly take her breath away. Memories of Kenny's violence were like all the debris that's carried with the wind during a terrible storm. What was it her grandfather use to tell her? It wasn't the wind in itself that killed you, it was all the fence posts and shingles and jagged tree branches and tin sheets of roofing that was suddenly spinning ninety miles an hour! Once she found a simple knitting needle completely embedded in the trunk of a tree.

Bonnie took a long, deep breath. No movement out there. As she looked at the table and saw a glass to wash, she watched her hand as though it didn't particularly belong to her. And as her fingers clutched it, she felt an identical pressure on her lungs. The tighter she held the glass, the tighter her lungs felt and it was hard to breathe. Bonnie recognized it as weariness and sorrow. Her eyes began to burn—absent of tears even though her heart demanded that they be shed. It helped just to squeeze her eyes shut and then to slowly open them, first, looking through lashes and then squinting.

No movement out there. Her fingertips were starting to shrivel and she became aware of the length of time she had been standing in one spot with her hands in water. Yet, it didn't matter. There wasn't anything else to do anyway. With a sigh she dipped the soapy glass in the rinse water. To be sure it was clean, she held it up to the light. A small substance was stuck on the inside. Reaching down into the glass she tried to scrape it with her fingernail. It wouldn't budge.

Now, her concentration was on the glass and whatever it was that was stuck there. Oatmeal? Caked sugar of some sort? She couldn't imagine what it was. But if Kenny saw it, he would smash the glass and then hit her and scream into her face how worthless she was. Scraping harder, the glass suddenly shattered in her hands. A number of jagged pieces fell into the soapy water. Very carefully, she felt for them and stacked them in her hand. The last piece came out of red, soapy water.

Bonnie was suddenly horrified that she had cut herself. Past experience made her take the stopper out of the sink immediately. If Kenny saw the blood in the water he would make her wash every single dish and pot and pan in the house. Even if she hadn't used the utensil in a week. He would reprimand her 'if you did it one time you probably did it twenty times and I'm not eatin' off no bloody dishes!' The water grew redder and redder. As the last bit drained, she saw a solid, red stream flowing from her hand.

Now what? It didn't hurt until she looked at it. And then she saw the deep gash between her thumb and finger. As though she was looking at a piece of chicken meat she lifted the flap and saw the meat and muscle of her own hand. Nothing to do but sew it closed. It was too deep just to put a bandage on it.

Without blinking, she scanned the room and saw her medicine kit. Using the tie string from her apron, she made a tourniquet of a sort to try and stop the bleeding. Then she found the candy-cane shaped vial that held the curved surgical needle and cat gut. Snapping the top off she wrinkled her nose at the smell of formaldehyde. Thank goodness it was her left hand that was cut. As though she were sewing on a quilt she pushed the needle through the flap of skin and then into the flesh. She wasn't sure if it was numb or if she just didn't care. Either way, there wasn't any more pain than if a honeybee had stung her. When she knotted the suture and cut it off, she tore off a strip of her petticoat and wrapped it around her hand to keep everything in place. Then she went back to the sink and cleaned it out.

Going outside, she picked up the spade and dug a small hole and buried the glass. It was hers anyway and she could drink from her coffee cup. Maybe one day she could sell enough eggs to buy another glass. Until then, she had to try and keep Kenny from noticing it was gone.

Still, no movement out there. She let her bare toes push the dirt and clump of grass back into place. He'd never notice. The sun was hot, but it felt good. She remembered how she would try to look at the sun when she was a child. Uncle Ronald told her once it was a ball of fire and if she looked too long it would burn her eyes out. He said he saw a mailman once who looked directly into the sun too long and his eyes were like two boiled eggs. Most horrible thing he ever saw!

For days after that she'd close her eyes and pretend to be blind. But she couldn't keep them closed for very long. It was awful not to be able to see. After that she kept her eyes down and just enjoyed the warmth. Now, she wondered if there was any truth to the old story. She wasn't sure what to believe any more—or even whom!

Kenny told her once he loved her. But that was after he beat her so bad she couldn't move for two days. That wasn't love, and his words were far from the truth. Yet, it wasn't hate either. It was more like a sickness and she felt sorry for him. Like her third baby, Collin, who had fits and thrashed about the floor. He couldn't help it and he really didn't know what he was doing. It took the boy about two days to recover after one of those spells. He hadn't been a threat to anyone and he only did the hurt to himself. She still loved her baby even though she hadn't seen him for a long time.

When Kenny saw the thrashing and drooling he said it was from the devil and she had a choice. He'd either beat the boy until he got the devil out of him or she could give him away. Kenny didn't believe in selling children, but he wouldn't keep them if there were any problems. She said she'd handle the matter and with all of little Collin's belongings she traveled for two days on foot and left him at the parsonage. It was hard to explain his condition and why she had to give him up. How long had it been since she'd seen him? One year? Two? She tried not to think about it because there were times she missed him dreadfully. But she knew that he'd be well taken care of. She had chosen a preacher and his wife because the poor woman loved children but was just as barren as Esther or Elizabeth, in the Holy Bible.

Bonnie looked down at her front and put her hand across her abdomen. It would have been better if she had been barren. She had given birth to five babies but hadn't been able to keep any of them! The first time she had only been fourteen and Kenny said a baby was too much trouble and he didn't want it around. In fact, he didn't want any children! He said he knew of a way to kill the baby before it was even born but she wouldn't allow that. The only way she was allowed to complete the pregnancy was by making a promise that as soon as it was born she'd give it away. It made no matter to him if it was a boy or girl. He tried to forbid her to give the child a name; she did anyway. He figured if the child didn't have a name, then it wasn't really a human being, but a thing. Kenny said there was no sense in her getting attached to the baby because it would never live in their home. He swore that one day she'd thank him, but that day hadn't come yet.

Bonnie had been frantic the last three months of her first pregnancy. Who would take her baby? And then she had an idea and pursued it. Just as Judith Ann had taken care of her, Bonnie persuaded her aunt to agree to take care of little Lucy Thomasina Parker. If Kenny didn't want to be a father, then her child wouldn't carry his name. Bonnie was going to make sure of that!

Giving birth to Lucy on a Thursday, Kenny demanded that she return on Sunday and resume all duties as a wife. Bonnie had less than three full days to cradle her first child. Judith Ann was livid about the arrangement and had begged Bonnie to leave Kenny.

"You can't allow a man to dictate your life like that; it just isn't right. That beautiful, little girl needs her own mother."

Bonnie knew she didn't have a choice so she tried to make it sound better. "Kenny says we'll take her back when she's older. He just doesn't do well with babies. And I don't know nothin' about them either."

Judith Ann was frowning. "There hasn't been one mother throughout the course of history that has gotten proper directions on takin' care of their child. It's just somethin' you learn as you go 'cause each young'n is different."

"But Kenny says I'm a child myself that needs takin' care of. He can't handle two of us. Please, Aunt Judith, for the sake of the baby, raise her for just a spell." Bonnie was in tears.

Judith Ann consented but wasn't very happy about it. Three months after Lucy was born, Bonnie was pregnant again. This time it made Kenny mad. The second after she told him he back handed her and called her stupid. Then he kicked her in the stomach. Throughout her pregnancy he constantly told her how ugly she was and that it was all her fault she had gotten pregnant again. From that time on he was always hitting or kicking her or causing her to fall. She tried to stay away from him as much as she could.

Bonnie made two trips to see Lucy but Kenny accused her of having an affair with another man so when the baby was born he refused to believe it was his. After that he forbid her to ever go to Judith Ann's again. In her ninth month he had taken her to a convent and paid the nuns to take care of her. Bonnie wasn't sure what other arrangements had been made but when she gave birth, she was told that she had a girl. Those in attendance wouldn't allow her to actually hold the child, but Bonnie did turn her head so that she could see the little shape of the infant. The baby had black hair and reminded her so much of Lucy!

"Her name will be Bernadette Marie Parker." Bonnie begged to touch her but was denied.

The nun told her to rest, that she was losing a lot of blood. When she woke up she asked about the baby and the nun sadly told her that the child had never taken a breath. Then she explained that they had baptized her and buried her, thinking it best that Bonnie never see her. But something in Bonnie's heart told her that Bernadette was alive and would probably be adopted. She went along with the death idea but every chance she had she said sternly "you be sure to call that child by the name I gave her! It's the least you can do." Once when she started roaming the corridors of the massive convent, she heard the cry of a newborn and was convinced that Bernadette was still alive. Early one morning she told one of the sisters that she had heard a child crying in the night. The sister denied the possibility and told her that she had only been dreaming. Bonnie pretended to sleep a lot so they would leave her alone. They did everything by a schedule and it was easy to determine the pattern of their comings and goings. While they were at mass, Bonnie would sneak out of her room. It didn't take her long to follow the cry and stand behind the locked doors that separated her and her child. She knew she was only torturing herself, but she wanted to memorize that cry so when she left the convent she would still be able to hear it.

On the fifth day she was weak from sorrow and didn't have the energy to walk the corridors. Kenny had left her at the door of the convent while she was in labor, and he returned on the sixth day.

"I need you at the house." He started putting her clothes in a bag. "I got about eight bushels of peas for you to shell and I'm hungry."

He never asked about the baby or even how she was. Bonnie went home feeling completely empty. It was the first time that she had entertained the idea of truly hating her husband.

Then, at sixteen years old, she found herself pregnant with her third child. This time she begged Kenny to let her keep it. She was older and wiser and not a child anymore. To her surprise, he agreed. The child's given name was Kenneth Collin. Bonnie had hoped that her husband might accept him since it was his firstborn son. But Kenny was offended that she talked more to the baby than to him so he made her call him Collin. Often times Kenny would come in and demand that she put the baby down and meet his needs. Then he referred to the child as 'the dupe'. Even though he was verbally hateful to the child, he never laid a hand on him. She truly believed Kenny would eventually accept the boy until she discovered that after Collin's third birthday there could be no denial that he was epileptic. Collin had been the love of her life. He had burly blond hair and huge, brown eyes that held incredible tenderness. Oh, the fit that Kenny had thrown when he saw the child had blond hair! He called him a freak of nature!

Nothing had been easy then. Bonnie was devastated when she found herself pregnant again when Collin wasn't even five months old! Kenny told her that one child was enough. If she wanted to keep the boy, then she had to give up this new baby.

Every time she had to make a choice, Bonnie died inside. She was tired of fighting so she went through the nine months no longer caring. In her seventh month she had found a young couple that wanted to take the child. Arnold Alexander was placed in the woman's arms an hour after he was born and Bonnie never saw him again.

She was consoled only by the fact that she had Collin. Knowing that he was prone to seizures she was especially guarded and protective of him. She use to pray constantly that Kenny wouldn't be home when the boy had a spell. It had only taken one time of seeing the boy roll on the floor, out of control, for Kenny to make up his mind that he wasn't going to live in the same house with a possessed child. Collin had to go! That's when Bonnie took him to Brother Bill's house.

When Bonnie found herself pregnant for the fifth time, and still no child in her arms, she tried to keep it secret for as long as she could. She even debated about leaving Kenny before he found out. In a moment of desperation she started packing her bags. She didn't have any idea where she'd go, but she knew she wanted to keep this child!

Kenny walked in on her just as she opened the front door to go out. He took one look at the suitcase and shoved her back inside. It was a wonder that he hadn't killed her then. As it was, she was in bed for two days hardly able to move. She was surprised that she hadn't lost the baby but she had protected her bulging abdomen the best she could. Then she refused to talk to him. Days went by without a word.

When Kenny demanded an explanation she screamed almost hysterically. "Don't you understand? I'm pregnant again and I want this baby!

This is my child and I want to raise it! Otherwise, I have nothing to say to you."

"Again?" he yelled back. "When will you stop having babies? Haven't you figured it out yet? I hate kids! As long as you're my wife there will be no children in our home! I should have never let you keep that little, demon possessed freak as long as you did! But I tried to be a good husband. I went out of my way so you could get this mothering thing out of your system! Well, I'm sick and tired of it! I took you as my wife, not some kid's mammy."

They argued for a long time but in the long run she thought she had won. Since she didn't have Collin anymore, she desperately wanted to keep this child. Just one. That's all she asked for. Kenny finally consented but his words seemed to be in defiance of his actions. Bonnie felt as though he was plotting something and she lived in continual fear.

On January 1, Patricia Catherine was born. Bonnie had no way of knowing what the new year would bring. But she was thankful for each day that the child was in her arms. Kenny didn't show any emotion one way or the other. He refused to acknowledge that Patricia had even been born. In fact, he expected Bonnie to do her daily chores and whatever else he asked of her.

"If you can't, then we'll have to get rid of the obstacle in your way, won't we?" he glared at her.

Six weeks went by and she considered every moment precious, but she never trusted him. Kenny was always looking for an excuse to get rid of the baby. Fortunately, Patricia seldom cried and wasn't demanding. Her disposition was almost too good. There were times that Bonnie wondered why she was so quiet, but she counted it as a blessing and went about her business. Patricia Catherine never got in Kenny's way so she was allowed to remain in the house.

Almost a year had passed. It was a horrible night. Thunder crashed and lightening split the sky so fierce that Bonnie was afraid a tree would be hit and catch on fire. The livestock were restless and at one time the rain was so hard that Bonnie would have sworn that a herd of cattle was stampeding over the roof! Kenny had crossed from the cabin to the barn and had nearly been knocked off his feet. He hadn't been more than four yards away from her and the rain had engulfed him from her sight! She had never in her life seen such a raging storm! Water was leaking everywhere and she had buckets and pans all through the cabin, trying to keep ahead of the flood!

Patricia was sitting on the floor in front of the fireplace as though nothing was going on around her. "Hey, baby girl," Bonnie cooed to her, smiling at the contented child. Patricia didn't look up or acknowledge that she had been spoken to.

"Patricia?" Bonnie went behind her and clapped her hands, hard. The baby reached across the floor and picked up a spoon she had been playing with. Then it dawned on Bonnie what the problem was. Her baby was deaf. Was this a curse or a blessing? Her silence and quiet way had kept Kenny away, but once he found out, what would he do?

Bonnie could hear his words, "I ain't livin' with no child that won't answer me when I talk to 'em."

Once again, she knew that the days were numbered. There was no way she could prevent Kenny from finding out that the child could not hear. No matter how much her heart protested she knew what the outcome would be. But who would want to adopt a deaf child? Bonnie found herself trying to think of a substitute mother. As she watched her precious child, the years of sorrow suddenly hardened her and a force of defiance created a parting between her and Kenny, just as surely as a fierce earthquake splits the ground. No! This time she wasn't going to do it! Never again would she give up her child. She'd leave Kenny before she left her child in another woman's arms.

Even though she had her mind made up, she lost complete control of the situation. Bonnie had just put Patricia to bed when she started shivering and aching all over. Knowing that she was getting sick, she did everything she could to prevent herself from getting worse. First, she drank broom tea with a teaspoonful of cream of tartar for her bowels. Bonnie figured if she could flush the sickness out of her body she'd be okay. By morning she was into a full sweat but still shivering. Kenny was disgusted with her inability to fix him breakfast and knocked her across the room as he stormed out. When she tried to get up, she found herself completely unsteady. Her knees buckled and she fell back down, knocking a potted plant over and spilling the dirt everywhere.

She had never felt like this before and had no idea what was wrong. It was all she could do to drag herself to a chair so she could use it for support to get up. Hanging on to the furniture she made her way across the room and assured herself that Patricia was okay. Then she collapsed on the bed. Bonnie didn't get any better. She heard Kenny come in and immediately go into a tirade about the mess she had made and never cleaned up.

Her heart nearly stopped! She tried to raise her head but was so dizzy she fell back down. He came in the room and tried to force her to get up but she couldn't do it. Finally, he just shoved her back onto the bed and stormed out, ranting and raving that he wasn't going to stick around. He cursed her as he told her he'd go get the doctor.

Hours must have gone by. At last she heard voices in the room. The doctor came in and Bonnie was relieved that Kenny had actually realized it was serious enough that she needed help. She was surprised he just hadn't let her lay there and die. The doctor examined her and told Kenny that she had dropsy, that seemed to be leading to Bright's Disease. The symptoms were all there; chills, convulsions, fever and albumin in the urine. Then he asked all kinds of questions; had she been exposed to wet and cold, scarlet fever, pneumonia or pregnancy.

"She stays pregnant half the time," Kenny complained as he made up his mind that the only thing wrong with her was that she was weakened from always being pregnant.

The doctor gave his prescription. "What you'll need to do is help her sweat it out. And then take salt for the bowels. If she'll stay covered up she'll be fine."

Kenny didn't like the idea of being a nursemaid. "I don't mind bringing her food but you're expecting me to come in from the fields and put corn towels on her, too? That's gonna take a lot of time, Doc. Can't the body just heal itself? It always has before."

The doctor knew Kenny well and felt compassion for his patient. He gave a stern look, "Not in this case. She'd never be able to take care of herself or the baby. She needs constant care."

Those were the last words Bonnie heard the doctor say before he walked out of the room with Kenny. The room was spinning again and she couldn't fight it. She knew Kenny wouldn't take the time to boil all the corn and wrap the cobs in towels. Corn sweats were good, in fact, most of the time she preferred that over the mustard plaster. It was too easy to blister the skin if the mustard was too strong or stayed on the skin too long. She remembered Kenny talking about an old man who blamed pneumonia on cold feet. He left the mustard plaster on his feet too long and the flesh peeled off like the skin on a new boiled potato. He couldn't walk for almost two weeks he was in so much pain! She was so sick she fell back asleep even though she had desperately tried to stay awake.

It was dark when Kenny came back in. He tried to get her to eat some soup but she couldn't. She was vaguely aware that morning came but she still slept. Each time she stirred enough to know she was awake she listened for Patricia but didn't hear anything. Thinking that only a few hours at the most had passed, she was thankful the child was sleeping so peacefully, and then she closed her own eyes again.

It was starting to get dark again. Kenny came in with something for her to drink.

"How's Patricia?" Bonnie asked.

"She's just fine."

"Did you feed her? I'm sure she's hungry by now."

His voice was harsh, "I just told you she was fine. Now drink this so you'll get better."

Bonnie sipped it and found it to have a horrible taste so she asked what it was. Kenny said it was medicine and forced her to continue sipping it.

"How'd you get it?" She was almost too weak to even talk. "Did the doctor come back?"

"No, I haven't seen hide nor hair from him. We're really fortunate, you know, to get this stuff. That quack doctor thinks he knows everything, but I'll tell you who knows everything there is to know and that's the Injuns. Old Little Claw was in town, and I was smart enough to go to him. He told me this would cure you. It's a remedy that works for his family so I don't know why it won't work for you, too."

Bonnie took as much of it as she possibly could and then she laid back. "I'm so tired," she mumbled.

Kenny covered her again and left the room. Two more times he came in with the bitter drink. Even though she was feeling closer to death than she did to life, she knew the concoction was working. She was somewhat aware of him coming to bed and then getting back up. She woke up once, thinking she had heard Patricia cry out, but then she wasn't sure if it had been reality or just a dream. If she wasn't crying, that meant Kenny was taking care of her. Maybe he had a change of heart. She was such a good child!

Four days had passed before Bonnie could actually make sense of time. The sun was shining in the window and she tried to sit up. Kenny came through the door.

"Well, at least you're acting like you're alive this morning. It's about time. I knew that old Indian medicine would work."

"I feel a little better, at least I don't ache to the core. What in the world happened to me?"

"Darned near died, I can tell you that. I was fixin' to start plotting out a burial place for ya and whittle some epitaph." He smiled, letting her know he was just teasing.

Bonnie was glad he was in a good mood. "I want to see Patricia; is she still asleep?"

"How should I know?" He answered as though she was stupid to be asking.

"What does that mean?" Bonnie was instantly alert! "Where's my baby, Kenny?"

"She's being taken care of."

"By who? Who's got Patricia?"

"I don't know her name but she lives with Little Claw and his family."

"The Indians have her?"

"Now I guess they would if they're taking care of her. That does make sense now, don't it? Surely you got your faculties enough to figure that out."

Bonnie was horror-stricken. "You gave my daughter to the Indians?"

Kenny was indignant. "Well, what was I supposed to do? You couldn't take care of yourself let alone that squalling kid. And I'm not havin' nothin' to do with her, you know that! Seemed like a good trade to me; your health for the kid. When Little Claw brought the medicine he had this squaw with him and she was more than glad to take the baby. You ought to be thanking me, you know? I would have let the little nuisance lay in her own filth and starve to death. I don't care! At least someone is taking care of her since you shirked your duties."

"I've been sick, Kenny, I wasn't avoiding my duties, you know that."

"Well, why did you get sick to begin with? You weren't taking care of yourself, were you? At least I was here for you! If I hadn't been here you would have died and you know it! You should be mighty grateful to me instead of fussing about something you don't have."

Bonnie leaned back on the bed. "I am thankful for you Kenny. At least the baby is being fed and she's safe. As soon as I'm strong enough I'll go get her. Where have they made camp?"

"I have no idea. They just pass through here a couple times a year; I don't keep track of them."

The reality of what he said terrified her. "If they were just passing through then how will I ever find Patricia?"

Kenny shrugged. "Do you think I care? If they came by once I'm sure they'll come back again. What's the big deal? Now that you're awake you can start fixin' my meals again. I'm tired of having to cook for myself."

Perhaps it was the anger more than the medicine that got Bonnie back up on her feet. Even though she did everything she knew to do, she never found out where the tribe was. The answer was always the same, 'they're out on the plains by now. Probably see them sometime next year." Once again she resolved herself to the fact that her child was gone. Memories were so painful! She shook her head, coming back to the present.

Bonnie continued to look out the kitchen window. She was almost twenty-three, which meant her first child, Lucy, would be almost nine years old. Was Collin going to school now? Oh, how her heart ached!

After the sickness she had gotten pregnant two more times, but she didn't carry either one more than four months. She never told Kenny of their existence or their demise. Something must have happened to her to cease child bearing. Either Kenny had permanently damaged her insides or God's mercy had drawn the line to suffering! In all truth, it was better they hadn't lived. It didn't seem like she could have a perfectly, healthy and normal child so no telling where they'd end up. Bonnie couldn't bear to give away another child! It just wasn't right! She was determined in her heart never to be cheated again. But what could she do? The time in her life had come that something had to change!

Kenny was still as mean as ever. If she hadn't been afraid of him, she would have left him a long time ago. But she didn't know where to go or what to do. She had been taught that a godly woman never left her man. That would be sin. She had thought about not being a godly woman but that scared her more than Kenny did! If God wasn't for her, then He'd be against her and the Holy Bible said it was a fearful thing to get God mad at you.

If anyone was ungodly, though, it was Kenny! She hadn't known that when she married him. They had their ceremony under a huge tree and she had been so happy that day. All her life she had been pushed to the side. She felt abandoned because her own mother had chosen a wild life in some New Orleans theater instead of being a mother to her.

Kenny had seemed like an answer to her lonely prayers. Judith Ann had always taken her to church. She'd been dressed up in her finest and Kenny had been attracted to her from the start. They had spent endless hours together and he had been loving and complimentary. He liked the wealth of the household, especially Uncle Ronnie's boat! Judith Ann accused Kenny of just wanting to marry into the money and that Bonnie was too young to realize it. Then Judith Ann came down with polio and all of life changed! They had to move to another town that had a hospital with equipment to treat polio. Kenny and Bonnie had to move out on their own. Kenny agreed to live in the cabin. There was good money in potatoes and he knew he could be a successful farmer. He wanted to be on his own anyway.

Now, Bonnie felt so defeated! Her mother didn't love her, her husband didn't love her, and she had been forced to give away all of her children. Now, as she stared out at the nothingness, she wondered what life was really all about; was it meant to be this cruel? There wasn't a day to go by that she didn't pray for Lucy, Bernadette, Collin, Arnold and Patricia. Her loneliness was intense. She sighed. Had God deserted her? Was He even there? For just a sick moment her stomach tightened into a knot as she thought of that possibility.

Maybe Judith Ann was wrong about God. If she had been a good, church-going woman, why did she come down with polio? Had she committed some terrible sin? Other people lived just fine and they didn't particularly believe in God. If Bonnie hadn't been afraid of God's wrath she probably would have kept her first baby and left Kenny. If she had stayed, and he continued to beat her, she probably would have killed him. There had been plenty of times she had prayed for his death! But then she felt guilty and felt as though God was punishing her for not appreciating the things she did have!

Bonnie was surprised to find that tears were rolling down her cheeks. She honestly didn't think she had any more left. But why was she crying this time? Was it because she was realizing just how cruel life was and how unfair she had been treated? Or was it because she was trying to convince herself that God didn't exist? Without Him she wouldn't have made it this far. She was a mother to five children, hopefully still alive, and the keeper of two memories that never took their first breath. She was a good person and she would have been a good mother to all of them! Suddenly it hit her; the problem was not in her but in Kenny! He was the one who had forced her to give her children away. The Holy Bible taught that the wife should be submissive to her husband and she had faithfully done that! So she knew in her heart that God wasn't punishing her for disobeying Him or anyone else.

Looking down at her body, she lifted her skirt to scratch her ankle a moment. As she did, her fingers felt an ugly scar and her thoughts went back to the time when the old sow attacked her. Bonnie hadn't been aware that the sow had given birth and she had boldly walked into the pen. The pig attacked, protecting its newborn. As she rubbed the itch and the scar, her eyes looked up into the sky. "Why can't you protect me like that, God? If you can save Daniel from the lions can't you save me from the beast that my husband has become?"

She found herself opening and closing her fingers as though she was desperate to have the touch of her children, and then she broke. Crumpling to the floor she sobbed, not caring if Kenny came home or not! Maybe he would call her insane and do away with her, too. She had always been so strong. A new thought suddenly filled her mind. She was still strong! Incredibly strong! If no one else would defend her, she would scream and rant and rave and shake her fist and defend herself! If Kenny hit her, she'd hit him back! If he told her 'no', she'd scream 'yes'! She'd act like a mad woman if she had to instead of being a shriveling, submissive coward! From this moment on, absolutely no one was going to bully her.

The more she thought about it, the more she felt her strength returning. If an old sow could defend her sucklings, then Bonnie was going to attack anyone she had to in order to defend what belonged to her! If it was sin, then she'd just have to be guilty of it. And if God condemned her and struck her dead, it couldn't be any worse than the hell she was already living in! Her mind was made up, she was going to get her children back! Just the thought of it gave her incredible strength. For the first time…it didn't feel wrong.

Bonnie got up off the floor and went to the front door and looked out. Where did she start? If she openly defied Kenny she knew that he'd react in violence and if she was injured again, it would only slow her down. She wasn't any good to her children if she was nursing wounds or couldn't walk. If she tried to fake her death or just disappear in some way, he would find her. Her eyes immediately went to the bed frame where the old chains still hung. Even though she was terrified of them, Kenny laughed as he made up stories of who he'd chain to the bed. There was always a gleam in his eye when he threatened that it could be her one day if she didn't continue to obey him! Bonnie knew that she didn't want to be treated like a captive.

And then the idea took root; she was going to act as though she had lost her mind! If she was good enough at convincing him, he would send her off just like he had the children. He'd find someone to take care of her. But, who or where? If he took her to the convent the nuns would be upset when they learned that she had deliberately deceived him! She'd be condemned to do penance the rest of her life! Which was worse, her body chained to the bed or her soul chained to a confessional?

Bonnie knew she had to be extremely sane in order to play the part of the insane! It had to be calculated and manipulative and yet beneficial. She had to be in control at all times so she could lure Kenny's thoughts down the path of her own. It would be constantly outguessing him and thinking before he could! She couldn't afford to be wrong or to even let him become suspicious of what she was doing.

She smiled as her mind raced through one scenario after another. Could she do it? Her memory almost materialized two little girls with black hair, a tender blond-headed child that had seizures, another boy that had a shape but no features, and then her precious deaf child. Being with her children and having them in her arms again was the only motivation she needed to do whatever she had to do!

When Kenny came riding up to the house she was ready for him! Four hours ago she was dreading his return; now she couldn't wait! She was wearing an old, brown sweater even though it must have been eighty degrees out. Right before he came into the house she pulled some pins from her hair and shook her head so that strands of hair were loose and falling haphazardly. Then she went to the kitchen to start cooking.

"I'm hungry, woman." Kenny burst through the door. "What have you been doing all day?"

"Just working," she greeted him, as usual.

"You look a mess. What's the sweater for? You getting sick again?"

"No, I just felt like wearing it. I'll take it off if you want me to."

"Then take it off. It's stupid to be wearing a sweater in a hot house. Hurry up and get my supper on the table. I'm going to go clean up."

He headed towards the bathroom and she watched him as she prayed "if you're watching, too, God, don't hold this against my account. I just want my babies back. And you can help me if'n you want to. I don't intend no one to get hurt." She ended with the thought, "Especially me!" Bonnie knew she couldn't make this change too fast. Kenny would have to figure it out over a period of time.

In the next three months Bonnie continually plotted each move. She might misbutton her blouse or wear two different socks. She put the coffeepot on the stove but failed to light the burner. She was constantly misplacing something and would have to ask Kenny if he had seen it. If they were having a conversation she would change the subject to something totally bizarre. She let him see her mind drift off until he almost had to yell at her to get her to listen to him. And then she started carrying a doll around and pretending that it was her baby. That seemed to distress him the most! He broke it and threw it outside. As soon as he left she retrieved it, singing to it and cuddling it even more.

"Mommy's little baby; don't you cry," she soothed the broken doll.

Then she quit talking to Kenny. She smiled at him constantly but didn't say a word. Eventually she began swaying and rocking herself and humming. Bonnie knew that was getting to him! At first he was angry with her, but then he started ignoring her, which made things even easier! She didn't want to go overboard so there were times when she'd have an intelligent conversation with him. One day he came in and she deliberately threw a temper tantrum and then as he stood and stared at her, she stopped abruptly and pushed out her lip in an exaggerated pout.

"I wanted some ice cream and we don't have any. Can you get me some?" she pleaded.

"Woman, you're crazy! We ain't got no ice cream here or anywhere close to here."

"But we just made some yesterday."

He turned around and went back outside. It was all she could do to keep from laughing. He was spending less and less time in the house with her. She knew better than to do anything else when he came back in. He was already agitated enough and would quickly reach his point of endurance.

It was fortunate for her that she didn't add to the insanity plot because Kenny stayed out in the barn for over an hour, drinking heavily. When he came inside he was carrying an ax.

"You gonna chop wood this late in the evening?" she innocently asked.

"I'm fixing to chop your head off if you make me mad. I ain't puttin' up with no crazy woman tonight!"

Her hand immediately flew to her open mouth as she staggered backwards. Bonnie didn't have to ask him if he was serious or not! She had never thought Kenny capable of murder but the look in his eyes warned her that he was a dangerous man and meant business.

"I'm not gonna make you mad, Kenny." She finally managed to make a complete sentence. But then she faked a smile. "But I got supper if you're hungry."

"Of course I'm hungry, you stupid idiot!" The alcohol was talking more than he was and she nodded her head as though he had spoken kindly to her and she was thrilled to please him.

The good Lord must have been on her side because she had known to have a good meal prepared. She quietly breathed a prayer of thanksgiving as she went to the stove and dished up chicken and dumplings. It had always been a rule of his that she had to sit down and eat with him, but she wasn't allowed to say anything until he finished. The only time she could talk was to answer a question.

After several mouthfuls of which he was still chewing on, he asked her "What's with you Bonnie? You sure have been acting strange lately."

"I get headaches real often," she spoke softly.

"Maybe you're getting a brain tumor or something. I swear there's times you act plumb crazy on me. I won't tolerate that! You know that, don't you?"

She wiped her mouth and looked down at her plate, her hands in her lap. "I suppose not. I know that you wouldn't tolerate nothing wrong with the babies. I try to be a good wife to you, Kenny."

"Most of the time you're a sorry wife but I ain't gonna live alone and you know that. But neither will I live every day of my life with someone touched in the head!" Suddenly his eyes burned into hers. "I'll kill you first, Bonnie, you can mark my word on that."

She chewed on a fingernail. "Wouldn't that be like killing a mockingbird?"

"Maybe so." He continued to eat in silence. Then he demanded another helping and another cup of coffee. He cursed her. "Why are you always so slow about everything you do? You use to didn't be that way!"

"I'm sorry, Kenny, I'm tryin' hard not to make you mad." Her hands were actually trembling and she almost spilled his coffee as she set the cup down.

For a moment she was terror stricken. The ax was at his feet and she knew he could grab it and swing before she could even defend herself. Would he really kill her? Even when he forced her to get rid of the babies he had never threatened to actually kill them. At least, not once they were born. So, why the threat on her life? She had to believe that he knew he was losing control and at that moment was too drunk to be rational. From then on, she had to constantly watch over her shoulder.

A week later she added another phase to her plan. She knew that he would be around the barn and working in the yard so she told him that she was going to walk down to the river and see if the patch of raspberries was ripe.

"Just don't fall in the river. If you do I'll let you drown and I won't pull your sorry body out of the river. You can become fish food for all I care."

"Raspberries don't grow in the water," she commented, then took a deep breath and blew it out slowly, shrugged and walked off with a bucket in hand. Bonnie knew she was pushing it but Kenny was sober and she had to see how far she could go.

She took her time in gathering the berries so if Kenny was watching her he'd see that she wasn't doing anything stupid; she was just incredibly slow. When the bucket was almost full, she started humming and then squatted down and watched the river current for awhile. Sitting would have been more ladylike and far more comfortable, but she merely squatted until her knees hurt so bad she was forced to stand back up. Then she swung the bucket a little and looked around as though she wasn't sure which direction to go. With a childlike smile she spun in a circle, her head back as she watched the clouds spin with her. After that she started walking in the wrong direction. As she suspected, Kenny was in the distance, watching her. His eyes were squinted in a fierce frown as he shook his head.

"That does it," he mumbled.

When he was drunk he thought about killing her with the ax and had already figured out where to bury her so no one would ever find her body, but now that he was sober, he thought better of it. He refused to live the rest of his life with her blood on his hands, but neither did he want to put up with her foolishness. He knew he couldn't survive on his own cooking, and he refused to go to bed alone. Men had to have a woman in the bed.

Leaving her, he went into Gough's Ridge with the sole purpose of finding him another woman. He headed to the new drinking establishment called Foxie's. The owner of the place was a fiery, red headed woman who loved to laugh. She was always out to have a good time and she didn't care who she had that good time with. Kenny wanted someone who would only have eyes for him. It hadn't been long before he drew the attention of a young, slender girl with bobbed, brown hair. Her eyes sparkled and though he thought she was a little too skinny, she acted as though she sure liked him. He bought her a drink and they laughed and had a good time. When they danced she didn't mind where he put his hands as long as he held her real close.

"A man like you should have a good woman lookin' after him," she whispered in his ear.

That's when he put on a pitiful act, whimpering that his wife was crazy and that he was so despondent he didn't know what to do! The girl's reaction was more than Kenny had ever hoped for! She immediately fell upon him and cradled his head and tried to comfort him. Becoming his advocate she generated so much concern that the bartender gave him a free drink. Kenny played it up! Before he left that night he and the girl had already decided to start meeting so she could help soothe his fretful state.

The next day he was coming out of the barn when he saw Bonnie leaving the garden. She wasn't coming back to the house and he wondered where she was headed. It didn't take him long to justify his choice in getting serious about someone else taking care of him. He rubbed his chin and gave a little 'humph', realizing that he had forgotten the girl's name. It could have been Charmaine or Marlene, he had no idea! As long as she could cook and clean and keep him satisfied he really didn't care. He'd call her Honey or Darlin' or something like that and she'd never know the difference.

Kenny went on to the house to get some water. If Bonnie wandered off and got lost, that would be her problem! It would make his tale even sadder if he could tell everyone that his beloved wife had wandered off and got herself lost and he was spending all kinds of money and energy on trying to get her back. If she was really lost, maybe he could even get a search party going or post a reward.

He spit on the ground. No, forget the reward. If there was any kind of money involved, he'd pay to make sure she stayed lost! He wasn't about to pay someone to find her and only add to his misery!

Kenny was sitting on a kitchen chair, lighting his third cigarette, as though he had been waiting for her.

"I got a whole bucket of berries," she smiled. "How about a cobbler for supper tonight?"

"Suit yourself, I'm going to Gough's Ridge. Do you even know how long you've been gone?"

"I don't think so. Was I gone too long?" she questioned. "I was kind of surprised to see the sun set so early."

"You fool, the sun don't set early, you're just late!"

"I am? I'm sorry, Kenny, I ah…" she looked down at the floor. "I guess I wandered off too far and ah, had a, ah, hard time gettin' back."

Then she looked at him with a gleam in her eyes. "But I didn't go to the river and drown myself. You told me not to do that."

He moaned and rubbed his jaw, then got up abruptly and went in the bedroom.

She called out to him, "I promise I won't do it again! I know that makes you mad and I swear I'll never leave the house again if you don't want me to."

She tensed up, expecting him to charge at her in fury or to start hitting or calling her names. His response totally took her by surprise. He came out swiftly but brushed right past her.

"You go ahead and leave the house all you want to, that's fine with me. I ain't sticking around here for you to fix supper. Cook for yourself but don't burn the house down." He didn't even look at her as he bolted out the door and headed to the barn for his horse.

Bonnie sank down in a chair. "Oh, my," she licked her lips and then rubbed her eye. "This is good."

She smiled, complimenting herself. No cuts, no bruises, no threats to kill her! He might get drunk in town but she'd be in bed by the time he got home and he never messed with her once she had the lights out. Even though she was taking the risk of making him mad, she had started sleeping with the broken doll. When he realized what she was doing he refused to share his bed with her anymore. Bonnie looked around the room and almost started to laugh. Life wasn't so bad after all! She had the rest of the evening to herself and she didn't have to be afraid. The raspberry cobbler would melt in her mouth and she didn't even have to share it!

When she woke up the next morning she soon discovered that Kenny hadn't come home during the night. That meant one of two things. He was either dead or he was with another woman. Even though she had only herself to blame for his unfaithfulness, it still left a knot in the pit of her stomach. As she stood in front of the mirror she scolded herself with condemnation, 'It's all your fault; you drove him away.' Her reflection promptly scolded right back with a backbone of determination, 'He has his life to lead, you have yours!'

The image in front of her wasn't a whiny coward any longer! There was no way she was going to back out now.

Setting her mind to the fact that Kenny was no longer hers, she detached herself so she could concentrate on the children that were hers! She went about cleaning and doing her chores and then she heard voices just as she was about to leave the hen house: Kenny's and a woman's. They obviously thought she was in the house. Bonnie pulled the door shut a bit as she stood inside the chicken coop.

"You sure this is right?" The girl was asking Kenny. She couldn't have been more than eighteen years old!

"You said you wanted to see her. I'm telling you the truth, by tomorrow she won't even remember that you were here. The woman is getting crazier by the day. She'll believe anything we tell her."

"Well, all right then."

Bonnie leaned against the wall with a grin on her face that she couldn't wipe off! Deciding to give them both a show she deliberately started laughing. Kenny would have been outraged if he had known she was really laughing at him! With her eyes filled with excitement she came dashing out of the hen house towards them.

"Kenny!" she squealed with delight and then acted shocked to see the girl with him. "Oh, hello. I'm sorry, I didn't realize we had company. It's so good to have you here, though."

"Bonnie, this is Sherlene Bishop."

She extended her hand, "Aren't you one of the cousins that live down south a bit?"

"Yeah, yeah, she's my cousin. She might be staying with us for a spell. Is that okay with you?" Kenny grinned.

"Oh, sure! I just love family!"

"What you got there in your apron?" Sherlene was trying to see what Bonnie was cradling so tenderly.

Bonnie's eyes grew wide with wonder. "I don't know! But look, I found them under the hen in there." She slowly and carefully revealed her precious bundle.

"Those are just eggs." Kenny started to ridicule her but held back since Sherlene was there. "See, Sherlene, see what I told you? She thinks she found a treasure or something! What am I going to do?"

"You poor dear; it's worse than I ever imagined!" she cooed to Kenny. "I know you told me she was losing it, but I had no idea of the extent of her derangement. Oh, you poor, poor soul."

Then she turned to Bonnie, who was still smiling. "Do you know what to do with those eggs?"

Bonnie looked down at them and debated on an answer. Kenny wasn't about to hurt her as long as the girl was there. Play it for all its worth, she thought. "I don't rightly remember."

"I can show you how to cook them."

"You cook them? These little things are something to eat? Why was that chicken in there sittin' on them?"

Sherlene giggled and then ruffled Kenny's hair. "Oh, she's precious, Kenny! Sad, but precious!"

Bonnie couldn't resist. In a little girl's voice she mimicked. "You're precious, too, cousin."

The two went into the house as Kenny excused himself to go to the barn for something. Bonnie was having a great time. When Sherlene cracked the egg, she acted horror stricken and tried to fix the broken pieces.

"Oh, you spilled it! Oh, my goodness! How in the world are you going to put it back together?"

Sherlene tried to calm her down. "You don't fix it, you throw the shell away and cook the rest. Just watch."

"Oh, no, no, no. Kenny don't like broke things. Hide it before he comes back in! He'll throw a terrible fit!"

"No, Bonnie, you don't have to hide anything. And believe me, I know that Kenny loves eggs. He has ever since…he was a little boy and I cooked for him." She chose her words carefully. Sherlene had a sweet, patient expression on her face as she gently removed Bonnie's hand from the handle of the skillet she was going to fry the egg in. "Now we need an onion and some sausage. We'll just fix up some breakfast right here and now."

"Oh, I like breakfast. Do you know how to make biscuits?"

"I sure do."

"Oh, Kenny loves biscuits for breakfast! In fact, Kenny could eat biscuits with everything! I was makin' some the other day but I must have left out one of the ingredients because they just didn't turn out like they should have. He throwed them in the trash."

"Maybe you left out the eggs?" She held the last one up before she cracked it.

"You put eggs in biscuits, too?" Bonnie's eyes roamed the room as though thinking it through, and then suddenly remembering, "Oh, of course you do! How in the world could I have missed that?"

"Maybe because you forgot what they were?" It was a gentle question that carried no mockery or criticism at all.

Bonnie just shrugged. "I've been forgettin' a lot lately. Well, I can tell you one thing. I'm sure glad you're here!" As long as Kenny was out of the room, Bonnie played her "insanity" to the hilt!

She had no idea what the two were actually up to but she wasn't about to pass up the chance to strengthen her scheme. For the time being she was going to ignore the hurt that Kenny would actually bring the girl into their home with the intention of making a mockery of her! And then it dawned on her; Kenny was padding his basket before he put all his eggs into it. He was merely checking out the size of the heifer before he built the stall.

With Sherlene now aware of her situation there was no way Kenny would kill her. That made her relax somewhat. But, Bonnie knew her time was limited. She had heard snatches of conversations and suspected that Kenny was talking to someone about an institution up north. Bonnie took a deep breath and held it as though it would help towards the deliberate hardening of her heart. Well, the sooner the better, she decided. Let the scrawny child be nurse and housemaid to the sorry likes of her husband. She'd face reality soon enough. The man didn't have sense enough to match his own socks let alone keep his house clean and his clothes washed. But he sure knew how others were supposed to do it! And he had ways to make them do it, too!

When Kenny finally came back into the house, Sherlene had fixed a generous brunch for all of them. Bonnie stayed silent as she ate. She was trying to decide how helpless she would become now that Sherlene was there. Not knowing if it was only a short visit or if the girl was moving in, she had to be cautious about embarrassing Kenny and having to pay for it later.

As Sherlene and Bonnie cleaned up the kitchen, Kenny announced he was going to feed the livestock. He tried to sneak a kiss to Sherlene, but Bonnie saw it. Even though she tried to disregard it, she couldn't deny the pain she felt as she was forced to admit that Kenny didn't care a thing about her. To bring the girl there was one thing, to openly show affection was quite another! Bonnie's whole demeanor changed and Sherlene was quick to pick up on it.

"I'm sorry you saw us kiss. It doesn't mean a thing. Haven't you heard that old phrase about kissin' cousins? It just means we really like each other. Family is like that, you know? You aren't mad, are you?"

Bonnie knew that the young girl didn't want the situation to blow up in her face. "No," she lied as she searched for an explanation for her change in behavior.

"Oh, good, I wouldn't want you mad at me." Sherlene was obviously relieved.

Bonnie forced a smile. "Now, why would that happen? You're a nice person. I'm just mad because I can't find my barrette and I know I left it on the counter here. My hair keeps getting in my eyes and I just hate that! It makes me so cross when I forget where I put things!"

"Oh, well, let me help you find it." Sherlene may have been a good cook but she was incredibly immature and gullible. Kenny would soon take advantage of that! It wouldn't take long before he would have Sherlene wrapped around his little finger.

Bonnie watched her a moment, thinking, those pretty brown eyes wouldn't be so innocent too much longer. Just make him mad once and the brown will take on a peculiar shade of black and blue, then a greenish yellow. If Bonnie wasn't plotting her freedom for the sake of her children, she would have scolded herself for being callous to the pain that Sherlene was about to discover. No woman should ever have to live with a man like Kenny!

Sherlene didn't go home. Bonnie excused herself early in the evening and turned out her light. Listening to the sounds in the night brought anguish and yet a strange kind of relief. It was hard to explain. For the first time in years, Bonnie slept in, knowing that the 'cousin' would make herself quite at home. During the morning she would wake up momentarily and hear snatches of quiet laughter but then would peacefully fall right back to sleep. To her astonishment she looked at the clock and discovered it was almost two in the afternoon! Without changing from her gown she shuffled out into the kitchen, carrying her doll.

"Well, we were beginning to think you were going to sleep the day away! I bet you're starved, aren't you?" Sherlene was talking to her as though she were a child. Fine. Play along.

"Baby is hungry, too." Bonnie held up the broken doll.

"Told you she still had that thing." Kenny was suddenly standing in the other doorway, watching and listening.

Sherlene smiled sweetly. "Well, bring baby into the kitchen and I'll get you both something to eat. What do you want to do today? Kenny and I are going into Gough's Ridge today to take care of some business. You could go, too, but I know you'd be terribly bored. Will you be okay by yourself?"

"Oh, sure. Daddy will be back soon. I'll wait for him." Bonnie smiled, knowing that Kenny wouldn't touch her now, regardless of how ridiculous she was. As much as she despised the situation on the one hand, she found herself grateful that Sherlene was there to balance out the anticipation and terror! She knew that her life was no longer in danger and that freed her mind to concentrate on what she was trying to accomplish. During the first two weeks that Sherlene was there, Bonnie became more and more helpless, as though confirming the decision the two had made to put her away.

Kenny now had all plans finalized. As Bonnie seemed to be absorbed in her own world, the two would talk as though she wasn't even there. It was through such unguarded discussions that Bonnie learned what was in store for her! Kenny had gotten advice from a lawyer and they were just waiting for an admission date to Sugget County Institute for the Mentally and Physically Impaired. Bonnie found out that the red tape and paperwork had been completed with her future being signed and sealed.

Before she went to bed that night, Sherlene and Kenny explained what was going to happen. In the morning, they were going to take her to the train station. She would be closely supervised until she got to a large town called Pearce. There she would be met by 'family members' who had a big house and lots and lots of relatives who lived there. They were anxious for her to visit and Kenny told her he had been saving for months so she could go on this trip! It was meant to be a surprise because he loved her so much! Bonnie didn't even have to pretend that she was thrilled! All she had to do was ask childish questions about having a bedroom and if it was okay if she could take the little bassinet to carry her baby in. Kenny was happy to agree to anything she wanted!

There was one last thing to do and as soon as Kenny left to milk the cow, Bonnie approached Sherlene.

"I really like you," she spoke in a soft voice.

It was true. In the last three weeks she had grown very fond of the young girl. There had been times when she had carried on a decent conversation with her. Once she had even heard Sherlene remark to Kenny that Bonnie had her lucid moments and what a shame it was that her mind had deteriorated so quickly.

"She must have been a wonderful wife at one time." Sherlene had been overly sympathetic. Kenny acted forlorn and rejected, as though life had dealt him a terrible blow.

Before Bonnie left this property and this cabin, she was going to make sure Sherlene was warned about Kenny's abusive behavior. Sherlene would have to decide if the advice came from a sound mind or not.

"Well, thank you, I like you, too, Bonnie." Sherlene was sitting on the porch swing and Bonnie sat down next to her.

"Can we talk a minute before we have to leave?" Bonnie didn't wait for an answer. "I want to say thank you for everything you've done for me and Kenny."

Then she sighed deeply and took Sherlene's hand. With her perfectly sane voice she began, "I've known a lot of heartache. And I've learned this; sometimes people aren't who you think they are. When you least expect it they show their fangs and attack. That means you might have to take drastic measures to survive. Never underestimate the power of anger. The inside can die even though the outside lives."

"Why are you saying this?" Sherlene was totally dumbfounded by this sudden change of manner. Bonnie could tell she was trying to grasp some kind of logical reasoning for this ominous warning.

"I had a terrible, terrible dream." Bonnie was cautious not to get too "sane". "You were in that dream and you were laughing. But then, the night fell and you lit a fire but the darkness wouldn't allow the light to glow. There was a face in the dark that was angry and a voice that yelled at you. With each hateful, evil word, your flesh began to scale over. But it was too late. You were turning into a monster, too, and you begged to die but the voice wouldn't allow it. You pleaded for the daylight to return but the evil had suffocated it."

"Stop it, Bonnie, you're scaring me!" Sherlene started to rise from the porch swing but Bonnie held her back.

She reverted to the childish demeanor. "I told you it was terrible! Some people call that kind of dream a nightmare, but I call it a lifemare because you never, never, never wake up. Have you ever had a scary dream to come true?"

"No, they're just dreams."

Bonnie sat silent for a moment and then shrugged. "If you don't go to sleep, then you can't dream. I don't think I'll ever go to bed again."

"But you have to sleep at some point in time. I'm sorry you had such a terrible dream, but you're awake now and you can see that its daylight and everything is okay."

Once again Bonnie used her sane voice. "Yes, for me it is. I woke up, but you're still in the dream. This place is darkness and if you don't leave while you can, the dream will destroy you." Bonnie went inside without another word. She had given Sherlene the best kind of warning she knew of. The girl would have to figure it all out and one day realize the truth that had just been spoken. The sad thing was, Bonnie knew that Sherlene would be enveloped in darkness before she even realized the sun had set!

And then, all of life seemed to take whirlwind speed as Bonnie was whisked away from her home and then suddenly found herself at the train station. She was relieved that she didn't have to conceal her excitement and yet apprehension. No one knew but her that she was tasting freedom with the finale of finding her children.

As soon as she got on the train she had to figure out how to carry out the rest of her plan. She was now racing against time because her only chance of freedom was not to reach the destination Kenny had planned for her. Once she was behind locked doors, she had no assurance she'd ever be released. Bonnie knew she'd have to prove her sanity first and no telling how long that would take.

She didn't know anything about an institution but she had overheard the two talking about the horrors and atrocities. Sherlene had been concerned about the shock treatments but Kenny had assured her that they wouldn't be necessary. He explained that Bonnie would immediately go under medication and would live out the remainder of her life drugged so she would feel no pain.

Kenny had it all figured out. "They say patients are usually there from three to five years. I can't put my life on hold for that long. To tell you the truth, the doctor suspects she has a brain tumor and won't even survive through the year. You've seen yourself how quickly her mind is going. We have to be honest about our feelings for each other and live our lives as though she didn't exist any longer. You may think it's cruel, but to me she's the same as dead. I'm just relying on you to help me through my suffering and to make the adjustment in my life without her. I'm trying so hard to be strong!"

Bonnie had almost gagged! But she couldn't fault him. Was her deceit any different than his? Just as Kenny had plotted to get rid of her, she had done the same to him! She truly believed that once she boarded the train and was out of sight, Kenny would dismiss her. Sherlene might try and contact her or even try to talk him into visiting, but Bonnie knew that in all actuality, she would never see Kenny again. He had signed a paper of divorcement and committal with Sherlene as a witness.

It was the law that if he committed her as his wife, he could never divorce her as long as she was a patient. In fact, he would also be responsible for the payment of her extended care, and when she was released, she would go back to him. By divorcing her, he relinquished all rights and claims to her as his wife. She now belonged to the state and there was no legal connection between her and Kenny any longer!

"Thank you God." She repeated the phrase as often as she took a breath and knew that she was alive! The full reality began to creep up on her. She wasn't married anymore! At one time she had feared this day, believing that God would punish her if she had left Kenny. The way things were turning out, Bonnie felt as though God was now defending her.

When she was getting dressed for the trip she had layered her clothes. Sherlene had laughed at her, trying to convince her that her suitcase was to hold all the extra clothes. But Bonnie stayed adamant, almost fiercely so! Sherlene finally gave up with the comment "look weird if you want to, who cares what happens after today, anyway?"

Bonnie took her seat in the train, playing the insane part for all she was worth! She pulled her hat low on her head and sat like a child. She was carefully watched the entire time. The ticket had been pinned to her collar. Once the conductor claimed all tickets, she knew the hardest part was about to begin. Thinking on the odds of failure nearly overwhelmed her! For a second she had to catch her breath as she left Gough's Ridge. She had known this area almost all her life.

Her heart nearly broke as she realized the train was taking her farther and farther away from her memories. She allowed herself to weep silently. Then she threw her head back. There was no need to be silent, she was supposed to be insane! Let the tears flow! Let the voice wail! With heart-rending agony she cried because she was being separated from everything she had ever known and with two signatures on a piece of paper she was now legally divorced. She moaned from all the beatings and she found herself rubbing away the hurt from swollen ankles, bruised arms, broken bones, and busted lips! Her fingers touched her eyes and nose as though touching each year of cruel oppression. And then, she allowed her body to shake and tremble and nearly convulse as she lamented over each of her children!

It didn't matter if people were staring! She let it all out and then she had an exhilarating cleansing and a refilling of excitement and determination. Bonnie started to laugh. She was going to find her children! She was free of Kenny! He would never, never hit her again! She laughed even harder! It wouldn't be long before she would be standing before Lucy, her first daughter. She knew that Judith Ann would applaud her and do everything she could to help. Somehow she would find Bernadette. And she would hold her precious Collin again. She didn't care if he was still having seizures. Arnold would be about five years old. She had no idea what he would even look like! But she would be able to feast her eyes upon him and memorize every little detail that she had never seen before! And then she would find Patricia! She had to find her deaf baby!

Bonnie took the broken doll from the bassinet and held it up. "Mommy's coming." She burst out in laughter. "Mommy's coming. And I'll never, never let you go."

The laughter was joined by tears again but this time they weren't painful. Then she fell into a peaceful, exhausted silence. By now, everyone was avoiding her! People asked to have their seats changed so they could get away from her noise and bizarre behavior! The car attendant tried to explain that she was a mental patient but totally harmless. It made no difference, the other passengers were uncomfortable and demanded to go to another car. Those who stayed acted as though they were totally mortified and deliberately averted their eyes.

"You're a genius." She silently complimented herself.

Bonnie looked around at only a few faces in what started out as a very full car. One elderly woman looked like she was having trouble breathing and the car attendant was intent on assisting her. Bonnie knew that this was the one chance in a million that she needed. She offered a sincere prayer for forgiveness in case her performance had brought on the woman's stress. Leaving her carry-on luggage and the doll and bassinet, she got out of her seat and headed to the little cubicle with the toilet.

"Stop! Where are you going?" The attendant that was responsible for her called out. He quickly recognized his predicament, knowing he had to keep his eyes on her but not able to leave the elderly woman.

"I gotta go!" she raised her eyebrows. "It's okay, I know where the potty is and I'll be right back. Baby is sleeping."

And then she hurried on, into the next car, bending over so no one could see her face. Maybe they thought she was about to be sick and was desperately trying to reach the washroom. As soon as she got inside the little cubicle she took off her hat and jammed it into the trash bin along with her sweater. In a pocket she had a comb and lipstick.

Exiting with her hair neatly combed she walked proudly through the adjoining car until she reached the next washroom. Again she went in and peeled off more clothes. By the time she reached the fourth car, no one would have ever recognized her as the distraught woman from the first car. Three more cars and three more bathrooms had helped a metamorphosis into a respectably dressed woman who obviously carried herself with pride and confidence. Even though Bonnie was aware of a lot of commotion going on in the aisles she tried to look as though she was totally undisturbed by it.

Bonnie had ended up in a car that was mostly populated by older women. She had honestly never seen so many women all in one location and she wondered if they were a group traveling together or just happened to be on the same car. Whatever the reason, she tried to blend in.

She sat down and acted as though she had been in that seat the entire time. There was a gentleman across the aisle reading the newspaper. Leaning across, she got his attention.

"Excuse me, do you have any idea what seems to be the problem? There certainly is a lot of activity going on."

He looked up the aisle, then down, then back at her. "To tell you the truth, Ma'am, I've been asleep and just now picked up my paper. I'm sure it's nothing to concern yourself over."

She was relieved that he didn't ask where she had come from or to make a comment that someone else had been sitting in that seat! He regarded her presence as perfectly natural. For an hour she sat with her head held high even though her spirit was somewhat cowering at the thought that at any minute someone would discover that she was a fraud. When the car attendant passed for the second time she greeted him and even asked him for the time. Bonnie wanted to make sure he recognized her as being in that location and would remember her as a soft-spoken woman. Nevertheless, her shoulder seemed poised in a ready position for someone to take hold of her and tell her she didn't belong there! If the train hadn't been so crowded she knew she would have never pulled it off! Not able to sit any longer she began to roam a bit.

Now she greeted the other passengers with an air of dignity and poise. For a good ten minutes she stood in the narrow aisle conversing with another female passenger, quite a bit older than she was. Bonnie introduced herself as Suzette Freeman.

"Where are you sitting?" Bonnie's new companion asked.

"Right there." Holding her breath, she tested all fate. "Oh, no, my clutchbag is gone!" Bonnie was pointing to her empty seat. Then she turned to the gentleman she had talked to earlier. "Sir, did you see anyone go by here and possibly take any of my belongings?"

He shrugged, "I honestly didn't pay any attention but I know there's been countless people going up and down these aisles like there was a parade or something!"

The older woman was extremely helpful as she called to the car attendant and explained that while they were talking, someone had snatched the pocketbook. With a calm but concerned manner, Bonnie explained to the car attendant that she was preparing to get off at the next stop but because of the theft had no identification or money! He tried to respond to her plea for help but wasn't sure what to do about it.

"Oh, I was so foolish for even leaving it there!" she chided herself.

Her new friend was quick to defend her, "Not your fault alone, my dear, don't be too hard on yourself. Who would have ever suspected there would be a common thief on a luxury rail liner like this one! It always amazes me that just any riffraff can buy a ticket."

The car attendant, now feeling guilty for not patrolling his area better, assured her that as soon as they got to the train station he would alert the proper authorities and they would try to find her stolen article and take care of all impending matters.

Another car attendant passed them and Bonnie overheard a quick exchange that the crazy lady couldn't be found. The woman with her was immediately alert and questioned them about it.

She tapped the man's shoulder. "Am I now to be subjected to lunacy as well as thievery? Please, please, get me off this train! I find I'm begging to be back in my own safe home and away from this preposterous fiasco." She almost swooned as she grabbed the back of a seat.

"Oh, nothing for you to worry yourselves over. We will have it under control in a matter of moments. You fine ladies won't be troubled at all. Please, have a seat, we're almost at the station now."

"Are you traveling alone?" Bonnie asked the woman.

"As a matter of fact I am; why don't you sit next to me? I'm getting off at the next stop, too, and perhaps I can assist you. I'm beginning to think the trains aren't as safe as they use to be! Imagine thieves and crazy people on the same train! What is this world coming to?"

"Indeed!" Bonnie stifled a chuckle.

Shortly after the whistle blew, Bonnie was able to see the outskirts of town. The car attendant approached them again.

"Excuse me madams, but the train will be temporarily delayed while they do a quick security check. I know you're anxious about your belongings but I have your description of it and there's no need to stay on board while they search. If you'll accompany me I'll take you to the stationmaster where you can fill out a report. Is that satisfactory?"

"Very much so." Bonnie answered first. "I can not tell you how distressed I am that someone on this train has stolen something so personal to me."

"We regret it deeply, but assure you that all matters will be taken care of expediently. I'm sure you will be compensated for your inconvenience. I'll personally have the porter secure your luggage for you and bring it to the office, all you'll need to do is identify it for him."

He led her to the luggage compartment, asking how many pieces she had. Now she was in trouble! The wrong reaction would immediately give her away. The porter might even deny seeing her and if she chose someone else's luggage she might get a man's! If the rightful party to the luggage saw the porter carrying it out they would cause a ruckus for sure!

There were two blue bags that looked almost identical. She chose the one on the top and then quickly departed the train.

"I'm so sorry," she apologized silently to whomever the luggage really belonged to. "But there's no other way." After the train pulled away, she could always act shocked as she discovered the porter had picked up the wrong suitcase! Still, she felt positively miserable. Her deception was involving more and more people.

True to the man's word, he escorted them off the train and got them out of the impending commotion. Bonnie's head was spinning as fast as her heart was racing! As it turned out, her new acquaintance was truly a godsend.

"Mrs. Mack, you've returned safely! Did you have a pleasant trip?" The stationmaster greeted her.

"It was divine, Mr. Brown, simply divine. But I fear my friend here has become terribly inconvenienced because of an unfortunate theft of her pocketbook. Can you imagine what it must be like for a woman of stature to be without identification? No, you probably wouldn't, but I can assure you that such a theft is parallel to finding yourself defiled! A clutchbag is a very private article of dress."

"Then we shall get on with reporting it and not waste precious time. Your name?" Even though the man looked directly at her, Bonnie couldn't get a word in.

"Her name is Suzette Freeman and she's from Willoughby. She's just here on business and doesn't know a soul." Mrs. Mack was clearly going to take control of the matter.

"Do you have anything at all to prove your identification?" the man asked. "Perhaps a letter or something in your luggage?"

Mrs. Mack was indignant. "No, of course she doesn't! We're not about to rummage through luggage right here in front of God and everyone just to try and prove who she is! Why would a person not be who they say they are? Really now! I will gladly vouch for her. Now, please get on with the paperwork. I'm sure Suzette is as famished as I am, aren't you dear?"

"Quite, I'm sure," she answered.

They were in the office for a good ten minutes before she heard the train whistle blow again. One of the attendants knocked on the door and Bonnie's heart stopped for a moment. Was her scam up? Had someone recognized her? He came in and set the blue luggage down and then motioned to speak privately with the stationmaster.

Mr. Brown went to the door and the two men tried to speak in hushed tones. All Bonnie could make out was that the missing pocketbook hadn't been found but they had discovered articles of women's clothing stashed in the bathrooms with no rhyme or reason as to why. The crazy woman hadn't been found but they suspected she had stolen the pocketbook. Since the passengers who had gotten off had been carefully screened they were quite sure the woman was still on board and would soon be found. Mr. Brown emphasized, a little louder that their rail line was extremely efficient and boasted that there was nothing to worry about! It was only a matter of time before all things would be settled!

"Could we have an address or phone number where we could reach you?" Mr. Brown asked Bonnie. Once again Mrs. Mack spoke up.

"Use my address. Without a pocketbook this poor woman doesn't have a dime to her name so she can't very well stay in a hotel. Unless of course, the business you work for has already made arrangements for your stay here?" It was both a statement and a question.

"No, they just gave me money so I could cover expenses when I arrived." Bonnie tried to sound like she knew exactly what she was talking about.

"Tragic, I tell you." Mrs. Mack shook her head and then stood. "Fred Brown, you do your Christian duty and make sure she's reimbursed! I have to make a phone call while you're settling matters."

And then Bonnie found herself alone, answering another myriad of questions. She wasn't nervous in the least because she had taken the last two months to plan her story. Suzette Freeman was nearly as real to her as an old school teacher, Mrs. Gerbling. If she did start to contradict, she merely excused it as fatigue and stress and Mr. Brown remained sympathetic.

In reality, she had only carried a pocketbook one time in her whole life and she had no idea what women carried in them. As she sat by Mrs. Mack she had asked for a tissue so the woman would have to open her purse and Bonnie could see what was inside. Mrs. Mack had been eager to nearly empty all the contents of her pocketbook to get out a drawing that one of her grandchildren had given her. Even though it was little more than a stick figure she was proud of the artwork.

When Mr. Brown asked Bonnie to catalog all contents of her pocketbook in order to estimate the loss value, Bonnie went down the list of everything from hairbrush to Bible, cosmetics to crackers!

"And some fruit. I get hungry on a long trip. Not that it was worth anything," she added.

When she left his office, she had a notarized document that she was Suzette Freeman with a post office box number in Willoughby which was a little town about ten miles from where Judith Ann lived. Uncle Ronnie had taken her there once for the State Fair. Bonnie also had fifty dollars and a return ticket. At least that would put her within ten miles of Lucy with no one being the wiser! At the moment she felt like the luckiest, richest person alive!

She stepped out of the office just in time to see the train pulling away from the station. Somewhere roaming the narrow aisles was a phantom crazy person being taken to the mental institution in Pearce, almost another hundred miles away from Archer with at least fourteen stops in between. Fourteen more possibilities for the distraught woman to disappear! Bonnie smiled, thinking about the nurses and attendants that would be at the station, ready to greet the poor deranged ex-wife of a potato farmer who carried a broken doll and had no idea what eggs were! And to think Kenny had assured them that she would be totally cooperative and wouldn't need special assistance!

"Please God, help Sherlene, she's sure gonna need You." Bonnie whispered. How could it be that Kenny and Sherlene already seemed like people from another time? Bonnie found Mrs. Mack and the two of them left the station and headed to her house in a taxi.

"Now you go ahead and use the phone and let your company know what's happened. What time do you have your first appointment?"

"Not until the morning. I told them I didn't want to feel rushed today."

"Smart woman! Very good, we'll have time to sit and have a cup of tea and unwind from such a harrowing experience!" They were friends! Bonnie didn't want to admit that she had never talked on the telephone. First she had been challenged to act crazy. Now she had to act as though she had a job and was there on business! Maybe she would have been better off to have been visiting a dying grandmother or something.

"I don't believe you told me what business you're into." Mrs. Mack prodded as she set the kettle on the stove to boil water for the tea.

"It's a private organization, actually, and we find missing children." Bonnie quickly gathered all the information she had heard from Sherlene and Kenny as they had discussed various government agencies and how they worked.

"Oh, how gallant! Jobs are so scarce these days. The men take the business jobs, as you well know, and the women here are left with little more than a factory job or teaching. Unless, of course, they can get on with the government. The pay is just horrendous but that's just the economy and the system. It's a wonder we can afford a pint of milk! You certainly are blessed. Do you work along with the government?"

"Sometimes, but we find that there's too much red tape and far too many secret files! Actually, we prefer to do our own research and that's why I was hired. There are just some homes that only a woman can get into. And we find that a woman will confide in another woman whereas they distrust a man. As you say, it's the system right now. Did you know that children are often taken to convents and within those entombed catacombs those children simply disappear?"

"Never to be heard from? Surely not."

"Oh, yes, it's quite common. I've been looking for one child for almost seven years now. I know the background she came from and why she was taken to the convent, but the knowledge stops there. It is nearly impossible to find out who has adopted these children so they can be returned."

"But once they're adopted, why in the world would the parents want them back? Doesn't that just add to the confusion of the child?"

"For most it probably does. Some cases, like the one I'm working on now, was more like a kidnapping. The child should have never been taken from the mother to begin with."

"Black market babies! I've heard of that!" Mrs. Mack took two cups out of the cupboard. Unfortunately, Bonnie had no idea what she was talking about. Time to quickly change the subject.

"Oh, enough business talk. Sometimes I get so wrapped up in my work I don't take time to stop and smell the roses. You know what I mean? Tell me, did you decorate this kitchen yourself? It's just the most darling kitchen I've ever sat in!" Bonnie took a deep breath and was determined to get Mrs. Mack talking instead of asking questions.

The house was a charming little Cape Cod with vines growing all along the outside of the fireplace. The arched doorways gave it a comfortable feel and the windows were wide with colorful sheer curtains rather than the heavy drapes. A cuckoo clock hung in the living room above a roll-topped desk. Bonnie was absolutely fascinated with the entire decorating scheme. She had never seen anything so simple and yet so stately! Upon their arrival, Mrs. Mack had immediately taken her to the spare bedroom and then showed her where she could wash up.

The four poster bed was covered with a beautiful handmade quilt while a lacy, white knitted afghan graced the back of a rocking chair. There was a fireplace in this room as well.

"Please feel free to hang up your dresses and just make yourself at home. Take your time and then meet me in the kitchen." Mrs. Mack's hospitality was congenial.

Bonnie stared at the blue suitcase. What would be inside? What if it was locked? She put her hands on it as though it were a time bomb! She just knew she'd open it to discover men's socks and underwear! But, blue was a woman's color and there had been a lot of women in that particular car, so the odds were 50/50. Remembering a dowdy, elderly woman she gave a quick prayer that she didn't have a suitcase full of granny dresses!

"Here goes," she whispered and then held her breath. The moment of truth was at hand! The catch released and she pulled up the top – women's clothes! Bonnie breathed but then thought of another problem. What if the clothes weren't the right size? At that moment she felt so terribly ashamed of what she had done she wanted to drop the lid of the suitcase and cry. There was going to be some poor woman getting off the train without a thing to wear!

For just a quick moment, Bonnie thought about being honest with Mrs. Mack and telling her the truth. She could hear her explanation "I pretended to be crazy so my husband would give me away instead of killing me so I could go find my babies and get them back!"

Why did the truth suddenly sound like some demented fairytale? No, she didn't dare say anything this soon. Her trail would be too easy to follow! She rightfully belonged to the state and once they found out she was missing they just might promote an all out search and stop at nothing until they found her! How soon would they be able to connect Bonnie Parker (she had been committed under her maiden name) to Suzette Freeman? Regardless of how sane she believed she was, maybe she had to be a little bit crazy to actually try and pull off what she was attempting! Who in their right mind would cause such a scene on the train and before the day was over have the nerve to ask assistance from the stationmaster? She had deliberately and calculatingly deceived Kenny and now she stood in a stranger's home with not only a new identify but cash and clothes as well! None of which she honestly deserved.

Blowing out her breath, which rode with an air stream of insecurity, she pulled out a blouse from the suitcase. It was not only her size but it was beautiful! The feel of it captivated her. Never had she owned anything so soft and well to do. There was a skirt under it that seemed to match. Like flowers in a rose garden! If she had had the time, she would have excitedly tried each item on but she knew Mrs. Mack was waiting for her. Bonnie closed her eyes a moment and rehearsed. "I am Suzette Freeman. I am Suzette Freeman."

As she convinced herself, she looked at the clothes again. She knew it wasn't right, but maybe this was a gift from God as she started her new identity. Just as God was helping her out, surely He would help out the woman the clothes really belonged to. Bonnie would feel somehow connected and indebted to that woman the rest of her life!

It was late evening when Bonnie finally crawled under the covers. What a day! The phone had rung several times and she had watched carefully to see how Mrs. Mack had handled it. The world suddenly became enormous as Bonnie realized how small and insignificant she really was. Life was totally different here. Judith Ann had a nice way about her but Bonnie had only been a child when she had lived there. At that age she had taken everything for granted with no interest in the things adults said or did.

The two women had a very pleasant visit over tea and butter biscuits and then Bonnie excused herself. It seemed so strange to her to spend the night in someone else's house. At first she had a hard time getting use to all the noises. But then she drifted into a good sleep and felt totally refreshed when she woke up.

Mrs. Mack was up bright and early, singing in the kitchen as she put on the coffee and started making breakfast. She had been a widower for the last five years and was quite comfortable living alone. Company was a welcome treat, however, and once Mrs. Mack started talking, it was hard to get a word in edgewise!

"Suzette?" she called. "Rise and shine my dear."

For a moment, Bonnie didn't respond to the name, and then she snapped back into the reality that she would have to identify with. She quickly put on a terry cloth robe and went into the kitchen.

"Slept like a baby," she yawned. "That's a fabulous bed."

Bonnie's day as Suzette Freeman had begun! After breakfast she took a bath and then ran a finger against the soft material of each item of clothing again. Holding a green sweater against her she spun in a circle and then got dressed. Looking at herself in the floor length mirror, she was truly amazed. If Kenny could only see her now….no! She wasn't going to think of him! If only her children could see her now! That was the way her mind had to work. As she left her room, she almost ran into Mrs. Mack in the hallway.

"Oh my, don't you look professional! What a slim figure you have," Mrs. Mack complimented her.

"Thank you," Bonnie almost blushed. "My....father" she had to come up with someone besides husband, "bought me this last Christmas. He has good taste in clothes, don't you think?"

"He certainly does. Oh, my Barney did, too. His favorite color was green and I believe he would have dressed me in green every hour of the day for every occasion that existed. Maybe that's why I have such a green thumb."

She held up her thumb and laughed. Just then the phone rang. Bonnie held her breath when she heard the name of Mr. Brown. Keeping a forced smile on her face she listened, though trying not to look as though she were eavesdropping.

"Good morning to you, too. Yes, we have both rested from that horrible experience yesterday. Say what now? The suitcase? You must be totally mistaken. Yes, she's standing right here in front of me and looking quite stunning I might add. What a very peculiar question: do they fit? Mr. Brown, a business woman has to look her best you know. Jobs are so hard to come by these days. She's ready to walk out the door this very minute to conduct a very important interview. No, I don't believe so. My goodness, no, I am not about to trouble her with your misfortunes! Isn't it bad enough that she had her pocketbook stolen? Yes, you were very gracious in how you settled that incident and I do respect you for that but I certainly don't want to be pulled into another charade of inefficiency. I wish I could help you but I'm afraid everything is exactly as it should be here. I hope you'll excuse me because I already have a thousand and one things to do today. Good day to you, Mr. Brown."

Bonnie poked her head out of the doorway. "Problems?"

Mrs. Mack laughed, "Nonsense stuff. Next thing you know they'll have an escaped convict on board and ask us to figure out who killed the porter! Men can have the strangest ideas!"

What would she have done without this precious woman? After getting simple directions to the courthouse Bonnie almost skipped out the front door. She had declined to use the telephone, explaining that a morning walk would do her good. Mrs. Mack went on out to putter around in her little greenhouse never suspecting a thing.

Bonnie's mind was constantly at work. She sat down on a bench at the bus stop as though waiting. It gave her a good place to stop and think about what to do next. Where did she even begin? Thanks to Mrs. Mack she had successfully established a new identity, but she knew that one wayward answer or one unanswered question would give birth to confusion and then someone would start putting pieces together. It was best not to stay here too long.

Mrs. Mack would probably be answering questions for the next couple of months from confused parties who were trying to make sense of what happened on the train! She knew, without a shadow of doubt, that Judith Ann would be the first person the authorities would go to for answers. Therefore, even though her heart begged to see her daughter, Lucy, she knew better than to go there too soon! Things had to calm down.

She tried to think it through. She was supposed to be here on business. The only reason she knew to go to the courthouse was because she and Kenny had gone there once when there had been a question about Arnold and they both had had to sign some papers. Bonnie decided it was best to leave right after she had asked some questions. She would tell Mrs. Mack she had a great lead and had to go back home immediately. Then she would use her return ticket before anyone suspected that she had never purchased it to begin with. She wondered if people kept records on the names of those who purchased tickets. If there was, it would only be a matter of time before someone discovered Suzette Freeman had never bought a round trip ticket in the first place! It seemed as though her lies and ill-gotten gains were about to suffocate her!

Before she left the bench she made a solemn vow. She would somehow return the suitcase and clothes, and she would pay the stationmaster back for the money he had so trustingly given her. And she would tell Mrs. Mack the truth. That only seemed right! She wasn't about to have other people tell her children that their mother was a liar and a con artist!

Bonnie sighed. What had she gotten herself into? She longed for the time that she didn't have to tell lies. But for now, she could neither condemn nor feel sorry for Bonnie Parker. Focusing on her children alone, she left the bus stop and headed to the courthouse.

The woman at the desk was a little bit older than she was. Bonnie couldn't imagine ever working in such a position. She marveled at the woman's ability to type and handle all the papers she had on her desk.

"May I help you?" a soft, patient voice came from behind bright red lips. Round, hazel eyes blinked as the woman flipped the hair off the back of her neck.

Bonnie identified herself as Suzette Freeman but didn't say a word about working for a company in Willoughby. She knew she couldn't be totally honest because the names of her children would immediately spark suspicion.

"I just need some help because I have no idea where to even start. If a person wants to find a missing child, where do they go?"

The woman thought a moment, chewing her gum. "Have you tried the police?"

"I believe it's more of a matter of adoption than a crime."

"Oh, I'm sorry, all of our adoption files are sealed and no one can see them."

"What if I wanted to adopt?"

"Oh, well, that's a different story." She shuffled through some papers and wrote down two names and handed the paper to Bonnie. "You need to talk to Mr. Kelley. He's our representative here in this county. His office is upstairs, and then down three doors to your left. Can't miss him."

Bonnie thanked her and headed up the stairs. Another lie was about to be told. Feeling totally out of place and overly cautious, she held her breath a moment to try and inhale courage and then exhale determination before she went through the door marked Winston Kelley. Another woman sat at a desk and looked up at her, greeting her very politely.

"Do you have an appointment?" she asked.

"No, I'm just passing through town. I live in Willoughby and will be returning on the next train. Is it possible to speak with Mr. Kelley?"

"You're in luck, he just came back from court. I think we can squeeze you in for about thirty minutes if you think that's sufficient."

It was just fine! Bonnie waited and then Mr. Kelley came out of his office. He was a young man but with gray streaked throughout the temples of his black hair. His eyes had a sparkle to them and he greeted Bonnie as though they had been old friends.

"Can I help you Miss Freeman?"

"I certainly hope so." Maybe this would be easier than she thought. His office was spacious and she sat down in a brown leather chair next to his desk. Pictures of his family were on the wall behind him along with his name and several certificates and photos with numerous children.

"Happy faces of adopted children eager to be loved," he explained as he watched Bonnie's eyes go around the room.

"I would like one of those children. Actually, I'm just looking for information and I have several questions." She sighed, sitting with her back straight and yet trying not to appear nervous. He nodded his head, ready to assist her.

She continued, "First of all, I have a question. Is a child considered legally adopted if there has never been any paperwork filled out?"

"Was the adoption through an agency?"

"No, just between the parents and the people that agreed to bring up the child."

"Nothing is legally binding there."

"So, it wouldn't be hard to get the child back?"

"By law a mother has the right to her child unless she has abandoned that child. If the child was placed in a home temporarily, it may be hard emotionally to separate them, but there wouldn't be any problem legally. Why do you ask?"

"Actually, I'm asking for an acquaintance who had to give her child up to relatives until she could take care of him herself. But that's been over five years."

"That's not considered a legal adoption. She can easily get him back."

"What if she doesn't know where he lives?"

Mr. Kelley rubbed his chin. "Well, that makes it a little more difficult but not impossible." They continued to talk and Bonnie kept asking questions. Then she asked the hardest question of all.

"Have you ever dealt with adoptions that are paid for at the convent?"

"Excuse me?"

She repeated her question but he quickly told her that such adoptions were not legal and if the convent received any money it was considered a donation to the church and nothing could be done about it. The only way to track down those children would be through the cooperation of the nuns. They worked through their own system which was not recognized as being legal in that particular state. Bonnie's heart felt an ember of hope but was soon drenched from the reality that records were not kept and after seven years memories might have faded.

Their time was soon up and Bonnie thanked him, not knowing for sure how she felt when she went back out the door. Would she ever be able to find Bernadette? Arnold was the only one who had been legally adopted. The parents had insisted on that and Kenny had taken care of all the details. Even if she couldn't be their mother, at least she wanted to see them, to hear their voice and to know that they were okay. Another plan began to develop as she walked back to Mrs. Mack's. Bonnie found her new friend still in the greenhouse.

"You weren't gone very long." Mrs. Mack looked up from a spider plant and smiled.

"Long enough to get a good lead on one of my children. I really hate to do this to you but I've got to go back home right away. If I don't follow it up quickly I may lose it."

"Oh, and I was so hoping to fix us a nice roast for supper."

"I would be delighted but duty calls. You just have no idea how important these children are to me! You've been so gracious, I know I can never repay you."

She tsk-tsked as though it were nothing. "Well, you do what you must. I have to admit you made the end of my journey quite enjoyable. A woman my age is always looking for a little adventure."

"If I come through here again, may I call on you?"

"I would be offended if you didn't, my dear. You come any time and you don't need to call first. I'm almost always home. Can I help you with anything?"

"Actually yes. While I'm getting ready would you call a cab for me?'

Mrs. Mack immediately put her shears down and slipped off her gardening gloves as she headed into the kitchen, more than glad to help out.

They continued to exchange trivial chitchat and then Bonnie scurried to the room, carefully put everything back into the suitcase, left a five dollar bill on the dresser with a little note of thanks and then left. Slipping into the back seat of the cab she told him she had to make one quick stop before she went to the train station.

That was to a department store. He was to wait for her as she quickly went in with bag in hand. One more lie. "Excuse me, I've managed to over pack my suitcase and the clasp simply isn't trustworthy. Would it be possible to buy a piece of luggage and repack the clothing before everything falls on the ground? I'm actually in a great hurry to catch the train."

The clerk was more than anxious to accommodate and within a matter of moments Bonnie had carefully separated the two outfits that Mrs. Mack had not seen and put them into a small floral bag before she left the store. Getting back into the cab she thanked the driver for waiting and then had him take her to the train station. Her explanation was that she had to get the suitcase to her niece who was leaving for college. The cab driver was asked one more time to wait.

Bonnie's heart was beating frantically as she looked for Mr. Brown. He was in his office but absorbed in some kind of paperwork. Going out on the loading dock she saw two men getting ready to load all the luggage. But they were talking more about fishing than they were paying attention to anything else around them. When their backs were turned, she inconspicuously set the blue suitcase down with all the other pieces and then scurried back to the cab. Somewhere along the line the suitcase would turn up as unclaimed and then the poor woman who had lost it to begin with would have almost everything returned. She seriously thought about using her return ticket to Willoughby but she just couldn't bear the thought of getting back on the train and facing the porters and car attendants. Someone would surely recognize her! Convinced that she needed to follow her instinct, she smiled at the cab driver and told him to take her to the bus depot, and silently prayed that she had enough money to buy a bus ticket.

Bonnie was leaning back against the headrest as the bus carried her to Willoughby. So far everything had worked out incredibly well. No one cared what her name was or what she was doing. She was no more than a face in the crowd. Closing her eyes she thought of the last time she had seen each child and remembered everything she possibly could about them. She knew the first thing she had to do was to get some kind of a job so she could have money and make amends to those she had cheated. Her mind was getting tired of all the stories she was telling but she had to work out all the details and to be confident in what she was saying. That took practice! She rehearsed the same story, over and over and over!

The next three hours gave her a good chance to think it all through and to even catch a twenty minute nap that allowed her to wake up feeling totally refreshed and invigorated! At last they got to Willoughby. The bus pulled in and Bonnie decided to get a sandwich before she looked for a room. She entered the little bus stop cafeteria and sat down at a booth. The waitress was slow to respond but she didn't care. There were several people there and she was quickly drawn into the atmosphere of confusion. The little, blond waitress was getting more and more agitated because three people were obviously into a heated argument. When she took their orders to them, the man being the most verbal of the trio, started yelling that the order wasn't what he wanted and he actually threw the plate on the floor.

The woman accompanying him was not only angry but humiliated and she raised her voice and started calling him names. Just as the waitress set down another plate the man backhanded the defiant woman and when the third party moved to get out of the way, another plate hit the floor. The waitress was crying and screaming at them. Then she turned towards the kitchen and hollered at a man standing by the in/out doors.

"I don't need this, Riley, I quit!" She untied her apron and threw it on the stool at the counter and she stomped out of the building.

The couple continued to yell at each other and both were hitting. This was more than Bonnie could stand! She had never been in a situation like this and she had no idea what people normally did to resolve it but she certainly knew how to handle it! Getting up from her booth she approached the angry trio. Bonnie put both hands on the table and with a firm voice told the man to stop. Where she got the courage, she had no idea. But this was no different than being around Kenny when he was drunk. He stared at her with cold eyes, stunned that anyone would interfere.

She couldn't back down now. Bonnie might have, but Suzette Freeman was a strong woman who wasn't going to let anyone bully her or anyone else. In a firm, deep voice she took on an authoritative, crisp tone that wasn't to be messed with.

"Don't you dare hit her again! This is not the time or place to create such a scene. Now sit down and let me clean up this mess so we can get your lunch. You'll feel a lot better once you've eaten."

"Who are you lady?"

"I'm nobody to you, okay? Just sit down."

"You sure are gutsy." He found himself more amused than angry. "What if I decide to knock you across the room for buttin' in my business where you don't belong?"

Bonnie didn't even so much as flinch. "I've been hit before; you don't scare me."

He stared at her for the longest time but then sat down.

"I just want a turkey sandwich, is that too much to ask?" The female partner was rubbing her jaw and whimpering. "If I can even eat it now."

"Shut up! You know better than to call me names."

Now Bonnie's voice was less authoritative and more pleading. "Come on, come on, let it rest. How about some coffee?"

"I didn't order coffee!" He practically snarled at her.

"Yeah, well, maybe you need it. You're drunk and you need something in that stomach."

"How do you know what I need?"

Bonnie laughed, remembering all the episodes with Kenny. She just shook her head and smiled. "Like I said, calm down and let's try to enjoy some lunch, okay?"

She didn't wait for an answer but looked around and saw a coffeepot with stacks of coffee cups. Without even acknowledging Riley she poured the man some coffee and took it to him.

"Go ahead, drink it, okay? Now, how did you want your order fixed?"

He told her and then she went over to the double doors where Riley was standing. "Would you please get that man another hamburger and fries? I'm going to clean up the mess…"

"Lady, you don't even work here, what are you doing?" Riley stopped her.

Bonnie stood up and looked at him as though he must be deaf and blind. "Your lady just walked out on you and you have a room full of hungry people."

She grabbed the apron on the stool and tied it around her waist. "I'm working for you now. My name is Suzette Freeman." And with that she turned and started picking up the broken plates. The cook looked out of the little window and smiled so big that if he had had false teeth he would have lost them!

And that's how her new life started! For the next five hours she learned how to be a waitress and found Riley to be a good person. The work wasn't hard but dealing with the people took a special touch. When money was left on the table she put it in the cash register. Finally the cook got her attention.

"What you doing that for?" He screwed up his mouth as though he was trying to chew his left jaw with his right teeth. "Don't you know that's your tip money? You keep that for yourself."

By the end of the day, Bonnie had three dollars in her pocket. For the last thirty minutes no one had come into the little café and Riley called her over to a booth.

"Okay, little lady, let's make this official. I really like your style! Where do you live?"

"I, ah, don't have an address yet. I just moved here…today."

"Okay, well, who's your next of kin?" He was met with a blank stare. "You got any kinfolk living in these parts?"

"No."

"Friends?"

"No."

"You just showed up in Willoughby not knowing a soul?"

She smiled, "Yes, sir, that's exactly what I did."

"May I ask why?"

This time she decided to be honest. "Because my abusive husband divorced me and I have to survive."

"Why Willoughby?"

Bonnie shrugged, not really knowing what to say. "Because the bus brought me here and this is where I got off."

He shook his head in disbelief. The smile revealed an admiration for her spunk. "You don't know anyone and you don't have a place to stay. Have you got any money?"

"Some." She smiled as she took the change out of her pocket. "I have three dollars."

"Then this is what we're going to do. You promise me you'll show up every day this week and I'll pay you in advance and then you go over to Billie's Boarding House and get yourself a room. Deal?"

"Deal! I only have one thing to ask of you first."

"Ask." His eyes were bright.

"Could I please have something to eat? When I got off the bus I was hungry and that was a long time ago."

"That's right, you did come in here as a customer, didn't you?" He got up and went to the little window and got the cook's attention. "You fix her anything she wants and give her generous portions. From now on she eats free anytime she wants."

"You got it," the cook called back.

When she left the Bus Stop Café she followed Riley's directions to Billie's. The house was a three-story structure with a balcony on the second and third level. In all truth, it looked more like a bordello she had seen in Gough's Ridge. But just the opposite was true. Her knock was answered by a heavyset woman who welcomed her in and showed her to a little room on the second floor. Bonnie immediately liked her. Billie had a fabulous sense of humor and the more Bonnie actually studied her features, the more she saw a kind of beauty she had never seen before. It was as though it was shining from the inside out.

The first day ended with Bonnie in an old feather bed, a homemade quilt covered her and a little nightstand and lamp was next to the bed. A desk and chest was by the window that overlooked the street and then a little dressing alcove, covered by a sheer curtain was close to a bathroom. There was a picture of Jesus on one wall and another picture of some lady with a lavender umbrella who was sitting on a plush, green lawn. Just the bare necessities of furnishings. But it was clean and quiet and it only took Bonnie ten minutes to fall asleep.

During the next six months, she worked at the Bus Stop Café and spent as little money as possible. She had amends to make before she could spend anything on herself. She had thought in her own mind that the state would quit looking for Bonnie Parker after three months. If she allowed three more to go by, she figured she would be in the clear. With the first fifty dollars she had saved she tucked it in an envelope and mailed it to Mr. Brown with a little note: Even though I appreciated your assistance, I just felt as though it was my own fault my pocketbook had been stolen and I would feel much better if you would kindly take your money back. I will be glad to travel on your train again.

She had tucked thirty dollars in the pocket of the suitcase when she had returned it, hoping that it would cover the clothes she knew she could never replace. Even that was probably generous but she had to consider the poor woman's stress as well. One day she would be able to tell Mrs. Mack the truth and clear her dishonest record completely!

It was time to go to Janesville where Judith Ann lived, but Bonnie honestly didn't know how to get there. That night at work she approached Riley.

"I've got some business to do there. Someone I want to see."

"An old lover maybe?" he winked at her.

"Yeah, sure," she blushed, but it was as good as anything else even though they both knew it wasn't true. "Only he can't know I'm there because he has this big wolfhound and the dog will eat me alive if he even smells me," she teased.

"Some dog, huh?"

"Oh, yeah. Real bad. We put a saddle on him once and let his boy rope all the stuffed animals for practice."

Riley never asked for the truth. He just agreed to drive her over to Janesville. She was so nervous she was almost sick to her stomach! The town had changed a lot but she was soon able to get her bearings and it wasn't long before the old house loomed before her. Tears came to her eyes. Riley watched her but he didn't say anything.

And then a young girl came out of the house. It was Lucy! Bonnie gasped and literally froze. The child was beautiful! Her dark hair hung to her waist in braids that were secured by little, pink ribbons. She was wearing a pink and green plaid dress with white bobby socks and brown shoes. Even though she had Kenny's chin and cheekbones, the rest of her features were a duplicate of Bonnie's.

"That's your child, isn't it?" Riley was bold enough to voice what he saw.

"Yes, she is." Bonnie had taken a deep breath but couldn't hold back the tears. She would never, never deny being the mother of her children again! But she knew she still had to be careful in trying to claim them. After six months of being with Riley, she knew she could trust him. "My husband wouldn't let me keep her so my aunt's got her here. I can't begin to tell you how much I've missed that child."

"She your only one? You must have been a baby when you had her."

"I was only fourteen. I got more. I just don't know where they are."

Riley reached over and put his hand on the back of her hand. "We could always try and find them."

Her eyes flashed to his face to see if he was serious. There was a slight frown and a genuine look of concern. "You don't know what you're saying."

He disagreed. "Yes, I do. A mother needs her children. I don't know your story, but I've sure been impressed with what I've seen in the last few months. What can I do?"

She had to swallow the lump in her throat before she could even talk. "No one can know, Riley. I belong to the state and if they ever find me I'll be locked up." There. She had said it.

"You kill someone or something?" Now he was looking down his nose at her with a worried look, more than just idle concern.

She laughed, "No, they just think I'm a little crazy, that's all."

He was obviously relieved. "Is that all? Well, isn't everyone? How about the man last night who ordered the cherry pie and smothered it in mustard?"

"That was awful, wasn't it? I appreciate your willingness to help me, but I'm not sure if I should get you involved. I don't want to cause trouble for anyone and I honestly don't know what I'm in for."

"You want her back?" Riley's eyes went back to Lucy.

"Sure I do, but I have to be able to take care of her first. She hasn't seen me in maybe eight years. I'm not even sure she would want to live with me." Bonnie started telling him about Lucy and then each year of heartache as she was forced to give her children away. It was as though her heart had to share its burden with someone and Riley was listening to every word she was saying! The expressions on his face revolved from disbelief to anger to laughter to compassion…even to murder!

"I would have killed him!" Riley was referring to Kenny. "Don't even tell me his name because I'd have to go lookin' for him!" His blood pressure rose as he thought of all the ways he would like to work out his hatred for the man!

"There is one good thing." Bonnie tried to calm him down. "His children will never know him because they don't carry his name. Collin was too little to even remember the man. But they'll have me. That's what I'm living for now."

"You absolutely amaze me." Riley was looking deeply into her eyes. "Most women that get beat up by their husband just cower down. What made you stand up and fight?"

"I'd had enough, Riley. I thought God would punish me but instead He defended me. I reckon that's what gave me the courage to fight back. You believe in God?"

"I sure do. I'd never be a preacher or nothin' but I know the Word like the back of my hand. Seems like between you and me and God Almighty, we can find those children of yours."

"Where do we even start?" Bonnie could barely contain her excitement.

"Right here, right now. We know that Lucy is alive and well. You know who has Collin, since you took him there yourself. So, let's see if he's home."

"Just like that?" Her fingers were bouncing at her lips, her breath fluttering and a new rush of tears falling freely.

"I'll get my brother to watch the café and I'll sweet talk Roberta into coming back just to cover for you. That's the girl you replaced. I got some savings that will put gas in the car and we can find your children."

"Riley, why are you doing this?"

He honestly couldn't say. "Well, I don't believe you can earn your way into Heaven but I don't think you can ever send up too many treasures ahead of you. It just seems like the right thing to do, that's all."

Before they left Janesville, they had both gone up to the door and knocked. A strange woman answered.

"What do you folks want?" she wasn't a bit friendly.

"We're with the Chamber of Commerce doing a city census. How many live at this address?" Riley was holding a clipboard with an inventory list from his café. As long as the woman didn't read the writing he figured it would look impressive enough.

"Two adults."

"We have this listed as the residence of Ronald and Judith Ann Stivers, is that correct?"

"No. Now it's Ronald and Delores Stivers. Judith Ann is dead."

"Do you have any children?" Bonnie asked.

"I got three of mine and he's got him this kid that stays with us but she ain't ours. Does she count?"

"As long as she's living with you she does. Do you have a telephone?"

"Sure we do."

"That's all we need to know. Thank you for your assistance."

She frowned and then shut the door without another word. Bonnie knew everything she needed to know. They walked back to the car, neither saying anything. As soon as Bonnie shut the door, Riley put the car into reverse and glanced at her from the corner of his eye.

"Lucy won't be here much longer; don't you fret for a moment. From the sound of that woman we won't have any trouble at all in getting her back! Piece of cake!"

"I can't let her know who I am, Riley." Bonnie's spirit was warning her of danger. The state authorities had probably already contacted Delores and was just waiting for Bonnie to show herself. There was no loyalty between them and Delores would have had no qualms about turning her in.

"Already got it figured out. If at all possible, my brother Rowland will come for her, then they'll remember his face, not ours. Now, let's get a map and see how far Collin is from us. Where did the preacher live back then?"

It was all happening! Riley still had no idea what Bonnie's real name was, but that didn't matter. He wouldn't have wanted to know. His quest was merely to reunite her with her children. Seeing Lucy again had torn at her heartstrings. How was she going to handle herself when she saw that blond headed boy who had been so dear to her? What if he had died like Judith Ann? Maybe one of his seizures had claimed him at a young age. It didn't matter, she had to know of either his existence or his death.

Riley stayed true to his word. As soon as they got back to Willoughby, he arranged time off for them from the café. Rowland was a mechanic and since times were slow he agreed to help out. Bonnie had never dreamed there were such good people in the world! Riley had gone to the bank and taken money out of his account as though he had been saving it for this purpose alone! She tried to convince him that she would pay him back but he wasn't interested. He said that seeing the joy on her face would be payment enough.

Bonnie had done her best to pinpoint the area where she had taken her son. Kenny had forbidden her to go into Gough's Ridge to find a family for any of the children. For one thing he didn't want people to talk about him; for another he didn't want the children close enough that Bonnie would keep sneaking off to see them.

The only other church was in the little community of Fuertes which was almost sixteen miles from the cabin. Kenny never went there so Bonnie knew that would be a safe place. Fuertes was still too small to show up on a map but Bonnie was sure that they could easily find it if they just headed in the right direction. Riley seemed to have a terrific sense of direction and before they knew it, there was a small, white sign with black letters. FUERTES. Population 32. Actually, the 32 had been crossed out and someone had painted in 33. No doubt the work of some proud father, Riley mused.
The church steeple was spotted above the treetops and they drove straight to it.

"I'm scared." Bonnie was holding her breath, fidgeting.

"It will be okay; he's been with good folks, right?"

"Hopefully the best."

"Then why are you so scared?"

Bonnie didn't even want to voice her fear of the child being dead. Neither would she admit she dreamed of asking for him and the man pointed to the graveyard. In the dream she had walked up a hill that had felt more like a mountain and among all the giant tombstones she found one, tiny, little cross that bore Collin's name. Date of death was only two days prior. She had just missed him. Bonnie shook her head to free it of the nightmare! It wasn't going to happen that way!

The church was quiet. Riley had gone up to the door and even went inside but Bonnie could tell by his walk that no one was around. He started to come back to the car but then saw someone in the back, taking care of the grounds. Riley motioned for Bonnie just to sit tight; he'd be right back. Within moments he was walking briskly back to the car and jumped in.

"Next stop is the preacher's house. By the way, he's got six kids. This should be fun."

"Then Collin is alive?" Bonnie was chewing on a fingernail.

Riley's smile was radiant. "He has been these last four years! You're fixin' to see your son!" He gave an unexpected warhoop and Bonnie wondered if a person could be intoxicated with joy! Riley was almost giddy as he turned the two-minute conversation with the groundskeeper into an explosive narrative of lifelong hope. Suddenly, they were in front of a two-story, white house with children in the yard. Bonnie searched for the blond head but didn't see one. She couldn't believe the conflict of emotions. A woman answered their knock.

"I remember you," she stared at Bonnie. "Though you look a might bit healthier now! You've come for your boy, haven't you?" There were immediate tears in her eyes.

"No." Bonnie answered so fast it even took her by surprise. "I just want to see him; not take him."

The woman's countenance brightened. "He's beautiful. Come on in, he's doing some studies with Brother Bill. What do you want me to tell him?"

"Is it okay if you just say we're your friends and we came by to say hello?"

"As you wish."

Riley followed behind Bonnie as they went towards a back bedroom. When they opened the door, both looked up. It was all Bonnie could do not to burst into tears. She clenched her teeth and took a deep breath and forced a smile.

"Yes, Mother?" Brother Bill stopped reading. "Do you need me?"

"Not at the moment. I have some friends here just passing through and they wanted to see how our children have grown. I thought I would find you in here. Collin, please come and say hello."

The boy got up and walked over to them, stretching out his hand to politely shake hands with Riley. Then Collin extended his hand to Bonnie. She took it gently at first and then she squeezed.

"My goodness you sure have grown!" Bonnie was at a loss for words.

"I have my own shotgun now and Dad takes me out hunting with him."

"He's my marksman." Brother Bill chimed in. "Next year he'll probably bring in more game than I do. I'm really proud of this boy."

Collin was a handsome child with impeccable manners. "Do you live around here?" he asked.

"No, it's a day's drive away."

"Oh, well, I hope you'll be able to come back some time soon. The church is having dinner on the grounds this Sunday. Will you still be here? We'd love to have you join us."

"I appreciate the invitation but we're going back tonight."

"You just got here. Won't you at least stay for supper?" Ruby invited them.

Bonnie started to protest but Riley quickly accepted. He was not only hungry but also prepared to spend as much time as possible. As usual, the men stayed together and Bonnie headed to the kitchen.

"My name is Ruby," she whispered, realizing that Bonnie had probably forgotten.

"I'm Suzette." She had a thousand questions to ask about Collin, so she was grateful for the time they had alone as they prepared the evening meal. "Does he still have seizures?"

Ruby handed her a big mixing bowl from the cupboard. "Yes, he does. But he handles them very well and the other children don't make sport of him. I want to assure you that he's well taken care of and he's very happy."

"Does he know anything about his birth or the early days?"

"As a matter of fact, he does. All of my six children have been left in my care and they have each been told that they were a special gift to us."

"Does he ever ask about me?"

Ruby smiled warmly. "He prays for his parents every night. His words are 'and God bless my real parents wherever they are and let them know I'm okay."

Bonnie's eyes suddenly filled with tears that she couldn't hold back any longer. Ruby embraced her as she sobbed. After a few moments she regained her composure. "I'm sorry," Bonnie apologized. "Would you let him know that his prayers have been answered?"

"Yes, of course. What do you plan to do next?"

"I honestly don't know. I have a job now but I'm not where I can properly take care of him." She had to choke back the tears again. "But, I do want my boy."

Ruby had a strength that Bonnie truly admired. "I understand that. Then, this is what we'll do. When you leave here I'll talk to him about living with his real mother; you know, prepare his little mind. Before you take him I'll tell you everything you need to know about his condition and how to care for him. He requires a lot of supervision. He doesn't have the seizures so often any more but you never know when one will overtake him.

"Ever since you brought him to my door I knew in my heart that you'd be back. I want you to know that I can't love him as much as you do, but he's never lacked in anything that was in my power to give. He's a good boy and if you do wrong he'll preach at you!" Ruby laughed, remembering the times when Collin had reminded one of the other children that the Lord would not be pleased with their actions.

"Don't be surprised if he becomes a man of the cloth. If you take him, you'll make sure he goes to church, won't you?"

"I promise you that." As much as her heart was rejoicing, she knew Ruby's was breaking. She had been a mother to him longer than Bonnie had! How could it be that one child could be loved so much? Ruby had five others, Bonnie had four. And yet, the love for Collin was as strong as though there wasn't another child in the world. Sometimes Bonnie was overwhelmed with the power of love. Hate was pretty powerful, too, but it was so destructive. Love was good. It was kind and understanding and unselfish. It only wanted the best that life had to offer. Ruby was going to let the boy go without a fight. And she was doing it out of love. Bonnie had to wonder if she would be able to do the same thing. Which would be loving him more? Leaving him in the home where she knew he was being taken care of, or having him with her? Did she have the wisdom or ability to take care of his physical and spiritual needs? It was something she would have to consider.

When they were all sitting around the table to eat, four adults and ten children (friends were included) they all joined hands as Brother Bill gave thanks. It was then that Bonnie realized what was missing in her life. When she closed her eyes for the prayer, she imagined what it would be like to be holding on to Lucy, Bernadette, Collin, Arnold, Patricia and Riley's hands. She wasn't sure why Riley was included, but he was there, too, just like a real family. And they were all thanking God for their many blessings. That's what was missing—the Comforter, the great Provider, the Invisible Guest at each meal! It wasn't enough just to think about God, those thoughts had to hold hands with a lifestyle! They had to live the thoughts through breath and deeds.

Bonnie tried to share her ideas with Ruby while they were cleaning up the kitchen. The children had gone back outside and Brother Bill and Riley were sitting on the front porch.

"You say you have more children?" Ruby handed her a plate to dry.

"Four more." She gave their names and explained about Lucy and then the quick glimpse of her second child when she was in the convent. "My husband forbid me to name the children, but I did anyway. I told the nuns that she was to be known as Bernadette Marie."

"Bernadette? That's not a common name and yet, I've heard it." Ruby's hands were suspended in midair as she searched her memory. Only her eyes darted back and forth as she tried to "see" the child that went with the name. "Oh, yes, I remember now. I don't want to get your hopes up but there is a young girl by the name of Bernadette that goes to school with the children." A broad grin brightened Ruby's face. "She's older than Collin and you can mark my words that that child has the blackest hair of any child I've ever seen! I wonder if she could be yours?"

"That would seem too good to be true! I had feared that the couple who took her probably lived a great distance from the convent so no one would ever be able to find them. I've only recently learned that such adoptions are not really legal." Bonnie stopped talking a moment, seeing that there were tears in Ruby's eyes. "I'm so sorry, I'm upsetting you with all this talk, aren't I?"

She shook her head, dismissing it. "It's okay, I'm just a softie. My heart just breaks to think that your husband would force you to give up each one of your children. I remember the night you showed up here with Collin. I told Brother Bill that very same night that you would be back for him. It was obvious then that your mothering instinct was far stronger than your vows of obedience. You'll never hear me say that your marriage vows are not sacred, but I do have to question the validity of obedience when God does not direct it. I believe that's why the Holy Book says we are to be equally yoked. The God I know would never ask you to submit to the kind of cruelty you've experienced. I think you've paid your dues, child. It's time for you to get your little ones back. If you saw this girl that I'm thinking of, do you think you would recognize her?"

"I know that Lucy looks an awful lot like me. And even though Collin has blond hair, he has my eyes and lips. Patricia looked more like her daddy and so did Arnold. At least I would like to see her. I kind of think my heart will know even if my eyes don't."

"Then why don't you two spend the night and I'll take you to the schoolhouse tomorrow and if the child is there, you can see her without anyone asking questions."

"That's surely taking advantage of your hospitality." Bonnie thought it too good to be true.

"What else do I have to do then to help out someone in need? The Bible says, 'when you do it to the least of these my brethren, you do it unto me'. If I were in your shoes, I would certainly want someone to help me."

"How can I ever repay you?"

Ruby laughed, "Oh, that's easy. You do the same thing for someone else. It's passing the kindness. Like a relay race the children play all the time. You pass it to them, and they pass it to another and then the other passes it to yet another, and the kindness never stops."

Once again Bonnie slept in a strange bed. But this time there was a tiny body next to her. Generally, two girls slept to a bed but the older one agreed to sleep on the floor. The little one was curled up next to Bonnie; a doll in one hand and her thumb in her mouth. Once she was asleep, Bonnie had to reach across and stroke her hair. In this one bedroom she was sleeping with four little girls. All through the night she was kicked and poked but when morning came she had to admit that she felt vibrant and excited. Morning chores were done without complaint and then the children got ready for school. Ruby and Bonnie walked behind them. Riley went with Brother Bill to visit an elderly man who had fallen off his front porch and had possibly broken a hip.

Bonnie saw the black haired child before Ruby even pointed her out. She could have been wearing a sign, her features were so much like Bonnie's! "That's just got to be her!" She was almost holding her breath. Or, was it just wishful thinking? Was Bonnie seeing things that weren't really there?

"Would you be so kind as to wait for me just a moment?" Ruby headed right into the schoolhouse without any hesitation. The teacher was cleaning the blackboard.

"Good morning, Sister Ruby. What brings you here this early?"

"Curiosity. You have to understand my question comes from a mother of six that are not my own. Do you know if Bernadette's parents are her own God-given parents?"

"Well, I honestly don't know but I do have my suspicions they aren't. You didn't hear this from me, but I could have sworn that about ten years ago I heard Roxeanna Harris say she'd be willing to sell her soul to the devil if she could just have a child. And the next thing you know they sell the land they inherited from her great granddaddy and Claude starts making baby furniture. Now, what do you think?"

"I suspected as much. Are there any other children that come from questionable backgrounds?"

"Not that I know of." She continued cleaning off the board and then hesitated. "Well, come to think of it, I do remember a child some years back. A little boy. He died during that horrible flu epidemic, you remember that?"

"I sure do, I almost lost one of mine to that dreaded curse. Well, thank you. You've been more help to me than you'll ever know."

Ruby bid her a good day and then went back out to Bonnie and relayed the information. Bonnie had never taken her eyes off the child.

"She's beautiful, don't you think?" Bonnie was lost in her own world of dreams and memories and hopes.

"You trust me and I'll find out everything I can about her. Next time you come visit, I'll have you some answers. As far as I know she comes from a good family. That Roxeanna wanted children ever since she was a child herself. I reckon she's older than me, now, which puts her in her late fifties. As far as I know, Bernadette is her only one. I remember at the time I thought she was a little bit too old to have that child but the angel wasn't going to catch me laughing! Brother Bill couldn't afford to be silenced for nine months!"

Bonnie had no idea what she was talking about but she gave a little laugh to match Ruby's and acted as though she understood. They walked back to the house and it wasn't long before Brother Bill and Riley came strolling up.

"You'll bring her back, won't you?" Ruby was holding onto Bonnie's hand with both of hers as she questioned Riley.

"As long as you have no objections I sure will."

"You do that because this mama needs her babies. Everything will work out just fine."

"Did God tell you that?" Bonnie asked as she wet her lips.

Ruby wrinkled her nose and looked at the sky. "I'd be in trouble if I told you He did. No, that's just from my heart to yours because I want it to be good."

Bonnie and Riley left right after that and they talked about the situation all the way home. Riley wasn't about to give any advise; he kept saying 'you follow your own heart. Then you'll know that you're doing the right thing.'

Bonnie wasn't ready to accept that. "What makes you think my heart knows? I appreciate your confidence in me, but I'm not convinced that I'll do the right thing whether I try to reason it all out or if I just rely on my own desires. If it was a math equation you would only have one correct answer. But we're involving people's lives here and there's as many answers as there are people."

"But doesn't a mother know?" Riley was watching the road and wouldn't look directly at her. "Collin and Bernadette are your flesh and blood and were taken wrongly from you. You have every right to take them back if you want to."

"Oh, I want them both, there's no arguing that. But my rights? Are my rights more important than theirs? And what about Roxeanna? If she spent every dime she had for that baby, how can I just take her away? She'd die from a broken heart, Riley. Or, she'd hate God and say it was a cruel joke He played on her; giving her a baby to love and then taking it away from her. I have no right to do that."

"You just amaze me," he was shaking his head. "You sure you're real?"

"Pinch me and see."

He reached over and pinched her arm and she immediately hit him. "Hey, what'd you do that for?"

"Did you feel it?"

"Of course I did."

"Then I must be real! I felt it and delivered it right back."

They both kind of settled back and remained in silence for the next thirty minutes. Bonnie had a lot of thinking to do and she appreciated the time to sort out her thoughts. And then they were home.

She thanked him. "What happens next?"

"Well, we found three out of the five. Surely the last two won't be any problem."

Bonnie sighed. She certainly hoped not.

Ruby was standing at the front window watching the children play outside. Brother Bill was in his favorite chair, reading. "I'm going to walk a bit," she told him and then went out the front door. She had been thinking and crying. Suzette Freeman had every right to her child but Ruby didn't know how she could bear to ever give Collin up. He was as much a part of her life as her husband of twenty-nine years! Hadn't she warned herself not to get too close to him? Hadn't she known that the mother would return? Yes, she had known it to be a definite possibility; she just wasn't prepared for the reality!

Her steps took her to the church and then behind it to the little cemetery. Something was bothering her. With the first familiar name she was distracted. Old man Hammond had been a man of God's own heart! Lived a good life and left a rich heritage for his children. His funeral had been a time of celebration, not sadness. Next to him was his beloved wife, Bessie. Ruby could see the two of them glad to be in Heaven but intent on looking into each other's eyes and sharing a silent kind of oneness again. Tombstone after tombstone brought back memory after memory. Towards the back of the cemetery was a section for all the little children. Tiny crosses stood before tiny mounds like little sentry soldiers. Ruby walked back and forth until she found the one she was looking for.

There it was. She bent down on one knee and talked to God a minute. Carved in letters bore the name and epithet:

BUSTER ARNOLD ALEXANDER AKINS
Born 1937 Died 1938
His initials spelled BAAA
and he will forever be our little lamb.

~~~~~

It started raining in Willoughby. The first two days the puddles and leaks were tolerated because everyone hoped that it would soon end. But the rain didn't quit. The puddles got deeper and some streets were flooded from curb to curb. Bonnie didn't own any galoshes so she put on old shoes and
~~~~~

carried ones she would work in. By the time she walked the four blocks to the café, she was drenched. The following four days of rain kept her clothes stuck to her from the dampness. She wasn't surprised when she came down sick. Bonnie had been tempted to stay home from work, but she knew she needed the money.

When the last bus came in she was going to go on home but by then her fate was already determined and there was nothing she could do about it. Even though a woman had come in, Bonnie hadn't actually looked at her until she put the glass of water in front of her and then it was too late. There was immediate recognition, but Bonnie simply felt too miserable to try and bluff her way out of it.

"I know you, don't I?" The woman grabbed Bonnie's wrist and held it tightly.

"No, Ma'am, I don't believe so. Do you live here?"

"You know perfectly well that I live in Janesville. And looky over there, isn't that Mr. Census-taker himself hidin' behind that door? Now, isn't this a peculiar turn of events?" She let go and Bonnie had to rub her wrist a moment it hurt so badly.

"I'm sorry, I have no idea, whatsoever, as to what you're talking about." Bonnie's heart was beating frantically and all she wanted to do was run. A lack of energy kept her glued to the floor.

Delores smiled as she sat back. "I want a hamburger and fries and make it quick. I got business to attend to while the rain is slacked off a bit." Nothing more was said, but Bonnie was worried. Deeply worried.

As soon as she had a moment with Riley she whispered "Delores is here and she recognized both of us."

"Just act normal. There's nothing that says we can't have two jobs. If you don't give her reason to suspect anything maybe she'll just let it pass."

But she didn't. She had no intention to. As soon as Delores left the café, leaving no tip for Bonnie, she finished her business in Willoughby and then drove back to Janesville. She kept running her tongue across her teeth, delighting in what was about to happen. Even though it was late, she headed straight to the police station.

"I know where that Bonnie Parker is," Delores told the first officer she saw. "What'll you give me now for turnin' her in?" She was already counting the money before he put it in her hand!

By the next morning, Bonnie didn't know if she was nauseated from having a cold or from fear. Either way, she didn't have the strength to even get up and get dressed. She took more medicine, trying to relieve some of the pain in her chest and head. All of a sudden there was a hard pounding, and it wasn't in her head! Her door was about to be pounded off its hinges.

"This is the police, open up immediately."

Bonnie staggered to the door and opened it just a crack. The man pushed his shoe in between the door and the frame and then shoved the door open even wider. "We have a warrant for the arrest of Bonnie Parker, ward of the state and a fugitive.

"I don't know who you're talking about. I'm Suzette Freeman, I can show you a notarized paper that proves it." She immediately started looking for it in the desk but she was so nervous her fingers were flipping through papers without meaning. The two officers wouldn't wait for her to locate it.

"Get your sweater, Ma'am, you've got to go with us."

"I can't! I'm too sick to even walk!"

"Yes, we understand your sickness. I'm sorry, but you're under arrest. If you need a physician's care it will be given to you."

"At least let me change clothes! I need more than just my sweater if I'm going outside." She stared at them as they stood motionless.

"So, change." The officer kept his eyes on her with a smirk. "But you have to stay within our sight. You won't pull a little disappearing act on us this time!"

They continued talking as she turned her back to them and tried to dress as modestly as she could. Matters were only complicated when she had to drop down into a chair for fear she was going to pass out. They thought she was just acting so yelled at her. As soon as she regained her balance and was dressed, it was only a matter of terrifying moments before she was going down the stairs and being escorted into the police car. Billie watched from her living room window, waiting to see which direction they went as she frantically dialed Riley's number.

Nothing Billie could have done would have helped the situation. Everything seemed to be running ten minutes late. As soon as Billie had called Riley, he was at the police station. Ten minutes earlier they had taken Bonnie to the train station. He had gone to her room and found her paper that stated she was Suzette Freeman, but when he arrived at the train station, she had boarded the train just ten minutes prior to that, wearing a straight jacket and being guarded the entire way. There wasn't another train until morning.

The jostling and noise of the train only made Bonnie feel worse. By the time she arrived in Pearce, she was almost doubled over. Still, no one took her seriously. A man in white uniform was waiting on the sidewalk with a wheelchair. The policeman helped her in; signed release papers and then left.

Bonnie was immediately taken to the infirmary. A woman followed her into the room and pulled the little curtain around the bed.

"Strip down, honey, you need an exam." Nurse Sharon waited for her to obey.

"Don't do this to me, please. I'm too sick to endure anymore today." Bonnie couldn't even hold her head up.

"You should have come here months ago; then your treatments could have started sooner and you wouldn't be in such bad condition."

"No, you don't understand. My mind is perfectly healthy; it's just that I have the flu or pneumonia or something. I tried to explain, I'm not Bonnie Parker, I'm Suzette Freeman. You've got the wrong person."

"Sure, honey, whatever name you want to go by is just fine. We'll call you Hiawatha if you like that name better. But you're the right person. You were sure a hard one to track down. But we don't give up. You might as well settle in because you're home now."

"No, I can't stay here. I have children…"

"Bonnie-Suzette-Hiawatha, whatever your name is, your life that went on outside these walls ended the moment you got picked up. From now until you're released, you are ours, your number is 2707, and the only thing that will change that is your cooperation and future health. Do I make myself clear?"

Bonnie looked at the nurse, then at the stained gray walls and the cold steel table she was supposed to be examined on. She thought they were in the basement; there were no windows. The ceiling tile was yellowed from dirt and age, with ugly water spots where it had leaked from the roof. She sneezed and then shivered. How could life change so drastically? Even though the room was bright there was an oppressing darkness that seemed to cocoon her. But what would she emerge as? Suzette had been the butterfly. Once again she was just Bonnie Parker. That fact actually terrified her! Did butterflies turn into something else or did they just die?

Delores walked into the house with a smile. Her hand was clutching her purse as though it held a million dollars. To her…it was! She had received the reward for turning in Ronnie's great niece. Even though she knew it would mean Lucy would have to stay longer, she delighted in the fact that she had the woman put away. Any mother that would abandon her own flesh and blood didn't deserve to have a life of her own and Delores let everyone know how she felt about it.

She clearly remembered that day that the two "census takers" had showed up at her door. At first she had believed the story, but then she wondered why her house had been the only one they had gone up to. Something about that woman had looked familiar but she didn't know why. It was only when Lucy made a comment about her looks that Delores began suspecting what was really going on. The child had seen the man and woman sitting out in the car and then had positioned herself behind a tree to watch them as they went up to the house. That night, Lucy had commented 'that woman looked so much like me it was spooky.'

That's what gave Delores the idea to start digging through pictures. She found one of Kenny and Bonnie when they first got married. The resemblance was indeed uncanny. Delores knew that Bonnie had come looking for her child, and she was going to do everything she possibly could to prevent it.

"She looked like a nice lady." Lucy raised her eyebrows as she chewed on the end of her pencil.

"Well, you don't want nothing to do with her, I can tell you that." Delores warned Lucy with a threat in her voice.

"Why not?" The question came from innocence.

"She dumped you here when you were a baby and hasn't seen you since. No birthday presents, nothing for Christmas, no money, no nothing! What makes you think she cares a thing about you now? If she did she would have identified herself like a responsible human being and spoken to you. Instead, she lied about who she was and what she was doing here. What kind of woman would do that, huh?"

"Maybe she didn't know who I was. Maybe she was scared to admit she's my ma."

"Or maybe too ashamed. Maybe she saw you and then decided she didn't want you after all. That woman is crazy and no good and you might as well accept that fact right now. The only reason she'd want you is to see how much money she could make off you. Look at your scrawny bones. You wouldn't even make a good parlor maid."

From that point on, if Bonnie's name came up, Delores was quick to put her down! Now, as she came in the house she saw Lucy sitting on the sofa, reading a book.

"Get your lazy self up and go do the laundry or something. You think time was made just so you could squander it away by reading some stupid book?"

"Where have you been?" Lucy reluctantly got up.

"Doing a good deed for society. You won't have to worry about that crazy woman comin' around here no more. She's right where she's supposed to be. In the nut house!"

"You mean my mom?"

Delores exploded. "I don't ever want to hear you call her that again! She's not your mom; all she ever did was just give birth to you, that's all! Like a dog givin' birth to a litter of pups! Judith Ann was your mom and now I've got you. And you better count your blessings that you have such a good home. You may think I'm unfair at times but it's a lot better than living with a crazy woman! No tellin' what she would have done to you! You'd probably starve to death or freeze or sleep out in some ally. I reckon I saved you from a fate worse than death."

There wasn't any reason why Lucy shouldn't believe Delores. Even though she didn't like her very well, she still respected adults and believed what they told her. Her lips were quivering as she walked away from Delores to gather up a load of laundry. Just as Delores had once taken a box, packed all her toys in it and stuffed it in the back of an unused closet, that's what Lucy did with the image of her mother. In the boxes of her imagination she stuffed the memory of the woman that had come to the house, along with all her hopes of one day being wanted by that same woman. Then she sealed each box and stacked them in the back of her mind's closet where things weren't needed anymore. Those thoughts were like outgrown toys and she wasn't going to think about them anymore.

As the days went by, if she did think about the woman, she gritted her teeth and scolded her thoughts. "I hate her!" Lucy didn't want to spend her entire life with Ronnie and Delores and it was all her mother's fault that she was there to begin with. It wasn't fair, and the more Lucy thought about it, the angrier she got.

CHAPTER 9

ଙ୍ଗ ଙ୍ଗ ଙ୍ଗ

1969

The sun was starting to set just as Phyllis and Will got back to the car. As she sat down, she immediately pulled her shoes off and propped her socked feet on the dashboard. "Wow, what a day! This has got to be one of the most thrilling days I've ever had in my entire life. Thank you, Will."

"My pleasure." He always liked to see her happy.

"Where do we go from here?"

"Home."

She played with her hair a minute, brushing it up with both hands and then running her fingers through it as she smoothed it back down. "Yes, but then what?"

"Seems like we need to talk to some people to try and fill in a lot of the gaps. Your mother for one."

"That could be interesting." She was hesitant.

Somehow, she didn't think Lucy would find this as exciting as she did. Nevertheless, she was determined to pursue it. For the next thirty minutes she became almost withdrawn as she searched her thoughts and rehearsed different ways to ask the questions she wanted answers to.

Lucy Parker was a determined woman who lived in her own world! Phyllis wouldn't say she had a deprived childhood, but she knew she had missed out on a lot! She'd never had a father and the early school days had been horrible. How many times had she avoided questions like 'who's your daddy?' or 'what does your daddy do for a living?' One time a lady had asked 'are you a daddy's girl? You sure don't look like your mother.'

Truth was, she didn't even know her father's name! All she knew was that her mother had gotten pregnant at fourteen or fifteen years old and hated men the rest of her life! As a child, Phyllis had never trusted men because of her mother's negative behavior. A school teacher had asked her once why she didn't like his class.

"I like social studies just fine. I just don't like men teachers." Her twelve years hadn't refined her bad manners or boldness. He hadn't taken it personally.

"But what if I told you something that was so terribly important that it would make your life the happiest life of anyone alive?"

"For sure I'd call you a liar and I wouldn't trust you! There ain't no such thing as that kind of happiness." She had looked at him as though he was crazy.

"Yes, there is," he persisted. "But, never mind, you wouldn't be interested."

"Why wouldn't I be?" she shot back in her own defense.

He seemed uninterested, "You wouldn't believe me even if I was telling the truth because you don't trust men."

"That's right, I don't." Phyllis had cocked her head and started to look away.

He sighed, "That's a real shame. You're gonna miss out on something that every child wishes they had and only a few are wise enough to get."

"What's that?" He had her attention.

"Can't tell you until you trust me."

"A person only becomes trustworthy when it's proven they aren't a liar." She quoted words she had heard before.

"Will you give me a chance to prove myself?" He had a look of expectancy and excitement.

"I suppose." She was quite reluctant, but at least consented to listen.

That's when her teacher began telling her about the love of Jesus Christ and how He could make a drastic change in her life. He said it didn't matter what her past was or who her relatives were. Jesus wanted her and her alone. Others could come, too, but He had a purpose for her and wanted to be a part of her life. This was all new to Phyllis. She'd never heard anything like it!

"I don't even have a friend, so how come this guy Jesus, all of a sudden, wants to get chummy with me?"

"He's been waiting a long time; it isn't sudden like."

"How come you're the first person to ever tell me this?" she challenged.

"Maybe no one else thought you would listen."

Then he told her about the church and how the people would be closer than family. Phyllis sighed; that was a long time ago and yet sometimes it still felt like yesterday. She could remember the first time her Sunday School teacher had told her that God was her Heavenly Father.

In her innocence, Phyllis had asked. "Does He ever come to earth to visit his children?"

The teacher had a warm smile, "Actually, His throne is in Heaven, but His residence is in our hearts, once we ask Him in. Did you know that your Father loves you?"

Phyllis shook her head; her eyes round with curiosity. "You know who my father is? Wow, you might want to tell my mom because she doesn't have a clue!"

It had taken her a long time to separate God from her earthly father! Her main question was why one father would love her when the other one didn't even want her. Phyllis was now convinced that if it hadn't been for her church family she would have never understood what love really meant. It was only through their concern and compassion that she could compare God as Father and friend. Lucy had never stopped Phyllis from going to church but she certainly wouldn't go with her! By the time Phyllis graduated from high school, she found herself far closer to her church family than to her own mother.

Now, Phyllis was going to ask questions about her past so that she could make sense of her future! When Will finally said good night, she locked the front door after him and then sat down next to the phone. With nerves on edge, she dialed her mother's phone number and waited with held breath.

"Yeah," the voice was deep and scratchy.

"Mom? Did I wake you?"

"Who's this?"

"Phyllis."

"What d'ya want?"

"I want to come by in the morning."

"You need money or something?"

"No, I just want to talk. Okay?"

"Suit yourself, I'll be here." She hung up.

Phyllis held the phone, not believing she had been disconnected so quickly.

"Fine. And thanks, I'll see you tomorrow," she told the receiver and then put it back in the cradle. It disturbed her, but she had learned a long time ago not to take it personally. Her mother was a sick woman and other than prayer and understanding, there wasn't a whole lot Phyllis could do about it.

Lucy seemed to live in anger and it ate at her existence like cancer. Phyllis was going to try and ask questions with as much sensitivity as possible. She knew she would be stepping on toes, but she didn't want to deliberately crush them. Besides, if she made Lucy mad, she knew she would instantly get kicked out of the apartment and achieve nothing! Why did it all have to be so difficult?

Maybe this was why she had never challenged the warning to stay out of the lives of her relatives. Bringing up the issue was going to create a lot of turmoil. Would it be worth it? Phyllis knew she would have to be gentle and yet strong. In her own Christian walk she knew the past could only be a monster if it wasn't leashed. It wasn't like a T-Rex that no man could tame or control. She knew that when God gave mankind dominion over his world, it meant having control over the past, present, and future as well. The present and future were pretty secure. But what was she going to do with the past?

The answers to that question began at eight o'clock the next morning when she got up and planned her day. Phyllis knew that her mother never got up before ten o'clock so she wasn't in any hurry. Sitting down at her desk, she pulled out a yellow legal pad and started writing down questions that she wanted to be sure and ask. At 9:30 she left her apartment and drove to the fish market; bought two pounds of oysters and headed across town to her mother's.

Finding a parking place was always difficult. She had to drive around the block twice before a couple leaving the apartment building finally got out to their car and left their space along the curb. She had slipped into a reserved space one time and almost got her car towed. Taking a deep breath and sighing a prayer for peace, she grabbed the white carryout bag and went into the building. The elevator took her to the sixth floor. Even before the doors opened she could smell the stale odor of garbage and mildew. How she hated it here! Endless protests had gotten her nowhere. The place was always filthy. Roaches and rats cohabited with the residents because there was a continual mound of trash left out. Phyllis shivered just thinking about it.

Her steps seemed to squish into the dirty carpet as she went four doors down from the elevator. Phyllis blew out her breath slowly and then knocked.

Lucy answered the door, wearing a faded green smock that was torn on the shoulder. Her hair was an uncombed mess. Cigarette in one hand, a beer in the other. The two stared at each other, and then Lucy noticed the bag.

"Is that what I think it is?" She took a drag from the cigarette and deliberately blew the smoke on her daughter.

"I always bring you oysters," she handed them to her.

"Yeah, especially when you want something. You think it will soften me up, huh?"

"No, I just know you like them and don't have a chance to buy them."

"If rat turds were oysters I'd be in luck, wouldn't I?" she laughed and then choked, immediately guzzling the beer to stop the cough.

Phyllis went on in the room and sat down at the kitchen table. Lucy's humor was always a good sign because Phyllis wouldn't have to pin up the skirt of depression before she exposed the petticoat of truth. She kind of hoped it would be the standard for the whole morning.

"You doing okay?" Phyllis tried to make eye contact but Lucy wasn't ready to look at her.

"What do you think? Coffee?"

"Sure."

Lucy turned and flicked a roach off the counter as she pulled the coffee maker out from the wall. Phyllis knew that as soon as she opened the cupboard door, roaches would scatter like pepper blown in the wind. She hated this place! Lucy was oblivious to it.

"So, what's on your mind? Why am I being graced with your presence this morning?"

Phyllis decided to plunge right in. "Will took me out to a little cabin that used to belong to our family. It's right outside of Gough's Ridge. Do you remember the place?"

Lucy stopped with her hand in midair with the coffee filter. She squinted her eyes and frowned. "Sure I do. I blew the damn place up." Then she remembered she wasn't allowed to cuss in front of her daughter. "Excuse the language but if a place can have a curse on it I suppose it's legitimate to say it's damned, right?"

Phyllis didn't even hear the vulgarity. "You blew it up?"

Lucy grinned as she bit on her lower lip and then continued to make the coffee. "I sure did. Didn't burn long enough, though. Never no mind, it was enough to satisfy my anger."

"Why'd you do it?" Her mother seemed to be in a talkative mood and Phyllis was going to take advantage of every moment.

"I hated it. I hated the people who lived in it. I hated everything about it. So, I blew it up."

"Didn't you get in trouble?"

"Why should I? It's my cabin so I reckon I can do what I want to with it. Kenny left it to me when he died; as though I would have wanted it! I was never so glad to see a sorry scum of a human being leave this earth. He didn't go soon enough, I can tell you that."

"Kenny was your father?"

"Nah, just the old man that physically gave me life and then mentally destroyed it." As she watched Phyllis's expression, her crudeness shifted to a serious murmur. "Yeah, Phyllis, he was your grandfather for whatever that's worth."

"How'd he die?"

Lucy thought about it for a minute and then laughed until she started choking. "His little concubine shot him. Guess he hit her one too many times because they called it self-defense and she came off cleaner than a whistle. Battered woman sympathy, you know? There she sat in court with her leg in a cast and her face lookin' like hell. Sorry. It's hard to talk without cussing. You still against that sort of thing?"

Phyllis raised her eyebrows as she confirmed it with a nod. Lucy scoffed and took a long drag on her cigarette. "At least you don't try and hide my beer anymore. So, why'd you come? I forgot."

Now was the time and Phyllis wasn't going to back down. "I'm going to write my autobiography and create a family tree. I really want to know who the Parkers are."

"And you expect me to tell you?" There was a flare of hostility in her voice.

"I was hoping you would."

Lucy suddenly had a sly smile. "Without cussin'? Can't do it. There's not enough nice words in my vocabulary. How well do you draw them little stars and bleeps and things that represent them naughty words?"

"You can do it," Phyllis had to smile, too. "You're in rare form this morning, how come?"

Lucy opened up the white bag and took out the container of oysters. Taking the lid off she smelled them first with a long ahhhhh. Without a fork she reached in and pulled out one of the slimy looking tidbits and popped one in her mouth, washing it down with beer. Then she wiped her fingers on her smock.

"Man, I love those things. They go down so smooth."

Phyllis almost shivered. She could eat them but only on a cracker with cocktail sauce. Never for breakfast! As soon as the coffee was ready, Lucy filled two cups and sat down at the table, one leg under her. Phyllis noticed that her mother's leg was scabby and must not have been shaved in months! She shook her head as though shaking out one thought so she could think clearly on another.

"You really blew up the cabin?" Phyllis asked.

"I sure did. It was evil and needed to be blown up. Why are you interested in it?"

"Will and I kind of wanted to restore it and maybe live out there."

"Have you completely lost your mind, child?" She scooped out another oyster and dropped it in her mouth. "Nobody would willingly live out there."

"We think it's beautiful and peaceful. Did you always live in Janesville?"

"I did until I ran away from that witch of a stepmother."

"What happened to your mom; my grandmother?"

"You tell me." Lucy was suddenly stern and her body was tense.

"No, Mother, you tell me. Here I am, and I don't even know my own grandmother's name! What happened to her?"

"She got what she deserved."

"Why are you so hateful towards her?"

"She never wanted me. Left me in the care of relatives who didn't want me either. She got into some kind of trouble and the state committed her. Crazy as a lunatic. You be sure and put that in that autobiography you're writing. She had her a friend by the name of Riley. He tried to get her out of that crazy house but it didn't do no good. That just tells ya she was there for a reason!"

"What made you decide to go back to the cabin?"

"I figured if my own mother didn't want me, maybe my father would." The older woman suddenly hit the table and with an angry, agonized face cursed him with a string of profanity. Then her attention went back to Phyllis.

"I wasn't there for twenty-four hours before I found out what he was all about! Wished I could have killed him myself! At least I got the satisfaction of seeing that cabin go up in smoke!" Lucy smiled as her eyes looked back into memory. "What a beautiful sight it was! You should have heard that boom! You'd a thought it was the grand finale to some 4th of July celebration or something and they set off a hundred fireworks. Prettiest thing I ever saw! And then I just walked away from there."

"How old were you?"

"Too young to be forced to have something like that in your memory for the rest of your life."

"Was that before you had me?"

Once again anger crossed her face and for a moment, Phyllis was afraid the woman was going to get violent. "You don't need to know nothin' about your birth or what was going on at the time. You understand me, girl?"

Each word was spit out in fury. Lucy was shaking. Normally, Phyllis would immediately back off and change the subject with an attempt to calm her mother down. Not this time.

Phyllis found herself almost rigid. "I'm truly sorry if it upsets you, but I'm going to find out about my past and I would like to hear it from your mouth first. I think you owe me that much respect."

"Respect?" she hollered. "What about what you owe me?"

"Don't turn it on me; I've respected you all my twenty years! This is important to me and I'm old enough to handle it. What can you possibly tell me that I haven't probably figured out on my own? Or worse yet, that I've imagined? Maybe I'm believing a lie simply because you won't tell me the truth!"

"Oh, no." Lucy shook her head as she opened another beer and drank half of it before she continued. "You don't need to know nothin', and you won't want to know, neither."

"Well, that may be true but I'm still going to find out. What's the deep, dark secret Mom? What have you tried to keep from me all these years? Surely, it's not all that horrible."

"You think not?" She lit another cigarette and then with cold contempt she sat down next to Phyllis and leaned across the table so their faces were no farther than three inches apart. If Phyllis hadn't been so intent on hearing the truth, she would have gagged at her mother's bad breath.

"Okay." Lucy seemed to be building the courage to tell her daughter the truth. "Okay. You want to know why I destroyed that cabin and why I drink like I do? You want to know who's to blame for how I live now?"

She gave a dramatic pause as she backed up a bit, licked her lips and then rubbed her eye and cheek. Through yellow, stained teeth she almost hissed the name. "Kenny Fisher."

Her gaze burned into Phyllis's heart, as though gloating in the struggle she was seeing in her daughter's comprehension. "That's right, your own grandfather." She blew out a stream of smoke with harshness behind it. "That's who your daddy is. And that's who destroyed my life at the tender age of fourteen. Now, aren't you glad you know?"

Phyllis hadn't been prepared for this information. She had always suspected her mother of having a childhood affair. One of those only-one-time situations that could change a life forever. But her own grandfather? No wonder Lucy never married. Now Phyllis understood why her mother always seemed to be mad at her. Her uncanny resemblance to her grandfather continually reminded Lucy of that horrible man! She was momentarily speechless as a million thoughts, that now seemed to hold hands with a matching explanation, went through her mind. Now it all made sense!

Gaining her composure she sat up straight. "Yes, yes I am glad I know! For your sake as well as my own, and maybe even my children's! Oh, Mother, what horrible things you must have endured in your silence. No one knew about Grandfather's behavior?"

Lucy swore again as she opened the refrigerator door and then slammed it shut without getting anything out of it. "Of course someone knew! That little bleached-blond step-mother knew all too well! For God's sake, Phyllis, she watched it all happen and said it was my fault. I shouldn't have seduced him! I didn't even know what that word meant! Then she told me how unfair life was and if anyone expected to survive they just had to learn how to deal with it! She said everyone is a victim and that I could be glad I learned it at a young age. Yeah, I was real glad!"

Phyllis's spirit was rebelling. It just wasn't right! Her heart was breaking for the injustice of the whole situation. Lucy apparently saw it in her face.

"If you think you're going to pity me now you can forget it! I don't need anything from you." She turned sideways in her chair, crossing her legs again.

Phyllis knew she had to break the tension so she smiled in a humorous defense. "Yes, you do. I'm the only one who brings you fresh oysters."

Lucy started to scowl but then gave in to a smile as well. "Okay, so maybe there is one thing."

Once again they sat in silence. Maybe a full five minutes. It didn't seem long or uncomfortable. For the first time in all of their time together, the two seemed to be at peace with each other.

Finally, Phyllis stood up and refilled her coffee cup. "I'm not feeling sorry for you, but I do realize what a horrible secret you've kept all these years. Thank you for telling me."

"I suppose you had to know at some point in your life." Lucy ran her fingers through her filthy hair. "Not that I want you to spread it around. Even though most people that it would affect are dead now."

"Where's Bonnie?"

"She's slowly dying in some kind of rest home or another. That institute fried her brain with all them drugs and stuff. Her daughter takes care of her."

"Daughter? That means you have a sister. You've never talked about a sister."

"I've never talked about none of the family, now, have I?" Her voice was edged again with crispness.

Phyllis nodded, that was very true. The thing Lucy most often had said was 'if you don't know nothin', then nothin' can hurt you.'

Lucy laughed at the thoughts that were going on in her head. "What a tangled web we weave! Yeah, there's family all right. You got aunts and an uncle living all over this county. But do you think you'll ever see them? Not a chance. Everyone is hidin' like a lizard on a branch. The only reason I know they exist is because Riley tried to help me once."

"What about your sister that takes care of Bonnie?"

Lucy shrugged and swayed for a moment, then one corner of her mouth lifted in a smirk. "The first time I met her I decided I wasn't about to have nothin' to do with her."

Phyllis wasn't going to ask why not, even though she was anxious to know. Lucy dug down into the container of oysters and ate three before she continued. "Her name is Patricia. She'd been brought up with the Indians and her ways are dad-blame strange. When Bonnie got out of the crazy bin this old Indian woman got the two of them together. What a pair! I guess Pat's been with her ever since. Makes me sick."

"Why's that?"

"Think about it. A crazy woman and a deaf and dumb retard. Maybe they deserve each other."

"How can you say such a horrible thing about your own sister?" Phyllis didn't want to sound righteous but she was stunned at such coldness. Oh, how she had yearned to have a sister!

Lucy cocked her head, her eyebrows raised. "Do I care? What I think about any of them ain't gonna change what they are! I'm better off without any of my family around me."

Phyllis wasn't about to go along with that! She knew there was a social stigma on those with mental problems, and the deaf weren't particularly accepted in the mainstream of life, but Lucy was talking about flesh and blood family!

The thought kept running through her mind 'but God loves them and I bet I could, too!' Chances are Patricia was probably more socially stable than Lucy was! She wondered what it would have been like to have been brought up by the Indians in a totally silent world.

"How did the Indian woman know Patricia belonged to Bonnie?" Phyllis asked.

Lucy wiped her nose on a dingy hand towel. "Because dear, when Patricia was a baby, her wonderful father gave her to a tribe of Indians when Bonnie got so sick she was practically dying! Story goes that when Bonnie got back up on her feet, the Indians were long gone and she had no idea where to find them. Kenny said she was mad at him for years after that for giving the baby away. But he didn't care. Nice daddy, wasn't he?"

"What was the Indian's name?"

Lucy scowled. "How should I know? And why should I even care? All I know is that they took care of her until Bonnie come out of that insane asylum."

"You know the names of the others?"

"Indians?"

"No," this time Phyllis scowled. "Of Bonnie's other kids." She was hoping that Lucy would stay with her and keep talking. The beer was beginning to have a negative effect on her.

"Don't know. Don't care," she said with a perky but resistant attitude.

Phyllis was silent a moment. "I heard about a Jonathan Parker that lived close to Gough's Ridge," she lied.

"Did not. Ain't no Parker living close to Gough's Ridge. Closest one is in Fuertes with that preacher family."

"Maybe it's his son then."

Lucy laughed scornfully. "Not unless his wife has been messing with another man. He can't have no kid in his condition." Then she suddenly realized that Phyllis had manipulated the information. "How dare you!" her eyes were hateful.

"How dare you deliberately lie to me. They're a part of my life as much as yours! How can you deny them as family?"

"It's real easy; they're a bunch of rejects, every one of them! You want to know Miss-Smarty-Pants? Fine, I'll tell you, so you can have an ear full! You got an aunt by the name of Sister Saint Something who has given her life to God Almighty and lives in that freezin' convent. As far as she's concerned she has no family. Thinks she married Jesus Christ Himself. Now, just what do you think we got in common, huh?

"At the opposite end of the spectrum is that demon possessed Collin that thrashes about in fits where he drools and bites his tongue and his eyes roll all crazy like. If you think I'll have anything to do with him you're crazy yourself! And then there's Patricia. Can't even carry on a conversation with her! She grunts as bad as Collin does. Makes my skin crawl, I tell you."

Phyllis had to bite her tongue, 'and then there's Lucy, the angry and bitter drunk', she thought to herself.

The young girl almost had tears in her eyes, so thankful that God had saved her from such a life! 'But why me?' She closed her eyes and addressed God privately. 'Why did you choose me to break the pattern? My life has been good and I'm happy and mentally sound and physically fit. But...what made the difference?' It was a question that she knew she would ponder for quite some time. Whatever the answer was, she felt incredibly blessed and unique.

"So, does that make me a wicked person in your eyes?" Lucy's voice snapped Phyllis out of her deep thinking.

"We all have our problems, Mom, some worse than others. I'm not going to sit here and condemn you for anything. I have no right to do that."

"Well, aren't you Miss Goody Two-shoes? Where's that boyfriend of yours?"

Phyllis was always glad to talk about Will! She welcomed a change in topic because she didn't think her mind could handle another thing. Lucy finished off the oysters and without rinsing the container threw it in the garbage. Phyllis looked at it, knowing the roaches would find it in a matter of moments. She eagerly talked about Will and gave her an update on the wedding plans.

"Mom, did you ever want to get married?"

Lucy was on the second pack of cigarettes. "I suppose I did at one time." She studied the pack a moment and selected a cigarette as though it was better than all the others. Striking a match she then shrugged. "Actually, I did. His name was Thaddeus Hyman Weatherford. He treated me real good and he had a respectable bit of money. I suppose we could have had a good life together."

"What happened?"

"He was too religious. Wanted to go to church every time the doors were open. He never told me I had to quit smoking or drinking but I knew he didn't approve of it." She laughed as she shifted positions in the chair, propping her feet up on the empty chair across from her and leaning back. "He sure did want to save my soul, I can tell you that."

Phyllis smiled, feeling the same sentiments. "So far you haven't told me anything bad about him."

Lucy frowned as though her daughter was stupid. "You're so narrow-minded. Just because you like going to church doesn't mean it's meant for everyone. You try walking in my shoes little lady and see how far it gets you. I walked into church with Thaddeus one day and everything was just fine until they found out you weren't my little sister. You can best believe they advised that boy to stay clear of me! So, I helped him out. I got out of his life real quick so he wouldn't get a bad name by seeing me. The church is nothing but hypocrites and I don't need them."

"Who does? Thank goodness the hypocrites are just a small minority of church members who have never matured. Don't judge us all because of one group of people. There are too many good people who really care."

Lucy picked up on the condescending tone, "I don't need to be preached to."

"No, you don't, but neither do you need to let one incident dictate your whole life."

"One incident?" Lucy totally lost it as she swore profusely. "Unwed mothers don't live with just one incident! It happens over and over and over!

We are never, and I mean never outside of the world's condemnation! Every time someone saw you they looked at me and passed judgment. No matter how clean I tried to keep you, they considered me filth! And them church people were the worse! So holier than thou! You know who took me in for awhile? A prostitute down on 7th Avenue, that's who. Nicest woman you ever met! She never put me down and she wasn't afraid to be seen with me! All those church people cared about was to ease their own conscience by getting my soul saved; like it was a feather in their cap or something. It's sick, Phyllis, just sick. "

Phyllis couldn't deny it. "I know, I've felt rejection too. But my prayer is that one day everyone will put all prejudice aside and love us for who we are. I can tell you there's good, honest, loving people in the church, too. People who really care and who stick closer to you than a brother. People who not only say God loves you, but then shows you how. I've got friends like that now, and I finally feel accepted with a positive sense of belonging. You're talking about me when you talk about the people of the church, because I'm one of them. I'm a Christian, Mom, and that doesn't mean I'm better than anyone else, it just means I give all my worries to God and let Him have control of my life. I hurt, too. I'm angry, too. And I make a lot of mistakes.

"You taught me that as long as I was under your roof you were responsible for me, but as soon as I left, then I couldn't blame anything on you because I was responsible for myself. You know you need God in your life and if He's not there then you're livin' with the biggest hypocrite of all and that's yourself."

Phyllis couldn't believe she was being so blunt! In fact, she had no idea why she even said what she did! Any other time, Lucy would have been furious. The older woman stared at her daughter, then dropped her feet to the floor, stood and opened the refrigerator door again. Both Phyllis and Lucy knew there wasn't anything in there that she wanted. When she turned back around she had tears in her eyes, but she wasn't angry.

"Some things you just can't help, now, can you? I made my bed, I'll lie in it."

"At least you could have clean sheets."

Lucy scoffed as she shut the refrigerator door and then went to the cupboard. Phyllis quickly closed her eyes as soon as her mother opened the cabinet door.

"If you've been wallerin' in filth all your life it really don't matter if the sheets are clean or dirty, now, does it? Stain is stain and it can't get washed away."

"Yes, it can. Whiter than snow, Mom, I've told you that before."

"So did Thaddeus. If other people hadn't interfered in our lives we'd probably be married and you'd have a last name. Maybe I wouldn't be living in this pig sty."

"Did you ever hear from him again?"

"Nope. I moved to Fuertes for about a year. That's how I found out about Collin and Bernadette. I did like that preacher lady that lived there. I suppose she was the first holier-than-thou-Bible-believer that wasn't a hypocrite." She noticed Phyllis was frowning. "Other than you, of course! You're okay even if I don't understand you."

Lucy paused for a moment and then continued as though her thoughts hadn't been interrupted. "Ruby was that woman's name. And she was a gem, just like her name. She liked you real well."

This was a story that Phyllis had never heard before! "Then why didn't we stay living there? I don't remember her at all."

"No, you wouldn't have. You were only about two, if that old." Lucy stared at the table for a long time, frozen with her hand still on the cupboard door. She gently closed it and then reached for her cigarettes again and sat down as she took another out of the pack.

"People who live a good life just have no idea what it's like to be shunned. When I was twelve I was so self-conscious I was humiliated if my socks drooped. For awhile I was a good student and makin' grades was important. I got treated with respect. But then more and more was expected of me and I came up short. All of a sudden, I was a dunce and told that I'd never amount to anything."

"People are cruel, I understand that."

"Do you?"

For a moment, Phyllis had to guard her temper. "Yes, Mother, I do! Maybe you lived with an illegitimate child but I was the one that never had a father! You've heard the name bastard I'm sure! I was the one who had to listen to all the rumors and slanderous remarks. I was never good enough to even be considered a friend even though I would have been a loyal companion for life! Were you ever aware of how lonely I was and how desperately I yearned to be loved and accepted?"

Lucy's mouth twitched and finally went into a half smile. "As much as I know my own loneliness and grief. Maybe we're both doomed to a lifetime of pain and misery."

"Not me! No, Ma'am! God has turned my life around and I'm going to marry Will who deeply loves me! And we're going to live happily ever after!"

"You do that Cinderella." She said it in an even tone without any emotion. The end of the cigarette was in the ashtray, motionless. Her eyes were gray and lifeless, her skin looking sallow. There were ugly, yellow stains on her fingers from the nicotine. Lucy looked sixty years old. She was only forty-six. For just a moment, Phyllis found incredible love for her mother, and yet undeniable repulsion for the life she felt forced to live. It didn't have to be that way!

Phyllis was overwhelmed with how choices affected a person's life. Too many wrong choices, as in Lucy's case, had spiraled her self-worth into an endless cycle of nothingness. Her life story was like taking a pen and drawing a continuous circle until it looked like an ink tunnel going across the page. Lucy was trapped somewhere in that never ending circle.

Whereas, the right choices, in Phyllis's case, had simply drawn a line across the page. There was a beginning, there would be a definite ending, and everything on that line was plain and simple. Even when there were occasional loops, nothing entangled her. Walls of insecurity didn't spiral around her. Did that make her a better person? Sadly, yes it did! But did she feel superior to this woman who existed in a roach infested house, a prisoner to the addiction of beer and cigarettes and worthlessness? Phyllis blinked slowly, not liking her answer. Yes. Yes, she did!

No! That's wrong! Phyllis scolded herself! 'I'm not superior, I'm just.....' she fought for the right word. What was she? Fortunate? Blessed? Lucky? Better off? Certainly all of that, but something else. Not superior, but...emotionally and spiritually above things not people. The love of God was the answer to all problems, all circumstances, all tragedies. It was sustaining and secure.

"So, what are you going to do next?" Lucy changed the subject, her voice lifting just a little. She actually made eye contact with Phyllis and waited for her to answer.

"Actually, Will and I want to write my autobiography and then see if we can do anything with the cabin. I truly did want to find out who it belonged to so I could see if there was any chance of buying it."

"I'm telling you, you don't want that place."

"I'm telling you I do."

This time Lucy was blazing with anger. "Why? So you can continue to rub it in my face? Don't you know the pain that existed in that cabin for everyone who lived there? There's not one soul that wasn't cursed by it!" Her eyes were hard and cold. "I would never come visit you! I don't need that kind of reminder."

That wasn't much of a threat! Lucy hadn't been in Phyllis's apartment since she had moved in! Phyllis shook her head and looked out the window as though it would help her to put her thoughts together.

"If you're sick, don't you want to get well? If something is broken, don't you want to fix it? If something is wrong, don't you want to make it right? The nightmare is over, Mom. The curse is going to be lifted. Will and I want to rebuild that cabin and fill it with love and goodness and let it be a garden for God.

Lucy gave a humph as she smiled. "Plan to grow any apple trees?"

"Now, aren't you clever?" Phyllis smiled back. "Sell us the place, Mom. If anyone can change it, we can."

"You're crazy."

"I suppose so." With tongue in cheek she teased again. "Sounds like I get it honestly, though."

Lucy let out a long sigh and just shook her head back and forth. "I'm not going to sell it to you."

Immediate defense made the question pique with frustration. "Why not? You don't want it."

Lucy ignored it. "Because I'll give it to you as a wedding present if that's okay."

Phyllis couldn't believe it! "Are you being serious?"

She coughed. "Right now I am. I might not be when I'm a little more sober so if you want me to stay true to my word here you better not complain about my drinking. I still won't step foot on that place, even if you turn it into the Garden Of Eden. For me it will always be hell on earth. I suppose if it don't bother you to look at them walls and know you were forcefully conceived there, then fine. Go ahead. You're a better person than me."

Phyllis chose her words carefully. "Living there doesn't mean I don't have respect for your pain. Maybe I was conceived in perversion, but I'll never regret you giving me life, when under those circumstances you could have aborted me."

"I may be the lowest scum on earth as a mother but at least I'm not a murderer."

"Thank you, it's going to turn out wonderful, you just wait and see! Oh, Mom, this makes me so incredibly happy! You just don't know!"

Phyllis wanted to jump up and hug her but she knew Lucy would push her away. She didn't like to be touched by anyone and showing emotion always disturbed her. Phyllis had hugged her once and she hollered 'Stop it! Stop it!' as she brushed imaginary cooties off. Actually it was rather humorous and they both had laughed.

"You still have to bring me oysters once a month." Lucy demanded.

"You know I will!"

Phyllis couldn't wait to tell Will everything that had just happened! Granted, she had learned some very disturbing facts about her childhood and her mother's life, but the fact that she was going to get the cabin made it all worth it! In her memory she could see the charred walls, the trap door under the old table, the chains on the bed. Yes, there had been pain within those walls, but she was going to write a new story! Without any explanation she suddenly saw a figure before her, as though a shadow.

"Mom, tell me something. How can I find out who that Indian woman was that seems to be popping up in all our lives?"

"Who?"

"The woman who protected Joe when he was a boy, and not only helped in Francine's birth but was there to comfort her after a tragedy. I bet it was the same woman who brought Patricia back to Grandma Bonnie. How can I find out who she was?"

Lucy squinted her eyes as she popped the top on another beer. Deep in concentration she looked at a picture on the wall, then down at the beer, then over at the bookshelf. Then she rubbed her nose.

"Tell you what. I think you should go to Fuertes and talk to that Ruby lady. She knows a lot of things about this family. Don't know how, for sure, but it seems like I can recall her saying something about the Indian askin' about Collin and Bernadette as well. I think Ruby might know something. She knew about little Arnold being dead."

"Who's Arnold?"

"Would have been your uncle if he hadn't died. He's the only one of us five kids that didn't make it. Sometimes I think he was the lucky one."

"Don't say that!" Phyllis objected. "Your life may change yet. There's a good world out there and the sun is shining." She picked up her purse and was getting ready to leave. "Want to go to church with me Sunday?"

"Huh?" The dumbfounded look on Lucy's face was a Kodak moment of life's oddest expressions.

Phyllis had a broad smile. "Never hurts to ask."

Lucy stomped on a roach that was scurrying across the kitchen floor. "Geez, girl, I give you a stupid cabin and you turn fanatical on me. What will you think of next?"

"How about accepting the Lord and getting baptized?"

Lucy closed her eyes in pretend exasperation. "Get out of here."

"I'm going. Can I do anything for you? Get you some groceries or something?" Phyllis offered.

Lucy waved her hand. "No, no, I'm fine. I get my check today or tomorrow and I got two good legs to take me where I want to go. Next time you come, don't forget the oysters. And bring some clams, okay?"

"You aren't going to eat them raw are you?" Phyllis grimaced.

"No! Good grief, I'm not crazy! Maybe I'll steam them and the oysters. That'll be a treat."

"Will do. Bye, Mom. I love you." Phyllis had her hand on the doorknob, ready to go out.

"Yeah, yeah." She shrugged and lit another cigarette as she raised her hand to say goodbye.

As Phyllis was walking out the door she thought, 'that's sad when your greatest pleasure in life is two pounds of oysters!' She started to take a deep breath but then realized where she was and knew it was better to actually hold her breath until she got out of the building! Terrible place to live! Absolutely wretched!

But then she saw the cabin in her mind and her excitement made her skip out of the building.

"Please, God," she begged, "don't let anything happen so Mom will change her mind."

As she went out to the car she imagined the scene where her own mother had placed some kind of explosive in the cabin to blow it up. Phyllis could see Lucy standing at a distance; eyes bright with the thrill of destruction. And then the boom! It must have rocked the ground she stood on!

Phyllis actually shuddered when she thought about her grandfather Kenny. What a wicked man he must have been. Well, he was dead and gone. That was the past which was only a stepping stone for the future. Then she thought about Will and how much she loved him. What a wonderful, enchanted future it was going to be!

Opening her car door and getting in, she looked at the steering wheel and knew that the next place this car was going would be to Fuertes, where a little gem of a lady lived; who just might know who the mysterious Indian was. To find her would be like finding the missing piece of the puzzle. In the meantime, she was going to go back to her apartment and read every page she possibly could that was still protected by the brown satchel.

CHAPTER 10

1969

Will was just about as excited as Phyllis was. It was a beautiful Saturday morning and they were only five miles outside of Fuertes. Phyllis had been up almost the entire night reading through the journal. Now, she knew it belonged to Landonelle Stivers Parker. The woman, who was also known as Nelle Parker was her great, great grandmother. If she was still alive she would be around eighty-six years old. Phyllis wasn't sure how to locate her but she sure wanted to try!

Along with the information she had gotten from her mother, Phyllis knew she had an accurate line up. Joe married Nelle, they had Francine who then gave birth to Bonnie. Lucy was the first of five children born to Bonnie and Kenny Fisher and Phyllis was the only daughter of Lucy. In each generation, someone had mentioned an Indian woman. Hopefully, Ruby had the answer as to who that woman was!

"But why would she be involved with each life all through the years?" Phyllis had asked herself that question probably fifteen times but she voiced it again for Will's benefit, even though she knew he disagreed with her.

"I don't deny there was an Indian, but I think it could have been several women, not just one." He had concluded.

Between the two of them they seemed to exist on entirely different wave lengths even though they had the same goal. They passed the sign that gave the name of the town and its statistics. FUERTES: Population 707.

Just as Bonnie and Riley had followed this exact road years before, Will and Phyllis headed down the main street looking for a steeple. They both knew that there wouldn't be that many churches. The first one they found was a Catholic church. Phyllis had a broad grin, "No need to stop there."

"Why not?"

"Priests don't marry. If there's no wife, there's no Ruby."

Will rolled his eyes. "Of course I knew that, I just wanted to make sure you weren't going to come up with another lame-brain story."

She smiled. He saw another church down the road and they slowed down. This one was a Methodist church. Phyllis couldn't explain it, but she didn't have the "right" feeling. Nevertheless, Will parked the car and went inside. Not more than five minutes later he returned.

"No Ruby there, the cleaning lady said to try the Baptist church."

"Where is it?"

Will backed up and then held up his finger to indicate 'just a minute'. He turned the corner and then went another block and there was the church with a beautiful steeple. This time Phyllis was too excited to stay in the car. When they went inside, it looked completely deserted. Then they heard someone moving around in the back.

"Hello?" Will called out. An elderly man came from around a corner with a questioning look on his face. "Sorry to bother you, but we're looking for the pastor's wife by the name of Ruby."

His grin went from one ear to the other. "That's my bride you're looking for. She's at the house. Follow me, I was just heading home."

Phyllis liked him immediately! If she had ever imagined a grandfatherly figure, he would have been it. He shuffled a little, not in any hurry at all. Will introduced himself and Phyllis and then discovered the man was Brother Bill.

The house was just a little over a block away so Will left the car and they enjoyed the walk. When Brother Bill found out they had never been to Fuertes before, he pointed out some of the historic sites and gave them some history. In all truth, Phyllis was fascinated with the small town. There was an old school building at the end of the block. A newer addition had been built, but the old remained intact and was well preserved. It had probably been one of the legendary one-room country schoolhouses with maybe thirteen students in the entire registry. Its name was Valley Home. The old structure was probably used now as an auditorium or a lunchroom.

Brother Bill grabbed the railing on his front porch and took each step at a time, making jokes about being old and decrepit. "Sure hope when I get to the pearly gates they'll give me a body with bulging muscles! I always wanted to be a weight lifter until I got in the ministry and then found out the weight of the world wasn't meant to be carried on my shoulders, no matter how strong I was!"

He stopped and opened the screen door and then gave a shove on the inner door. "Here we go, let's go find my little woman."

Ruby was sitting in the living room, looking at the newspaper. Her smile was genuine and even though Will told her not to get up, she did. She crossed the room and greeted them as though they were her own grandchildren. Ruby then insisted to get them all something to drink before they sat down to chat. Phyllis fell in love with the hospitality and the comfort and ease of the little home. Her mind immediately flashed back to her mother's apartment with all the roaches and stench. If Lucy could have had even a tenth of this…no, even one hundredth of it, she would have felt as though she was living on top of the world! What made the difference?

And then it suddenly hit her. God was in this home through the lives of Brother Bill and Ruby. God was in her and Will's life. Never before had she seen the light conquering darkness more than she did right then! It had nothing to do with her determination to make something of herself by having the things her mother never had. It had everything to do with her conviction that Jesus Christ was both Savior and Lord and that she had pledged a willing obedience to Him for the rest of her life.

When they finally settled down, Phyllis wasn't sure where to start. She took a sip of the sweet tea and then squared her shoulders. Ruby was looking at her with expectation. Looking quickly over at Will, she could sense that he was going to remain quiet and let her do the talking.

"Well," she lifted her shoulders and then relaxed. "Will and I are looking for a woman that you may have met quite a few years back. I have no idea what her name is; all I do know is that she is an Indian and apparently knows a lot about my family."

"Then you must be of the Parker clan that my pride and joy comes from." Ruby sat back and folded her hands in her lap as though remembering years and years of special times. Then she leaned forward and tilted her head to the side. Raising her hand, one finger pointed towards Phyllis. "But, you my dear, are different from the other Parkers."

"Why do you say that?" Phyllis voiced it at the same time Will was mouthing the exact words.

"I know my sisters." She stated matter-of-factly.

"Are you related somehow to the Parkers, too?" Will asked.

"Oh, no." She opened her hand, shaking all five fingers as though 'wrong, wrong'. "I'm talking about my spiritual family. You're a child of God, are you not?"

"I certainly am."

"Then I can share my heart with you and you'll understand. Let me tell you about this woman you're asking about, as well as the ones she has protected. I know this story because she came here—oh, several years ago, I believe—and we had a wonderful talk. She is a most remarkable woman!" Ruby sighed and even though she made eye contact with both Will and Phyllis, she seemed to be looking more at the past as though it were an exquisite mural enveloping them in that very room.

"It all began somewhere around 1886, about sixteen miles from here in a little, log cabin nestled in the woods."

"We've been to that cabin!" Phyllis almost came out of her seat! "In fact, my mother is going to give it to Will and me as a wedding gift."

"Then you should know it's history. Ira Parker lived there and he had one son living with him, and this Indian girl that he kidnapped and held hostage. Even though he called her AnnaBelinda her real name was Wind In Mourning. Beautiful name, don't you think?"

Phyllis had a shiver run through her! She knew she had been right! Just the name of the woman somehow brought her close and as real in her own life as Will was.

Ruby continued. "All the time she stayed with that evil man I'm sure the wind did mourn for her. But she escaped and ended up with a Christian family in Gough's Ridge. Frothworth returned her to her people, but first she was introduced to Jesus Christ and he told her that the great Spirit she worshipped was really God, the Father. This was knowledge that she had to nurture on her own. Just like cultivating a crop, she watered it and fertilized it and tenderly took care of each little shoot of faith that sprang up from the foundation and truth of Christianity.

"Even though her people traveled quite a bit, she stayed with Frothworth at least once a year. She was always checking on little Joe, Ira's son. Wind In Mourning had pledged in her heart that she did not want Joe to be evil like his father. Frothworth had a son named Gunther and if there was something special happening, Gunther knew where to find Wind In Mourning and he would ride out and get her."

"Then it was Wind In Mourning who helped Nelle give birth to Francine." Phyllis cut her eyes over to Will and grinned.

Ruby's eyes sparkled as she sat back in the rocker for a moment. "Oh, what a beautiful story that was! No sooner had she swaddled that baby girl than she heard the doctor coming. Barely got out of the house in time. Wind In Mourning never wanted to be seen. She had followed Joe as he made the journey to his uncle's. That was an exciting trip, I can tell you! She left him food and at night she would cover him and touch his hair. If he woke up she would tell him she was the night spirit watching over him and that he had to go back to sleep so she could keep the bears away. He protested, 'no, you're AnnaBelinda' but she told him she only looked like AnnaBelinda so he wouldn't be afraid of her. Clever, don't you think? Anyway, once Joe was safely at his uncle's house she went back to Frothworth and then rejoined her people.

"No one in town liked Indians so she was always cautious that she didn't cause trouble for her white family. By all rights, Wind In Mourning would have been vindicated if she had hated every white person alive! But she had a remarkable spirit within her that kept her doing the right thing. If ever there was a true missionary, Wind In Mourning was a precious example! All the hate and anger and revenge that you would have expected from her became love and patience and blessings. Why? Because Gunther became Christlike to her and through example helped her to understand the miracle of grace and salvation and got her out of her heathen beliefs.

"That's why she ventured to that cabin on the night Francine was born. She loved that boy, Joe, and she didn't want him to bury his first child. Later on, she would go into Gough's Ridge when Francine was there singing. Frothworth kept a close eye on everything. Wind In Mourning was there when Thomas was tragically struck down and killed."

"And was it her tribe that Patricia was given to?" Will jumped the story just a bit.

"Yes, it was."

"Wow, what's the odds of that happening by coincidence?" Phyllis asked out loud.

"Actually, it wasn't what you think, though I agree that God had His hand in it. These people traveled two or three times a year and there was only one other tribe that did, too, but they were farther south. Well, Wind In Mourning knew that baby the moment she laid eyes on her. But she also knew that Bonnie's husband was a wicked man. Little Claw's woman was barren and that little girl couldn't have been more loved. You see, Wind In Mourning and I talked about this because I was given a boy to raise. Bonnie's first son, Collin."

"Bonnie is my grandmother and Mom said something about Collin having fits or something."

"Yes, he's epileptic. Patricia is deaf. Two of the most precious children in this entire world! When Bonnie stood at my front door with him, my heart broke for her. Oh, she hated to give him up. I could hear her wailing when she left him! She came back for him when he was eight or ten, I forget now. Oh, I did some wailing myself, I can tell you! But I knew he had only been loaned to me. I'm just Collin's caretaker. Anyway, even though I had found peace in myself about him being returned to his mother, it never happened."

"She was put in the insane asylum, wasn't she?" Phyllis asked.

"Yes, even though her mind was just as sane as yours and mine. My, how she fought for those children! I decided not to say anything to young Collin. He was content living with Brother Bill and me and I didn't see why I should upset him. He still has seizures, you know. But now he has a wife and they work so hard for the Lord. I just know that Collin will be a preacher one day! Anyway, Wind In Mourning shared with me how Patricia had been brought up. As you probably know, Indians use a lot of sign language so it wasn't anything for them to learn to communicate with this special child."

"Why did Wind In Mourning come to you?" Once again Will was jumping ahead of the story. "And where is she now?"

"Oh, my, I have no idea where she is living now. She came here because she was trying to get all of Bonnie's children together. As soon as that poor woman was released, Wind In Mourning did everything she could to take those children to their mother."

Phyllis had her face buried in her hands and Will noticed that she was trembling.

"What's wrong?" he tenderly asked.

"Mom said that her mother never wanted her and she's believed that all her life."

"It's simply not true," Ruby almost whispered. "Your mother was deeply loved and wanted. It was only because of Kenny that she was forced to live with relatives. I know this to be true, child."

Phyllis bit hard on her lip even though she couldn't hold back the tears. "All this time Mom has believed a lie? Her life would have been so different if she had only known the truth! MY life would have been different!"

Once again Will kept the story moving. "How did Wind In Mourning know where to start?"

"Riley and Gunther were cousins! Isn't it a small world? Or, maybe an example of God's compassion and providence. The two got together because Riley was deeply in love with Bonnie."

"Where's Riley now?"

Ruby's body seemed to wilt before their very eyes. "He's dead."

"Oh, no!" Phyllis didn't want to hear that!

"I was a little upset about that myself. In fact, I had to question God a little—not in rudeness you understand, but out of the need to settle my mind! Bonnie had come so close to freedom and to having her children back! So terribly close! And because of one woman, she lost absolutely everything, even the man she could have loved and who would have gladly been a father to all her children! I simply had to ask God, why?"

"And what did God say?" Will had a sadness on his face that was like a dam holding back the force of raging waters.

"Wait, wait. How did he die?" Phyllis wanted to know.

"Riley was heading up there to the hospital to see Bonnie and it was raining really hard. It was the woman who raised Lucy, Delores Stivers, who I blame for all this. She had told Riley something that upset him almost to the point of hysteria. Riley should have never been driving by himself under those circumstances. Got himself into a head-on collision and died before he ever got there. And I was afraid that was just going to send Bonnie over the edge and I cried out to God! 'God, why? How much more can this poor woman take?' Oh, how my heart ached for Bonnie Parker! And then, to answer your question, young man, God simply reassured me 'it's okay'."

Will and Phyllis both were waiting for more, but Ruby remained silent. "That's all? Just, it's okay?" he finally asked.

"What more did He have to say?" She was frowning at them as though His answer had been more than sufficient.

"And that gave you peace of mind?"

Ruby shook her head, "Oh, yes," then she thought for a moment. "Children, you seldom find peace because it's a form of comfort from a heartache, you find peace in spite of the heartache."

"What in the world did Delores tell Riley to get him so upset?"

"She had already given consent that Bonnie was to be given shock treatments as needed, but then she began to insist that they do a lobotomy as well. Doctors were doing that a lot at that time. Terrifying! Riley knew that he was going to be too late to stop it. You see, because of Bonnie's absolute insistence that she had to find her children, the medical authorities were convinced that she was still delusional. Kenny Fisher had told them the truth, that they did not have any children at home. What he held back was that the children did, indeed, exist. Upon physical examination, the doctors determined that Bonnie had given birth, but once again, Kenny declared that the children had died.

"Well, the story goes that the doctors kept her heavily sedated because when she wasn't drugged she was almost violently adamant about getting out. Being next of kin, Delores and Ronnie both signed papers that absolutely no one could visit. Delores knew that Riley would do his best to get Bonnie out of there, so she conveniently put a stop to all his attempts."

"No one saw through her vehemence?"

"Apparently not. Sometimes there's just nothing a human can do."

"Oh, that's so cruel!" Phyllis had to actually put her hand on her knee to stop from shaking.

"Yes, by all standards what happened to Bonnie was cruel and unfair, even somewhat barbaric. And I have no doubt in my heart that God was quite saddened by the whole affair too. But, you see, we can only see this side of it. God sees the top and bottom and sides and even knows the width and depth of our suffering! He's not going to allow anything that can possibly get out of His control. Have you ever noticed that if life gives you soup He gives you a spoon? And if you get tough meat He'll give you a knife? In all my life, He's never expected me to eat my soup with a knife."

There was silence for a moment as they all agreed. Then Will asked, "Did Bonnie ever know that Riley was killed?"

"No, not that I know of. After the shock treatments I understand she did quite well. There was always something not quite right, though. It was through all the testing and extended treatments that they discovered she had an inoperable brain tumor. Chances are she had it all along and it was only through the treatments for insanity that they discovered it when they did. You see, things have a way of working out." Ruby sat back, smiling.

"So, Bonnie was never told that Riley was killed in an accident?" Phyllis was still having a hard time processing it all.

"As it turned out, Bonnie didn't even remember Riley so it wasn't necessary. To this day, her babies are still just babies and she's only twenty-one years old. Nothing else has happened in her life. Sad, isn't it?"

Not only sad, but so tragic that Phyllis found herself angry! "It's not fair! Are you telling me that Bonnie went into that institution with a sane mind and came out insane? And no one did anything about it?"

Phyllis was becoming quite livid about the whole thing. Will wanted to get up and embrace her, but he knew that in her agitation she would only push him away from her. This was turmoil that had to be physically worked out.

"They tried, my dear. I understand that Matthew Nader, he's the president of the Institute where she went, fell in love with her and made sure she received the best medical care she could possibly have. Other than that, nothing else could be done."

"No! I can't accept that." Phyllis had her fists clenched as she hit the air. She had to stand she was so upset. She paced the room for a moment as thoughts went through her head. Tears blurred her eyes and she could feel a ringing in her ears.

"No," she repeated softly, "it's just not right. From what I understand, it wasn't Bonnie's fault. She desperately tried to do what was right. She was a defenseless victim! How could God turn His back on her like that? I can understand everyone else failing her, but not God! He should have defended her. Riley should have gotten her out of that place before they destroyed her mind and then they could have gotten married and kept those children together. And my mother would have known she was loved! Why didn't God intervene? It didn't have to end like that!"

"Yes, it did." Brother Bill suddenly joined the conversation. "In all the time I've been a minister of the living gospel I've learned that, regardless of how we interpret it, God divinely ordains the patterns of our destiny. Even though He has to work through the choices we make, nothing can take us out of His hand. I believe in my heart that Bonnie was a child of God, therefore, I can rest assured that He has given her a special endurance and coping ability.

"The Jews were in a physical bondage but the Germans couldn't weaken their spiritual strength. Those who endured the concentration camps will tell you that in all the unfairness and wicked cruelty, God was there to uplift their tortured minds. We can't possibly understand it because our thoughts are not His thoughts. And our ways are not His ways."

Brother Bill sat back and took a long drink of lemonade as though he had nothing more to say.

Phyllis was somewhat consoled even though her spirit was still crying out. "How can you possibly see any good in this?"

Ruby tried to comfort her. "Bonnie is not suffering, my dear. Granted, what happened to her seems to be complete injustice but even though we say her mind is gone, her mind is actually safeguarded. No one can hurt her anymore. If things hadn't happened as they did, chances are Collin wouldn't have met Christina, and Bernadette wouldn't have become a nun. There's a good chance that you wouldn't have met William there because your mother would have probably taken you to New Orleans. I remember now that you were about two years old when Lucy knocked on my door. She wanted to run. Run long and hard. Every choice involves a consequence. It wasn't Bonnie's choice to be institutionalized, but God did work it out for her good, just as the scriptures promise. If it hadn't been for the state taking care of all her medical bills, she would probably be dead by now. One day maybe even your mother will understand."

"Yeah, when she lets go of the anger and gives her life to the Lord."

"How old is she now?"

"Thirty-six." Phyllis answered.

"Yes, that's right, because Collin is now thirty-four. Time goes so quickly. To Bonnie, they haven't aged a bit and it's the love for them that keeps her going. Like Brother Bill said, she's not suffering. She says she's looking for them, but it's only in her mind. Even if we took each child to her, she wouldn't know them. My precious Collin went once with his wife Christina, and Bonnie couldn't make the connection. She believed that he had the same name as her boy. It's like her mind is frozen and nothing goes beyond 1940. Except for Patricia!" Ruby's eyes brightened as she remembered Bonnie's response to her youngest daughter. "God has allowed Bonnie to accept Patricia as her daughter. She talks to her as a child, but that doesn't really matter since Patricia is deaf anyway."

"Does Patricia have a man in her life to support her?"

"You mean like a husband or boyfriend? No, I don't think so. But I haven't seen her in a couple of years so of course things could have changed by now."

"Do you think there's any way I could go see her?"

"I don't see why not." Ruby had a compassionate demeanor that filled Phyllis with renewed hope. "Brother Bill, please go to the desk and get my address book. I'm not sure of the name of that home where Bonnie lives, but we know some folks that live in Archer and they'll help you. Now, Phyllis and Will, if you talk to these people, they'll help you with anything you need. Good people! You'll think they've been your friends your whole life!"

It was dark when they finally said goodbye and Phyllis found herself heading back home. Her mind was still spinning. "Will, it's still early in the day, what's our chances of going to Archer today and talking to those people?"

He certainly didn't want to deny her, but he also knew that Archer was going to be a good four hour drive. Getting there wouldn't be a problem; getting back home at a decent hour would be!

"Do you really think it would be beneficial right now?" he questioned. "I mean, Patricia is deaf so you wouldn't be able to ask her too many questions. And it's debatable if she knows that much about family history. Sounds like Bonnie wouldn't be any help at all."

"But they are my aunt and grandmother." Phyllis sighed. She knew Will was right, she just wasn't ready to end her search. And deep down, she did want to meet every relative she had! "If nothing else, I bet Patricia would be able to tell us where Wind In Mourning is. Or Gunther!" Her eyes were bright with sudden hopefulness! "He just lives in Gough's Ridge! Oh, no!" she frowned, her deep eyes narrowing into mere slits.

"What?" Will had to take his eyes from the road to understand the sudden change in her voice.

"We don't have a last name. Or, do you suppose Gunther is his last name? Ruby mentioned Frothworth. Is that a first or last name? Could it be Gunther Frothworth?"

Will just shrugged. It was an unusual name and surely people in the town would recognize it. "I have an idea." He nodded as though confirming the thoughts in his head. "We'll go to Gough's Ridge and head straight for the church."

"Why there?"

"Because Ruby said that Gunther was a wonderful Christian man. That means anyone in the church should know him, right?"

"Right! Oh, Will." Once again her eyes were downcast.

"Now what?" He looked at her momentarily before his eyes went back to the road.

"What if Gunther is dead, too?"

"Neither Ruby nor Brother Bill indicated that. Surely they would have said something. You're just being pessimistic now."

"Can't help it." She started to chew on a fingernail but Will touched her hand which made her withdraw it. "I mean, this whole story is so tragic! A poor Indian child was kidnapped and probably tortured and treated like an animal. One woman loses the only man she ever loved. Another woman loses all her children and her mind! Then my own mother blew up the cabin because my grandfather is really my father! Lives were devastated as though the curse had threatened to destroy our heritage as surely as the explosion ripped apart those log walls. It would be perfectly in line with this tale of woe to find out that Gunther died two days ago!"

"And you didn't believe me when I told you there was a curse."

Phyllis propped both feet up on the dashboard and put her hands behind her head as she stretched. "You're right, Will. A terrible curse has been placed on the Parker family. But there's one thread of decency and almost righteousness that seems to be woven in this tapestry of human tragedy."

"Which is?"

"The undeniable goodness of Wind In Mourning. I just have to meet her."

"But, Phyllis," now he was frowning, "you just put Gunther into the clutches of death. The chances of Wind In Mourning being dead are just as great as Gunther, you know what I mean? She'd be an old, old lady by now."

"Oh, I can't stand it!" Phyllis put her feet down with a thud and blew out her breath, exasperated. "We get so close only to find out we're farther away than when we started! Do you know how disappointed I would be if Wind In Mourning is deceased and we'll never know her story? Oh, Will, what if we're too late? In such a short time I've been introduced to relatives I didn't even know I had; only to find out that half of them are already dead and buried! What a waste."

He wanted to make sure he understood her. "A waste of what? Your time? Their lives? The situation? What?"

Phyllis tried to explain but every time she opened her mouth nothing sensible came out and her thoughts were so fragmented she couldn't even make a complete sentence. She ran her fingers through her short hair and ruffled it as though trying to smooth out the confusion by shaking it up!

"Okay. Here goes. I think it all boils down to this." She stopped and cocked her head as though finally seeing it all in alignment. "If the family had just honored one another, lives would have been so different! When adversity struck, they separated and tried to deal with it on their own instead of uniting. Hopeless, you know? They were defeated before they even knew the race had begun! Except for Wind In Mourning. Why is it that the one person who had every excuse to turn out as a drunk or a prostitute or sentenced to life for murder ended up living happily ever after? Even if she is dead, she won the race! Am I making any sense at all?"

At first he was going to tease her but then decided she was much too serious to accept any verbal jousting. "Okay, so what's such a waste?"

"Wasted relationships, Will. Each generation of the Parkers had so many opportunities to bond as family but they wasted them. Instead, Mom drinks herself to oblivion and makes me feel like I'm an orphan." Suddenly, tears were spilling over from her tender eyes. She wiped her cheek, embarrassed. "A large part of my life was wasted because I never knew my aunts and uncles and grandparents. I can never reclaim those years. It's not like I can go back and say 'hi, I'm your granddaughter. I'm not a child but spoil me anyway. Read to me, teach me things, stay up late with me and giggle all night! Take me for walks and let's go to the zoo or on a picnic. Come to my school concert and listen to me play…" she couldn't talk anymore, her voice was broken and so high pitched it wasn't intelligible.

Will checked the traffic and then carefully pulled over to the side of the road. He didn't have to say anything. He just reached over for her and she met his embrace as she actually sobbed. His fingers automatically raked through her hair in soothing strokes. Never had he imagined the discovery of the cabin would come to this. He wasn't sorry about taking her to it. On the contrary, if it hadn't been for the discovery of a demolished cabin, she may have never had the ability to reconstruct her heritage. At last, her life was going to have profound meaning! But he sure didn't like to see her cry! After awhile she took a deep breath and then regained her composure.

"I owe a lot to Wind In Mourning, don't I?" she smiled at him. "Let's go find Gunther and discover where she is."

The turn off was just three miles farther. Will was confident it would be easy to find him. Once they found him they'd go back to Fuertes and actually meet Collin and his wife, and then he'd go with her to meet Patricia and her grandmother Bonnie. It was debatable if they could meet Bernadette, but they might even give that a try. History was going to be rewritten!

CHAPTER 11

ঌঌঌঌঌ

1969

Within thirty minutes, Will was driving into Gough's Ridge. He knew every street and business that was established. The population was continually changing, but the community was comfortable. There were now four churches within the city limits. On this particular Saturday they all looked deserted.

"Now what?" Phyllis wasn't about to give up.

"After church you go out to eat. Let's check at the biggest restaurant first because generally church folks like to go in big groups."

"That's easy enough." Phyllis automatically looked down the street to an establishment that was owned and operated by two brothers. She and Will had eaten there many times even though they didn't know any of the help personally. "And, good thinking, too, because I'm hungry!"

She was always hungry! "How about some fries and a strawberry shake?" he suggested.

"I was thinking more in the line of a hot meatloaf sandwich."

"With potatoes and gravy?"

"But of course."

For the first few minutes she was so eager to order something to eat she temporarily forgot about their search for Gunther. Deep down, she was almost afraid to ask for fear of getting a negative reply. Chances are, Will felt the same way because he seemed to deliberately keep an easy-going conversation between them about trivial things. After they ordered, they talked a bit about Ruby and Brother Bill.

When the waitress brought their order, Phyllis finally decided to risk it. "Do you live here?"

"Sure do. In fact, I don't know any other place. I think my family goes back six generations in this little town."

"Then you probably know everyone. We're looking for someone that is probably a pretty old man by now. Do you by chance know of a man named Gunther or Frothworth?"

She thought and then shrugged. "Not personally. Is that the first name or last?"

"We honestly don't know."

"Then I take it he isn't a friend."

"No, not yet. But he knows someone we're trying to locate."

"Missing person?" She seemed eager to get into a good mystery.

"No," Will disappointed her. "We're just tracking down relatives."

"Oh." She set a ketchup bottle between them. "Personally, I'd like to lose mine! They can be such a bother at times!"

Phyllis was tempted to say something contradictory but decided it wasn't worth it. The waitress started to walk off but then came back.

"I don't know how you feel about talking to strangers but that's Mr. Gocken over there and he's lived here all his life, too. If anyone would know who you're looking for, it would be him."

Will looked in the direction she indicated and saw the back of an elderly man sitting alone at the table. "You don't think he'd mind?"

"Goodness, no, the man loves to talk! That's why he comes in here every day. He doesn't miss a thing, I can tell you that!"

Will thanked her and then grinned at Phyllis. "We'll find Gunther, you'll see." He bit into his turkey club sandwich. If the man started to leave, he'd get up and go over to him, but it didn't look like Mr. Gocken was going anywhere soon. They were able to finish their meal, though both were really too excited to have to sit still for long. Will approached him as Phyllis stayed at the table. In only a matter of seconds, Will waved her over. She practically skipped over, eager to meet him.

He almost laughed, "Just looky here, I'm being blessed by the most beautiful young lady these eyes have seen in three plowin's! You say you're lookin' for someone that lives here in Gough's Ridge?"

"Yes, sir, a man by the name of Gunther."

A big smile crept out on his withered lips. "My old buddy Gunther? What you searching his feeble bones out for?"

"We think he might be able to tell us where someone lives."

"What I don't know, he knows! Between the two of us we keep this town covered."

"Where would we find him?" Phyllis was so thankful the man was still alive!

"Home. Sittin' on his front porch talkin' to his hound dog. That's where you'll find him. Me? I like sittin' here and watchin' people come and go. Don't got me a little woman to wile away the hours with and dogs are fine company but they don't have much of a vocabulary!" He leaned back in his chair and stretched a moment which produced an involuntary deep belch. "Pardon my manners little missy. Now, how is it you know the likes of Gunther?"

They could be there the rest of the night explaining the story if they weren't careful! Phyllis shot a glance at Will to make sure he wasn't about to embark on a lengthy explanation. He obviously had it already figured out.

"Distant friend of a relative, that's all. Where did you say he lived?"

"I don't think I did say. Of course, this old mind sometimes plays tricks on me. But it won't be hard to find him. He just lives about a block from the old mill. You go back outside and turn towards the school and you'll see his place."

Will raised up a bit to look out the window where the old man was pointing. He must have been frowning because Mr. Gocken interpreted his movements as being confused. Trying to be helpful, he started to get up and walk over to the window with Will. No sooner had he gotten out of his chair than he unavoidably expelled gas.

Puckering his lips and frowning, he jerked his head so that he could look behind him as he scolded, "you be quiet back there! There's a lady present!" Then he apologized and shuffled over to the window. It was all Phyllis could do not to laugh!

Even though Will was quite sure he could find Gunther's house, he followed Mr. Gocken and listened politely. They thanked him and left as quickly as they could. Phyllis was so excited she was practically bouncing! Long before they could actually see the house number, they saw the old man sitting on his porch, just like Mr. Gocken said he would be. Will greeted him and asked if he had the time of day to talk a spell.

"I reckon I can talk till I either die or get raptured. You goin' with me if the trumpet blows?"

"Sure am."

"Then I reckon we got time to talk as long as we want. Sit yourself up here a spell. This here is Ruthless." He bent down and patted the hound's head. "He won't bite you unless you bite him first. You got all your shots? Sure don't want my dog sick."

Will loved his sense of humor. "I'm up to date except for those worm tablets. Nasty things."

A broad grin spread from ear to ear. "You're my kind of young feller. Now, what can I do fer ya?"

"We're looking for an Indian woman by the name of Wind In Mourning. We were hoping you'd know where she lives."

Just then a woman came out of the house and joined them. "This here is my little woman, Amanda."

"You young folks want anythin' to drink or eat? I got some leftovers in the kitchen I can warm up for you."

"No, thanks; we just finished eating. We just wanted to ask about a woman we're trying to locate."

"Yes, Mother, they're asking about Wind In Mourning." Gunther's eyes closed a moment as though recalling pleasant memories. "Would have married her myself if I hadn't been so much in love with Amanda here."

"Is she still alive?" Phyllis drew up the courage to ask.

He frowned. "Is she? I'm not rightly sure."

Phyllis's hopes plunged. Gunther scratched his chin and looked off in the distance. "About three years back there was this horrible outbreak of influenza in her tribe and nearly wiped out all the aged and newborns. Buried thirteen of them that year. Sad, sad. Seems like Wind In Mourning might have been one of them."

Once again Phyllis was protesting! It just couldn't be! She was just sickened by his words.

Amanda was shaking her head. "Now, Gunther, darlin' you might be a little confused here. Wasn't it Windy's sister that died?"

His eyes suddenly brightened. "Yes, Mother! You're absolutely right! It was her sister! I must be getting old." Then he shook his head "'bout to make a hundred years on this earth! That's why I took me a child bride…so she could take care of me. I planned to live a long time!"

"She's alive?" Phyllis had her hopes sprouting again.

Amanda eased into the rocking chair and settled herself. "She is as far as I know. Poor health, though. To the best of my knowledge she's living in a nursing home. We're blood sisters you know. She bled her finger and I bled mine and we mixed our blood. That's a lifelong pact you know?"

"Yes, I know. Do you see her very often?"

"No, not, as much as I would like. We old people don't get around as much as we used to. These bones just won't cooperate. If you're wanting to see her I'm sure she'd love to have you visit. She's just over in Cameron, you know where that's at?"

Phyllis nearly dropped her teeth as she gasped. "Yes! That's where Will and I live."

Amanda laughed with a kind of twitter and giggle. "Well, now aren't you blessed! You two better hurry home. Looks like rain in the air and you know the streets get wet when it rains."

"Yes, Ma'am, they sure do." Will nodded. He started to leave but then was caught by the expression on Gunther's face. "Is there something you want to tell me before we go?"

"No, I was just thinking about the old days when I first met Wind In Mourning. They're not so clear, but I do know that God has blessed me with her friendship. How is it that you're lookin' for her?"

"She's been a part of my family since the days of Ira Parker. I decided it was time to meet her."

"Well Lord God Almighty." He whispered, not in vain but in awesome wonder. "You get to Wind In Mourning as soon as you can young lady. Yes, Ma'am, she's been in your family a long time! Told me some stories, too! Imagine that. You're one of the Parkers."

"Yes, sir, I sure am."

"Well, it's time the two of you should meet." Gunther reached down and patted the dog's head again. "And you give her our love, would you? And tell her we say hey."

Will shook his hand again and assured him that the greeting would be given. No sooner was the car door shut than Phyllis burst out.

"Cameron?"

"Right in our own backyard and we never knew!"

The morning started out unusually windy and cool. When Phyllis looked outside she knew that she could be in the middle of a hurricane and not be discouraged about getting outside! Her heart was already racing with anticipation!

Today was going to be the day! Will had dropped her off late the night before, right after they had finalized plans in going to the nursing home. Then he had called, close to midnight, to let her know that he had to change his plans.

"I'm so sorry, but something's come up and I can't go with you."

"Something terrible?" She was instantly alert to impending doom.

"No, just something important. But it's okay because you can do this by yourself. In fact, it might even be better this way. Maybe the woman will be able to talk to you a little bit easier if I'm not with you."

There was something in his voice that concerned her. "Will, tell me, what's wrong?"

He seemed to force a laugh. "Nothing is wrong, my sweet. Tell you what, we'll get together and have supper tonight and you can tell me all about your visit with Wind In Mourning. I'm really excited about this whole adventure!"

"Yes, I know. Why can't I see you before five, though?"

"Well," he paused a moment and spoke to someone else in the room, then got back to her. "I've got to go out of town and I don't think I'll be back sooner than that. In fact, if you can't reach me, don't worry. Okay?"

"Not really. I wanted you to be with me."

"Believe me, Babe, I'm more involved than you realize!"

"I don't know," she started to whine.

Will took a deep breath and tried to keep his voice light. "Phyllis Parker, you're about to meet Wind In Mourning. You know, the woman that you told me all along was an intricate part of everyone's lives? Focus on that and nothing else. I would love to be with you, but I just can't. But I will be anxious to hear how everything went! Trust me, okay?"

She agreed, but she still wasn't very happy about the change in plans. After she hung up she stared at the phone, wondering if she was being paranoid or if he was trying to keep something from her. He had been so excited the night before! All the way home from Gunther's they had talked and made plans; they had laughed and carried on like two kids planning a surprise party for their best friend!

"Oh, well." She finally shrugged and then looked in the closet to see what she was going to wear. Deciding on a bright summer dress, she took extra care with her hair and makeup. Thirty minutes later she looked in the mirror and was satisfied. She looked good! Shoulders back, head high, she licked the bright red lipstick and noticed there was a real sparkle in her eyes! Just as she opened the door, she looked to the sky. "Please, Lord, let this woman be alert enough to talk to me."

All morning, Phyllis had tried to rehearse what she wanted to say. What if the woman had lost her ability to communicate? What if she had become senile and didn't remember a thing? No! That just couldn't be! This was just too important. Phyllis refused to entertain the thought that the woman wouldn't be all that she expected.

Her eyes automatically checked her speed as she drove across town. She let the last few days play through her mind. Things seemed to happen so fast! How could it be that this woman lived in her very own town and she'd never known it? Or had she?

All of a sudden she realized the light had just turned red and she had to quickly hit her brakes. Her thoughts had hit their own red light. "No." she shook her head, disbelieving the thought that went through her mind. "No!" she spoke out loud. "That would be just too, too uncanny to say the least!" But the more she wanted to discredit the thought the more she convinced herself it was a possibility! Then she finally voiced it, just to actually hear the words. "Is Wind In Mourning here because of Mom?" Somehow, some way, the Indian woman had always been somewhere in the background of each of her ancestors. It was as if Wind In Mourning was weaving a thread through all the tapestries of their lives.

It made sense, and yet Lucy's own attitude contradicted it. From their earlier conversation, Lucy didn't even know the woman's name. How could that be possible? Then another thought hit her with a blow so intense it nearly took her breath away!

"Is Wind In Mourning here because of me?" Everything that Phyllis had wanted to say totally disappeared from her mind. As sure as she knew her own name, she was sure it wasn't by accident or even coincidence that Wind In Mourning lived in the very town Phyllis did. She started thinking back through her past to see if there had ever been a time that a mysterious woman had played a part in her life. Before she could entertain that thought, she realized she was pulling into the parking lot of the nursing home. Phyllis stopped the car and sat there, almost frozen. As though her mind suddenly became crystal clear she remembered a specific time when she was only fourteen and had taken on the responsibility of a paper route. Lucy seldom gave her spending money and she had her heart set on buying her very own flute. Even if she had saved up the little bit that Lucy would give her, she knew she wouldn't have more than fifty dollars by the end of the year. So, Phyllis was determined to buy the flute herself. Having the paper route was hard work but she fixed up the basket on her bicycle so she could stack papers in it and she had a little book she kept the accounts in. For six months she had worked that route with no complications or interference from anyone.

Everything she made she put in a special box, and she kept a chart posted on her bedroom door as to how close she was getting to her goal. She got up every morning at five o'clock, rode her bike to the Journal and took off. She had twenty-five people on her route. On this particular morning, she wasn't feeling too well but she pushed herself anyway. Halfway through the route it started to rain. In her desire to get done quicker and to keep all the papers from getting wet, she started to get careless. She knew the curve and the hill was tricky even in dry weather. Just as she dreaded, she began to slide and before she could even react her bike was out of control; papers were flying out of the basket and in her panic she ran right into a tree! Knocked her off the bike with a horrible thud! Phyllis remembered sitting in the rain and crying. She was disgusted with herself for allowing the accident to happen. It was still dark and with the remaining few papers in the basket she held them tightly against her and walked to the next set of houses where she was suppose to deliver them. Leaving her bike twisted around the tree, she wasn't even aware of both knees bleeding as she limped down the hill to the other houses. She remembered crying the whole time. To make matters worse, she was six papers short, but she wasn't going to trudge back up the hill to try and find them. By then, she knew that they would be soaking wet anyway. It was time to go home.

Lucy hadn't even stirred from her bed. Phyllis silently took her wet clothes off at the backdoor and still in tears went into the bathroom to dry off and clean up. She was a muddy mess! She must have debated for a half-hour about waking up her mother. Finally, she did, explaining that she needed a ride to the Journal so she could get six more papers and finish her route. Lucy had been angry and at first refused but Phyllis had eventually talked her into it. To make matters worse, Lucy stormed into the Journal office and wanted to know how anyone in their right mind could send a poor fourteen year old child out in that kind of weather and expect them not to get hurt!

"And she better not have to pay for them papers neither!" Lucy had shouted.

Mr. Kulhanek seemed positively perplexed. He apologized for the fall that Phyllis took and looked her over to make sure she was okay. Then he said, "Well, little lady, someone must have been looking out for you because they came in and bought six papers and I haven't gotten any calls from anyone on your route saying they didn't get their morning paper. I sure wondered what she needed six papers for but now I guess I know."

Phyllis had been so relieved that she hadn't disappointed anyone, she didn't think much more about it. It was only when she was older that she realized the significance of someone helping her out like that. Later in the day she had gone back for her bike and realized that she'd never be able to ride it again. Lucy wouldn't even think about getting it fixed so that ended her paper route.

Suddenly, Phyllis had another revelation. Her mouth actually dropped open as she took a quick breath. She had gone back to the music store several weeks later and was standing there looking at the flute that she wanted so desperately. With tears in her eyes she knew that without the paper route she'd never have enough money to buy it. Miss Glenda had been working there at the time and asked her what was wrong.

"Nothing. I just got my heart set on something I can't have."

"You mean that flute?"

"Yes, Ma'am. I saved up money…worked hard for it…but I don't have the job no more. And I know I'll never have enough money."

"I wasn't supposed to tell you this, but someone put that flute on layaway and has been paying for it each month."

"Well, you see there! I couldn't have had it anyway." Phyllis was in tears as she started to leave.

"No, you don't understand. The layaway is in your name. You're Phyllis Parker, aren't you?"

"Yes!" She spun back around, quickly wiping her eyes.

"How much money did you save?"

"Seventy-four dollars and eighteen cents."

Miss Glenda pulled a book out from behind the counter and thumbed through it. Her small, round face became radiant as her finger pointed to a figure. Phyllis could clearly see her name was written there with about six entries of payments.

"Looks to me like if you bring me sixty-four dollars and eighteen cents you'll still have ten dollars and your flute. Do you have any sheet music?"

"No, Ma'am."

"Then you'll have money to even get some music so you can play."

"Honest?"

Now as Phyllis remembered that day, she realized she had only assumed that Lucy had been paying on it. Come to think of it, when she had thanked her mother for secretly putting money aside, her comment had been "as if I had some, right?"

Phyllis had been so excited about having the flute, she had never even thought to question her mother's response. "Who really paid for that flute?" She questioned out loud. Realizing that she had spent enough time in the car, she checked her appearance in the rearview mirror and then blew out both cheeks. "Here we go."

She had never liked this particular nursing home. It was better than Lucy's apartment but there was still something depressing about it. It was an old brick building, two-story, but the rooms upstairs looked vacant. One window was broken in the corner with the remains of an abandoned bird nest.

Rebuttoning her top button, Phyllis tried to keep her emotions under control. Her heels clicked against the tiled floors. The smell of age, incontinency and antiseptics assaulted her. Dreadful place! A nurse passed her and smiled but remained silent. Phyllis went to the front desk.

"Excuse me, I'm here to visit a friend of mine. At least I think she's still here. She's an Indian woman by the name of…"

"Oh, Winny Moore! That's what we call her here. Do you know that Indians don't have last names? And we can't have accurate records without last names! We did have another Indian here but it was a man and he died a year ago. We don't get too many Indians so it's easy to remember. Usually only family members come to visit. I don't think they welcome just anyone."

Phyllis was silently praying, please, Lord, don't let this woman deny me a visit! Could a person get arrested for trespassing on public property? At this point in time, Phyllis would risk just about anything to meet this woman! "It is all right if I visit, isn't it?"

"Well, I suppose so. She's not accustomed to having visitors. Do you think she'll know you?"

"That all depends on her memory. I'm hoping she will."

"Well, Miss Winny surprises us all the time."

At last, Phyllis breathed a sigh of relief, knowing that she wasn't going to be denied. "It's really important that I see her."

"If she tires though, please extend the courtesy to end your visit until another day. She's in her nineties you know."

"Yes, I understand."

Somewhat reluctantly the nurse got up and started walking down the long corridor. Phyllis looked in the rooms whenever a door was open. So many of the residents were in bed, staring from unseeing eyes.

At last the nurse stopped in front of the door marked 23. She opened the door and poked her head in. "Miss Winny, are you awake?" Phyllis couldn't hear a reply. "You have a visitor today to see you." She stepped in the room but motioned for Phyllis to wait a moment. In one quick motion, the nurse went to the window and pulled back the drapes so the sun could brighten the room. Then she came back and only then allowed Phyllis to enter. "Remember, don't tire her too much."

Phyllis nodded as she bit the inside of her cheek. She wanted to ask, "why? Is she running a marathon later today?" But she respectfully remained quiet. The nurse made sure the door was propped open before she went back down the hallway. Phyllis watched her go before she turned and looked directly at the aging woman sitting in a chair by the bed.

"Oh, my." Phyllis fiddled with her top button again. She had expected the worse; a shriveled, crumpled woman with dull eyes, and a sagging spirit that matched a listless life. Sitting before her was a woman meticulously dressed with her hair neatly pinned up in crisscrossing braids. She had been reading. The gray eyes were warm and alive with tenderness as she took off her glasses and smiled at Phyllis.

"Good morning, my dear child. How is it that I am honored with your visit today? Should I know you?"

"I'm honestly not sure. If not, I bet you know my mother."

The woman smiled. A beautiful smile. "Then sit down there on the bed and let's talk about it. What is your mother's name?"

Phyllis liked her immediately as her hopes soared. "Lucy Parker."

Miss Winny was obviously taken by surprise. In fact, the look of surprise was quickly exchanged with a forced frown. Her eyes were downcast and she obviously debated if she wanted to continue the conversation or not. "I'm old; my memory isn't as good as it use to be."

Phyllis ignored the remark as she jumped right in. "If you are who I think you are, I would like to thank you for being such an incredible influence. You're a very remarkable woman whom I admire deeply."

The smile returned. "I thank you for such kindness, but I believe you have me mixed up with someone else."

Somehow, Phyllis knew she didn't. "Do I? Let me officially introduce myself. I'm Phyllis Parker, the daughter of Lucy Parker, the granddaughter of Bonnie Parker and the great granddaughter of Francine Parker. I found a journal that Landonelle wrote when she first married Joe. And of course, we both know your connection to Joe." She extended her hand and clasped the old woman's wrinkled hand gently. "I'm incredibly honored to meet you, Wind In Mourning."

The gray eyes stared as tears filled them. Her mouth dropped open as she gasped while at the same time her hand went to her heart. She tried to talk but couldn't. Phyllis was worried that it had been too much.

"Oh, I'm fine." She gave reassurance. After a couple of swallows she regained her composure. "It's been a long time since anyone, other than my people, has addressed me by my given name."

"I think it's beautiful. Oh, I have so many questions for you, but I was told that I wasn't supposed to tire you. I've probably already over-extended my welcome by nearly giving you a heart attack just now."

"Oh, no, no, no, I'm just fine. It was a very pleasant surprise. And I must honor your openness with honesty. You are not unknown to me, my dear child; I just didn't recognize you at first because you've grown into quite an elegant, young lady. I want to share something with you, if I may." She closed the book in her lap and set it on the nightstand.

"Please, do."

"A long time ago, I knew a man by the name of Frothworth. I had it in my heart that I wanted young Joe to be a good man and Frothworth told me that bad often just begat bad. Every once in awhile, God says enough. The cycle ends. I think, my dear, that before you were conceived, God spoke. And your goodness has broken the cycle." Her words were carefully chosen and she spoke slowly and deliberately. "From what I know, you have responded to God's choice and you have honored Him in your life."

"The same as you." Phyllis studied her a moment and then broke the gaze as she turned to resituate herself on the bed, hoping the nurse wouldn't come in and tell her to get off! "You are such a remarkable woman. I know parts of the story, but there are so many gaps. Could you help me to understand?"

Wind In Mourning laughed more in the movements of her shoulders than in an audible voice. "Oh, my, where do I even begin? If I go back to the beginning, I'm afraid the good Lord will call me home before I even cross the river! Let's start with what concerns you the most."

Phyllis had to think a moment. Where did she even begin with her concerns? "I know you wanted to stay in Joe's life and to help him, but what made you stay with the rest of us, too?"

Her eyes widened as she shrugged. "I suppose it's because I saw the curse destroying one life after another and I was waiting to meet the one person who could end it."

"That's me! That's my whole intention!" Her eyes were beaming.

"Then you'll succeed. You white folks are a peculiar people. Oh, such tragedies to those who lived in that cabin! Broke my heart! I think it was the sadness that made me so determined to help. When I was a little girl, I searched for my purpose in life. And one day I found it."

"Helping us."

She nodded in agreement. "I devoted my whole life to sharing the goodness that I had found in my wonderful friend and white brother, Gunther."

Phyllis almost giggled. "We met him, and he sends his love."

"Is he well?"

"Oh, I guess as good as can be expected at his age. We found him sitting on his front porch with his dog beside him and his wife bringing him something cool to drink. He's very happy." Phyllis could see a gleam of total devotion in the woman's eyes. A thought suddenly came to mind. "There really was a curse?"

"Oh, yes." Wind In Mourning kind of rocked back and forth a moment. "From Jeremiah's dying lips. Do you know they never found him? I looked, too! Searched for years and years. I have always wondered what Ira did with him. I knew that the curse would remain until it was righted. Now, that's not from my Christian beliefs but my tribal religion. Some things are so ingrained you can't change them."

"Well, Will and I are going to restore that cabin and clean out all the demons. The land is so beautiful! And we can do it, because we know that God is on our side." She crossed her legs and settled back a bit. "What ever happened to Joe?"

Wind In Mourning looked up at the ceiling and then into her own thoughts. "He was loved by a special woman who didn't necessarily change him, but she understood him. She went through some real hard times with her daughter and at first Joe was completely oblivious to her suffering. You know how men can be. But I kind of grew proud of that boy. When Francine left for New Orleans he took care of his wife like he should have from the beginning. Never did have any more children though. And I think that made Nelle kind of sad but she'd had a special time in her life. Got a book published!"

"Really?" Phyllis couldn't believe it. "Under her own name?"

"Yes, but you don't find it in book stores much. Nevertheless, that book seemed to fulfill her in ways that motherhood never had. It always disturbed me that she didn't bond to Francine. I thought she would have. When Francine showed signs of being a daddy's girl, Nelle could relate to that and didn't even try to sway her daughter more towards her. I guess since she was a daddy's girl herself she knew how special that relationship could be. Since her own mama died she never had an example to live by. I have to tell you, though, Nelle and my Joe were a good couple. He died before she did. Pneumonia, I think. And she lived alone for maybe ten years after that. Always writing. Died with a pen in her hand and a story in her mind."

"What was the name of her book? I've just got to have it!"

"I have my own copy right over there." She pointed to a nightstand that held about ten books. Phyllis nearly raced to it, her hands shaking with excitement. When she touched the brown book, it was almost the same electric surge she had felt when she touched the satchel. Gently picking it up she turned it to look at the title.

"In The Footsteps Of Fireflys." She read out loud. Then she thumbed through and discovered that it was a collection of short stories and poetry by Landonelle Parker.

"Look at the cover page. She autographed it for me."

Phyllis immediately turned back and sure enough, there was the same handwriting she was so familiar with. But now it was alive and energetic. "This is such a treasure!" She had to remind herself that coveting was a sin.

"Well, when I'm dead and gone you make sure you have it. I'll tell the nurses that you are to have all my books. Pleasant reading. If anyone appreciated it I suppose it would be you."

"Oh, I could never thank you enough! This will be in a place of honor for my whole life." She held it against her for a moment and then put it back down.

"It's just a book. But a special book because it belonged to my Nelle."

"Your Nelle? From what I understand you seemed to stay in the shadows of our lives. Did Nelle actually meet you?"

"No. Even when she autographed the book, she had no idea who I really was."

"Haven't you wanted to reveal yourself? All of us would be so grateful for everything you've done."

She gave a little humph. "Oh, I suppose so, but I didn't want any credit. It was enough just to see you all grow up."

"What about Francine?" Phyllis went into a quick explanation that she had been forbidden to have anything to do with her relatives and had just found out that she had aunts and uncles.

"Francine had quite a career in singing and for maybe five years she managed herself quite well. But then fame and fortune became her ruin. She lived high and mighty when she knew her family was starving to death. Wouldn't share a dime of it. Caused a lot of trouble. Mostly with her daughter, Bonnie."

"You helped Bonnie get her kids back, didn't you?"

"Oh, I tried. I suppose I did some good. At least Patricia is taking care of her."

"According to Miss Ruby you did a tremendous amount of good! She told us a lot about you."

"Well, Miss Ruby is a woman after my own heart! She's a little one-sided though." She picked up on Phyllis frowning so explained herself. "She can only see the good in people, never the bad." A thought suddenly crossed her mind. "I think I finally decided I was a good person when I taught Patricia to pray. She couldn't hear one word I said and yet she understood. Oh, you should have seen her signing. It was as though her hands became her voice, just booming with praise! Every movement was majestic and magnified! And then, when she was asking for repentance or lifting the heartfelt needs for others, she was like a swan with the most grace and elegance you could ever imagine. Her whole life changed when she personally met the Lord."

"I had no idea that Aunt Pat was a Christian." All she could remember was the slander from her mother's lips about her being deaf and not making intellectual sounds!

"She takes care of Bonnie which is full time; but she also teaches deaf children in Sunday School."

"So, she's happy?"

"Remarkably so. And blessed. I thought she might be bitter because of Bonnie's insanity but she actually says it has made her stronger in her faith. She has learned what true compassion means and why the scriptures say God has made the simple things a stumbling block to the wise, while the foolish understand great mysteries."

Phyllis almost wasn't listening; her mind had gotten hung up on the fact that Lucy's misguided opinion of family had robbed her of so much! Oh, how she wanted to know each one of her relatives! A sudden silence made her aware that she had been absorbed in her own thoughts.

"So, what else do you want to know?" Wind In Mourning stretched her back a bit and Phyllis knew she was getting tired.

Once again her mind went through a myriad of thoughts. "Did you help buy my flute?"

Wind In Mourning dropped her head and chuckled. "I knew it would be a good investment. I've heard you play and I was right."

"When did you hear me?"

"I was in the audience at every concert you were in. And I clapped the loudest!"

"Oh, wow. See," Phyllis almost wagged her finger at the little woman, "See, you're always there! In all of our lives! I've never, never known anyone like you! You truly amaze me. Absolutely, truly amaze me. How did you do it? For instance, how did you know Nelle was in labor?"

"Gunther came and got me and I stayed with them during her last days. I had been camping out for the last two days waiting for that baby to be born. Suddenly, no one was around and Nelle commenced to screaming." Wind In Mourning's eyes were large as her thumb rubbed the back of her hand. "I had to help." Then she held out her hands as though holding the newborn. "That baby girl was a miracle and it was then I made up my mind I wanted to be a part of as many miracles as I could."

"Oh," Phyllis was frowning and leaning forward getting as close as she could, "please, tell me, were you there when I was born? Mom has never told me a thing about my birth. And I just found out who my father was."

"Your mother is a very troubled woman. I don't think she will ever recover from that injustice. She rejected my help. There wasn't anything remarkable about your birth. At first, Lucy didn't want you and I believe she would have left you in the trash somewhere. She came mighty close to doing exactly that. But then she wept from the memories of what her mother had done to her and she took you back up in her arms and never let you go. I know she's made a lot of wrong choices and I know she seems to be bitter with the whole world, but I don't doubt for in instant that she loves you. She just didn't know how to show it."

"I've never doubted her love, either. A lot of times I don't understand her but then, I've never walked in her shoes. And neither do I want to!" She added with emphasis. "So, tell me more about Francine."

Wind In Mourning smiled at the memories. "She was kind of special to me. I watched her grow up and I listened to her sing as often as I could. You have to understand that I wasn't welcome in Gough's Ridge so I always had to be very careful about where I went and who saw me. But that's beside the point. I didn't like Thomas much. That man lived in a darkness that only came to our people when the witchdoctor threw overlapping claws. I ran into Thomas once in the woods." She closed her eyes, rubbed her nose, and then shook her head.

"He was as surprised to see me as I was to see him. I was good at staying out of sight but Thomas seemed to come out of nowhere. He asked me 'you real or some spirit?'. If I was real, I knew he'd hurt me because I could see it in his eyes, so I told him I was the walking spirit of mournful women. He asked me what I was doing there and I told him I had come to avenge Nelle. If anyone hurt her I was to release my demons of pain. It sounded good. Well, I had nothing to do with it but all of a sudden that young man let out a shriek and grabbed his head and fell to the ground!

"I stood there totally dumbfounded! He begged me to stop the pain and that he'd never, never go near Nelle Parker again." Wind In Mourning lowered her voice and leaned forward as though whispering a secret. "In all truth, honey, I had no idea what he was talking about but I squared my shoulders as though he was watching me and challenged him. I said, I don't believe you Thomas Gardiner. Oh, he begged all the harder! Pathetic! So, I pronounced mercy on him and then disappeared before he could get back up on his feet. I reckon he believed me because to the best of my knowledge he never went inside the Parker household unless he was with Francine." She sat back and let her shoulders sag.

"Are you okay?" Phyllis was sensitive to her condition.

"I'm fine." Nevertheless, she sat quiet for a few moments, then opened her eyes and smiled. "Now, I didn't see Bonnie as an infant, but I did see each one of her babies. I was so scared of Kenny. Lord of Mercy, I thought Ira had done come back to life and took over the flesh and bones of Kenny Fisher. I had leg chains once that kept me trapped, but she had chains on her mind. I couldn't do much with her until she made up her mind to stand up for herself. After she left, I come down sickly myself. Years went by but Gunther promised to keep me informed. It was a sad day when he told me Lucy showed up at the cabin. I feared for her life but I couldn't do anything."

"What was wrong with you?"

"Got polio." She pulled her skirt up, exposing a shriveled leg. Phyllis couldn't help but stare. "Came close to meeting my Maker. He would have sent me back though, because He wasn't finished with me."

"For my sake, I'm certainly glad! I don't know if you'll ever understand how special you are to me! I feel as though I've known you all my life but at the same time I've been cheated of a relationship."

"Well, dear, you can't reclaim lost time but don't concern yourself with that since we'll have an eternity together. I suppose that will be enough time to tell our stories… and then some!" She let a yawn escape.

"Oh, I'm tiring you, and I didn't want to do that."

"Well, I'm not cooking supper tonight or going out on the town so I suppose it won't hurt me to be a little tired. It's the curse of old age. One day, though, I'll just close my eyes and look to the Lord and be dismissed."

Phyllis didn't want to think of the possibility of that. She wanted to spend time with this special woman even though she knew time was the one thing that Wind In Mourning didn't have much of! A thought came out of the clear blue and she smiled.

"Will and I are getting married real soon. If the Lord permits, will you come to our wedding? It seems only right to have you there." She was preparing herself for negative excuses. Can't leave the nursing home. Too frail. No energy. That sort of thing.

"Yes, I'll come, as long as I don't have to stay in the background and watch from a distance." She had a beautiful smile.

Phyllis couldn't believe it! "You'll be on the front pew! Are you really serious? You'll come?" Wind In Mourning nodded that she would. "Oh, wow!" Phyllis had to actually hold back tears. "What an honor."

"But I have to wear purple. Will you buy me a purple dress for the occasion?"

Phyllis was ecstatic! "With shoes to match!"

They continued talking and then Phyllis knew it was time to leave. When she leaned over to kiss Wind In Mourning's forehead, the thought that went through her mind was, this woman is real! And she couldn't wait to share everything with Will. Phyllis nearly skipped out of the nursing home. It wasn't until later that afternoon that she began to think again of what Will had told her that morning.

What bothered her about the conversation was that it was so unlike him not to clarify everything in specific details. He had not only been vague but somewhat mysterious! Three different times she caught herself going to the phone only to realize it wasn't five o'clock yet. And then she went three more times before five-thirty.

At six-fifteen the phone rang and she dashed to it, almost breathless as she answered.

"Hey, what are you doing, running the fifty yard dash or something?" His voice sounded light and carefree.

"Just waiting on you to call; I was getting worried. Where have you been?"

"Well, at first I was afraid I was on a wild goose chase but it turned out quite productive."

"Oh, tell me." She almost squealed with delight. Phyllis bounced into the easy chair and propped her feet up on the arm.

"Not on the phone. This has to be done in person. Are you hungry?"

"Sure, I always am." Her feet hit the floor in one swoop.

"So are we."

"We?" She immediately caught the plural. "Who's we?"

"The three of us."

"Will, please." She drew out please in a pitiful tone.

"Meet us at LaMere's in twenty minutes. Oh, and be sure to look really good."

"What's going on? I'm ready now and I can be there in ten. Unless of course you'd rather I put on my blue Mainbocher dress with the diamonds you gave me."

"No, I'm sure you're fine; as long as you aren't wearing Mickey Mouse. You could always get us a table; that would be fine."

"Want me to order, too?"

She expected him to laugh and decline the offer since she was just teasing but he surprised her. "Sure, go ahead. Prime rib for all of us."

"Will!" She sat upright. "What is this all about? Did you come into some money or something?"

"Later, Babe. Got to go now." And then he hung up. Phyllis dropped the phone to her side, not having a clue as to what was going on. If it was prime rib then that meant something incredibly special. She had only eaten it twice in her whole life; one time at an elaborate wedding banquet and another time at a company Christmas dinner. Dashing into the bedroom she refreshed her makeup and debated about changing clothes. Her mind was spinning with all the possibilities of this mysterious trio she was meeting!

By the time she pulled into the plush restaurant she had taken all of the twenty minutes Will had given her, but it looked as though he hadn't arrived. She was actually disappointed when she didn't see his car in the parking lot. There was a limo at the side of the restaurant that caught her eye but she didn't pay much attention to it. Chewing on the inside of her lip she frowned, still wondering what was going on. Reluctantly, she went inside, wondering how much longer she'd be kept in suspense. As soon as she walked through the double doors and started to look for a place to sit, Will stood at the back and waved to her. Her heart skipped a beat. As she crossed the restaurant she was silently begging the woman to turn around but she never moved. Will's eyes were actually luminous!

"Darling!" He reached out for her hand. Darling? He didn't use that name very often. Maybe Babe or Sugar, but certainly not Darling.

"Will?" Her voice held fifteen questions just within the one syllable of his name.

At last the woman turned. Even though Phyllis could clearly say she had never met the woman before, she easily recognized something familiar about her.

Will pulled her chair out for her. "It took some doing, but we're all here. Do you have any idea who this is?"

Phyllis felt somewhat awkward and put on the spot. What if she voiced her thoughts and was wrong? She didn't want to be humiliated as well.

Will was quick to pick up on the second of hesitation and plunged right in. "This is Mr. and Mrs. Dennis Johns." The woman didn't stand, but she held her head high and the smile was warm and congenial. She stretched out a hand, which Phyllis immediately took, noticing that there was a slight trembling. Was it from age or from being slightly nervous? The woman looked to be in her sixties. It was the shape of her mouth as well as the eyes that gave her away.

"Better known as Dennis and Francine Johns." Will just beamed putting special emphasis on the name Francine.

Phyllis sat down with a thud. She didn't mean to but the realization that she was holding her great grandmother's hand zapped every bit of strength from her. She couldn't help but stare. Francine didn't take offense at all.

"How? Uh, when, uh, who….."

Will got tickled at her stammering. "Speechless, huh? Let me explain."

"Please do." She looked at him and then back at Francine and suddenly remembered she hadn't formally greeted Dennis and she quickly stretched out her hand to shake hands with Francine's husband. "I'm so glad to meet you. What a tremendously wonderful surprise!"

Francine spoke next. "It was our surprise as well when your fiancé here knocked at our motel door. I knew you existed but I had no idea how to find you."

"Would you have wanted to?" After she said it, she realized that it wasn't a polite thing to ask. She immediately started to apologize and clarify herself but Francine stopped her. For a moment the two of them locked gazes and Phyllis could see years of wisdom and hardness in the deep-set eyes, and yet there was a gentleness that was even stronger.

"I'm sure you've heard all kinds of horrible stories about me and I'm equally sure that 90% of those stories are perfectly correct. You have every right to hate me as much as the rest of the family does. When Will asked if we would come to meet you I said no at first, but then I changed my mind. I think I have distanced myself enough from the family. He told me how important it has become to you to know your heritage." She cocked her head to the side and winked at Dennis before she looked back at Phyllis. "So, here I am. I wish I could give you endless hours but I have to be back in Willoughby by ten tonight so that my crew can set up for a concert tomorrow."

"So, you're still singing?" Phyllis asked.

"Only for very special occasions. My voice isn't what it used to be…but then, neither am I." A sad look crossed her face as she reached out and touched Phyllis's hand for just a second. "It's hard to believe that you're my great granddaughter and this is the first time I've ever met you. Will you forgive me for never being a part of your life?"

She was serious! Once again, Phyllis searched the face and could only find sincerity in the expression. "Yes, of course! But—"

"No, no." she didn't want Phyllis to speak. It was quite clear that Francine was use to being in the spotlight and taking control. "I'm not going to promise you anything because I've only recently started making promises that I intend to keep." She looked lovingly at Dennis and then explained that they had only been married less than a year.

"Chances are we'll have a good time tonight and then I'll get back into my lifestyle and I may not see you again for six months or more. It's not because I will intentionally neglect you; it's just that it's mighty hard to teach an old dog new tricks! I have been selfish my entire life and I have made choices that should have put me behind bars. I have failed at nearly everything I've done except for singing and staying alive. Fortunately, Dennis rescued me from myself.

"At sixty-six years old I have finally stepped out of myself to discover what else the world has to offer. Now, in your quest to learn, what do you want most to know?" She set back as though she had said her piece and was content to carry on an actual conversation between the four of them.

This was just too good to be true! Phyllis was still practically speechless that the woman in front of her was Francine. They had the same hands. Francine's fingernails were tapered exactly like hers.

"Well, say something." Will encouraged her.

"I don't know which question to ask first." Her mind was literally spinning. "Do you remember the Indian woman that came to you in the dressing room when Thomas was killed?"

"Yes, I remember. Why?"

"I met her today." This time Phyllis shot a glance at Will. "She's absolutely incredible! Was that the only time you ever saw her?"

"Yes and no. One time I did get a letter from her. I saved that letter and to this day I have it in my keepsake box. She told me that she brought me into this world and that I was special to her. I think I kept it because I needed to know that someone in this world cared about me. Frothworth was another special friend. He gave me the money to get started in New Orleans and once when I had surgery he and Emma, and Wind In Mourning sat in the waiting room until they knew I was going to make it. I was just coming out of it but even in the haze of anesthesia I recognized Wind In Mourning. She left before I could actually speak to her. The three of them were incredibly generous people."

"Frothworth and Gunther have been key players in all of your lives." Will interjected.

"I can tell you, the world experienced a great tragedy when it lost Frothworth and Emma! But life has a way of filling in the gaps and charging on ahead."

"I do have a question." Phyllis had just remembered being out at the river with Will on the day they had found the cabin. "Do you have any idea whose house was on the other side of the river? There isn't even a bridge there anymore."

"Give me a moment to think about it." She began to search her memory and then suddenly it dawned on her. "You must be referring to Martha's house. I think she was the only one who lived on the other side. Snakes were bad over there. And there was always trouble with that bridge. Martha would get a wild streak and her daddy would get a mean streak. If boys tried to court her, her daddy would tear down the bridge. They'd be isolated for months before he'd build it back. Wasted effort if you ask me."

"What happened to Martha?"

"Probably died from some social disease. She owned a bordello about twenty years ago. I never had any use for her." Francine went into the explanation of catching Martha and Thomas in the cave and how he had been shot and she thought he was dead.

"If you had it to do over again, what would you change?" Phyllis asked.

Francine immediately laughed. "Oh, my goodness! So many things I'd have to have another life time to accomplish them all! But, the clock's hands don't go in reverse or stand still. At least I have no regrets now. Dennis has been my knight in shining armor. Imagine getting married at the age of sixty-five and feeling like life has just begun. It's a trip."

Just then the waitress came back to take their orders. Phyllis had to think a moment. What more could she possibly want? How could she even eat at such a time? She wanted to spend every moment she could listening to Francine talk and watch her expressions and gestures. The thought that kept going over and over in her mind was 'this is my great grandmother'. She was truly spellbound by the whole encounter!

For the next hour, every question posed had an answer given. All too soon, Dennis and Francine were whisked away in the limo.

"I can't believe you." Phyllis bit her bottom lip as she stood next to Will.

"I knew you'd like that," he grinned. "And to think I actually pulled it off. Okay, let's go home because I want to hear all about your visit with Wind In Mourning. Was she practically on her death bed?"

"Nope. She plans to dance at our wedding." Phyllis teased.

∽∽∽∽∽

It seemed like a month before the next weekend came when Will and Phyllis could go back out to the cabin. Now that she knew it was hers, she was even more interested in it. As they both walked towards it, her mind was only on one thing. She had to touch it again and stand within the remaining walls. This time she would know that even though it was her own mother who had blown it up, she and Will were going to restore it! What had really shocked her was when she had mentioned that desire to Francine, she and Dennis were all for it.

"Now, how in the world are you two newlyweds going to undertake such a financial monkey on your back when you're just starting out? Even with your combined incomes, do you honestly make enough to be able to restore that old place?" Francine was wiping her lips with the cloth napkin.

Phyllis sighed, knowing that Francine was posing a legitimate question. "I know that we have to count the cost before we plunge into it, but we agreed that even if it takes our entire lifetime we still want to make that cabin a blessing instead of a curse."

Without even discussing it with Dennis, Francine put her napkin back in her lap, opened her pocketbook and pulled out her checkbook. "I understand that you're getting married within the next four months, is that right?"

Will smiled at the thought of it. "We sure are."

"Well, I don't know where I'll be in four months. I don't even know if I'll be alive or not! So, this is what I'll do. I'll give you a wedding present from the two of us and you can decide to do whatever you want to with it; whenever you want to do it. If I don't make it to the wedding, at least I'll feel as though I didn't miss out entirely. Can we agree on that?"

"Sure." Phyllis didn't know if her heart would ever quit racing! She took the check that her great grandmother handed her and didn't look at it at first. Then she noticed that Francine was obviously waiting for her reaction, so she turned it over.

"Oh, my!" She was totally speechless as she handed the check to Will, who looked at it and had to catch his breath as well!

Francine was amused. "My goodness, children, that's nothing when I can bring in three times that in one performance! Just think of it as my contribution to a lifetime of happiness."

"I honestly don't know what to say!" Phyllis was still trying to recover from seeing the five-digit figure.

"I believe that a thank you is sufficient enough." Francine raised her eyebrows somewhat.

"Yes, thank you, but mere words don't hardly seem enough." Phyllis noticed that her hands were actually trembling.

"Well, then." Francine had a deliberate stern look to her expression as her eyes narrowed, a deep frown creasing her forehead. "I want you to do something that you've never done before in your entire lifetime."

"Which is?" Her voice raised somewhat, which was also a giveaway that it wasn't just her hands that were trembling.

Francine's dour look suddenly broke into a smile. "Give your great grandmother a hug." At that, Phyllis practically knocked the chair over as she got up and graciously hugged the woman she had never dreamed of meeting personally, let alone receiving such an extravagant gift from.

"Oh, I thought you'd never ask! You'll never know how much you mean to me! And really, the money has nothing to do with it! I wouldn't care if you had gone bankrupt and had to ask us for money! Just the fact that I know you means a great deal. I feel as though I've been cheated all my life. Well, I can promise you this, our children will know every relative they have! Every aunt, uncle, cousin, grandparent, and great grandparent. If they exist, our kids will know them!"

That had all happened a week ago. Now, as Phyllis walked to the cabin with Will close beside her, she remembered how enraptured she had been throughout the rest of the meal. Even the next day, she kept repeating, 'wow, unbelievable'.

She still felt that way when she looked at the countryside all around her. It wasn't hard to find the cabin and at first she was going to rush to it, but then she stopped, looking at it from a distance.

"What are you thinking?" Will asked.

"This is only the second time we've seen that place. I wonder how Wind In Mourning felt when she stood out here and looked at the cabin after she had escaped. Or what the others thought when they came back. Do you suppose once we fix it up Mom just might come and see what all we've done?"

"That's questionable. She tried to destroy it; I'm not sure she'll be too keen on seeing it restored."

"Why do you suppose Francine was so generous?"

"Dennis said she was trying to be the kind of person she had once been, you know, before her career actually started. This is where she fell in love and had such a strong character. For her, you're not only restoring the cabin but her good memories."

"She must have really loved Thomas." Phyllis sighed but then grabbed hold of Will. "But not any more than I love you!" She looked into his eyes a moment and then kissed him, her lips giving evidence to the joy and security she felt in being with him. Then she broke away and practically ran to the cabin. "Come on, Will, one day you'll be able to carry me across the threshold."

She stopped abruptly as she reached the doorframe. "History says that terrible things happened here. But I proclaim that from this day forward, only good things will happen! It will be the turn of a new century. A new book will be written!" She leaned against the wall, her shoulder against the rough bark. The joy within her was bubbling over.

Wind In Morning

1975

Phyllis was leaning against the doorframe, watching her daughter tagging behind Will as they were collecting toys that might blow away. "Better hurry, that storm is coming in fast!" She called to them as she looked at the sky again and frowned. Heavy, black clouds were actually swirling as though they weren't sure which direction they should be moving. Even though Phyllis was somewhat worried, Will and Jillian were having a great time! He was shouting 'hurry, hurry, the storm's coming' and in her three year old way, Jillian was imitating his movements as well as his voice, her little legs running as fast as they could!

At last the toys were secured and they burst through the front door. "We made it!" Will swooped the child up in his arms and headed to the kitchen. "And now it's time for some chocolate milk and cookies. Come on, Mommy."

"Is everything unplugged?" Phyllis was already at the cupboards getting some glasses for them."

"Should be. And we have flashlights all over the house and a lantern on the mantel. There's three jugs of drinking water and enough food for an army! We're going to have the best time of our lives."

"Or the worse."

Will frowned and tickled Jillian under the chin. "Listen to ol' gloom and doom Mommy. She needs something to cheer her up so she'll have a party with us."

Jillian stretched forward so Phyllis would have to take her. "You need some lovin' Mommy? We got lots and lots of lovin'. This storm will soon be over, you'll see. And Daddy and I will take good care of you."

"How do you know it will be over soon?" Phyllis playfully frowned and pursed her lips in an exaggerated pout.

"Daddy told me so."

Phyllis smiled. Whatever Daddy said, his daughter believed with all her heart and mind! Phyllis really couldn't explain why she was so jittery. It wasn't like she hadn't been in terrible storms before.

"Do you think Mom will be okay?" Phyllis poured the milk.

"Lucy? In all truth, it would be a blessing if the storm blew that wretched apartment building over! Maybe she'd live in a decent place. Yes, Phyllis, she'll be just fine, too."

She tried to perk up and relax but there was still a tension in the air that she felt as surely as she felt the warmth from the sun. Just then a roll of thunder echoed through the air which actually shook the glasses on a shelf. It was such an unexpected boom that Phyllis not only jumped but let out a little yelp, spilling a little of the chocolate milk.

"You are scared, aren't you?" Will had picked up the washcloth and was cleaning up the milk. This time he wasn't teasing her.

"Can't explain it." She tried to shrug it off. "I'll be okay." Jillian had put a blanket on the floor so they could sit in front of the fireplace and have their indoor picnic.

No sooner had they stepped in the living room than lightening flashed and all the power went out leaving them in unexpected darkness. The wind seemed to pick up and started a viscous assault on the outside of the house.

"Okay, where's that lantern? We get to eat our cookies by fire light!" Will quickly struck a match and got the lantern glowing. Jillian wasn't in the least bit afraid. "I think this is quite special. Years and years and more years ago, the only light in this cabin was from lanterns and candles. So, we'll just go back in time for awhile. Isn't that exciting Mommy? Your imagination has always loved to venture to the past." Will smiled as he held up a glass of chocolate milk as though giving a toast.

"How far back in time do we want to go?" She sat cross-legged and raised her glass as well.

"How about when Joe was born? I bet that was a good time. Life was probably pretty happy at that point in history. I know this little girl has sure made us happy!" Another lightening flash lit up the sky, followed by an incredible boom of thunder which brought on yet another flash! Jillian scrambled into Will's lap.

"Let's watch the fireworks together." She snuggled in, the same as when she crawled in his lap to watch a movie.

From that point on it was a succession of lightening and thunder as closely spaced together as though someone were sneezing! It was the wind that made Phyllis uneasy. There were times when it sounded as though the roof was going to be ripped right off. If it hadn't been for a new roof she would have seriously doubted if it would have withstood the onslaught of the fierce winds.

And then there was an explosion as lightening hit a tree and the huge branch cracked and was ripped off the trunk. It came crashing down next to the house. The sound of the kitchen window shattering brought the three of them to their feet! Will raced into the kitchen. Part of the tree limb was poking into the kitchen through the window like a camel sticking his head inside. The wind had carried glass shards everywhere.

"Don't let Jillian come in." Will warned her. The floor was covered in pieces of glass. He tried to think of what to do. Finally, he decided to get the shower curtain and secure it at the window until he could get his saw and cut the limb out of the way. "We'll just have to ride this one out." He told Phyllis. The shower curtain helped to keep the rain out somewhat. Now that the storm had actually invaded their house, Jillian was a little scared.

"I don't like this anymore." She whimpered. Phyllis cradled her in her arms and went back to the living room and sat in the rocker with her. Closing her eyes she thought back of all the other moms that had sat in front of this very same fireplace, rocking their children. As she ran her fingers through the hair of her daughter Jillian, she was suddenly Anna, running her fingers through Joe's hair. Anna, who was murdered by Wind In Mourning's brother. Had Wind In Mourning possibly become like a mother to Joe because of that? Was it a way of reconciling what her brother had done? Maybe so. And then she became Nelle, rocking her daughter Francine. Phyllis immediately looked up to the shelf where Landonelle Stiver Parker's book was displayed. How many stories had Nelle thought of as she sat and held her daughter? There was a precious poem about Francine when she had only been three or four years old. There was also a sketch of a child kneeling to touch a flower in an open field, though Phyllis had no idea if Nelle had done the sketching or if it was by an artist. The few lines said:

One tiny, yellow flower looked
out over a meadow of green and
brown. It was so small it could
barely be seen. But as
little Francine skipped through
the meadow, the flower stood on
tiptoe until it was ten feet tall, and
its radiant smile stretched two
feet wide. That's why the child
stopped to touch the flower.
It was the biggest, most beautiful

flower in the whole wide world.

As the wind continued to beat against the house, Phyllis remembered another bit of prose that Nelle had written about the wind. Each word came to memory:

The wind is calling, calling,
leading you to glide,
glide into the wisps of
enchanted, weaving webs of laughter.
The wind entices, entices,
dancing through golden valleys
of billowy, willowy tresses,
caressed in earth's freedom of living.
Calling, calling, enticing,
Ever dancing through golden
valleys of billowy, willowy tresses,
caressed in earth's freedom of living.

Phyllis thought it had a musical quality to it. Perhaps Nelle had created a tune to go with it. And then Francine grew up but Phyllis knew that Bonnie had probably never been rocked in front of this fireplace. How many times had Francine wished she could have had Bonnie on her lap and been able to run her fingers through her hair? Maybe that's when the real sadness began. No, it didn't do any good to dwell on the past. Phyllis shook her head and then kissed the top of her daughter's head. Life was good.

Yet, the wind seemed to blow her right back with its moaning and howling. What had gone wrong? There had been storms in everyone's lives, but the others seemed to have battled things far more devastating than wind and rain! Lucy still hadn't stepped foot in their home. It didn't matter that new walls were up and the place didn't even look the same. Francine and Dennis had been out several times and were very pleased with the construction and renewal.

Phyllis let her mind wander as the past blew closer to the present. Long ago she had set a goal to meet each of her relatives and she had succeeded in doing exactly that. Including Bernadette! It had been a short visit, but at least Phyllis was able to meet her. Lucy still wouldn't have a thing to do with any of them. It didn't matter to her if they had risen from their afflictions or not. She was determined to keep them just as miserable and downtrodden as she was!

"Listen." Will came back in the room.

"To what?" Phyllis looked up, realizing she had been absorbed in her own thinking.

"The storm's over."

Jillian perked up immediately and even Phyllis sat up straight and listened. Sure enough, there wasn't even so much as raindrops hitting the windowpanes any longer.

"What about the kitchen window?"

"Well, it's secure for tonight. Since it's not raining anymore I'll deal with it in the morning when I can see what I'm doing. It'll be okay."

They got ready for bed and Jillian started out in her own bed but was quickly snuggled in between Phyllis and Will. Of course, Phyllis didn't mind. She liked to have the tiny body curled up next to her. Jillian had always been her pride and joy! It took her awhile before she could fall asleep. Her mind kept wandering to the damage the storm had caused. Her eyes were heavy, and even though she thought she was just going to close them for a second; she suddenly awoke to the alarm going off. It was six o'clock.

"Is today Monday?" Will mumbled.

"No, I just forgot to turn the alarm off. It's Saturday."

"Good, I can sleep in."

Phyllis shoved him. "No you can't, we have to check out what all the storm did last night."

"That was just a nightmare. A very vivid nightmare. There was no storm."

"You wish! Get up lazy bones, we have work to do!"

Jillian stirred, too. The first words out of her mouth was to let them know she was hungry and then asked how soon could she go in the kitchen! Then Will remembered the glass and the tree branch poking in the window.

"Okay, let's get up and see what all happened." Will was already rolling out of the covers and reaching for his jeans on the floor. Phyllis slipped a smock over her pajama top. She'd get dressed later.

The appearance of the yard was devastating! Limbs were everywhere. The shed by the garage had blown over and the yard was littered with cans and bottles and small tools. The roof on the barn was lifted up on one edge as though a giant can opener had pried it up. Shingles were everywhere! The tractor was facing a different direction from the way Will had parked it.

"Where's my pool?" Jillian broke the silence.

Both Will and Phyllis looked at the spot where the pool had been. They had left it set up because it was quite large and full of water. At first, neither one saw it.

"There it is." Phyllis pointed to the top of a tree where the pool was hanging like a beret.

Jillian started laughing. "How silly! The wind was playing with my toys!" Phyllis decided she might as well see humor in the situation as well! They continued to walk around the property. In the back there had been several little outbuildings. Two didn't look to be in bad shape, but one had completely collapsed. But it hadn't fallen in the place where it had once stood. The wooden structure seemed to have been stretched until it finally tore loose from its "roots" and then collapsed.

"I'll get help to help clean up this mess." Will spoke. He had never been afraid of hard work but he knew this was something that he wouldn't be able to handle by himself.

"Look at this. It took us years to put it together and in just half an hour it's torn apart."

"Well, Mother Nature is like that; no respect for our achievements. At least it wasn't worse! What we lose isn't important; it's what we have left. And our house is still intact, other than the kitchen window." Will looked at the tree branch that had fallen. The base of it that had been stripped off was at least three feet around. They were incredibly fortunate that the branch had fallen the way it had. If it had rotated even a foot, part of the roof would have given way to its destructive fall as well!

When they went back inside, Will went to the phone but only to discover the lines were dead. "Looks like I'll have to go to town and get my brother. You two want to go?"

"No, Jillian and I will be just fine. We can start on the little things."

"Okay, I'll be back in a couple of hours. If Eric can't help, I'll get someone else."

"If the storm went through Cameron they might be cleaning up from the damage, too."

Will rubbed his eyes and then his whole face. Blowing out his breath he stretched his back. "Well, if I have to help him first I will, but I promise you I'll be back as soon as I can."

"That's fine." Phyllis assured him. Without phones or neighbors she really felt closed off from civilization but she tried to shrug off the foreboding sense of isolation.

She watched Will drive away. Looking about the yard, she didn't feel quite as safe as she use to. Strange how the invasion of the storm also affected the sense of her confidence. They had worked so hard to beautify the place and now it was as though the forces of darkness were mocking them. For some reason she started thinking about Ira Parker. In her mind she made him out to be the meanest looking, most vile person she could possibly imagine. As she stood at the front door of her home, she remembered what the cabin had looked like when they had first found it. She pictured Ira coming upon it and finding his family dead. And then she pictured Ira making the Indian child drag those dead and decomposed bodies out of the house. According to Wind In Mourning, he had just dumped them into hastily dug graves. No words. No markers. No evidence of lives once lived.

Phyllis looked out across the landscape. She wondered where those graves had been dug. Of course, by this time they would have Biblically turned back to the dust they were made of. How could he have done such a thing? Did he ever stand at the front door and look out and grieve for his wife and child? It made her shudder just to think of the callousness.

How she had loved to talk to Wind In Mourning. They had had a good year getting to know each other before the little woman died. Her people came and got her and they had a tremendous celebration in full tribal regalia. Wind in Mourning had actually become a legend among her people. Oh, the stories she told! Phyllis was spellbound whenever they talked! Just as promised, she got the books that Wind In Mourning had treasured. Nelle's book was in a glass display case along with the satchel and a baby shoe that had once belonged to Patricia. When Bonnie died, Patricia sold everything except for those things of sentimental value and then went back to the Indians as a missionary.

Phyllis had never ended her quest to learn about the lives of her ancestors. There was always something new to discover. The storm had seemed to blow in a lot of memories and contemplative thoughts. She went back inside; Jillian was eager for breakfast. The power had come back on sometime in the night and she was grateful for that. It wasn't long before the child was in the living room, listening to her music and going through all her books.

Phyllis stood at the sink; her hands submerged in water, but her eyes looking out the window at a world that was motionless. There wasn't a blade of grass blowing, not a cloud in the sky, not a bird or even a cricket. It was as though time had stopped and was standing perfectly still. Exactly as it had for Bonnie when she had stood at this very same window so many years ago!

"Mommy?" The voice broke Phyllis out of the time suspension.

"Yes, dear?" Phyllis turned around, hearing the clock ticking, a dog barking way off in the distance, and the music playing 'the wheels on the bus go round and round, round and round...." Jillian looked at her with the most precious eyes she had ever seen.

"I sure do love you," she grinned.

"Wow, Sugarbear, I love you, too." The gloom was gone! Suddenly, Phyllis was filled with unexplainable joy and peace. "Daddy will be home soon and then we have some work to do."

"I know. That yard is worse than my room!"

Phyllis hadn't expected him to return in less than a couple of hours so she was quite surprised when she heard a car coming down the long driveway. When she looked out the window she didn't recognize it.

"Who's coming?" Jillian asked as she stood at the front window.

"I honestly don't know. You stay inside until I call you." Phyllis watched and then decided to go out on the front porch and wait to see who got out. From a distance she thought she recognized the passenger as her mother! "Couldn't be!" she vocalized her unbelief. But as the car got closer, she saw that it indeed was Lucy!

"Mom?" Phyllis was walking down the steps just as the car door opened.

"So, you are alive and well." Lucy stepped out of the car.

"Yeah, we're just fine."

"Well, you could have never proved it by me! The phones are down and I was afraid you might be laying out here dead or next to it."

"Wow, Mom, you really do care." Phyllis quickly walked to her and gave her a big hug. She didn't care if the woman did try to push her away, which of course, she did. Lucy backed her off.

"Now don't get mushy on me."

"Introduce me." Phyllis nodded towards the man who had just gotten out of the car as well.

Lucy smiled. "This here is Alan Lopatka. Friend of mine."

Phyllis went to him and extended her hand. "Thank you so much for bringing Mom out here. It's good to meet you."

"I wasn't going to come and you know why!" Lucy was stern as she lit up a cigarette. She inhaled, blew out the smoke and then shook her head. "The place still looks a mess."

"We just had a terrible storm that ripped through here!" Phyllis laughed. "Of course it looks awful! But we're okay and as soon as Will gets back we'll clean up this place! It's beautiful here and we dearly love it."

"I know, I know, that's what you keep telling me. Well, now I can see for myself just what's so great about it. You made some changes."

"We sure did."

"Where's that grandbaby of mine?"

Phyllis called to her daughter and Jillian popped out of the doorway as though she had been anxiously waiting for her name to be called.

"Grammy!" she yelled as she rushed into the woman's arms. Jillian had always loved Lucy, though Phyllis had never understood the bond. It must have been some kind of silent communication between them. "Come see my room." Jillian tugged on her arm, her excitement making her little feet almost dance.

"Sure, Baby, Grammy's coming." But she hesitated as though it was going to take a little time to build up enough courage to go inside.

"It's okay, Mom, the whole place is totally changed. Love lives here now."

The one bedroom cabin had been transformed into a three-bedroom house! A wrap-around porch welcomed any visitor with comfortable rockers and a porch swing. Phyllis had wanted to keep the front door in exactly the same place, but instead of walking into one large room that served as kitchen and living area, you entered a spacious family room. The kitchen was off to the right so that its window looked out to the same scenery the first window had. The fireplace was now the centerpiece to both the living room and dining room. You could walk around it on both sides. What had once been the bedroom was now a screened in porch, bright and sunny with flowers in the window boxes. Walls would never be able to conceal secrets again. To the left was a winding stairway that led up to the loft. It was large enough for Will's study as well as a small guest bedroom. To the right were the other two bedrooms.

Lucy was visibly impressed. "Well, now, aren't you kids proud of yourselves?"

"We sure are. It's nice, isn't it?"

"It's okay." She shrugged, but then laughed. "Yes, it's beautiful. You got any oysters in that fancy kitchen of yours?"

"As a matter of fact I do!" Phyllis led the little group back to the kitchen and went to the freezer. "But they're frozen."

Lucy started to change her mind but didn't. "Well, okay, I suppose I can stay long enough till they thaw."

Phyllis took them out of the freezer and ran cold water over them, submerging the package in a bowl of water. Then they went back outside so Lucy could smoke. She chose the porch swing and pulled her feet up under her. Alan hadn't said much but he seemed content. He declined anything to eat but he did take a cup of coffee.

"So, how do you two know each other?" Phyllis finally asked.

"We play Bingo together. I decided to get out of my apartment for awhile."

"You look nice, Mom." Phyllis was sincere with her compliment. For the first time in months, Lucy had her hair combed nicely and wasn't wearing anything torn or stained. Her fingernails were still a little dirty but it was obvious that Lucy had taken some time on her appearance. Was it because of Alan?

They talked for about an hour and then Will drove up with a van following close behind. His expression was a giant grin as he got out.

"Well, Lucy Parker, how wonderful to have you at our home."

"No big deal." She waved her hand to dismiss it. "I came out to make sure you kids were okay." Then she introduced Alan and the two men shook hands.

"Well, we have help!" Will turned as five others climbed out of the van. "We can get this job done in no time, now!" He was so proud that family and friends had come to his assistance. Because they were able to organize themselves and create a plan in only a matter of moments, the work began. Phyllis chose to stay on the porch with Jillian and Lucy. Alan quickly got involved in the clean up.

Not more than an hour later there was a loud crash and Phyllis could tell by the excited voices that something terrible had happened. Will came running from the back of the house and headed to the barn.

"What's wrong?" Phyllis shouted.

"It's Robert; he fell in some kind of hole or well or something." Will was hanging onto an eight-foot rope and running back.

Phyllis and Lucy both shot off the porch and headed to the backyard. Robert was a nephew who was only seventeen. All the men had gathered around the collapsed shed, moving boards and rubbish.

"We were trying to clean this up and all of a sudden Robert broke through and disappeared. What in the world is under there?" One of the men questioned Phyllis.

"I have no idea; that shed has been there since the day we moved in."

"It's been there since I was a little girl." Lucy added.

"Never trusted the floor boards, though. Something about it always felt weird to me." Will added as he got down on his stomach and gently lowered the rope into the dark hole. "Robert, you okay?"

"He wasn't talking a minute ago." Eric told Phyllis.

They all listened for the assurance that the boy was okay. Will had noted that the walls were definitely dug out by man, not by nature. At last a voice came from deep below the surface. "I'm okay, just get me out of here!"

"Anything broken?" Will hollered again.

"No! Just get me out!" the voice sounded almost frantic. "I'm not alone down here."

Phyllis looked at the others, wondering what he meant by that! Was he referring to snakes or spiders or what?

"What do you mean?" Will questioned.

"There's a body down here! And it's cold! I'm freezing, okay?"

The rope wasn't long enough! Robert couldn't even reach it. He said it was about six feet short. The men debated what to do.

"Can we pull two people up at the same time?"

"Too risky. Besides, there's too many roots, just look at it down there."

There wasn't any more rope.

Phyllis had an idea. "Lengthen the rope by tying a couple of sheets together, that will work!" She went racing into the house to get them. It wasn't long before they had made the appropriate knots and they tried to lower the sheets but they kept getting caught on the roots. Finally, Will made a pouch in the end and put a heavy rock in it for weight. As soon as he did that they were able to lower the sheets enough that Robert could get a grip on them and climb out.

Even though he was scratched and bruised, he was okay. All he could talk about was the body down there. "There's not much to it, but I can tell it was a man. Mostly bones and what's left of an old coat. It kind of blends into the dirt and all. Scared me to death when I found myself looking at a skull! I wonder who it could be?"

Phyllis knew exactly who it was…or at least, she sure hoped she was right. "I bet you just found Jeremiah Davis. He's been down there about eighty years."

"Impossible."

"Maybe not." Robert involuntarily shivered. "It's as cold as ice down there! And once it was sealed, there wasn't much air I bet. I think a body could have been preserved."

Now Will joined in with the speculations. "So, Ira dumped his body down the shaft and then sealed it and built a shed over it. No wonder no one was able to find him."

"There are really bones and all?" Lucy grimaced.

"Guaranteed."

"Then this is historic! We can't touch them until we get a medical examiner out here! Oh, how I wish Wind In Mourning was still alive to know this!" Phyllis was excited, but then suddenly grabbed Will's arm. "Will! Do you realize the significance of this?"

"Maybe, but tell me what you're specifically referring to?"

"The curse! Now Jeremiah can be properly buried and that means the curse is lifted!" then she winked at him. "That is, if there was such a thing as a curse."

"I sure don't believe in such superstition." He acted innocent.

"We would have never found him if it hadn't been for that horrible storm. Now, all mysteries have been solved."

"Well, all but one." Will cocked his head, holding out one finger.

"What's that?"

He looked over towards the river. "Did I ever tell you about this eerie howling in the woods that happens once every year? Some say it's the Legend of Silverfoot."

"Who's Silverfoot?" Phyllis wasn't about to be gullible to the point of embarrassment.

"That's the name of the wolf-dog that used to belong to a man by the name of Ezerius Miller. He use to live among the wolves and would take money to set up dog fights. Silverfoot was a champion of champions; never lost a fight. Until one mysterious night…."

"Sure, Will, sure."

"It's true." He stood tall with determination. "Just as sure as I knew about this cabin, I also know about Silverfoot. I'll tell you about it one day."

Another story, she thought.

About the author:

Sandra Killian, who writes as Delibia, lives in Gainesville, Florida with her husband, Michael, of almost 40 years. Writing both fiction and nonfiction, she has dedicated herself to being God's "written witness". *Wind in Mourning* is the first novel in a series, taking the reader through the experiences of those who are not only believable but endearing.

Made in the USA
Middletown, DE
23 March 2020